OFFERINGS

The Trilogy
by
<u>Christine Sunderland</u>

Pilgrimage

Offerings

Inheritance

OFFERINGS

Christine Sunderland

OakTara

WATERFORD, VIRGINIA

Offerings

Published in the U.S. by:
OakTara Publishers
P.O. Box 8
Waterford, VA 20197

Visit Oak Tara at
www.oaktara.com

Cover design by David LaPlaca/debest design co.
Cover image © iStockphoto/Katarzyna Mazurowska
Author photo © 2007 by Brittany Sunderland

All scriptural references are taken from the King James Bible; all services are taken from the *Book of Common Prayer, 1928, for use in the Episcopal Church* (apologies to Roman Catholics for not using a Roman Catholic translation); all hymns are from *The 1940 Church Hymnal,* Church Pension Corp., New York.

ISBN: 978-1-60290-171-1

Offerings is a work of fiction. References to real people, events, establishments, organizations, or locales are intended only to provide a sense of authenticity and are used fictitiously. All other characters, incidents, and dialogue are drawn from the author's imagination.

Acknowledgments

I wish to acknowledge with gratitude:

Friends and family, who patiently read my many drafts and gave me invaluable suggestions.

Clergy and laity who have, by their example and their instruction, showed me the sacramental nature of life and love.

Editor John Ross Bush, who gave me my first tutorial on writing a novel and whose constructive evaluation of *Offerings* in its infancy put me on the right track.

Editors Margaret Lucke and Alfred J. Garrotto, who worked with me to make *Offerings* into a book folks might actually read.

Ramona Tucker and Jeff Nesbit of OakTara, who believed in my work and have walked me through the publishing process with patience and skill.

My dear husband, Harry, who continues to show me the amazing worlds of Italy, France, and England, and has been my rock of encouragement, humor, and love.

And here we offer and present unto thee,
O Lord, our selves, our souls and bodies,
to be a reasonable, holy and living sacrifice...

Canon of the Mass,
EPISCOPAL BOOK OF COMMON PRAYER, 1928

Preface

In my descriptions of historical persons and places I have tried to be accurate. Saint Thomas's rectory, the San Francisco Medical Center, the Chateau de Cure, the war memorial in the Pommery caves, the hospice at the Chapel of the Miraculous Medal are fictional.

I have also attempted to accurately describe (at least in their essence) the chateaux and restaurants visited by Jack, Madeleine, Elena, and Rachelle in their travels through France.

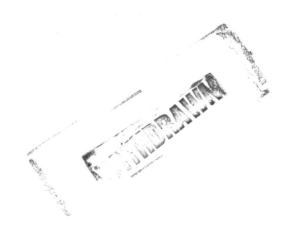

Prologue

"Papa!" Jack Seymour whispered. The boy, nearly twelve, stood by the bed and stared at his father who lay too still, his face too pale and gray. His father's eyes looked as though someone had rubbed coal under them. "Papa, wake up."

His mother said Papa would get better. Why didn't he? Papa took many pills, but he only grew thinner and grayer. He was thin when he came home from the war two years ago, but not this thin. Mama had fed him "back to his old self" and he was fine most of the time. Japan and Germany had surrendered and Papa was a hero! Mama had framed the Medal of Honor and hung it on the wall.

But now a lot of his hair had fallen out and he stayed in bed, except when they helped him to the bathroom.

"Papa, I have good news."

The body stirred and the eyes opened. He groaned and with shaking fingers beckoned the boy closer.

Jack leaned forward in spite of the sour odor. Why didn't Papa get up? Why didn't they play ball or go to the park on Saturdays? His mother brought soup on a tray to the bedroom and spooned the liquid into his father's dry mouth. A nurse visited from the hospital, her lips pinched, her body stiff. She frowned a lot, and most of the time she told Jack and his sister, Meg, to go away.

At night, as Jack lay in his bed in the attic room, he could hear the moaning below. He heard his mother crying, too, in the other room where she now slept. Little Meg, just seven, would climb the stairs when the sounds grew loud and crawl into her brother's cot. Sometimes she would cry too, little whimpers and gasps of air, and Jack would stroke her hair until she fell asleep.

He often turned on his crystal set radio to cover up the terrible wailing below.

"Papa, wake up." Jack knelt by the bed. He needed to tell his father the news. He had made the team—he made pitcher!

"Jack," John Seymour gasped as he grabbed the boy's hand with his own. "I love you, Jack. Don't ever forget that." His face was all twisted.

Where was his papa? The boy wanted his real papa back.

"I love you too."

"I have to go away," he breathed and Jack read his lips.

"Why?" The boy's heart pounded. "Why don't you get better? Like Mama says?"

"Look after Meg."

"I will, Papa."

"She's too young to understand."

"Understand what?"

"Jack, it's time. I'm going home. Home to God."

"No, you can't. Mama says you're better. She prays for you in church. You're wrong! God will heal you!"

"Look after her too, son. I'm dying. Cancer always wins." His speech was thick and hoarse, his breath foul, and he squirmed as though trying to escape a biting snake. "I'm sorry, Jack."

"No!" Jack wrenched his hand from his father's and beat upon the sick man's chest. "You can't die. I won't let you. I need you, Papa! We all need you!"

"It's better this way—too much pain." His father's eyes fixed on Jack. "Promise me you'll look after them. Be strong now. You're the man of the family."

"I promise. But...Papa..."

His father closed his eyes and gulped air. His chest rattled and his body grew suddenly quiet.

The boy laid his head on his father's chest. He sobbed. "I made the team, Papa. I'm pitcher."

The body was still.

"Mama!" Jack screamed. "Come quickly, Mama!"

Chapter One
San Francisco

This is my commandment,
that ye love one another as I have loved you.
John 15:12

On the first Saturday in September, Madeleine Seymour sat in the second pew of Saint Thomas' Anglican Church. Soon her son Justin would enter from the sacristy, followed by her husband, Jack. With that thought, she caught her breath, suddenly filled with a curious joy, for her son had asked his stepfather to be his best man.

Madeleine touched her rings, a diamond solitaire and a simple gold band, and recalled the day she married Jack in this chapel—February 6, 1982, over seventeen years ago. Her boy, a strapping nine-year-old, stiff in his first tuxedo, had carried the pillow holding the rings. In that ceremony they formed a new family, and now, Justin had chosen Jack.

And it was here at Saint Thomas' that she had first *met* Jack. As she and Justin walked toward the park on a Sunday in 1977 her boisterous son had pulled her into the white sanctuary, drawn by the organ music thundering into the street. She had never regretted it. As a struggling single parent, she welcomed Saint Thomas' friendly fellowship. And the beauty of the Sunday mass was a colorful contrast to her clerical job. The liturgy washed her with its sweet-smelling incense, flaming candles, and joyous song. She entered needy and tired; she left filled with new life, stronger.

Madeleine prayed that today's ceremony would go smoothly, that Jack would be okay. Only last week he had doubled over in pain. "A little heartburn," he said. But in the night he tossed and turned, and she worried. Now she watched and waited, as though her fierce attention could ensure a good result.

The church had once been an old Victorian, one of many on

Sacramento Street. Gone were the bay windows and neat front steps. Gone was the broken interior—walls, floors, and narrow halls—open now to vaulted space, high and holy, where incense swirled about the people, drawing them together, pulling them up. An arched entrance led to a small narthex and domed sanctuary. Skylights opened to the heavens, green tiles covered the earth, and twenty-four oak pews faced an antique tabernacle on a stone altar. Near the altar, a red candle burned. White roses in terra cotta vases sat on classical pedestals on either side, and tapers flamed beneath a wooden crucifix above. A sculpted Madonna stood in the left corner niche—the Gospel side. Blue votives flickered at her feet.

The nave was nearly full now, the pews packed with family and friends. Elena Coronati, their young houseguest from Rome, sat next to Madeleine, and Jack's three sons and their families took over the third and fourth pews.

Madeleine breathed in yesterday's incense mingled with today's roses. The air seemed also laced with anticipation and memory; her years with her son stretched back from this moment, years of grief and joy, of fear and trust, of love. The past formed a chapter, a unit of time framed by his birth and this ceremony, time marked off before it slipped away. She had taken part in the miracle of his creation, and now she would witness his re-creation in this sacrament of body and soul. *Marriage.*

She pushed a strand of hair behind her ear as the organ played the first notes of Pachelbel's *Canon in G.* Then her son, tall and serious, entered from the right—the Epistle side—his blue eyes trained down the aisle. Her husband, his flushed face mapped with a gentle satisfaction, entered next, followed by three groomsmen and the priest. Madeleine smiled, seeing her boy and his stepfather before the tabernacle. Jack had helped raise her Justin, pulling him through braces and baseball and report cards, through driving and dates and danger. He accepted the boy's initial distrust and jealousy, dishing out a bit himself, but the turmoil of those years and Jack's quiet support had woven strong threads of family. She swallowed hard as she stared at the two men who were her world, then studied her husband closely. He touched his chest and folded his hands. He seemed okay—for now.

Father Michaels looked pleased and purposeful; he cradled his prayer book and smoothed his wedding stole. She liked the young priest, although who could replace Father Rinaldi? With that thought, Madeleine looked beyond to the tabernacle, embedded with amber and

2

aquamarine, then to the red candle signifying the Blessed Sacrament—Christ himself—in the tabernacle.

"Lord, thank you," she whispered. "Thank you for this place, thank you for your Presence."

Turning, she watched the flower girls lead the bridesmaids toward the altar. Finally, as the organ shifted to Handel's *Trumpet Voluntary*, Lisa Jane and her father paused in the doorway. The bride, a statuesque brunette flowing in cream satin and antique lace, stepped serenely, as though her hands held the world to give to her lover.

"*Dearly beloved,*" Father Michaels began, "*we are gathered together here in the sight of God, and in the face of this company, to join together this man and this woman in holy matrimony...*"

Madeleine absorbed each sixteenth-century word that summoned the holy into their lives, enshrining their passage through time. As she watched Justin make his vows, the familiar voice, the voice of the child no longer, echoed in her ears.

The bride and groom exchanged rings and the priest wrapped his stole around their hands. "*Those whom God hath joined together let no man put asunder...I pronounce that they are Man and Wife, In the Name of the Father, and of the Son, and of the Holy Ghost.*"

The ceremony over, Jack followed the wedding party down the aisle, and Madeleine joined him. As she glanced at the Madonna and Child, she thought how glad she was for Mary's presence, the sacred feminine. She said a silent *Hail Mary* and slipped her arm through Jack's, touching the fine wool of his jacket and noticing a tear stuck in a crevice in his cheek. She handed him her tissue.

The social hall in the back of the church opened onto a redwood deck, and, beyond the deck, a lawn bordered with rosebushes. Tables draped in blue linen were loaded with canapés and delicate sandwiches, fruit cornucopias, platters of stuffed tomatoes in beds of greens, and plates of fanning asparagus. Justin and Lisa Jane's friends from school, their friends from work, and family from both sides mingled through overlapping worlds, as a band played Beatles tunes.

The receiving line dispersed, and Madeleine chatted with the guests, looking up from time to time to her husband, who stood behind a table tilting in the uneven grass, pouring champagne from bottles stashed in a washtub of ice. He had packed their old Volvo with cases of Moët his supplier had discounted to Seymour Wines, and now, having neatly arranged his champagne flutes, he turned to the next guest, gallantly holding an empty glass against the light and filling it with sparkling bubbles.

A gray pallor had replaced his flush. He touched his forehead gently and ran his long fingers through his silver-streaked hair, as though to regain his balance. She crossed the lawn, concerned, and noticed he wasn't wearing his sun cap.

Madeleine loved her husband. She loved his blue eyes, which possessed a confidence born of time—time spent analyzing ways and means to achieve his dreams. His threadbare schooldays had fed those visions of financial security, and his acute perception of others and why they behaved the way they did—his street smarts, he called it—had realized them. She loved that about Jack, his coming from nothing and making something of himself, his moving from rags to riches, his building a business from the ground up.

She also loved his chin, chiseled and determined, but softened with a charming dimple. His nose was fine-boned, and he said it was too long, but she thought it rather genteel. His cheek still bore a small scar where a bit of cancerous tissue had been removed, but for the most part, the jagged white line had merged into his freckles.

But what Madeleine loved most about her husband of seventeen years was that he never gave up his simple ways once he became successful. He rode the bus when he could, helped with church coffee hours, took the Scouts to Giants games where he bought them popcorn and hot dogs, sunscreen and caps. He had been awarded Father of the Year for his work with children's charities. At home he stocked the pantry with canned tuna and peanut butter, never forgetting his childhood war rations and his hungry college days.

"You okay?" she asked, touching his arm. "You're a little pale."

"I'm fine. And this one's for you, my dear." He gave her a glass and sipped from his own. "It's going well, I think. The day's warming up. We may get our September heat early this year."

Madeleine frowned. "Jack..." She picked up his Giants cap from the table and handed it to him.

He smoothed his hair down with one hand and slipped the cap over his head with the other. "Just a little bubbly, Maddie. After all, I've given up the hard stuff. I'm still allowed some wine now and again."

4

"Doctor Lau said—"

"Doctor Lau said to cut back, and I *am* cutting back."

Justin joined them, his face glowing with happiness. He hugged his mother, and she caught a whiff of spicy cologne.

She leaned back and touched his receding hairline, a genetic gift from her father. "Have I told you how proud you make me?"

"Once or twice." His grin held many grins from many days past: playgrounds, soccer, Christmas.

Madeleine looked into his blue eyes, certain her son had matured years with this single ceremony, as though he had graduated, become a different person, a true adult. "I wish your grandfather were here." Her pastor father had blessed many couples as they made their wedding vows, before he lost his faith, left the Church, and taught "values clarification" to grade school teachers. "Do you remember him? He died when you were nine, and your grandmother shortly after. He was a good man." Madeleine spoke as though to herself; this was not news to Justin. She bit her lip. Why bring this up, today of all days?

"I remember him a little—he took me to the circus."

"I remember that, too." Her father had not been well even then. The early stages of Lou Gehrig's disease were showing—slurred speech, twitching muscles. And, even so, he took her son to see Ringling Brothers' circus.

Madeleine pointed to Lisa Jane, who was welcoming an elderly aunt into her circle. "But you'd better help your bride over there. That's Aunt Edith she's talking to."

Jack hugged Justin and poured him a glass of champagne. As he watched Justin cross the lawn, he shook his head as though amazed at the miracle of time. "And now here comes our Elena."

"I saw her dancing earlier," Madeleine said. Elena and fifteen-year-old Bethany, Jack's oldest granddaughter, had organized the younger ones in a circle dance.

Their young friend approached slowly, raising her long flowered skirt to keep from tripping.

Jack touched his chest. "One would never know she was born crippled."

"God works in amazing ways." In her mind Madeleine saw the Rome chapel where they had met Elena—the teenage girl in her wheelchair, playing a refitted organ, her golden retriever peeking from her side. Fifteen years earlier, the nuns had found her, a baby, on the convent doorstep, swaddled in rags, sleeping in a vegetable crate. They gave her the name Elena Coronati—Elena after Saint Helen, for it was Helen's feast day, and Coronati after their convent. They raised her as their own in spite of her spinal defect.

"It was so beautiful," Elena said, her thick ponytail swinging. "They are so in love!"

"Miss Elena," Jack asked, holding up two bottles, "would you care for champagne or sparkling apple juice?"

"Juice, please." Elena raised dark brows. "The legal drinking age here is twenty-one, isn't it? I'm only nineteen *and* on a student visa. I don't want to do anything that might make me lose it." She looked at the bottles in the bin. "But thanks."

"You are wise," Madeleine said. "I know there's no age limit in Italy."

Jack handed the glass to Elena. "Very wise. Although this champagne is a special one—my former brokers gave me a bargain price when they heard it was for Justin's wedding."

"Are you still involved with the new owners?" Elena asked.

Madeleine watched his reaction. When Mandalay Foods bought their import business, she and Jack retired to a comfortable life, enjoying a slower day. But soon she returned to teaching history at the university and researching her book. She was fascinated by accounts of miracles, those amazing moments when the supernatural intersected the natural.

At first, Jack didn't seem to miss work. He played more golf and his handicap decreased. He did some fundraising for Coronati Foundation, the trust that supported Elena's orphanage. Lately, however, Madeleine sensed an increased restlessness in her husband.

"I do a little consulting," he said with obvious satisfaction, "and who am I to turn them down? Anyway, I own their stock—I have a vested interest."

"He keeps busy," Madeleine added.

Elena's face grew thoughtful. "It's important to use your talents."

"It is. I'm grateful Justin's found his niche in the building trade." She turned to Jack. "Can you believe it?"

"Believe what?" Jack asked.

"That Justin's married. My—our—little boy is married."

He kissed her on the forehead. "The years have slipped away, haven't they? But you look just the same, just a little gray here and over there." He touched her hairline, teasing. "One would think you were thirty-something."

"Thanks, but I'm afraid I'm not quite as trim as thirty-something."

Madeleine smoothed her skirt over her hips. How had fifty-two come so suddenly? How had she grown from size six to ten?

"Who *is*?" Jack asked, as though there were safety in numbers.

"But *you're* older. You have a better excuse."

"Only by twelve years. I married a child." He winked at Elena and she grinned, her wide smile white against her olive skin.

"And you jog." Madeleine patted his hard tummy. "You're in good shape, Jack, mostly. Maybe I should go to the gym with you."

"After you finish the book?" Jack squinted as though he knew the answer.

"*After* I finish the book. With this semester off, I might make some progress. Say, I decided on a title, at least a working title. Elena helped."

"Good girl, Maddie."

"Which one did you choose?" Elena asked.

"*Holy Manifestations: God's Presence in Our World.*"

Elena grinned. "That was my first choice."

Jack rubbed his chest. "Sounds good. I knew it would have religion in there somewhere."

Elena turned toward the buffet. "Let me get a plate of sandwiches for us."

"Thanks, Elena." Jack gazed at the bride and groom. "I'm so proud of him."

"Me too."

"He means the world to me, Maddie. I've grown to love that boy like he was my own."

"I know you have, honey."

Jack rubbed his chest and shook his head. "Do you think I was too demanding?"

"You set high standards—you wanted him to have the best, be the best."

"True."

"You set those standards for yourself as well."

"As did my mother for herself—caring for the neighborhood kids and organizing the local PTA."

"And your father?" Madeleine had never met Jack's father, who died shortly after the war. Jack didn't often speak of him.

Jack paused and stared at the grass, then at his black shoes.

"Sorry," Madeleine said, sensing she had trespassed.

"It's okay." Jack's lower lip twitched. "This seems a day for reminiscing. My father worked hard at the post office, but he played hard too. We tossed a ball on Saturdays—mostly baseball but in the fall a little football too. He was pitcher in the local league. I worshiped him."

"Then it was your mother who insisted on the violin lessons?"

Jack seemed relieved at the change of subject. "She was the one. Did you know I played a violin solo in the youth orchestra at the Paramount when I was fourteen?"

"You excelled at everything, I think."

"I tried. I wanted a better life. We were *so* poor. Always scrimping and saving." Jack poured a glass for a guest then turned to refill Madeleine's.

"You got your better life, I'd say."

"I did—I bought my mother and Meg new Sunday dresses with my first summer job. And our first TV. My first car at seventeen."

Madeleine fingered the gold cross Jack had given her at Easter. It was a Greek cross, the arms of equal length. "And you rescued Justin and me."

Jack chuckled and rubbed his chest. "That was a pleasure indeed. You two made it all worthwhile, although I have to admit Justin was a challenge at times. And here comes Elena, loaded with food."

"I wish she wasn't leaving. It's like having a daughter in the house."

"She had to return to Rome sooner or later, now that school is over."

Elena set a plate of sandwiches in front of Jack.

"Why, thanks, Elena, don't mind if I do." He popped a ham-on-wheat triangle into his mouth. "We saw you dancing earlier. You looked great out there."

"It's a miracle for sure. My legs don't recall ever being in a wheelchair."

"You had good doctors," Jack said.

"It *was* a miracle, Elena," Madeleine said, her tone too serious.

Jack raised a napkin to his lips and looked at Elena as though sharing secret knowledge. "And I recall one doctor who was very fond of you. An American helping out at the Rome convent?"

Madeleine frowned, fearing Elena's embarrassment. It had been two years since Garvey McGinty asked Elena to marry him and she turned him down. Elena blushed and looked away.

"Jack, she was barely seventeen. Elena, let's find a place to sit and eat and people-watch. We can leave the romantic skeptic to pour champagne."

Jack smiled and turned to serve another guest. The women found a

8

bench next to a newly planted maple tree, its young trunk bound to a stake.

Elena reached for a sandwich. "I don't mind Jack's teasing, Madeleine. I shall always be grateful to both of you. I'll *never* be able to thank you enough."

"Your being here is thanks enough. We've loved having you for the summer. And you'll be a tremendous help at the orphanage with the accounting certificate." Madeleine sipped her champagne. Tingles gathered and skipped down her throat.

"I'll be happy to help, but I meant your fundraising for Coronati House. You were so generous—you saved us."

"Jack enjoyed the challenge." The project had helped her too. "And we were both so thankful for my healing." The deep anguish Madeleine had known since her baby drowned would always be with her. *Had it really been twenty-four years since that summer of '75? Since she left Mollie in the wading pool?* Some days it seemed like yesterday—she would never forget. But on that pilgrimage she had accepted God's love.

"Are your nightmares truly gone?" Elena asked.

"Mostly. The journey through Italy worked miracles. But helping the orphanage has...how can I say it? Helping *continues* the healing."

"I'm glad."

"The convent does wonderful work in Rome, with all the babies and new mothers."

Elena looked into the distance. "Perhaps I shall take vows, become a nun one day."

Madeleine gazed at the young woman, so untouched by the world. Elena seemed unaware of her own beauty—her dark eyes, strong nose, full lips, and smooth skin. "You have time to work that out." Could she give up marriage, motherhood, family?

Elena tilted her head, unconvinced.

Jack joined them and took a seat beside Madeleine. "I was getting a bit tired, so George is relieving me." His face was white as he pulled out his blood pressure monitor and wrapped it around his wrist.

Madeleine waited for his reaction to the numbers. Medication had kept things under control, but he checked his heart rate regularly. He nodded an okay.

A young boy ran toward Jack, proudly waving a badge, his slacks grass-stained at the knees. "Mr. Seymour, Mr. Seymour! I got it. I got it. Thank you for helping me!" He lisped, his front teeth missing.

"And what did you get, Max?" Jack examined the cloth emblem. "It looks mighty like a fish, it does."

"It *is* a fish, Mr. Seymour. It's my fishing badge."

Madeleine grinned. She recalled the weekend Jack helped with the Russian River trip. He had come home aching and itching and sunburned and complaining he was too old for this.

"Congratulations, Max. We worked hard for that one, didn't we?"

"Yeah."

"And we'll work hard on the next one, won't we?" He handed the badge to the boy and tousled his hair.

"Yeah," Max said and ran back to his mother.

Jack smiled weakly and touched his forehead. "Cute kid."

"You okay?" Madeleine reached for his shoulder.

He leaned forward, swaying slightly. His glass slipped from his hand and onto the lawn. The clear liquid poured into the green grass.

"Sorry, not feeling too good." His speech was hoarse, raspy.

"Perhaps we'd better go home."

"My chest hurts...don't want to alarm you...all the same, a bit dizzy. Let me rest a minute."

"I'll get Father Michaels." Elena hurried away.

"Is it like last time?" Madeleine leaned over him, her arm around his shoulders, seeing the Emergency Room and feeling the fear. Doctor Lau had diagnosed acute gastritis and bathed his gastro-intestinal tract with an intravenous antacid.

"Yes and no...oh..." He doubled over, his hand on his chest. "I think I need to lie down. Don't let Justin see me—don't want to spoil things."

The young vicar approached. He studied Jack's face and felt his pulse. "Let's take him to the rectory." He motioned toward the house next door and helped Jack to his feet.

10

Chapter Two
San Francisco Medical

We find suffering and love
twined so closely together,
that we cannot wrench them apart: and if we try...
the love is maimed in the process.
Evelyn Underhill

Tuesday morning the rain fell in gusts, freak swirls of moisture carried over the sea by high winds. The red brick buildings of San Francisco Medical stood against the cold sky, solid and staid, suggesting permanence where there were no guarantees, only hopes, prayers, and goodly efforts.

Jack had survived his fainting spell, but tests were ordered. His EKG was normal. Even so, Conrad Lau ordered an endoscopy; the doctor would insert a minute camera through Jack's esophagus and stomach.

Madeleine followed Jack to the hospital entrance, through a crowded lobby, and into an elevator as the doors began to close. Their collapsed umbrellas dripped, water pooling at their feet. A woman in a wheelchair stared at the floor, creating an open space surrounded by tall, tense bodies. For thirty seconds they were a closed society of eight, travelers in a steel cage.

A bell rang, the door opened, and a disembodied voice announced the third floor. Jack and Madeleine squeezed out and walked down the wide, empty corridor to the end of the hall. Through swinging double doors, they entered the Diagnostic Center and took seats in a small waiting room crammed with empty plastic chairs.

Madeleine looked about the room. A sign on the wall read *Patients Rights and Responsibilities* in English, Chinese, and Spanish, the linguistic colors of San Francisco. A tattered *Good Housekeeping* magazine sat in a plastic wall rack, *Hispanic* in the slot below. A disconnected lamp stood in the corner, décor without light. Air whirred through ceiling vents in the windowless room as they waited in the silence under long florescent tubes.

"I'm glad Justin didn't see me faint," Jack said, "and we were able to send him off on his honeymoon." He focused on the opposite wall as though it held his future.

"We'll have to let him know at some point." Madeleine studied Jack's strong profile, his jaw set, determined. "And your sons as well, for that matter."

He rubbed his hands. "Not yet, not Justin and Lisa Jane, at least not until they get back. Doctor Lau insists it's not my heart, but the pain sure feels like it."

"I'm thankful it's *not* your heart."

"It could be worse."

"Nothing's worse than heart disease. Well, cancer, maybe, but Barrett's Esophagitis isn't cancer." She tried to keep the tension out of her tone, the pleading.

He rubbed his chest. "Close enough—pre-cancer."

"The doctor thinks you can help control the reflux with diet and stress reduction. Maybe you worry too much, honey."

A wave of anger—or simply panic—crossed his face. "I have a lot to worry about. The market's going crazy. Those stocks and bonds are our retirement, Maddie, at least what's left of them." He handed Madeleine his wallet, ring, and watch. "Be sure and talk to the doctor afterwards. He dopes me up and I don't remember what he tells me."

"I will."

He covered his face with his palms. "I just retired and now all this keeps happening. I worked so hard, Maddie."

"I know." She shivered.

"It's all so unfair. We finally can do things we never had time for or could afford. I wanted to travel a bit."

"Jack, maybe you should try praying." Madeleine reached for his hand. He withdrew it.

"Not now, Maddie, not now." If it was panic before, now it was anger.

"Please, Jack."

"This could be the real thing, Maddie." He turned, his eyes imploring her to understand.

She touched his shoulder. "I know."

The door opened and a nurse looked in. "Jack Seymour?" And to Madeleine, "He'll be about two hours. The cafeteria's on the second floor."

Madeleine watched Jack disappear down the hall.

She pulled from her bag a slim paperback Father Rinaldi had given her—Evelyn Underhill's *The School of Charity*. Today, she thought, it would be called *The School of Love*, for this earlier meaning of "charity" had faded with disuse. Perhaps she would find answers in these words to questions of life and death, why life *was* death, why man's dying began the day he was born.

Where was Father Rinaldi now? She missed him, his comfort, his wise words. She saw in her mind the day he died, as he consecrated the bread and wine. Such a moment to die—in the midst of the great sacrifice of the mass. His heart gave out—he was, after all, quite elderly—and God allowed him this peaceful passing. Even so, his leaving them left a hole in their lives, an empty space that could never be filled. She would see him again, she often told herself.

The book lay open in her palms. She pulled out a pencil and notepad and soon was folding page corners, fearing she would forget the words, wanting to hold the visions of this Anglican mystic close and real and available.

Suddenly Madeleine put the book down, clasped her hands together, and closed her eyes.

She prayed for Jack's peace, his comfort, the dulling of his pain. She saw the tube go down his throat and into his erupting stomach, where uncontrolled worry-explosions searched for a target and, finding none, destroyed the walls of his insides. The camera at the end of the tube would diagnose the present and predict the future. *Dear God, help us.*

Madeleine noticed other patients take seats and wait tensely, carrying their own revelations of mortality hidden, skeletons in a dark closet. Here, in this sterile space lit by cold rays, their bodies confronted their souls, thrusting them into the half-light, the physical facing the spiritual, as though meeting unexpectedly for the first time.

Time loomed precious as the sand fell faster through the hourglass, like rocks in an avalanche.

"Mrs. Seymour," the nurse said from the doorway, "could you come with me, please?"

Madeleine followed her down the hall of carts and linens and electronic boxes to a small room with computer monitors hanging from the walls, cords snaking through the air, and more electronic boxes. She recognized the heart rate screen with its jagged black line pronouncing life or death. Jack lay on his side, covered by a blanket, a tube dangling from his mouth, his eyes half-shut as he stared dully at the mattress edge. Madeleine turned toward the doctor.

Conrad Lau was a tight-knit man, middle-aged with lively eyes behind thick lenses. He stood beside the bed. He held a long wand that guided the camera, exploring Jack's stomach. He shifted his gaze from the monitor to Madeleine. "Please sit over here. I want to show you something."

Madeleine sat on a stool and stared at the screen. The pale tissue pulsated wet and bloody, as firm rounded masses of slippery matter worked in time to the beat of Jack's heart. The doctor directed the camera through the esophagus, and the tissue closed behind. Entranced, Madeleine sensed she was a traveler in a hidden universe, an unseen world suddenly seen.

"Now, here," he said, "you see the sphincter muscle. It's next to the opening that allows food to enter the stomach. This hole also releases gas from the stomach when we burp. The sphincter is made to open and close as needed, to keep food from coming up from the stomach. In some cases, for varying reasons, the sphincter becomes lazy, either slow to close, or not closing at all, allowing the walls of the esophagus to be bathed in stomach acid. Eventually the walls form a stomach-type lining and can become ulcerous, pre-cancerous. This is Barrett's esophagus and must be watched closely. Jack's sphincter remains open."

Madeleine leaned forward, mesmerized by the flesh and the blood. The tissue around Jack's sphincter was red and blistering as though it had been burned.

"The red area," Doctor Lau said, "is caused by the rising acids."

"Oh dear."

Looking at the screen, she followed the camera's path through the esophageal opening into the stomach, to a landscape of plains and valleys where peaks flared into pimply rashes. Shiny with moisture and splotched with bloody crevices, the tissue pulsed with the beat of her husband's heart.

But where was Jack, *her* Jack? His eyes were glazed. She reached out her hand, covering his. *I'm here.*

"This is an ulcer." Doctor Lau pointed to a crevice leading to a dark hole, then motioned to the nurse for the syringe and sent a bath of liquid through Jack's system, washing the blood away.

Jack coughed.

"I want to take some biopsies," Doctor Lau said, "and then we'll know for sure. Try not to cough, Jack. You must stay still while I do this."

He maneuvered tiny clippers to a red patch and snipped a bit of tissue. The camera lens filled with blood, followed by a wash of more fluid. Find and snip, wash, find and snip, wash. Blood and water, blood and water.

Doctor Lau's voice was calm, as though wrapping up a day's work. "We're just about done, Jack. Hold on."

A final wash poured through his stomach, and the tissue pulsed with life, glistening and clean, the red patches swelling and retreating, swelling and retreating.

"We're out." The doctor pulled the cord slowly through the esophagus, past the epiglottis, and over the tongue.

"He needs to rest. I'll call you."

"But..."

"I have to check the biopsies, Madeleine." His eyes were kind.

"Can't you tell me anything?" She glanced at her husband, who appeared to be dozing.

"I'm afraid it's a waiting game at this point." Doctor Lau put his hand in the small of her back and gently walked her to the door.

She returned to the sterile room of plastic chairs, the avalanche louder than ever.

Chapter Three
Sea Cliff

Charity suffereth long, and is kind;
charity envieth not;
charity vaunteth not itself, is not puffed up.
1 Corinthians 13:4

Wednesday evening Madeleine waited for the water to boil, for the bird spout to whistle in the white enamel kettle. She set out the mugs and tea bags—one chamomile and one Earl Grey—with a bowl of sweetener and a pitcher of milk on a bamboo tray, and added a plate of Elena's oatmeal cookies. They had finished their supper and Jack sat on the deck, stroking their tabby, Miss Kitty, as he stared into the dusk. The moist air was warm with a smell of salt from the ocean, carrying a promise of September heat. A waning crescent moon climbed behind the dark pillars of the Golden Gate Bridge, as the black surf rolled below.

In spite of recent events—or maybe because of them—it was one of those moments of deep contentment. Madeleine's eyes roved tenderly over the familiar kitchen and beyond, into the living room. Their home on the cliff was not large, but well situated west of the bridge, looking over the pounding Pacific. They had found it the weekend Madeleine proposed (she wanted to know Jack's intentions) and proceeded to pour their lives into it, painting and papering here, remodeling there, tearing out and adding on. Each bit of the house spoke of their years, their children, their grandchildren. The dining room table, a heavy mahogany piece from Jack's great aunt, hosted weaving conversations as platters of Christmas turkey and Easter ham passed from hand to hand. The bedrooms welcomed grandbabies and nieces and nephews and aunts and cousins. The compact kitchen was somehow big enough, and bodies bumped as corks popped and cooks stirred, a symphony of family. The paneled den cosseted 'Niners and Giants fans, the sportscasters bellowing through two floors to the attic where Madeleine read, the sea breeze blowing sweetly through open dormer windows. The breakfast nook, with its ivy wallpaper, opened to a wooden deck where Madeleine and Jack sipped cocktails as they watched the sun set or the fog roll in.

Madeleine lifted the kettle and poured the boiling water into their mugs. She carried the tray outside and set it on the table. "The tea needs to steep a bit."

"You said Doctor Lau was coming by?" Jack asked.

"He should be here soon," she said, reaching for a cookie.

"Why couldn't he call with the results?"

"He wanted to see us. He has pictures."

"It makes me worry." Jack tapped his fingers together.

"He said we're on his way home."

"I like Conrad Lau—always have, even if he does beat me at golf. He's a hard worker, a self-made man. I trust him, but what's he going to say?"

The doorbell rang and Elena shouted, "I'll get it."

Madeleine heard her pound up the steps from her basement apartment, speak a few muffled words, then pound back down.

Conrad Lau appeared in the doorway, holding a large manila envelope. "I hope I didn't alarm you by stopping by."

"Of course not," Madeleine said. "We appreciate the house call. Will you have some tea?"

"No, thank you. I'll just be a minute." He pulled a chair closer to Jack. "Madeleine saw the movie, as I like to say." He smiled, but Jack didn't respond. The doctor pulled out several five-by-seven glossy photos. "Look, now..."

Madeleine turned on the porch light and Miss Kitty jumped from Jack's lap.

"Jack, see the redness along the walls of the esophagus and around the opening to the stomach? This is the source of your pain. Your heartburn has progressed to Barrett's esophagus, caused by a weak sphincter muscle that won't close properly. We need to close that opening a bit."

"It's still esophagitis?" Jack asked as he studied the images of his own insides. "That's the cause of the pain? So how do we close the opening?"

"We wrap it with tissue from the stomach wall."

As Madeleine stood behind Jack, listening to Doctor Lau explain what she had seen, she felt her life falling, caught by the tide and washed to unknown depths. "Who does this operation?" she asked, her whisper sounding distant, apart from her self.

"I've brought resumes of two surgeons who are very good. You choose, and we'll set it up."

"Two? There are just two?" Jack scanned the sheets. "They're both under thirty. You've got to be joking. They're only kids."

Conrad Lau wrinkled his brow. "They're here at SF Medical and are covered by your insurance. There *is* one other, who specializes in this sort of thing, but I don't recommend her."

"*Her?*" Jack asked.

"You really *don't* want to use her. She has experience, but perhaps too much. In fact, she's Chief of Surgery. But she...er...may be unavailable."

Jack leaned forward. "She sounds good. What do you mean, too much experience? I *want* experience."

Madeleine breathed deeply, her chest tight. "Tell us about her. We need to know everything in order to choose."

Doctor Lau stood and slipped his glasses into their case. "I've said too much already. It has to be your decision."

Jack shook his head, determined. "But Conrad, at least give us her resume."

"Okay, but I advise against her." He pulled a third sheet from the envelope.

Madeleine read the words over Jack's shoulder.

Rachelle DuPres
Born 1942, Crillon-le-Brave, France; naturalized U.S. citizen through adoption.

Columbia, BA Pre-Med, Magna Cum Laude; Harvard Medical School 1968 Honors; Johns Hopkins Gastro-Intestinal Unit 1969-1978; San Francisco Medical 1978-1985, Department Head, Gastro-Intestinal Unit; 1985-present, Chief of Surgery.

Madeleine looked at the surgeon's photo: large dark eyes behind horn-rimmed glasses, long nose, high cheekbones, short hair, a serious expression.

Jack rubbed his hands together. "She looks good to me. She looks smart. She also looks familiar. I've seen her in the paper—was she in the *Chronicle?*"

18

"Might have been. Trust me, Jack," Conrad said, standing. "Choose one of the others. You may keep this material. And, Jack, don't take any over-the-counter antacids. Just take your Prevacid, okay? And try not to worry. Let a few responsibilities go, let others do things for *you* for a change. Learn to relax. Are you still jogging?"

"I try to make it twice a week up to Lincoln Park and back."

"Good. And continue with the diet: no alcohol, no sodas; no milk products, unless cultured like cheese, yogurt, or cottage cheese; no caffeine and that means chocolate too, no tomatoes or juices, apple is okay. You have the list I gave you. Let me know who you want and we'll set a date. It's really the best course."

The phone rang, parting the night.

"It's for you, Mr. Seymour," Elena called. "It's your broker."

"Will you excuse me?" Jack asked, his voice rising. "We'll let you know. And Conrad—thank you." They shook hands and Jack headed for the kitchen phone. "It's probably that Neotex again," he said under his breath.

"I'll walk you out," Madeleine said to the doctor.

They paused on the front porch, and Conrad said quietly, "Madeleine, it's a bit more serious than I let on." He pulled a lab report from his case. "But we don't need to add to Jack's worries. We need to do this operation as soon as possible. One biopsy came back positive." He handed her the report. "I want that tissue removed and the wrap done. Otherwise, I couldn't guarantee more than six months. This stuff grows like wildfire."

"One biopsy came back positive? Six months? What do you mean, six months?" Madeleine searched his eyes, then tried to read the paper in the dim light.

"Six months to live, Madeleine. I'm sorry." He rested his hand on her arm. "But we do this procedure, and he'll have years ahead of him. He'll be fine. You understand?"

"I understand." She was queasy.

"Call me tomorrow with a name. And Madeleine..."

"Yes?"

"He'll be okay. I've seen a lot worse, but I don't want him worrying. We don't need to tell Jack just yet."

"But I can't keep something like this from him."

"You *can*, Madeleine. You must." His eyes were commanding, then imploring.

"But he has a right to know."

Conrad Lau looked into the dark. "Not necessarily. There's plenty of precedent for withholding a diagnosis. As a matter of fact, it once was part of the Medical Code. It still is in parts of Asia. My father was a doctor, you know, in Hong Kong. He didn't always tell his patients the whole story."

"But that's not right." She peered at him in the shadows.

Doctor Lau shook his head. "I had a patient like Jack once."

"You did? How was he like Jack?" she whispered, glancing back into the house.

The doctor's face was pale and twisted as though he relived something long ago buried, something he wanted to keep buried.

"Madeleine, he took an overdose. We never had a chance to operate. I shouldn't have told him. He overreacted. And his temperament was like Jack's—he needed to be in control, constantly in control." Doctor Lau shook his head and stared at the porch steps. "I still blame myself."

"I see." She swallowed hard, her throat dry.

"Didn't his father die when he was young?"

"He doesn't like to talk about it. I think he was around twelve."

"Cancer, wasn't it?" He looked up, probing gently.

Madeleine gazed into his almond eyes. Jack hadn't told *her*. "I don't know. Did he tell you? What else did he say?"

"I learned from his medical history. And he said once that his father died in a lot of pain."

"Oh dear."

"Madeleine, he told me another thing—"

"What was that?" Her heart pounded as she listened for footsteps.

"He said he couldn't understand why people would want to live, if their quality of life seriously deteriorated. 'Quality, not quantity,' he told me. Madeleine, I took the Hippocratic oath—I won't be a part of assisted suicide." His eyes were pleading.

"But *would* the quality of his life deteriorate?"

Doctor Lau raised his brows in a gesture of compromise. "Some would say so. Restricted diet. Flatulence. Chest pain. And of course we would monitor him closely with regular endoscopies, etc."

"I understand." *Regular endoscopies. Restricted diet.* The kind of regimen that would suffocate her husband. "He wouldn't like it—I can see your point, but still—"

"We'll tell him, Madeleine, but not just yet. We'll operate and he'll be fine, trust me. Let's set it up, okay?"

Madeleine breathed deeply, resigned. "Okay, we'll tell him, but not just yet." She felt for the cross around her neck and managed a thin smile. "We'll set it up."

He patted her arm. "Good girl. Call me tomorrow with that name, and leave the rest to me."

His compact figure faded into the dark, the Lexus door slammed, and the engine hummed to life. Numb, Madeleine folded the paper and put it in her pocket. *Dear God, help us.*

The taillights shrank to tiny red eyes, then disappeared around a bend.

Thursday morning Madeleine clutched the seatbelt as Jack drove the Volvo up 19th Avenue toward the medical center. "Jack, please, choose one of the two recommended doctors. They're both well qualified."

"When I can have the Chief of Surgery? And I called around—she's famous for this wrap procedure. Nearly invented it. Considered to have perfected it. Her resume looked wonderful—Harvard, top student. I'll bet she *teaches* this operation."

"But Doctor Lau said she may not be available."

"She's certainly not answering her phone."

"So you think you can simply walk into her office with no appointment?"

"No, I'm walking into her office to obtain an appointment."

They parked in the cavernous garage and found their way to the office building. Doctor Rachelle DuPres was listed in the lobby directory.

They entered the elevator and Jack punched *10*. "She must be good. She has the top floor."

They found the surgeon's door open. A young man stood behind a desk, filling a banker's box with files.

"Is this the office of Doctor DuPres?" Jack asked. "What's going on here?"

"We'd like to schedule an appointment, please," Madeleine said.

The man looked up. A hospital ID badge hung from his neck. "I'm her assistant. I'm sorry, but she's on vacation."

Jack frowned. "Vacation? Doctor Lau didn't say anything about that."

"It was a sudden decision. If you go down to the lobby, they can refer you—"

Jack's voice rose. "I don't want to go down to the lobby and I don't want a referral. When is she coming back?"

"We aren't sure. Please, if you'll go..."

The inner door was ajar, and Madeleine slipped in. The walls were bare except for an old clock, the kind hanging in a classroom, and a floor-to-ceiling map of the gastrointestinal tract. She studied the colored diagram: the esophageal tunnel reached into the stomach, the huge red liver nested to its left, the fat pudgy colon grabbed the lower stomach wall and wound down and around, then looped up to the maze of small intestine cradled by the pelvic bones.

Next to the diagram, a bookcase held thick texts wedged under binders and memo pads. Dusty mini-blinds tilted, throwing narrow bands of light onto an oak desk littered with papers and charts. A glossy paperback weighted the sheets. Madeleine read the title upside down from long force of habit: *Lourdes, the Ultimate Guide.*

"Lourdes," she whispered to herself, picking up the book. "I've been researching Lourdes, but I've never been there." She opened it. An airline ticket rested in the fold. She glanced back at the door and quickly read the inside of the ticket: San Francisco-Paris-Bordeaux, September 13. *Father Benedict O'Reilly* was printed neatly on a yellow slip clipped to the page. She closed the book, replaced it, and returned to the outer office.

"You really must leave, sir, or I'll have to call Security." The young man was picking up the phone.

Jack threw his hands up. "What next?"

"Let's go, honey." Gently, Madeleine laid her hand on his sleeve.

They walked toward the elevator, and she noticed her husband's flushed face as a slow throb moved through the back of her head, the sure sign of an oncoming migraine.

"Jack, let's choose another surgeon. We're fortunate to have a choice—it's a new procedure and you know our insurance is limited."

"I want the best. We've got time to find DuPres, and *we will find her.* I won't have some child opening me up, some student learning on me."

"They're fully trained, not students. And they put you out completely."

"I don't care. Experience is important. I should know from forty years in business. It makes all the difference between success and failure."

"Experience is important, but—"

They reached the elevator and Jack pushed the call button. He turned to Madeleine, his features full of anguish. "My father had three surgeries. They didn't help. Just made him worse. Mother was never sure exactly what happened on that operating table." Jack shook his head, as though stung by the memories.

"You never mentioned that before." She looked up at his agitated face. Why did it take a crisis to truly know the heart of someone you loved?

"I guess not. Mama made vague accusations. And I suppose she couldn't prove anything. We learned later that the surgeon had been sued for malpractice. Meg and I always wondered." He stared at the light panel over the door. "Where's this elevator, anyway? It's stopping at every floor—some kid must have played with the buttons."

The elevator arrived, and they entered the empty cage. Jack looked at her with his earnest blue eyes, his brows pinched with conviction. "So you see why this doctor is important—she knows what she's doing. She's irreplaceable."

"I see." At least, Madeleine could see Jack's thinking. To her, he traveled through a narrow tunnel of necessary certainty. No risks. But weren't there risks in not taking risks?

The door opened to the lobby, and Madeleine noticed signs to the chapel. She recalled this building had been part of a Catholic hospital before the merger.

"Jack, I want to visit the chapel."

"Sure. Meet me here—I need a few things in the pharmacy."

Madeleine entered the small sanctuary and paused in the back. A red lamp burned, suspended near a modern bronze box on the left wall, and she knew this box, sculpted with jagged ridges, held the Presence of Christ. The altar stood in a window-apse that curved outwards to a memorial garden. Above the altar, a simple crucifix hung in the still air. She could see, through the wall of glass, a marble Madonna and Child presiding over the garden of red roses and white benches.

Inside, the pews fanned in a semicircle, and Madeleine knelt in the back row, near the door. *Dear Lord, thank you for my life, thank you for Jack. Each day is a blessing. But Lord, do not let him die...Let me help him...I lost Mollie so long ago, my sweet baby girl, but you gave me Jack to heal the wounds. Now I'm losing him. Dear Lord, I cannot bear another loss.*

She genuflected in the aisle, and, as she stood, she glimpsed the white Madonna through the glass. Outside, Mary held her infant son, as she gazed upon her grown son inside, nailed to the cross, the two figures encapsulating time.

Madeleine found Jack in the lobby, and they walked to the car parked in the gray maze of concrete stalls. As Jack turned the ignition, Madeleine breathed deeply, her head still pounding.

"Jack..."

"Madeleine, no more arguments. I'm calling Lau when we get back. He's got to know how to reach her."

"Jack, I think I know where she is, or at least where she's headed."

Jack turned to Madeleine as she entered the den. "I want to see her in person. I have more influence that way."

It was Friday and Jack was making calls. His den was his command center, as he called it, the hub of his retired life. From his massive oak desk, he called his broker to argue over stocks. He set up meetings with the Scout board. He even called parents about their boys, reminding them of events. He wrote letters to the editor. He organized fundraising dinners for Coronati House.

Madeleine sat on a leather couch with her second cup of morning coffee. Miss Kitty had been fed and let out; the dishes were done. They had held many serious conversations in this room, she thought, made many decisions. Some better than others.

"You worry too much." She could see that her husband was going to be obstinate, challenged as he was by the search for the elusive doctor. It didn't help that Conrad Lau refused to give out her home number.

"Of course I worry. That's how I get things done. At least get them done right. One of us has to worry." He looked at her fondly. "And I don't want you doing it."

"So you have to see her to interview her?" They might be able to track her down on the phone. "Maybe we should hire someone to find her. That would save time."

"A needless expense."

Madeleine gave up the fight, as she usually did. Her parents had fought and she had cowered in a corner, waiting for the cold silence, waiting for one to submit, to keep the peace. She had pursued this argument with Jack as far as she could. She needed a break. "Who were you calling?"

"Travel agents. You said she was in Lourdes, right? It would be fun to go back to France, get my mind off things, taste a little wine—just a little, mind you."

"How about Hank Harvey? He worked at United. He might still have connections."

Jack smiled. "I should have thought of Hank. I'll call him."

Madeleine watched him dial his law school buddy. Hank had trained for trial law and set up his own practice, but the pressure gave him ulcers. He finally accepted a job as United's in-house counsel. "Best thing I ever did," he often said. He got discounted airline tickets as well.

Jack hung up and turned to Madeleine. "We have three seats to Paris, connecting to Bordeaux, next Wednesday. From Bordeaux, we drive to Lourdes. Hank's calling back to confirm, but it looks good. You wanted Elena to come with us, right?"

"She knows the language. She'd be invaluable."

Jack rubbed his hands in anticipation. "And let's spend some time in Paris—after we find the doctor. I made a few dollars on that Internet merger last week."

"Sounds good." But would it be good? Would the trip help or hinder? Lourdes itself was a place of healing, but she had no idea how to find this Father O'Reilley and they might never locate the mysterious doctor. She would be relieved if Elena could come along. Some days Elena seemed like a daughter—had Mollie lived, she would be close to Elena's age. With that thought, the old heartache returned and Madeleine headed for the laundry room to pull the last load from the dryer.

Elena was already there, folding.

"I heard the timer go off," she said. Her hair was pulled into a clip and she wore running shorts and a cotton tee.

"We got the tickets."

"Really? We're going to Lourdes?" She rolled the last pair of socks and slipped them into a corner of the rubber basket. Her eyes were wide with expectation.

"It looks like it. And maybe Paris. After we find this doctor."

Chapter Four
Alameda

Pain, or at least the willingness to risk pain,
alone gives dignity to human love, and is the price of its creative power:
without this, it is mere emotional enjoyment.
Evelyn Underhill

On the second Saturday of September, Doctor Rachelle DuPres charged the net and deftly sliced the ball down to her left, where it landed two feet into Conrad Lau's forehand service court. Her old friend had made the mistake of playing a safe baseline game when he felt threatened, and Rachelle had taken full advantage. *Game, set, match.*

The ball continued its hop across their neighbor's court, totally unreachable. Connie threw his racquet in the air in defeat.

"How did you do that?" he asked as he approached the net to shake her hand. "Still, seven to five in a tiebreaker isn't bad after splitting sets."

Rachelle grasped Connie's sweaty palm. "Not bad. But thanks, Doc, I needed that."

"And you haven't even played recently—I've missed our Saturday matches."

She smiled thinly, pulled off her visor, and ran her fingers through her thick short hair. It was good to be on the courts again. Tennis had been a regular part of her life, her old life. But this morning her body moved as though drugged, stepping through routine maneuvers, dipping and swinging, turning and twisting, lobbing and slamming down. All the while she watched herself as though from a distance. The final score was a surprise.

They toweled off and drank deeply from their water bottles. The morning fog had evaporated, the sun was hitting them hard, and it was only eleven.

"Thanks for taking the time," Connie said as they rested on the courtside bench. "You must be busy packing. When do you leave? Your secret is safe with me, although I have several patients who desire your services. But we've been friends too long to ask questions. I won't pry."

It *had* been a long friendship, Rachelle thought. They had met at Harvard grad school over thirty years ago, and when Rachelle was appointed Chief of Surgery at San Francisco Medical, Connie and his wife urged her to buy into their Alameda neighborhood across the bay. She had never regretted it; she needed friends—she had few enough.

She slipped her racquet into its case. "Connie, I need to talk. Can we walk along the coastal trail?"

"Sure," he replied, his brow wrinkling.

The sun beat on their backs as they walked in silence along the estuary. Rachelle gazed at San Francisco's skyline rising in the distance, a fairy-tale collection of spires shooting out of the mist. A light breeze rippled the water, and a few sails dotted the bay, catching a last chance of summer. She took a deep breath. The air smelled of sea salt. Gulls soared, crying to one another.

How could she find the words to describe what was happening to her? The phrases seemed impossibly elusive, but she owed Conrad some sort of explanation.

Since the failed surgery, darkness had eclipsed her thoughts and governed her actions. Her ward routines merged into distant patterns apart from her center, and she recognized the sure signs of depression: separation, distrust, sadness. That last surgery flashed through her consciousness. It replayed and replayed.

Her colleagues had urged her to seek help, having noticed uncharacteristic lapses in her judgment. She had not returned calls, had missed patient appointments. She had forgotten meals and lost weight. Her fitness routine, tennis followed by thirty laps in the club pool, had become irrelevant. She slept little as masked faces, chrome monitors, and...blood...flashed through her night. She had considered therapy, but fled from such a public statement of distress, for wouldn't her peers find out? She refused tranquilizers and feared alcohol, having seen their toll on her father.

Conrad stopped and faced her. "So Rachelle, what's going on? You know we're all worried."

She stared at the gravel path, then out to the bay. "Who's we? The Board?"

"Naturally they're concerned."

"Has the press gotten to *you* too?"

"The press gets to everyone, Rachelle, but, no, I haven't spoken to them, and I don't intend to. This will all be forgotten in time. Mrs. Steinhoff has no case, no case at all."

"Okay. Here it is. I'm taking a sabbatical. Going to France. Monday, the day after tomorrow." *September 13,* she thought—her birthday, a date she rarely celebrated.

"France? Monday? Fine. We'll manage here. Take as long as you need. But why France?"

"I'm going to visit an old friend, Father Benedict." She had dreamed of him, she suddenly realized.

"Father Benedict?"

"My parish priest from home, from Massachusetts."

"I didn't realize you were Catholic."

Rachelle examined her fine-boned hands. "I'm not. I was raised Catholic, but it was mostly routine. We didn't attend church regularly. Our adoptive parents were lapsed Irish Catholics, you could say. Still, there was First Communion, Confirmation, social occasions."

"So why are you visiting this priest?"

"My own sort of pilgrimage, I guess. He was always easy to talk to. He sent a card last Christmas—he's in Lourdes."

"Is he? Lourdes is amazing."

"You go there, don't you? I'd forgotten." She regarded him with a vague curiosity.

"Every May with the Knights of Malta. We fly patients...and pilgrims. It's a remarkable place, Rachelle."

"Is it? After Lourdes, I might visit my sister and her family. She settled in a village in Provence." Rachelle had paid little attention to her twin sister in the last few years, rarely answering Rebecca's letters, engrossed as she was in her work at the hospital.

"Excellent. Where in Provence?"

"Crillon-le-Brave? Near Avignon? They grow grapes." She had found the place on a map.

Conrad looked out to the bay as though slipping into another world. "We've been to Burgundy, farther north. The countryside's charming, the wines fabulous. Su-Lynn and I wanted to buy a farmhouse, but it hasn't happened yet." He glanced at her as though expecting a laugh, but Rachelle didn't laugh.

They continued past the large custom-built houses that swallowed the small lots. Giant windows stared vacantly out to sea like glass eyes. She was like those empty houses, staring out to...to where?

28

They came to a point of land jutting into the bay. Rachelle welcomed the wind and spray, as the sea washed the rocks.

"So tell me about your sister," Conrad said, his tone gentle. "I don't recall you mentioning her."

It was true. Their friendship had revolved around work, tennis, and Su-Lynn's wonderful cooking. It was as though Conrad's family had become hers. She was grateful.

"She's different." Rachelle tried to form a picture of Rebecca. Freckles. Wide-set dreamy eyes. Thick dark hair, untamable. "She's my fraternal twin. We were smuggled out of France as babies. During the war, during the Nazi occupation. Through Lourdes and Spain to America. The Kennedys adopted us. They were good parents."

"But Rebecca returned to France?"

"She met Philippe in Paris—at the Sorbonne. He wanted to grow grapes. She wanted to find her roots. So they settled in Crillon, northeast of Avignon. I have two nieces and two nephews I haven't seen since they were children. Although I feel close to Pierre, the younger boy. He must be around twenty-five now. We've exchanged e-mails over the last few years. He's interested in medicine."

They paused in pensive silence, Conrad seeming to mull over her last words and Rachelle thinking of Pierre. She turned to her friend. "You need to get home, Connie. Su-Lynn will wonder what happened to you."

"Right. Rachelle, don't burn your bridges. You're a talented surgeon, and we need you. Keep your options open, okay?"

They headed back, shouldering their bags.

"Thanks, Connie, for listening. I'll find something French for the children. And I'll come by the house before I leave."

Rachelle trimmed her short hair shorter. She packed an extra pair of reading glasses, a Eurail guide, and foreign currency. She found her passport. She placed toothbrush, toothpaste, and sunscreen in a plastic freezer bag. She slipped her documents and wallet into an inner pocket of her backpack. She stopped the mail. She took no paper, owned no pets. The hasty preparations renewed her energy and hope; the suddenness of it appeased her, shaped her anger, and channeled her despair. Perhaps she was merely escaping, or trying to. Maybe she wanted to change something, to forcibly explode her habits of life, to shock herself out of this malaise, this gray, grisly hell.

By eight Sunday night she was packed, except for toiletries and a guidebook, which would go in her carry-on. She checked her e-mail and almost smiled when she saw Pierre's stilted message.

To: Rdupres@healthlink.net
From: Stones@aol.com
Subject: You

Ma tante chèrie, I learned you are coming! Very fine news! When?
Need for you to talk about internships. And spécialités. Et autres choses.
Helped deliver baby last week. Awesome as you say there.
We meet your plane in Lyons? Or train in Avignon?
Pierre

Pierre's words touched her, and for the moment she held on to a pleasant sense of anticipation. Could she help her nephew? Then came a rush of sadness. Unlikely.

Rachelle moved to the kitchen and poured herself a glass of Chardonnay from a bottle she had been nursing all week. She opened a can of minestrone, poured it into a pot, and set it on an electric burner. Perched on a counter stool, she watched the six o'clock news while her soup heated.

It would be good to flee, she thought, gazing at the flickering screen without seeing it. Flee the hospital, flee herself, find some sort of peace. She wondered if there might be life after death, as the Catholics believed. Indeed, even the Jews believed in life after death. Muslims too, for that matter.

In her mind, Judy Steinhoff's face appeared, accusing her. The woman's eyes were red and watery, her face puffy, her skin blotched. She had barged through Rachelle's outer office, looming suddenly large and threatening over her desk. A baby was strapped to her back and a young child clutched her skirt. Mrs. Steinhoff waved her hand as her voice rose, shattering the close office air. "Who do you think you are? God?"

A hissing of hot liquid hitting enamel pulled Rachelle to the present. She darted to the stove and yanked the pot away from the burner as the soup overflowed.

Chapter Five
Lourdes, France

I did not ask you to believe it,
I only told you what I had seen.
Bernadette of Lourdes

O n Wednesday, the fifteenth of September, Madeleine, Jack, and Elena flew San Francisco-Paris-Bordeaux. Madeleine sat by the window, Jack took the aisle seat to accommodate his long legs, and Elena the seat behind him. Jack put on earphones and watched the news on the small screen overhead as Madeleine opened her laptop and looked up the Lourdes chapter she had drafted for her book. Would Mary speak to them, here in this place where she had spoken to the young Bernadette?

Holy Manifestations: the Virgin Mary
Man has long been drawn to the holy, to that which is greater than himself, the Other. It was the People of Israel who first learned that the Other was one, not many, and this phenomenal change in the course of mankind's thinking changed the world.

Around 1900 BC, Abraham and his family left the sophisticated city of Ur, the Sumerian capital in the lush Euphrates River valley, heading for "the Land of Canaan." Old Testament accounts of his journey, histories with named individuals acting in chronological time, show little resemblance to the mythic writings of the period such as the *Epic of Gilgamesh*. The histories tell how Abraham's people worshiped one God, not many gods as was common in Sumer.

The God of Abraham led his people, speaking through prophets and prophetesses, kings and queens, accepting their innocent sacrifices burned on his altars in expiation of Adam's (and their own) sin, preparing them for the great Coming of the Holy One in Bethlehem. The woman chosen to carry the divine seed and to give him birth—the new Eve in the world of man—was Mary, a young, devout girl from the royal line of David.

Madeleine pictured the rustic Madonna in Saint Thomas'. What had the real Mary been like? She glanced back at Elena, deep in her book. She may have been like Elena, with her dark hair and skin. One day Madeleine would know, she would meet the mother of Jesus, of that she was certain.

Jack's screen pulsed with bright images moving about in quick succession. Madeleine turned to her own screen and focused on the quiescent words that moved in a different way, following her singular pattern of thought, her own manner of imaging.

Mary of Nazareth, daughter of Anne and Joachim, was obedient to the call. When Gabriel appeared and announced she would bear God's Son, she said "yes." Her obedience has rung down through the centuries, an Eve who welcomed the touch of the Holy. She endured the sacrifices that were required with such obedience: the shame of her condition in a society of strict law (and the fear of death by stoning), her difficult ride to Bethlehem in her last week, giving birth in the straw amidst the cattle (the dung, the flies, the lack of privacy, the isolation from her family). Through it all, she endured, obedient, trusting she was blessed among women.

Madeleine paused. Mary was indeed obedient and trusting, two qualities considered foolish today.

Mary watched her son grow to manhood, and when he hung on the cross she wept tears of grief, a sword piercing her heart. She rejoiced with the apostles in the upper room when he reappeared to them. She retreated with the young John to Ephesus (today Kusadasi, Turkey) where legend claims she lived to an old age and was bodily assumed to heaven.

Mary is the patron saint of France, a beloved mother and friend, the sacred feminine. As the mother of Jesus, she is the mother of God, the *Theotokos*, the *God-bearer*. She is mother to all Christians, who make up Christ's body on earth. In the nearly two thousand years since her assumption to heaven, she has intervened in our world again and again through visions and miracles. God has worked through the young girl who said *yes*. The evidence is plentiful.

In the same mysterious way, God has also worked through his saints, those who burned with love for him and in him, to lighten the dark, to alleviate suffering, to rescue, to heal, and to give hope in a world of despair. We do not know how, but we know why: he loves us. We do not know whether the saint blesses us or it is God working through the saint, or if there is even a difference between the two, but we know that miracles happen. The testimony is powerful.

Madeleine glanced at Jack, who had fallen asleep with his mouth open; a slow rattle escaped his lips and his head bobbed. Would they find this Doctor DuPres in Lourdes? Or would they find something else entirely? Would they encounter Mary in a new way, a healing light? *Hail Mary...*

She returned to her manuscript, pleased to see the next passage. The story of Bernadette touched her. The child was so poor, so simple, so earnest.

Holy Manifestations: Saint Bernadette

On February 18, 1858, fourteen-year-old Bernadette Soubirous saw a "beautiful Lady" in the Massabielle grotto on the River Gave southeast of Bordeaux.

The Gave had witnessed wonders before. In the fourteenth century, shepherds found a statue of the Virgin Mary in a burning bush along its banks and built a chapel to honor the mother of Jesus. Legend claimed that shortly thereafter, a young girl, drowning in the river, was saved by a branch held out by Mary herself. The girl cried, "*O, lou beth arram!*," meaning "Oh, the lovely branch!" and the place came to be known as Bétharram. By the time of Bernadette, a seminary and shrine were well established.

A miraculous stream. A burning bush. A statue of the Virgin. A drowning girl saved by Mary. Signs and wonders.

The nearly destitute Soubirous family had moved from a mill to a former jail, the *cachot*. A chronic asthmatic and of simple intelligence, Bernadette was unschooled until age thirteen. On that extraordinary day in February, as she gathered firewood with her sister and a friend, a "gust of wind" drew her gaze to the grotto where she saw "a Lady in white." Bernadette prayed the rosary with the Lady. The Lady asked her to return.

The visions continued, and on February 24, Bernadette witnessed the eighth apparition. The Lady asked her to kiss the ground, scratch the soil, and wash in its waters. A curious crowd had gathered by this time, and they watched the young girl eat dirt and smear her face. The following day a spring bubbled from the earth.

Healings began. On March 1, Catherine Latapie, thirty-eight, thrust her deformed hand into the pool from the spring, and the hand returned to normal. Bouriette Louis, fifty-four, was cured of blindness in his right eye, and Henri Busquet, fifteen, was healed of tuberculosis tumors of the neck.[1]

On March 2, during the thirteenth apparition in the grotto, the Lady commanded, "Let the people come in procession and let a chapel be built here." Bernadette reported this to her parish priest, but he did not believe her. She urged him again that evening. He replied she must ask the Lady her name.

On March 25, the Lady answered, "I am the Immaculate Conception."[2]

When Bernadette reported this, the priest said, "But what are you saying? Do you know what that means?"

"No, but I kept saying the name to myself all the way here," Bernadette replied.[3]

The dogma of the Immaculate Conception, decreed by Pope Pius IX four years earlier and a popular belief since the early Middle Ages, claimed that the Virgin Mary was conceived without sin, a condition necessary, it was thought, for her son to be born without sin. Bernadette's clear ignorance of this doctrine convinced the priest that the apparitions were real, and he told his bishop.[4]

Bernadette trusted the Lady; Bernadette obeyed. Naturally, eventually, she would be believed. Bernadette was like Mary.

The healings continued. On July 6, two-year-old Justin Bouhort was cured of terminal paralysis when his mother immersed him in the spring.[5]

The local authorities began to interrogate Bernadette.

Throughout months of intense scrutiny and badgering (for the popularity of the spring had drawn thousands, threatening civil unrest in the village of Lourdes), she remained simple and straightforward. Finally, she was believed.

The devout Empress Eugenie in nearby Biarritz heard about the miraculous waters and gave some to her child suffering from tuberculosis. The boy recovered the following day. On October 5, 1858, his father, Napoleon III, opened the grotto to the public.

The healings of Lourdes were well documented, Madeleine recalled. But why were some healed and others not?

The waters of the shrine of Our Lady of Lourdes continue to heal, the sixty-fifth documented miracle announced September 21, 2005. It is estimated that approximately four thousand were cured in the fifty years following the shrine's opening (see *www.Lourdes-France.com*). The waters draw pilgrims, sick in soul as well as body, and healings of the heart would be impossible to document and too numerous to count. The waters baptize both the outer and inner man as they cleanse him of disease and sin, in an ongoing sacrament of healing, an ongoing manifestation of God on earth.

From Easter through October, Lourdes, population seventeen thousand, hosts five million pilgrims and tourists from all over the world, including seventy thousand sick and handicapped.

A tingle traveled through Madeleine's spine. Surely, Lourdes would speak to them. She glanced up the aisle as the dinner cart clattered toward them. Madeleine nudged Jack gently.

They arrived in Bordeaux on Thursday and drove southeast to Lourdes the following morning. Jack took the wheel and Madeleine navigated from the front seat, gripping the map and guidebook in her lap. Elena sat in the back.

Following the A62 through Sauterne vineyards, they turned south toward Pau and entered the Landes pine forests. They wound through rolling pasturelands, heading toward the Pyrenees. Finally, they threaded through the crowded pilgrim town of Lourdes and turned left at the River Gave. Madeleine directed Jack to a hotel on the Avenue Paradis, Jack checked them in, and they agreed to meet Elena in the lobby at six for an early dinner.

Once in their sparsely furnished room, Madeleine gazed through a foggy window to the Victorian town of neat hotels and immaculate streets.

Jack unzipped his garment bag. "I can't believe we passed through Bordeaux without a taste."

"I was thinking the same." Madeleine unpacked, and as she hung her tan slacks in the closet, a folded paper fell to the floor. She picked it up—the biopsy report. Quickly refolding it, she slipped it back into the pocket, glancing at Jack. Should she throw it away? Destroy the evidence? But she might need the evidence to convince him time was of the essence.

"Do you remember the village of Saint-Emilion?" Jack asked.

She recalled the local broker who had showed them around, accompanied by his pert wife, wrapped in silk scarves.

"I remember wonderful macaroons, giant puffy coconut mounds."

Jack walked to the window. "It seems longer than ten years ago. Saint-Emilion was on the Left Bank, but we toured the Right Bank too, the Cote d'Argent, remember? We visited the great house of Mouton Rothschild. What a trip that was—I still have some of those bottles in our cellar."

Madeleine joined him. "I kept the macaroon bag and lots of pictures. It seems like yesterday. Say, did you remember to pack the camera?"

"Sure did, but doubt I'll use it much. Can't get too interested in pictures these days."

"Maybe Elena would like to take a few. You enjoyed taking pictures, Jack. We have some nice enlargements at home. Are you sure?"

"I'm afraid those days are over, Maddie. But we did pretty well, didn't we? We took advantage of the opportunities. I had to, starting from nothing. I don't miss the stress, but I sure do miss the wine."

Madeleine turned and wrapped her arms around him. "You never passed up a chance. I loved that about you then and I love that now. There will be other challenges, just different ones."

He gazed over her head and out the window, his profile outlined by the afternoon light.

"Hey, Mr. Seymour," she teased. "*Look* at me." She touched the

36

scratchy stubble on his chin. "What are you thinking?"

"Maddie, it's worse." He turned, and his eyes probed hers. He stroked her hair, a familiar and comforting motion.

"Worse?"

"I'm getting more reflux, more liquid coming up. Let's prop up the bed really good tonight."

"Oh dear. And the pain?"

"My chest—it's on fire."

"We'll stuff the couch pillows under the mattress, create an angle. You'll breathe easier."

"What would I do without you?"

He pulled her close, and she rested her head on his heart, staring at the rain spattering the window. "I've had a good life, you know."

"And you will continue to have a good life, Jack."

"So many things." He spoke to her from a great distance, one formed by time and memory.

She listened, waiting.

"In some ways I was a real child star. That violin solo in the Paramount really made my mother proud."

Madeleine looked up at his face, full of another life, redeemed by the innocence of childhood.

"And then there was baseball," he continued, stroking her hair. "I wasn't half bad—had my share of home runs, sliding to home plate just in time."

Madeleine smiled, listening to the beat of his heart. "I'm not surprised." She wanted to hold this moment, capture it, live in it forever.

"And did you know, at one point, I tried to run the local Methodist church? I was eighteen when they elected me to chair the Board. It seems incredible now."

"I wish I had been there." Madeleine tried to imagine him, explaining to his elders the best plan, the year's goals.

"But we were so poor, Maddie. So poor. We scrimped and saved, we watched and counted every penny. We never had enough. I hated that Mama wore the same dress every Sunday."

"I'll bet she didn't mind."

"She never said a word."

"She would be proud of you today, Jack."

"Would she? I'm not so sure. Anyway, it's all going to be over soon enough."

"Don't say that." His words thrust them into the present. She could touch his anguish, full of vague remorse mingled with excuse.

The three travelers dined in a small café that served a reasonable *menu du jour* featuring the local cuisine. Outside, a light rain fell as Madeleine watched Elena ladle white bean soup into their bowls.

"So," Elena said, "I've found Father O'Reilley. He was listed with the Visitor's Bureau."

"Did you really?" Madeleine raised her brows. "That was quick— nice job."

"He's in the Franciscan house here in town. He runs a retreat kitchen for pilgrims. I called him."

"And?" Jack poured a glass of wine for Madeleine.

"He will meet us at Saint Michael's Gate at ten in the morning. We're in Lourdes, and we have a guide! I can't believe I am really here, *in Lourdes!*"

"And Doctor DuPres?" Madeleine asked. "Did he know anything about her?"

Elena played with a loose strand of hair. "He did, but he said he would explain when he saw us."

"It's a beginning," Madeleine said. "I wonder what their relationship is." Was she Catholic? Maybe she was helping at one of the clinics.

Jack sipped his water. "I'm looking forward to meeting her," he said hopefully. "She may be able to give us a rough date for the surgery."

"I am too." Madeleine stirred her soup, watching the mushroom flakes follow her spoon in the spiraling eddies of white puree.

Elena looked at Madeleine, then Jack, her eyes bright. "I hope we can see Bernadette's grotto. Sister Agnes spoke of Lourdes. She described the night procession to the grotto where Bernadette saw Mary. The *malades*, the sick, carry lanterns in the dark."

Madeleine caught Jack's skeptical look. "I'd like to see the grotto, too, Elena," she said quickly. "Many have been healed by these waters, both body *and* soul. Many hearts have been healed as well."

Jack smiled thinly. "Hearts? How can hearts be healed? Sounds like poetic license."

"Broken hearts need healing," Elena said.

Madeleine looked about the room. "Unhappiness, confusion, grief, despair—there are many forms of heartbreak." Travelers clustered at tables, each bringing pieces of themselves to this shrine, broken pieces to be fit back together. "For me, understanding why so many are broken helps me believe in the mending."

Jack rubbed his chest. "Understand? Now you're talking about your mind."

"It's all *me*." Madeleine sipped her wine. "How can I separate my mind from my soul from my body from my heart?"

"Not without serious consequences." Jack smiled.

Elena laughed. "I agree, Mr. Seymour. But I know what Madeleine means. It *is* a mystery. Sister Agnes said the heart, mind, body, and soul only come together perfectly in the Eucharist."

"I've read that somewhere," Madeleine said, trying to remember the source, "or heard it in a sermon. We've been broken since Adam's fall—our bodies and souls split apart—and God gives us this chance to be whole again, holy, as it were."

"Right," Jack said, his tone edged with sarcasm. "Say, Elena, Madeleine wants you to be the trip photographer. I'm not really up to it. Would you like to take a few pictures?"

Elena grinned. "I'd love to. But you'll have to show me how."

The waitress set out a large bowl of greens and a basket of baguette slices, thick and crusty. Here, so close to Spain, olive oil was served in small bowls, and they tore bits of the fragrant bread, warm from the oven, and dipped them in the oil. Elena served the salad, which was dressed in lemon, oil, and sugar. Jack handed Madeleine a platter of lamb cutlets on a bed of rosemary sprigs. Aromas of garlic and onion drifted about them.

"So what do you know about Bernadette?" Jack took a small bite of lamb. "I saw the movie."

Chapter Six
The Esplanade

You will find all that is lacking in your heart
in the heart of Jesus.
F. Fénelon

aturday morning promised to be dry, and the village of young
Bernadette, so changed since her time, was quietly alive with
activity. Elena left early to find Father O'Reilly's hospice, and
Madeleine and Jack set out after a light breakfast in their room.
Breathing in the watered air, they walked down the Rue de la Grotte,
past curio shops and hotels, toward the entrance to the Cité Religieuse.
Others walked with them, serious white-clad attendants pushing
wheelchairs, the wounds of each person sometimes visible, sometimes
hidden. A sense of peaceful purpose drifted through the throngs as they
moved slowly forward this mild September day.

Madeleine handed Jack his cap and pointed up the street. "There's
Elena and that must be Father O'Reilly next to her. She remembered the
camera—it's around her neck."

Elena led a thickset man of medium height toward them; he was
probably in his eighties, Madeleine guessed. His dark cassock didn't
quite cover his black running shoes. "Father O'Reilly," Elena said, "may
I present Madeleine and Jack Seymour." She handed them empty plastic
bottles.

"Welcome to Lourdes! I'm Benedict O'Reilly." The priest shook
their hands as he appraised Jack. His thick white hair framed a ruddy
face, bushy black brows, a bulbous nose, and a small mouth that formed
his words with precision. "Elena has been telling me about your quest to
be healed."

"It's a pleasure to meet you, Father," Madeleine said. "We hoped
you could help us find Doctor DuPres—we understand she came here to

see you?" She couldn't quite read his face, but something was going on behind his cheerful countenance.

"We were hoping," Jack said, removing his hat, "to meet with her, if she has a few minutes."

"We know she's on vacation," added Madeleine. "We won't take much of her time."

Elena stared at Father Benedict and Jack rubbed his hands. Madeleine touched the cross about her neck, her eyes locked on the priest; clearly there was hesitation beneath his calm. Should she speak to him alone?

Benedict broke into a reassuring smile. "Please, let me show you around." He motioned toward the wide Esplanade des Processions, two straight paths on either side of a long strip of grass, surrounded by more parkland, leading to a Gothic basilica at the far end. "I understand this is your first visit to Lourdes, so I took the morning off in your honor. However, I'm sorry to say, Rachelle DuPres is not here." He glanced at each of them.

"Oh, no." Elena looked at Madeleine, then Jack. She fiddled with the camera strap.

"Not here?" Madeleine asked, her heart racing.

"Where is she, then?" Jack's voice rose with impatience. He glanced at the sun and slipped his hat back on, pulling the brim down firmly.

Father Benedict gestured toward a giant bronze crucifix standing at the foot of the pathways. "I'm glad they have this crucifix here, you know. We don't want to forget the main point."

"*Was* she here?" Madeleine asked, determined.

Benedict touched his chest, as though feeling for something under his cassock. "She *was* here, but...she left yesterday." He studied his shoes.

"And where did she go?" Jack's eyes bored into him.

Father O'Reilly looked from Jack to Madeleine to Elena. "It was wonderful to see Rachelle again. I was her parish priest in Massachusetts. Lots of Irish settled there and many clergy. But I was more Rachelle's teacher. She was forced to sit in my classroom several years for history and Latin."

"But, Father," Madeleine began again. Why was he avoiding their questions? She prayed for patience, for trust.

"A serious child," he continued, leading them up the Esplanade, "yet I remember her on the soccer field—could she run! I was delighted to hear she'd been accepted by Harvard Medical. I've kept in touch with her folks over the years but lost touch with her. I sensed she drifted away—from the Church—on purpose. You can't push belief, you know. Although something prompted me to send a card last Christmas to an old address. She said she received it."

Father O'Reilly, his eyes twinkling through deep crow's feet, gazed at Jack. Madeleine watched the two men study each other, as she and Elena followed them up the wide pathway. At the far end of the path, church spires rose into the sky, like beacons of hope connecting earth and heaven.

"I'm sorry," Elena whispered. "He's not very helpful." She focused the camera on the spires and clicked.

"It's okay. We'll manage. We must simply pay attention."

"Pay attention?"

"To God. You know—*the still, small voice of God*—like Elijah."

Father Benedict's words boomed through the crisp air. "Ahead you see the Basilique Notre Dame du Rosaire. It's an amazing structure, really. You have the Rosary Basilica on the ground floor, then above that, the crypt, the first chapel finished in 1866, and above that, the Basilique Supérieure, consecrated in 1871. All remarkable." He waved his arms through the air as though summoning angels to bear witness.

"But where is the grotto," Elena asked, "where Bernadette had her visions, where she saw the 'beautiful Lady'?"

He winked. "I'm saving the best for last. Follow me."

They descended steep stairs to the riverbank, where, under a cliff supporting the basilica, a shallow limestone cave had been carved out by the currents.

"The Grotto of Massabielle," Benedict said.

Above and to the right of the cave, a life-size statue of Mary stood on a ledge in a small recess. The Virgin wore a white robe wrapped with a pale blue sash, and yellow roses rested on her bare feet. On the ground below, a pyramid of white candles burned on an iron stand near an altar.

"That's where Mary stood when Bernadette saw her," Elena said.

Madeleine wrapped her arm around Elena as she gazed at the image of Mary. The dark cave with its bubbling spring, the lady of hope with the triangle of light flaming before her, and the altar where Christ would materialize in the bread and wine—they all merged into some kind of answer.

"The grotto," Father Benedict said, "remains much as it was then, except they diverted the river to pave a terrace for the crowds and install the thirty-four taps."

Elena ran to the dripping cliff-face, turned a handle, and filled her flask with the spring water. Other pilgrims—probably close to fifteen or so, Madeleine thought—filled bottles and gallon jugs, splashing the water on their hands and faces.

Jack and Madeleine joined Elena at the taps. They too filled their bottles and drank some. It tasted light and clear, fresh mountain water.

"The water was analyzed," Madeleine said, "and found to be normal. It doesn't even have those natural spa salts they look for."

Elena dried her hands in the breeze. "So the healings were not actually from the water itself."

Jack shook his head in disbelief and moved toward Father Benedict, who was chatting with a visitor.

Elena, her eyes serious, turned to Madeleine. "I can't believe I'm here, washing in these waters, drinking from this spring."

Madeleine sipped from her bottle. "I know. It's truly a material blessing. And a chance to intercede."

"And to thank God for my own healing. And yes, I will pray...for Jack."

"Pray for his belief that God loves him and will make all things right for him, whether or not his body is healed. But I think somehow belief affects our bodies, not just our souls. I'm not sure how, but when we believe, we give up something harmful to us, some need for control, some part of our pride. Belief comes at a price...and in turn grants the believer an even greater prize. I haven't found the right words yet." She gazed at Mary on the ledge. Would Mary give her the words? Surely Mary would know what words to use.

They joined Jack and Father Benedict. Jack was staring at rows of abandoned crutches that dangled from the limestone cliff.

Father Benedict led them to a booth near the grotto entrance. "Here are the prayer candles. You light one and carry it into the grotto with your prayers. Proceeds go to the upkeep of the shrine."

Jack purchased their candles, and they joined a line of pilgrims winding into the cave. Madeleine led Elena along the rock wall that curved behind the altar, carrying her candle silently through the damp and smoke as water tumbled underground. Through an oval pane of glass in the cavern floor, they could see the miraculous spring bubble over lichen-covered rocks.

"That's Bernadette's spring," Elena whispered.

"Today most of it's been diverted into the spigots and baths." Madeleine tried to hold her candle straight as wax dripped onto the paper holder.

Elena watched her own flickering flame as though it might reveal an image, paint a picture of that time. "I wonder what it was like for her."

Madeleine paused, thoughtful. "She was younger than you—she must have been astonished, a little afraid, and...probably entranced by joy, by love." She glanced back at Jack and Father Benedict. Jack looked about the cave as he pulled some tablets from his pocket and slipped them in his mouth.

They emerged into the light. An attendant inserted their four candles into the giant candelabra, adding their flames to the flames of others. Then, sitting on a low stone wall facing the grotto, they watched the candles burn bright against the dark; the tall white tapers leaned imperfectly, earthy matter reaching, groping toward God.

"You see those booths over there," Father Benedict said. "In the summer months they're filled with burning candles. Over three million candles are consumed every year. In summer there are often too many to burn, so they're stored for the winter months—summer prayers reaching into winter, you could say." He grinned, clearly pleased with his image.

"Is this where the famous processions end up?" Madeleine asked.

Benedict glanced at Jack. "Indeed they do. Every evening, with candles burning, come the sick, the lame, the blind...and the sick-at-heart. Farther down are the baths." He pointed to low buildings beyond the candle stands.

"Please, tell us about the processions," Elena said as she focused the camera on the grotto.

"The Marian processions are the torchlight ones. They go back to 1858, the time of Bernadette. Pilgrims meet at the grotto and walk to the gates, carrying their lanterns, singing to Our Lady. Then they return to the Rosary Basilica."

"Every night?" Elena asked.

"From Easter through October. They gather at 8:45."

"Let's do it, Jack," Madeleine said.

"I don't know. I'm pretty tired. Jet lag, you know—it's only our second day in Europe." He shoved his hand into his pocket.

"It would take your mind off things," Madeleine said.

"It *does* sound dramatic," he admitted, rubbing his chin.

"Please, Mr. Seymour," Elena said.

"I'll be your guide," said Father Benedict. "Meet me at eight tonight. Saint Michael's Gate." He checked his watch. "But now I'd better get back and help with lunch. It's been a pleasure for sure." He nodded to Jack. "Lourdes can heal in many ways." Raising his hand in blessing, he walked away, his short stride determined.

"Now what did he mean by that?" Jack asked. "And we didn't find out where Doctor DuPres went."

"Tonight, my love, tonight. Patience."

Madeleine took Jack's hand and they began to climb the stairs to the Esplanade. Glancing back at the flames in the cave, she saw Elena staring at the grotto, her hands on her hips, as though searching for herself.

"Elena!" Madeleine cried.

"I'm coming!" she shouted and ran to catch up with them. Her thick hair flew in the breeze and one hand held the camera tight against her chest.

A waxing crescent moon rose over Saint Michael's Gate.

Elena zipped her jacket. "We're early—our supper didn't take long. Father Benedict's coming soon, I am sure."

"I feel like a kid," Jack said, "being out in the night air, with a parade and all, and the moon just a sliver up there." He pulled out a large handkerchief and coughed a loose wet cough.

Madeleine looked up to the moon. "It *is* kind of fun, isn't it? Remember the Fourth of July parades when Justin was little?"

"He loved them. We'd wave flags and buy hot dogs."

Elena smiled at Jack.

Jack continued to gaze up at the night sky. He wiped his eyes.

"Are you okay?"

"Yeah, I was just thinking about my father and the war..."

"You didn't have much time with him, did you?"

"Not enough. Not nearly enough." He rubbed his chest with his index finger.

"Did your father die in the war?" Elena asked tentatively.

"No, but shortly after. I often think the cancer came from the stress of being on that cruiser in the South Pacific. Kamikazes attacked often in the waters off Okinawa, narrowly missing the ship."

Elena's eyes grew large. "Wow. That must have been terrifying."

"Let's not talk about that on this lovely night," Jack said.

"Of course," Madeleine agreed, trying to see his history, his images, his losses, more clues to the Jack she loved. How did a person's past create his present, make him who he was? The layers of time wound through each person in different ways, changing, coloring. Each journey was such a complex miracle, she thought, such a complex and powerful mix of minutes and hours and days. And choices made along the way.

Elena gazed into the distance. "There's Father Benedict."

Madeleine squinted, spotting the stocky priest as he hurried toward them. "I see him too."

Jack scratched his chin. "So Elena, do you believe this procession to the grotto will heal any of these people, these *malades* as they call them?"

"It could," she said, her eyes bright. "Some, I'm sure."

Madeleine watched Father Benedict draw near, grateful for his sturdy presence, an anchor in a rolling sea. "It's an opportunity to ask Our Lady to pray for us. I believe she really did appear to Bernadette. Mary cares about us."

"It's encouraging," Elena added, smiling at Jack hopefully.

"I don't know about all of that." Jack frowned. "I was taught this was hocus pocus, that we shouldn't pray to anyone but God...or was it worship only God?"

"We should *worship* only God," Madeleine said.

"I believe Our Lady appeared to Bernadette," Elena said. "Bernadette would not have lied. She was too innocent...." She broke into a grin. "*Bonsoir, mon père!*"

"*Bonsoir, mes amis.*" Benedict shook their hands. "Am I late? I'm so sorry if I am. I had the clean-up duty tonight, and wouldn't you know it, one of the crippled insisted on clearing the tables." He waved his arms in the air, his thick fingers splayed, as his curious eyes moved to each of them in turn. "Can you imagine? What could I say? It just took a bit longer. Our Lord taught me another lesson in patience and humility, my major shortcomings. I like to run the show, I suppose, and feel in control. Do you find that true for you too, Jack?"

The priest's words were like a warm waterfall. Madeleine waited, watching Jack.

"Precisely, control is key. The trick is to control but delegate. I don't envy you. You can't exactly choose your staff."

"Father," Madeleine said, "could you tell us where—"

"You were in business, Jack?" Benedict led them toward the grotto.

Madeleine swallowed her question. *Six months.* The words haunted her.

"I worked for Gilpin's Fine Foods, then started my own wine shops.

I sold our stores three years ago last May and retired."

"Congratulations. I know Gilpin's. They're nationwide. You have an MBA?"

"No, law degree. I handled their contracts, and later moved into finance."

"Are they still headquartered in San Francisco?"

"They are indeed."

"Wasn't there some trouble with Gilpin's? My aunt had some stock..."

"You bet. I'm proud to say I helped turn the company around, moved it from the red to the black."

Benedict raised his brows in appreciation. "It's a tough business, I'm sure."

"It's cutthroat. But I owe them a great deal. They hired me right out of school and I needed the job."

Madeleine laughed, giving up her urgency. "Tell the best part."

Jack smiled ruefully. "I couldn't afford a raincoat at the time of the interview, and it was pouring. The personnel officer said that since I was hungry—and wet—I would work harder than the other applicants."

Madeleine smiled. "And you had a family to support. I love that story."

In the same way, he cared for his mother and sister when his father died. Jack had always been the one to look to for help, the one to count on.

They descended the stairs to the grotto where hundreds of pilgrims chanted the rosary, holding lanterns that cast an otherworldly glow upon their features. Far below, the river rolled, sparkling with reflected light from the basilica above. Jack gazed up to the bright Madonna on the ledge, then down to the river that washed the banks. Madeleine followed his gaze to the rushing waters.

She touched his arm, turning him aside. "Jack, maybe you should pray for healing while you're here."

"I suppose...it can't hurt."

"But don't you believe—"

"I drank the water, didn't I? No change. If anything, I'm worse. Don't these healings happen right away?"

"Even so, pray, Jack, pray, and keep your heart open." Madeleine's eyes held his, as though she could will her faith into him.

Jack retreated into a familiar silence. Madeleine took his hand in hers, praying silently. *Hail Mary, full of grace, the Lord is with thee. Blessed art thou among women, and blessed is the fruit of thy womb, Jesus. Intercede for us, Mary, that Jack may find peace, and I may know how to help him.*

Carrying lanterns, they moved forward with the crowd, their faces shining in the reflected light, pulled into the swelling chorus of the *Ave Maria*. The *malades* surrounded them, those sick in heart or body, some pushed in wheelchairs. Madeleine gazed at the suffering pilgrims, humbly hopeful in the dark. Did each penitent share the wounds of Christ?

They passed the giant cross, bowing their heads in veneration. She looked at Jesus' frail body hanging against the heavy sky, the glow of candles flickering at his feet. She realized the crucifix was only metal and these candles only wax. But how the material helped her with the spiritual: Jesus hung there for her, with her, and, in some mysterious way, she met him there, in the cold and the dark, before the fiery basilica.

They continued down the Esplanade to the broad parvis where the crowd gathered, singing a different chant, its lilting melody floating about them, linking them with one another. They recited the Creed. *I believe in God the Father Almighty, maker of heaven and earth, and in Jesus Christ his only son our Lord, who was conceived by the Holy Ghost, born of the Virgin Mary...*

Several priests raised their hands in blessing, parting the damp night, releasing God's power like a flock of doves. Tears streamed down Jack's cheeks and Madeleine reached for a tissue in her purse. Jack wiped his face, shook his head in amazement, and smiled as he stared up at the bright steeples. He had opened his heart. He had allowed God to touch him.

Thank you, Lord, thank you. And thank you, Mary.

Jack turned to Father Benedict. "Let's get you something to eat," he whispered with a grin.

The priest grinned and clapped Jack on the back. "Don't mind if I do. Thank you very much."

Chapter Seven
The Grotto of Massabielle

When we love
we live less in ourselves than in that which we love;
and the more we establish our life beyond ourselves...
Charles de Foucauld

They found a café that was still open, the red-checkered tables empty at this late hour. The air smelled of stale smoke; from somewhere in the back, pans clattered and workers shouted.

Father Benedict had missed his dinner and Jack suggested the marinated beefsteak and garlic potatoes. The priest rubbed his thick hands with anticipation. Jack ordered a plate of pastries, decaf cappuccinos, and herbal tea, since they had eaten earlier.

Madeleine watched Benedict settle into his chair like a boy home from college.

"Thank you so much, dear friends." The priest smiled as he cut into his thick steak. "This meal is a real treat."

Jack sipped his tea. "It's our pleasure, Father. We are in your debt. That was quite extraordinary, especially for this old Methodist. If my mother could see me now, praying to the Virgin Mary, but something touched me back there."

Benedict raised his fork in the air. "Did it now? I'm very glad to hear it! But it's so sad, how judgmental Christians can be with their own. Of course idolatry is a sin and worthy to be feared. But the use of images and intercessors to aid prayer is common throughout the world and throughout history, and is most beneficial, in my opinion." His eyes rested on theirs as he held them with his words. "We don't worship a plaster figure on a ledge. We use it as a focus. We ask that God or the saint be present, making the image a channel for our prayer. I don't believe anything's too lowly for God to enter."

"Like in the sacraments," added Madeleine.

Father Benedict leaned forward, his bushy brows rising and falling. "To be sure, the sacraments! Water, wine, bread, oil. Simple things. Earthy things. Manifestations of God help us immensely. God's presence in our material world! It's easy to say and a great mystery. But there you have it, a great mystery."

"Madeleine is writing a book about that," Elena said.

"*Are* you now, Mrs. Seymour? That's one I will read for sure."

Madeleine grew thoughtful. The subject often overwhelmed her. "I'm still researching, but it *is* a great mystery—God working through matter." Who was *she* to write such a book? She grew small just thinking about it.

Father Benedict gulped some of his beer, then stared into the sudsy liquid. "My father liked to wash his beef down with beer, that is, when he could get beef—and beer for that matter. You would have liked my dad, Jack, a no-nonsense man of business. He immigrated to America from Ireland in '14. Spent some time on Ellis Island." The priest shook his head, as though to think back through two countries and eight decades a mystery in itself.

"Miracles still happen in Lourdes, don't they, Father?" Elena asked as she stirred two sugars into her coffee.

"They happen all the time, all the time." But now Benedict looked more intent on finishing his boiled potatoes than explaining the secrets of miraculous cures.

"Could you tell us about one?"

"And maybe after that," Madeleine said, "we could hear more about Doctor DuPres?" She searched his face for clues as she twisted the napkin in her lap.

"We do need to find her." Jack frowned.

"Indeed." Benedict rested his eyes on Madeleine.

Had she made some sort of connection? Madeleine wondered.

The priest pushed away from the table and leaned back in his chair, his hands clasped comfortably on his ample chest. "There are many cures in Lourdes. There are cures of heart and cures of body. But I think you're interested in a physical cure documented by the Bureau of Medical Observations. Not all the cures are documented."

Madeleine leaned forward, investing her seconds. "One that is physical and has gone through all the tests."

Jack seemed to be resigned to the diversion as well. Or was he interested in the cures?

"Yes, please," Elena agreed, her eyes glued to Father Benedict.

"So here you go. First, the Medical Bureau is made up of doctors from all over the world and of differing religious beliefs. They establish whether the patient was sick before coming to Lourdes. Afterwards, they establish if the patient was completely cured, without medical treatment, and that *the cure was instant and lasting*. Then the case goes to the International Medical Committee, made up of thirty doctors who meet yearly. The committee determines whether any other explanation is possible." His eye rested on Jack. "If the cure is considered genuine, the case goes to the patient's bishop, and finally to the canonical commission, who make the final decree, whether it's a sign from God, a miracle."

Jack slipped two white tablets into his mouth. "The process sounds worse than working with the government."

"That's for sure!" Benedict laughed, slapping the table and reaching for his double espresso. "So here is one for you, Elena. Her name was Jeanne Fretel, and she was Lourdes' fifty-second miraculous cure. I know the story well, since I'm friends with Father Roques, the priest in charge of the case. On October 8, 1948, Jeanne came to Lourdes in a coma, on a stretcher, suffering from tuberculosis peritonitis."

"Tuberculosis peritonitis?" Jack rubbed his chest.

"Peritonitis is tuberculosis tumors in the stomach lining."

"How awful for her."

"Indeed. So a *hospitalier*, one of the volunteer nurses, took her to mass. When Father Roques approached her with the host she did not respond. Black blood ran from her nose and mouth. He asked her three times: did she wish to receive the Eucharist? Finally, the *hospitalier* opened her mouth with a spoon, and Father Roques laid a bit of the host on her tongue, then closed her mouth. Instantly she opened her eyes and asked, 'Where am I?' Father Roques replied, 'You're in Lourdes.'" Father Benedict clapped his hands in delight, as he watched their faces. "Just like in the Gospels!"

Madeleine recalled the story. "You mean when Jesus healed the blind man by touching his eyes?"

"Instantly," added Elena.

"Right, that's the one!" Father Benedict said.

"Amazing." Jack stared at the priest. "So what happened then?"

Benedict beamed. "She got up and walked, just like another Gospel account. She took one of the baths, and they gave her three helpings of lunch—she was starving since she hadn't eaten much in six months. They found some clothes for her—she only had nightgowns. She went home to Rennes, back to her old job. She's still living, as far as I know."

"But she wasn't healed by the waters?" Elena asked, her words tinged with disappointment.

"They call it a Eucharistic Miracle." Father Benedict raised an open palm. "She was healed by Christ in the mass, actually a more direct intervention than the spring. You can learn about other cures in the Medical Office."

Elena looked at Madeleine; Madeleine looked at Jack; Jack continued to stare at Father Benedict.

"That's amazing," Jack repeated.

"And *you*, Mr. Seymour? You would like to be healed as well, I think."

Jack breathed deeply, arching his fine brows. He leaned back and gripped the arms of his chair. "I need surgery on my esophagus. We hoped Doctor DuPres would do it."

"Rachelle didn't want anyone to know her whereabouts."

"Why, Father?" Madeleine asked, relieved to learn more.

"She left the hospital, you must understand, for good reasons, haunting reasons. I don't know if I helped her, but I tried."

Madeleine searched his eyes. "We thought she was on vacation."

"She is, my dear, she is." He cleared his throat and looked away.

"If we could speak to her, maybe simply on the phone," Madeleine said.

"Tomorrow is Sunday, my friends," Benedict said, "and I have an eight o'clock mass in the grotto. It's in English, for an American group. Jack, would you like to come? It might do you good."

"We'd like that," Madeleine said, accepting the diversion, not wanting to push the priest any further. He must have good reasons for withholding information. "But we're not Roman Catholic. Are we allowed to receive the Eucharist?"

"We make exceptions," the priest said. "This is a place of healing. If you are believers in Christ's Presence in the host, then we welcome you."

"Thank you," Madeleine said, watching Jack as he figured the bill.

Jack raised his brows. "Why not? What's there to lose?" He stood and shook Father O'Reilly's hand. "I'll get the coats," he said, and walked toward the foyer.

Elena exchanged glances with Madeleine. "I'll go with him."

Madeleine nodded, her eyes on the priest. "Father, *please* tell us where the doctor is. The situation is more urgent than Jack realizes."

"I guessed there might be more to it."

"His doctor gives him less than six months if we don't operate. Jack has acute esophagitis, and a biopsy came back positive."

"And he doesn't know?"

"He doesn't know about the biopsy. The doctor insisted I not say anything, and I'm regretting I agreed. Jack worries so, and Doctor Lau thought his knowing would aggravate the situation unnecessarily. He had a patient once who took an overdose." And then there was Jack's father.

"I see. Why don't you choose another surgeon?"

"Jack insists Doctor DuPres is the most qualified, and he's too stubborn to settle for less. He believes his father died at the hands of an incompetent surgeon."

Father Benedict shook his head slowly, rubbing his chin. "Perhaps she *is* the most qualified." He looked toward the foyer, then turned to Madeleine. "She experienced a great failure, and I think she's running away."

"Failure? What do you mean?"

"I'm not at liberty to tell you, my dear. But be honest with Jack. Also, find Rachelle. She's too talented not to practice. She should use her gifts."

"But where is she?"

He heaved a sigh of resignation. "She's gone to Rocamadour to see my grandnephew, Brother Anthony. I'll call him tonight and see if she's still there."

"Rocamadour?"

"It's about a day's drive into the mountains, north of here."

"Thank you, Father, thank you."

They joined Elena and Jack at the café entrance. Jack held the door open for the ladies, then Father Benedict.

"I look forward," Father Benedict said, "to seeing you all in the morning—hopefully I'll have some good news."

He made the Sign of the Cross over them and strode into the night.

"Good news?" Jack asked.

"I learned more about Rachelle DuPres."

As they walked toward their hotel, Madeleine sorted her words, arranging them to form half-lies and half-truths, her remorse growing as she stepped deeper into a dark labyrinth. Her head throbbed.

In the night, Madeleine's heart fluttered as she woke slowly...reluctantly...longingly hugging her dream. A warm bright light, full of fragrant sweetness, shone around her, covering her like a mantle. A metal crucifix stood in the foreground; somehow she knew the Beautiful Lady shone through the light behind. Jack was drawn into the left arm of the crucifix, silently, effortlessly, unknowingly. The petals of Madeleine's heart opened as she watched, and closed softly as she floated awake...such a yearning to go back, such a tangible loss. Yet somehow she knew Jack would be all right. But when? And where? In this world or the next? Should it matter? Did it matter?

She gazed at her husband who was half sitting up in bed, propped by couch pillows, his head tilted awkwardly to the side, a raspy wheeze escaping his tangled lungs. His periodic cough, cacophonous cries parting the dark, had torn the night into pieces of heartache.

Dear Lord, let me bear some of this. Let me carry him for a while. Let him sleep.

The sun rose over the grotto, bathing the world in its early light. Madeleine sat between Jack and Elena on a wooden bench in the outdoor chapel. Our Lady of Lourdes presided from her ledge, watching over the timeless sacrifice, offered by God to man, and by man to God, in the mass.

Father Benedict stood behind the linen-covered altar, his back to the grotto, and intoned the Prayer of Consecration. With these words, Madeleine knew, Christ intersected time and space.

An acolyte shook the Sanctus bells, three golden balls trilling into the crisp morning, and Madeleine bowed her head.

The priest held the plate of unconsecrated hosts in his hands, reading the Gospel words of institution. "*For in the night in which he was betrayed, he took bread; and when he had given thanks, he brake it, and gave it to his disciples, saying, take, eat; this is my body, which is given for you; do this in remembrance of me.*"

At this moment, the glorious transformation occurred, and Madeleine was suspended in time.

The bells trilled again, and the priest raised the consecrated host. Madeleine looked up and traced the Sign of the Cross over her head and heart as she worshiped Christ, the Son of God, mystically united with the bread, the infinite at one with the finite.

The bells trilled, and she bowed her head.

Father Benedict held the chalice as he read from the missal. *"Likewise, he took the cup, and when he had given thanks, he gave it to them, saying drink ye all of this, for this is my blood of the New Testament, which is shed for you, and for many, for the remission of sins; do this, as oft as ye shall drink it, in remembrance of me."*

The bells trilled a fourth time, and the priest raised the consecrated wine.

Madeleine made the Sign of the Cross and glanced at Jack who had fixed his gaze on the crutches hanging from the cliff.

The bells trilled, and Madeleine bowed her head.

They joined the line to receive the Eucharist, and as the priest placed the host on her tongue, she knew she was not alone on her journey.

"The Body of Christ," Father Benedict said.

The host dissolved and traveled into her flesh, a union, a communion, of the mortal and the immortal. She was one with Christ and, through him, one with his bride, the Church, the community of believers throughout time, the communion of saints. *Lord, teach me to trust, teach me to wait, teach me to have patience. Use me to heal Jack. Thank you for this moment of joy, this moment of peace, this moment of knowing.* All things would work out, for God would give her what she needed, and it would be enough, no matter what. Of this, at that moment, she was sure.

Father Benedict, his face glowing, met them beneath the Madonna. "I'm so glad you came." He shook their hands.

Madeleine looked into his eyes with hopeful expectation. "Me too. And thank you for your help."

"And for showing us Lourdes," added Elena. "I will never forget this place and this mass."

"Every mass opens new doors." The priest fingered his stole. He turned to Jack.

"New doors?" Jack glanced at the crutches. "I'm afraid, Father, I'm a bit of a skeptic, but you knew that, didn't you?"

"I guessed."

"Father, did you call your grandnephew?" Madeleine said, her impatience returning.

"I'm afraid I couldn't get through, but I'll try again and let you know. Rocamadour is remote, high on a cliff, and they sometimes lose power."

"Father," Jack asked as they turned toward the stairs, "do you think God makes bargains?"

"What do you mean?"

"Did the owners of those crutches promise God something?"

"They did."

"What do you think they promised?"

"They offered their bodies and souls, Jack, nothing less."

Jack shook his head. "I promised God something else, something bigger than that."

"There's nothing bigger than that."

Madeleine, Jack, and Elena spent the rest of their Sunday browsing for souvenirs—icons, rosaries, miniature figures of saints called *santons*. They checked their messages regularly, waiting for news of Doctor DuPres.

Father Benedict called as Jack napped. "Rachelle's still in Rocamadour."

"Thank goodness," Madeleine said. They could leave first thing in the morning.

"Anthony couldn't promise how long she'd stay."

"Thank you, Father, for finding out. And for everything."

"A pleasure, my dear. Find Rachelle and I shall be in *your* debt." His speech carried the pain of both loss and guilt. "You might be interested in visiting the Black Madonna there. I shall keep all of you in my prayers. May God go with you, Mrs. Seymour."

The Black Madonna? Late that evening Madeleine considered Benedict's words as she watched Jack finish packing. She had removed her contact lenses, slipped on her glasses, and, wrapped in a robe, had settled into a lumpy armchair in the corner of their room. Her Underhill paperback and her prayer book lay on the nightstand. She knew she should be praying the evening Psalms, but instead she had settled into a quiet reverie, watching Jack, as often happened when her life was overwhelmed with new experience. What had she learned in Lourdes? Would the Black Madonna speak to her?

She considered Mary's response to the Angel Gabriel: "Be it unto me according to thy word." Obedience. Bernadette, in turn, had obeyed Mary. Could Madeleine obey God's call? What was his call for her at this moment in time? To trust, she thought, to trust him to work out all things for good. She recalled a hymn from her childhood, "Trust and obey, for there's no other way, to be happy in Jesus...." But, unlike the Virgin Mary, Madeleine had been conceived as all other humanity had been conceived—*with* sin, not *without*. That made obedience difficult, but not impossible.

Madeleine prayed a *Hail Mary*, and asked for help to be obedient to God's call. She prayed an *Our Father* and asked for an increased measure of faith, that she could trust him completely.

Would the Black Madonna help too? She opened her laptop and found her notes on Rocamadour. She was certain she had a bit on the Black Madonna in this remote mountain shrine.

Holy Manifestations: Miraculous Madonnas

In 1166, high up the side of a mountainous gorge in the desolate region of Quercy to the east of Bordeaux, villagers discovered an incorrupt body—one that had not decomposed. They had been digging a grave and found the body resting in a crevice of the limestone rock face, near the entrance to the Shrine of the Black Madonna.

Thought to be a pre-Christian Druid site,[6] the cliff cave formed a natural hermitage. With the discovery of the body, the fame of the chapel spread, for incorruption was a sign of sainthood. The eleventh-century Madonna and Child, carved from walnut and blackened by flaming votives, was soon credited with miracle cures and sea rescues.[7]

The monks claimed Amadour was first-century Zaccheus, husband of Veronica, who, escaping persecution in Jerusalem, had sailed to the southern coast of France. Soon kings and bishops led pilgrimages to Rocamadour, some continuing to the shrine of Saint James the Apostle in Santiago de Compostela, Spain. It was believed, in this age of faith, that saints healed through their bones[8] and that such a journey ensured salvation. All the while the Black Madonna healed the faithful.[9]

So it *was* a place of healing. Would this shrine help Jack? Would the Madonna soothe her fears?

Henry II of England, among the more famous pilgrims, journeyed here with his chancellor, Thomas Becket. Other penitents included Saint Dominic, Saint Bernard, Saint Louis IX with his queen, Blanche of Castille, and the French kings Philip the Fair, Philip VI, and Louis XI.

After the kings, came their people, seeking divine answers to earthly problems. They came on foot and by horse, carrying their walking sticks and satchels, protected by knights from robbers and wolves. They purchased badges of the Virgin, proud emblems of their journeys, often useful as tickets of safe passage.[10] In Rocamadour, hostelries provided lodging, blacksmiths shod horses, and thousands of candles were dipped and sold. Soon a town arose near the monastery, and six chapels and churches were built with income from pilgrims.

In the fifteenth century, the Hundred Years War with England devastated the countryside, and the French sought help from the Black Madonna of Rocamadour. On Easter Sunday, 1428, they made a national pilgrimage to her shrine and petitioned the Mother of God to intercede with her Son to save France not only from England but also from famine and its aftermath—plague, leprosy, and cholera—that swept the country.

Then, in the spring of 1429, the young Joan of Arc met with the heir to the French throne, the *dauphin* Charles, who hid with his court in Chinon. She explained that Saint Margaret and Saint Catherine had appeared to her in a vision, telling her to lead the prince to victory, to his rightful crown. Charles took heart and marched to Reims where he was crowned, and the Hundred Years War with England came to an end. Many said these events were more than coincidence and were a direct answer to the national prayers of Rocamadour.

In the sixteenth century Protestants sacked Rocamadour and burned Amadour's body to ash. In the later eighteenth, the shrine was desecrated by the Revolution, but through it all, survived. Today the craggy village of chapels gives hope to returning pilgrims, sick in body or soul, and the rustic Black Madonna, her son on her knee, is again a channel for man's conversation with God. Through the centuries, the millions of candles burning at her feet have continued to blacken the oxidized silver, a startling contrast to the white robe and yellow flowers of Our Lady of Lourdes.

The many pilgrims coming to Rocamadour had such faith, Madeleine thought. They saw the world and their place in it so clearly. Jeanne d'Arc obeyed. How Madeleine longed for such certainty.

She closed her computer, reached for her prayer book, and turned to the Psalms appointed for the nineteenth day of the month.

Chapter Eight
Crillon-le-Brave

Charity...beareth all things, believeth all things,
hopeth all things, endureth all things
1 Corinthians 13:7

octor Rachelle DuPres examined the red scales on her palms and gazed out the train window. She shifted her slight frame in the seat, feeling a broken spring, and rubbed her eyes with the back of her knuckles. Running her fingers through her hair, she was glad she'd had it cut before leaving town. She recalled her hairdresser's dismay when, once again, Rachelle refused to color the gray. Why should she be ashamed of her hair? She was not ashamed of being fifty-seven. Aging well meant accepting wrinkles and cellulite, not fighting what should be badges of honor.

She checked her bag for her reading glasses—her power glasses, as she called them, useful for intimidating the male culture around her—and affirmed they were in their case in the side pocket. She rezipped the pocket and placed the bag carefully with her duffel on the seat next to her. She refolded her tweed blazer and laid it on top. Touching a soiled spot on her black jeans, she wondered where she had gotten them dirty—maybe on the Rocamadour trail.

Rachelle studied her palms again. Until recently, she had taken care of herself, exercising and reading food labels—following her own advice to patients—and this outbreak on her hands was rare. She peeled some of the chafe, hoping to remove the unsightly skin.

The train would soon arrive in Avignon. Would this visit to her sister help? It was Monday morning, September 20, and she had come so far in the last week.

She had seen Father Benedict in Lourdes, who, when she was young, had been like a second father. His Christmas card had warmed her heart, in spite of her doubts in matters of religion. When she arrived, she feared what he would say. But when he met her at the train last Tuesday in the rain, his welcoming grin eased her nervousness. He showed her around, and she confessed her failures, appreciating his good ear. He talked her into visiting Rocamadour. "It's a spectacular setting not to be missed," he said. Her dulled mind did not protest; it was a relief to be told what to do and Rebecca wasn't expecting her for another few days.

But Lourdes and Rocamadour had disturbed Rachelle with their stories of unseen forces and partially understood phenomena. Her agnosticism, tinged by atheism, argued against such belief, supported as it was by undergraduate readings in Sigmund Freud, Bertrand Russell, and Paul Tillich. The existence of God was, at the very least, problematic in light of the suffering of mankind; that these superstitions, these fairy tales, survived in the late twentieth century remained a shocking mystery to her. Belief in God was silly enough, but apparitions of Mary and healing relics and miraculous waters were insane. Still, she was polite to her former priest and his nephew.

She had hiked the trails of Rocamadour, stretching her calves and hamstrings, inhaling the crisp mountain air. The room was cheap enough, the food simple, and the isolation welcoming, far better than crowded Lourdes. She met with the boy monk the day before she left and found Anthony a young innocent, probably one of the last of his kind. He could have been a hermit from the Middle Ages, the way his eyes were so distant and close at the same time, as though he lived in overlapping worlds. Puzzling and quaint, and definitely one for the psychiatric journals.

The mountains of Quercy, with their trickling falls and rocky promontories, their great gorges and soaring peaks, provided a much more satisfying balm for Rachelle's weary soul. She had hoped to leave her sadness there, as though the wild country would absorb it into its vastness, but it still gripped her, and she caught the Monday train for Avignon.

Now, through the window, Rachelle searched the platform for Pierre, Rebecca's youngest, as they rolled smoothly to a halt and the air brakes whistled. *Avignon.* The name sounded mysterious and very French with the silent *g*, the *n* disappearing into a sweet nasal nothingness.

Rachelle made her way to the exit doors, holding her duffel in one hand and slinging her backpack over her shoulder. As she stepped onto the station platform, a tall young man with curly black hair strode toward her. He smiled and kissed her on each cheek.

"*Bonjour et bienvenue, ma tante! Comment ça va? Bien?*"

Rachelle reached for his face and gazed into his brown eyes. "Pierre, it's so good to see you. Look at you! You've grown so—I might not have recognized you. You're much taller than I remember."

Blushing, he slid out of her grasp and grabbed her bag. "I was a child when we visited San Francisco. The car is in the first lot. Please, come with me."

"And you are well?" Rachelle ran to keep up with him, and they maneuvered to the car park.

She settled into the front passenger seat of a late-model Renault, avoiding the tear in the upholstery, then ratcheted the seat with the lever below, smiling as Pierre tuned the radio to a station with American music. His profile was strong, his hands small like hers, doctor's hands. He gripped the wheel firmly.

"We turn off at Carpentras." Pierre pointed to the sign as they sped south on the A7. "Then take the road north to Bedouin. You have never visited Crillon-le-Brave?"

"I'm afraid I never made it." She hadn't seen any point in digging up the past. It had been Rebecca who cared about Crillon, cared about their ancestry. The sisters grew up knowing their biological parents had died in the war, part of the Resistance. They knew little else.

"We have vineyards. You like wine?"

"I do. A glass now and again."

"We make wine, *vous savez.*"

"That's good." She gazed at the rolling hills, the grapes heavy and ready for picking. The road narrowed, following riverbeds and dry-stone walls. So this was the world of her twin sister, a world much like the Napa Valley, but older and more rural. This was the world Philippe gave to Rebecca after they met in Paris that summer. When they married, it must have seemed natural to grow grapes, like Philippe's father, and natural they should settle in the village of Rebecca's ancestors.

"You don't want to grow grapes, Pierre? This is lovely country."

"I want to see the world." He frowned, his voice edged with envy.

"Are you still interested in medicine?"

"*Oui, ma tante,* I want to be great, like you." He darted a glance at her.

Rachelle fixed her gaze on the neat orchards and lush vineyards. "You want to be great like me?"

"*Oui.* You are successful, are you not? You are chief of the doctors at the hospital? That is a great thing."

"I am Chief of Surgery, yes. But, Pierre, I may leave that position."

"You may leave?"

"We will see. I'm taking some time off."

"*Des vacances.* A holiday. That is good. You need to rest, then you return."

"We'll see."

"Mount Ventoux," Pierre said, pointing. He shifted into second gear and gunned the car up a steep slope.

"Your mother wrote of Mount Ventoux." Rachelle gazed at the barren peak rising above the valley. She had entered a foreign world of sense, a landscape of green vines and gray stone and blue sky. The air smelled of freshly mown grass.

"We hike and picnic on Ventoux in the summer. Maybe *le soleil* stay? We take you. *Et voilà.* Crillon-le-Brave. *Mon petit village. Très petit.*"

Pierre shifted down and the car grunted up a lane winding between stone houses. At the peak of the rise, he maneuvered alongside a thick wall and set the gear in park, scraping the quiet September air. A brisk breeze had cleared the afternoon skies to a startling blue. "This good for now. We find *ma mère.*"

A green door, number *16* painted neatly in black, opened to reveal a short woman with an open countenance. She looked with expectation at Pierre, then beyond to Rachelle. With her dark braid swinging behind her, she ran down steps bordered with red geraniums. "Shelley! Shelley!" A tortoise shell cat bounded after her.

Rachelle ran to meet her sister, and the two fell together, erasing time. "Becca," she whispered, catching the scent of lavender in Rebecca's thick hair.

Rachelle leaned back and gazed at the woman who had chosen such a different path from her own. Rebecca's brown eyes beamed from a tanned face; a flowered blouse ballooned over her jeans, not quite concealing her full figure. A silver cross lay in the vee of her blouse.

"Rachelle, are you okay?" Rebecca asked, her expression full of worry.

"Just a little tired." Rachelle smiled weakly. "Long trip."

"You're so pale...and so slim. We'll change all that. Let me show you your room—you have an hour to rest and freshen up before dinner. Alphonse—you remember my chubby redhead—has taken to cooking, so look forward to a gourmet meal, country style of course."

Rachelle took Rebecca's arm. The sisters walked up the steps between the flowers and into the small chateau that perched on the rocky cliff of Crillon-le-Brave. The house seemed part of the crag, merging into the medieval fortress that once guarded the town and the valley below.

"Amazing, isn't it?" Rebecca read her thoughts.

"I've never seen anything like it." The cat nuzzled Rachelle's legs and she pushed it away with her foot.

"There are many of these hilltop villages in France and Italy—where homes are built into mountainsides, carved out of cliffs. They were built for defense, not luxury or space. When peace returned, people settled in the valleys, closer to their crops."

Catching aromas of lemon oil and rosemary, Rachelle passed through a dining room with breezy yellow curtains. Through tall windows she glimpsed the valley and the mountain beyond. She followed her sister up spiraling stairs to the top floor, as Pierre thumped behind her with the duffel and pack, the cat following. Rebecca threw open the shutters with a practiced gesture and pointed to the men working in the vineyards along the base of the mountain.

"Look, Shelley."

"It's beautiful."

"Yesterday they began bringing in the grapes. It will be a busy few days—rain is expected soon. The trick is to harvest at the last moment possible, giving the fruit maximum sun and sugar, so we wait and pray we aren't caught in a hailstorm. A bit of a gamble."

"Is winter so close?"

"It is here, so near the Alps, and it's already the third week of September. That's Philippe out there in the white van, giving orders, just like his father did in Burgundy, God rest his soul." She made the Sign of the Cross and turned to Rachelle. "It's a good life, Shelley, but a lot of work. I'll leave you for now—I promised Alphonse I'd watch his cassoulet while he helps his father." Rebecca paused as she searched her sister's eyes. "Oh, Shelley, it *is* good to see you. I've missed you so."

"I've missed you too." Rachelle told a half-lie.

Rebecca kissed her on each cheek, swept up the cat in one arm, and disappeared through the door. Pierre glanced back, then followed his mother.

Rachelle gazed over the valley. A few puffy clouds floated beyond Mount Ventoux. White vans waited in the fields, and men bent over wagons of dark purple mounds that would one day turn into wine. In the distance, bells clanged six o'clock, the notes moving from village to village, coming closer and closer, marking the end of the day. The off-key tones suited her mood.

She felt a twinge of envy as she considered her sister's world. Children and cooking and housekeeping and...faith...were not Rachelle's choices. Rebecca looked happy, but somehow Rachelle's happiness had eluded her, as she chased a dream never fully realized, always out there, a distant and potent promise. Certainly her work satisfied her mind and occupied her hours, but recently, even before the failed surgery, she had wondered if there was more. Then Steinhoff.

She unzipped her duffel, placed a second pair of jeans and several shirts in the bottom drawer of an antique dresser, and hung a black linen sheath in the closet. She splashed water on her face from a porcelain bowl and stared into a cradled table mirror, its lead wearing through the glass, scratching and darkening her image. Smoothing down her hair with the water, she noted more gray, and thought how Rebecca's hair was still the same deep brown. She looked at her image closely: crow's feet lined the edges of her eyes, and red veins mapped the whites.

Discouraged, she scrubbed her hands thoroughly. With this familiar motion, the operating room flashed before her. She dried them quickly, slammed the door behind her, and trudged down the stairs with heavy feet, gripping the wooden rail with anguish and dread, quarantining her fevered thoughts with determination, regretting she had come to such a foreign land.

Rachelle stepped into the breezy dining room as her sister entered from the kitchen. Rebecca carried a deep bowl of steaming stew, fragrant with thyme and onions, and carefully set it down on the long plank table. She took the seat closest to the kitchen, wiping her hands on her apron.

At the opposite end, Philippe pulled out a sturdy wooden chair for Rachelle next to his own. "*Bienvenue*, Madame Rachelle, welcome to our home." He lowered his ample frame into his chair and smiled at his wife. His thinning black hair, combed over his bald spot, framed a tanned face, serious eyes, and a close-cropped beard.

Pierre entered with bowls of carrots and potatoes, and took the seat next to Rachelle. Alphonse, a stocky young man with a ruddy complexion, carried a platter of sausages and mushrooms, and sat opposite, alongside a dark-haired girl, heavy with child. He nodded to his aunt. "*Bienvenue, ma tante*, I remember you well. We rode the cable cars to Fisherman's Wharf—I will never forget the crab pots! Please, I present my wife, Josephine."

Josephine was piling food onto Alphonse's plate, her eyes adoring. She turned to Rachelle. "*Avèc plaisir, Madame.*"

"A pleasure for me too." Rachelle smiled, thinking that Josephine must be in her last trimester.

Philippe raised his hand. "May God bless this food to our use, *au nom du Père, et du Fils, et du Saint-Esprit*. Amen." He made the Sign of the Cross over the meal and passed a carafe of red wine.

Rachelle looked from face to face and spoke slowly, sensing their English was minimal. "Thank you everyone. I'm happy to be here. How did the picking go?"

"We made a start," Philippe said, his voice lined with worry. "More help comes tomorrow."

Rebecca raised her glass. "To bringing in the grapes."

"To bringing in the grapes," they echoed, the French and English mingling as their glasses clinked.

Rachelle watched Pierre ladle the cassoulet, thick with lamb, beans, and onions. As warm brown bread, cut into wedges, was passed down the table, followed by a bottle of green olive oil, she slipped silently into the life of her sister, seeing the care each took for the other, their delight in simple things, their ordinary celebration of love.

"They say a storm is coming," Philippe said, his brow pulled together.

"You'll manage, my dear. I know you will," Rebecca said. "You always do."

Chapter Nine
Rocamadour

The whole world would die of love
for so amiable a God if I could make it feel the sweetness
which a soul tastes in loving him.
Jane de Chantal

Monday morning was overcast, and an icy breeze warned of a storm from the Pyrenees. Shivering, Madeleine zipped her jacket. Elena loaded the luggage into the car.

"Elena, let me get that." Jack reached for the garment bag in her hand.

"Allow me, Mr. Seymour. Madeleine asked me to help."

Madeleine turned to Jack. "Let Elena wait on us. I suggested she drive today, so we might relax. You didn't sleep much last night."

Jack frowned. "That's true enough. But I'm quite capable..."

"It would be less worrying for you."

Jack took the front passenger seat, slammed the door, moved the seat back to accommodate his legs, and stared silently out the window.

Madeleine slipped into the seat behind Elena. "Jack, you can navigate the route." She handed him a folded road map.

"*Allons-y*, here we go." Elena turned the key in the ignition. "Next stop, Rocamadour. I packed a lunch. It will be a long day, but I think we can make it before nightfall. I read that it was best to see the sanctuary in daylight from the cliff terrace above."

Jack latched his seatbelt. "And we want to get there before the doctor disappears again. Let's invite her to dinner with Brother Anthony."

"That's a good idea." Madeleine watched the village of Lourdes pass by, the neat facades disappearing into the distance. What would they find in the home of the Black Madonna? And should she break her promise to Doctor Lau and tell Jack the diagnosis? Father Benedict thought so. *Six months.*

"Have you heard from Justin?" Elena asked, pulling Madeleine from her thoughts.

"I did," she said, thankful for the diversion. "The front desk hooked my computer to their digital phone line so I could check my e-mail."

"Are they back from Hawaii, rested and tan?"

"They're back, planning their lives, setting up savings accounts, working on goals. They're both employed full-time, thank God—Lisa loves teaching Kindergarten. They hope to buy a house in a few years. Justin said they were even considering baby names."

Jack shook his head. "Good for them, but I hope they delay having children for a few years."

Madeleine considered his words. "I do want to become a grandmother again, but sometimes it's dangerous to plan too much." She had planned on more children and when she couldn't conceive, she and Jack had considered adoption. But time slipped away—or caught up with them—and soon they sensed they were too old to begin a second family. Even so, God had blessed her in other ways. Jack's six grandchildren were dear to her and visited often—Bethany, fifteen; the twins Gillian and Audrey, twelve; Tod, Tina, and Andrew, ten, eight, and seven.

"Planning is good," Jack said. He studied the map, refolded it neatly, and slid it into the door panel. Clearing his throat, he pulled his heart monitor from his shirt pocket and wrapped the Velcro strap tightly about his wrist. "I think the A64 is coming up, Elena."

As the tiny machine hummed, Madeleine watched Jack's reaction to the numbers on the digital face. "Justin wanted to know how Jack's doing," she said. "I gave him an update on our doctor search."

Elena glanced back at Madeleine. "Was there anything from Rome?"

"Not yet. Are you a little homesick?"

The Velcro pulled away, tearing the air. Jack looked satisfied. He slipped the monitor into his shirt pocket.

"A little," Elena said, turning onto the main highway.

"We also heard from Daniel, Jack's youngest. He wished us *bon voyage* and wanted to know if he could carry our bags next time."

Elena laughed. Jack shook his head. "He's got his hands full with his own teaching schedule, but he's a dear boy to remember us."

Elena glanced at Jack. "What about the others—Johnny and Alex? Do they know about the trip?"

"We sent them rough itineraries," Madeleine said. "But they're closer to Pamela, their mother, than Jack, even settled near her home in San Mateo. They don't know the reason for the trip."

"No need to make them worry," Jack said. "And we've all got e-mail and phone numbers for emergencies."

They drove all day, through farmlands to Toulouse, north to Cahors, and finally across a vast limestone plateau known as the Causse de Gramat. When they reached the cliff's edge, they parked and walked to a viewing terrace to gaze over the deep Alzou Canyon. The medieval village of Rocamadour clung to the rock face below them and to their right, and far, far down, a river wound through the gorge. The sun dropped behind the three travelers, casting the canyon in shadow but bathing the opposite ridge in the evening light.

"I've heard," Elena said, leaning over the railing, "that the best time to see the village is in the morning, but even now..."

"Awesome, as Justin would say." Madeleine stared at the play of light and dark upon the ancient shrine jutting from the craggy mountainside.

They paused, listening to the silence in the cool of the early evening.

Jack rubbed his chin. "That's really something."

"Makes you feel a kind of reverence," Madeleine added.

"Like you're small but part of something big." Elena pulled out the camera, focused, and squeezed the button. "Hope that comes out."

They drove down the switchback, weary, but relieved to have arrived. Locating the Hotel Bellevue, Elena checked them in, and they located their simply furnished rooms. Madeleine walked to the window and gazed down to the shadowy gorge at the base of steep, slate-blue mountains.

"Did you inquire about Brother Anthony, Elena?" Jack surveyed the narrow space. "This room is a closet."

"He's in the monastery at the top of the village. I will call him tonight and hopefully we can see him tomorrow." She checked her watch. "Dinner downstairs at eight? *C'est très rustique, mes amis.* I'm wearing what I have on." She regarded her jeans and her running shoes. "Maybe I'll change my shoes."

"We'll come by your room at eight," Madeleine said, and closed the door behind Elena.

Jack unzipped his garment bag. "Why did I bring all these ties? And two sports jackets I'll never wear."

Madeleine began to unpack. She glanced at the thin mattress and the threadbare throw rugs on uneven planks. A dim light flickered in a single lamp. A cockroach scuttled along the wall.

"You'll wear those ties," she said, "in Paris."

Jack looked up. "Perhaps. How do you do it, Maddie? How do you take it all in stride? Here we are in a godforsaken hole—not even clean—and you see the best, you never complain. I wish I could do that."

"You could, Jack. I'm sure you could."

"After the operation, after the healing—when this burning stops—maybe then." He walked to the window and leaned on the sill, his hands forming tight fists. "Where *is* this doctor?" He pushed the window open and inhaled the brisk air.

"Do you think it might rain?" Madeleine asked as she unzipped her toiletry bag.

"It's too cold to rain, too clear. I can even see a few stars. Look!" He pointed. A quarter moon climbed into the night sky.

Suddenly the wind slammed the window shut, whistling around the cliff-hanging *auberge*.

"Remember the village of Eze?" Madeleine struggled with a warped drawer in the nightstand and finally yanked it open. She set her clock and mini-light on the top of the stand and her Underhill paperback on the shelf beneath. How she appreciated this Anglican mystic. Here was a married woman, like Madeleine, searching for answers to the mysteries of life. It was this readable scholar who convinced Madeleine that God worked through matter, through the real world. As the God of love and suffering he was present in the heart of life's ordinary routines and problems, in the crucible of human relationships. Dr. Underhill called the idea "practical mysticism."

Jack turned toward her. "Eze was high up the mountainside, wasn't it? Like here, but overlooking the Mediterranean. We had tea as I recall."

"We sat on a terrace that hung from a cliff. I remember the fog clearing bit by bit, as the sun shone on the sea far below."

"It stormed that night." He latched the window and pulled the muslin curtains in one tense movement, then strapped on his heart monitor. "It could storm tonight."

Madeleine searched for his pre-dinner pill and bottled water.

"We'll be blown off the mountain," he said. "We'd better have someone close the outside shutters as well. Elena can ask at dinner."

Madeleine watched his face as the monitor whirred, and the digital numbers appeared on the tiny screen. Okay for now. She handed him his pill and then his water.

70

They returned from dinner to find the shutters tightly latched. Taking two foam pillows from a chair, Madeleine shoved them under the mattress, creating an incline.

They settled into the lumpy bed and soon the night closed about them. Jack slept a troubled sleep, and his breathing was hoarse as he tossed in pain. The wind howled and the rain battered the shutters, and Madeleine dozed fitfully. In the thick dark she thought of other rooms of wakefulness where nightmares had terrified her, when Mollie, her skeleton shrinking, ran through closed doors into unreachable lands. Madeleine was thankful the old dreams had not returned. *This* black night held only the clamor of wind and rain, of material substance, of weather. And, of course, her husband's pain.

Jack's illness was like those dreams, it was that awful, flesh corrupted, aging, dying. But was there a spiritual side to his suffering? Was there always one and we simply didn't see it? She began an *Our Father*, pulled up the rough blanket, settled it around Jack's shoulders, and waited for dawn, reciting the comforting words she had memorized over the years, words that bundled her, warming her soul.

Finally, as a pale light pierced the shutters, Madeleine snuggled into her husband's back and wrapped her body around his. He pulled her arm over his chest and laced his fingers in hers. Drifting into the warmth of his skin, she inhaled his sweet Armani spice as her arms cradled the thumping of their hearts. At last, she slept. Deeply, without dreaming.

The morning skies were clear when they joined Elena for breakfast in the small lobby. A portly woman with pockmarked skin served muesli and canned milk, thick slices of grilled ham, a pot of goat cheese and bowls of strong coffee. A mangy black spaniel settled at Jack's feet, waiting for scraps and a scratch behind the ears.

Elena had reached Brother Anthony, and now she questioned their hostess. The woman smiled a toothless grin and pointed outside toward the pilgrims' Great Staircase.

Within the hour they were climbing two hundred sixteen stairs worn smooth through the centuries by knees and bare feet. Madeleine imagined the thousands of travelers to this mountain shrine, climbing and crawling, in rags and in silks, bringing their lives to be healed. But today, she and her companions were alone on the stairs, alone in the silence of the morning, as the sun burned through the crisp damp air. With each step, she said a silent prayer.

Elena fingered something in her pocket. Probably her rosary, thought Madeleine.

Jack grasped the railing, taking the steps slowly, his cap shielding his face from the bright sun. "Watch out—these steps are slippery from the rain." He pulled out his dark glasses.

They reached a landing, stopped to rest, and turned toward the valley below. Sunlight streamed over the opposite ridge, and Madeleine inhaled the fresh air. Elena focused her camera on the meandering river, a thin ribbon seeking the sea. Far away, a motor scooter broke the quiet, and at the top of the village, someone hammered, sending staccato notes into the air. Madeleine looked beyond to the monastery. It perched on the mountainside like a giant dove, pausing in its flight between heaven and earth.

Jack, having caught his breath, doggedly resumed his climb, his eyes fixed on each step. "This Brother Anthony," he gasped, "where do we meet him?"

Elena joined him. "At the top of the stairs—it's not far now. He's a contemplative, so he's kind to see us."

"Aren't they the ones who pray all the time?"

Elena laughed, and her ponytail, bound by a red scarf, swung about her shoulders. "They feel they do more by praying for the world than by working in the world. Their prayers are their own kind of work. This must be Anthony, now."

A slight figure in a black cassock appeared at the top of the Great Staircase. He pushed back his cowl to reveal a blond tonsure and a young, freckled face. As Jack joined him, he took off his cap in respect.

The young monk shook Jack's hand. "I'm Brother Anthony. You must be Mr. Seymour. I'm pleased to meet you, sir, and Mrs. Seymour." His green eyes searched Jack's, then Madeleine's. He turned to Elena. "And you, I believe, are Elena—I spoke with you on the phone. May I show you around? My uncle said this is your first visit to Rocamadour."

Jack frowned. "Thanks, but could you tell us where Doctor DuPres is? We wanted to have a few words with her." He pulled two white tablets out of his shirt pocket.

Elena glanced at Madeleine. "We *would* love to see the Black Madonna."

"Jack, I want to see the Madonna too," Madeleine said. "Brother Anthony, is the doctor still here? Are we in time?"

"Come with me," Anthony said.

They followed him across a shallow courtyard enclosed by stone buildings and entered a dark chapel smelling of wax and smoke. Small *remercie* plaques of thanksgiving surrounded the Black Madonna, her child on her hip. Candles burned at the figure's base in a teetering iron stand. The primitive Virgin was elongated, the arms slim, the face gaunt. The Child sat on her knee, his figure also slight. Both wore crowns of gold. But the severity of the image belied the thoughtful expression of Mary and the knowing expression of the Child.

Madeleine lit a candle and said a silent *Hail Mary*.

"This is the Lady Chapel," Anthony explained to Jack and Elena. "It's larger than the original one, which was probably the size of a small stable. Crowds of pilgrims waited their turn in the courtyard and on the staircase. They carried chains—representing their sins—and left them behind at the chapel door. They were set free."

Madeleine, hearing the words, turned toward Anthony. Transported into another time, she gazed about the chapel, merging the two worlds. "Such a small space for so many people."

Anthony folded his hands as though summoning the scene. "They came from all over France to this cave. They came to give thanks for blessings in their lives, for prayers answered. They came to be healed."

Madeleine could see them all, pulled by love, pulled by hope, pulled by obedience.

Anthony gestured with open palms. "The commotion must have been great. Singing psalms and hymns. Some wept for sorrows or sins. Some shouted their requests to Our Lady." He grinned. "It was a colorful time, to say the least."

Jack shifted his weight from side to side, clutching his dark glasses, watching the young monk and gazing at the vacant space.

"And it's so quiet today." Elena moved toward the Madonna and Child. It was her turn to light a candle, to say a prayer.

"It's not always this quiet," Anthony said. "We have a renewed interest in the shrine. Many groups come on pilgrimage. We're even on the Internet." He gazed at Jack with concern, clearly sensing his impatience, a restless urgency that filled the chapel.

Jack scratched his chin. "That's remarkable, son, but—"

"She answers prayers all the time," the monk added. "Maybe I should leave you here for a while?"

Jack raised his brows and tilted his head, as he often did when approaching a delicate question or a subtle demand. "Brother Anthony, we've come a long way. We would appreciate it immensely if you could arrange a meeting with Doctor DuPres—she's here, isn't she?"

"We'll take only a few minutes of her time." Madeleine looked at the rustic Madonna and Child, then Jack, then Anthony. She waited. Elena rejoined them.

"Of course." Anthony studied the older man thoughtfully. "I understand. Please, come this way, where we can talk." He led them into the sacristy, a small room off a side aisle. "This back door leads to a secret stairwell that connects to the monastery above the village."

"Wow," Elena said, her eyes growing large. "I've heard of these passages."

"They used it during the German occupation."

They sat around a small table. Colored light shafted through a high window and landed on a crucifix above an antique armoire. Madeleine watched the pattern of light dance on the suffering image of Christ as leaves from a tree brushed the outside wall, casting shadows that broke up the light. *What is thy will, Lord?*

Anthony rested his hands on the table. "I'm sorry to say this, but Doctor DuPres has left."

"Oh no," Madeleine said. *Again?*

Jack rubbed his chest and whistled through his teeth. "She's a slippery one, isn't she?"

Madeleine winced but could feel his disappointment, his exhaustion.

Anthony gazed at the crucifix. "I tried to help her. I don't know if I did."

Jack stood, his hands on his hips. "Where did she go?"

The young monk looked at Elena, then Madeleine. He rose and stepped toward the chapel door. "She went to her sister's. Yesterday."

Elena touched his sleeve. "Please, Brother, where does this sister live? We need to find the doctor."

They followed the monk into the chapel where he paused before the Madonna. "Mr. and Mrs. Seymour," he said, his features pulled together in worry, "I'm truly torn. My uncle told me to help you find Rachelle, and I trust his judgment. But I fear I may be breaking an agreement I had with Doctor DuPres, if not a clear vow."

They waited in the silence as he looked upon the Black Madonna. "She's gone to Crillon-le-Brave, a village near Avignon," he said. He pulled out a scrap of paper from his pocket and turned to face them. "I once visited the Morins with my uncle. They are good people, Rebecca and Philippe and their family. I believe Doctor DuPres mentioned she was close to Pierre, the youngest. Here's the address and general directions. It's about a day's drive from here."

"Crillon-le-Brave?" Jack asked. "That's near Carpentras, isn't it? We bought some Chateauneuf-du-Pape from a dealer in the valley."

"It's not far from Carpentras."

"Thank you, Brother Anthony," Madeleine said, relieved. "We do appreciate this."

"I wish you a safe journey," Anthony said, checking his watch. "Now I must leave you—it has been a pleasure." He raised his hand in blessing and disappeared into the sacristy.

Jack slipped on his dark glasses. "I'll meet you ladies outside. I need some air." He pulled on the heavy door and stepped into the blinding light, his figure a black silhouette.

"I'll come with you." Madeleine glanced back at Elena, who stood before the Madonna and Child. Her beads hung over her hand and her chestnut hair caught a ray of sunshine slanting through a high window.

Madeleine followed Jack across the courtyard, pushing against an icy wind. They paused at the top the Great Staircase.

Jack strapped on his monitor. "You'd better wait for Elena."

They listened in the silence to the whir of the tiny machine.

"How are the numbers?" Madeleine asked.

"Heart rate high."

"At least we know more about Doctor DuPres."

Jack frowned. "If we can believe this young fellow."

"Why can't we believe him?"

"Father Benedict wasn't too forthcoming. We had to pry the information out of him."

Madeleine sighed. It was true—the priest had skirted their questions. His loyalties were clearly divided, but understandably so. Much like his nephew.

Jack kissed her on the forehead. "You're too good, sweetie. You believe *everyone*. The real world isn't like that. Listen, I'm going back to the hotel. The front desk might have a paper by now and I can check the stocks. You wait for Elena." He began his descent.

Madeleine shivered as she watched Jack leave. Did she wear rose-colored glasses to view the world? Should she not trust Doctor Lau's judgment? Should she follow her own intuition—and Father Benedict's advice—and tell Jack the diagnosis? But Jack's father had such a painful, lingering death...and suffered those terrible surgeries...and then there were Jack's words to Conrad Lau about not wanting to live. But still, it seemed her husband had the right to know. What should she do?

Bells clanged noon, and Elena emerged from the chapel. She seemed self-conscious, as though concealing an interior delight. Tears streamed down her cheeks.

Madeleine wrapped an arm around her. "Are you okay?"

Elena dried her eyes with her fingers. "Sometimes, when I pray, I feel such joy. It overwhelms me—in a good way."

"Did Our Lady help you?"

"She comforted me."

"Good. Mary has often been a comfort to me as well. And now, the doctor has eluded us again. I wonder why she left her practice?"

"I don't know, but secrets come out in the end."

"Do you think so?" Madeleine swallowed hard. What would Jack say when her secret came out?

"It's only a question of time. We'll find her, Madeleine. Jack will be all right. I'm sure of it."

How Madeleine wanted to believe her. "I can't imagine my life without him."

"Is it that serious?"

Madeleine looked out over the gorge. She couldn't ask Elena to share this burden, to lie to Jack. "Thank you for your prayers, Elena."

"Jack—he is worse than you have said? Than even he knows?"

"I'm afraid so."

Arm in arm, the two women started down the stairs of the faithful, one step at a time, Madeleine certain her climb was only beginning.

Chapter Ten
Mount Ventoux

And above all these things put on charity,
which is the bond of perfectness...
Colossians 3:14

Tuesday remained dry, but a moist breeze hinted of rain. Rachelle sat next to Rebecca on a blanket spread over brown grass on the lower slopes of Mount Ventoux. The sisters unwrapped packets of cold chicken and sausage, opened a plastic tub of cherry tomatoes, and set out a loaf of crusty bread on a cutting board alongside a pot of black olive *tapenade* and a serrated knife; they laid out utensils and paper plates, and poured minted iced tea. They worked together, Rachelle thought, as they did when they were young, setting out a tea service for their dolls on the back porch; it was that natural. Time vanished.

Rachelle leaned against a granite outcrop and gazed up at Mount Ventoux, then down to the valley below. "It was good of Pierre to take over your lunch duties, not to mention pack us a picnic. Don't they need him to help with the harvest?"

Rebecca slathered a thick layer of tapenade on a slice of bread, handed it to Rachelle, then made one for herself. "He dislikes it, and his father won't force him. Alphonse doesn't mind, and there will be plenty of men, women too, from the village. They move from vineyard to vineyard until the entire crop is in."

"He's not interested in farming, is he, Becca?"

Rebecca sighed as though giving up a long-waged battle, a long-desired dream. "Pierre goes to Paris next week to arrange his schooling to be a nurse, at this point."

"But *you* don't want him to go into medicine?" Rachelle savored the tapenade, tangy with garlic.

"Maybe he has your talent. I can't stop him."

"But you aren't happy with his choice?"

Rebecca shook her head. "It's his decision, isn't it? He's ambitious. He's rejected our way of life, our values, our beliefs. He no longer comes to church with us."

"I see."

"Now my Alphonse—he *likes* Crillon-le-Brave, and family, and even cooking. He wants to open a restaurant in Carpentras. I wish you could have come to his wedding last year." She laughed at a memory Rachelle couldn't share. "You met Josephine. The baby—my first grandbaby—is due around Christmas."

"Congratulations. You've done well here, Becca."

"We aren't rich, but we have enough to live simply and comfortably, what with the summer guests and the harvest."

"And my nieces, Nicole and Erica? Do they still live nearby? Will I see them?"

"They live in the next village, and help out occasionally with the grapes and the guests—they should stop by tonight. And Alphonse is close. But you've done well too, haven't you, Shelley? Pierre follows your career."

Rachelle swallowed hard, then sipped her tea, watching the lemon slice bob in the dark liquid. "Of course. I've been successful." Her heart pounded.

Rebecca patted her sister's knee. "I wish you'd come sooner, Shelley. I've really missed you. We were so close growing up. It isn't the same, writing and phoning."

Rachelle feigned a smile. She tried to sound sincere, but her sister's world had never seemed important, until now, when her own had diminished. "I know. I've been too caught up in my work, I guess, and couldn't find the time. Now I wonder why." She looked out over the valley of vines, across to the rocky promontory of Crillon-le-Brave and the chateau that seemed to grow from the rock itself. "This is *so* beautiful."

"Pierre idolizes you, you know."

"Maybe I can spend some time with him before I leave. He's very quiet."

"He's like you, driven to succeed. Intense. He loves e-mailing, when he can get online at the library."

They sat in silence, watching a hawk glide toward the mountain, its wings unfurled in the wind current.

"Pierre mentioned you saw Father Benedict," Rebecca said,

sounding tentative, "at Lourdes, no less."

Rachelle looked at her hands. "I'm through doctoring, Becca."

"I can't believe that."

"You...don't understand..."

"Try me."

"I...I killed a man." Rachelle buried her face in her hands.

"Shelley, what happened?" Rebecca touched her sister's shoulder.

Rachelle stared at the brown blades bordering the blanket. "The procedure was in the operating theater, a lesson for the students. They saw it all."

"What did they see, Shelley?"

"It was his third time...he had Barrett's disease. To do the wrap, we had to open the esophagus and clear out the tissue..." She shook her head to make the scene go away.

"You've done this operation before, right?"

"Many times."

"And?"

She stared at the village opposite. "We lost him. I couldn't stop the bleeding. I should never have attempted the surgery. I should have refused him. I thought I could do anything. They all warned me."

"Rachelle." Rebecca rubbed her sister's back.

"He was only thirty-three, with two children, young children."

"Come here," Rebecca whispered. She pulled Rachelle close.

With this movement, Rachelle went limp as if some interior flooring had collapsed and the walls imploded. She wept—deep, wrenching tears, tears that rushed through her, choking. Her sister rocked her and slowly, her shaking lessened.

Finally, Rebecca sat back, her face grave, and took Rachelle's hands in her own. Rachelle braced herself for judgment. She pulled away. Her nose was running and her eyes felt swollen. She reached for a napkin to blot her face.

"Perhaps you expect too much from yourself," Rebecca said softly.

"That's what a colleague told me." She blew her nose. How long had it been since she cried like that? How long since she let go? The pieces of her center lay scattered on the grass—she needed to gather them and fit them back together. She breathed deeply, not liking this new vulnerability. Her sister was speaking—what was she saying?

"Shelley, everything has been easy for you, your rise to the top. You've had perfect schooling, a perfect career."

"So what does that have to do with it?" Her speech mimicked her, sounding hoarse, congested.

Rebecca looked away, fingering her cross. "We all make mistakes. Every one of us does."

"But I killed a man."

"It sounds like an accident, if that."

"I don't know, Becca."

"It was bound to come sooner or later."

"What would come? What are you talking about?"

"Failure, Shelley, despair, accepting the ordinary, being human like the rest of us."

"How can you say that?" Anger rose inside Rachelle like an ugly tumor. "You've never been responsible for a man's death."

"I've known death and near-death—Philippe was very sick once. I've known failure. But I have a way to deal with it."

Rebecca's eyes were imploring now—sickeningly sweet.

"Oh? And how would you deal with a failure like this?"

Rebecca opened her palms. "I'd give it to God. It's pride that's eating you up, Rachelle. Get rid of it. Pride will kill you."

"You're certainly straightforward, aren't you?" And flippant as well.

"I never could lie." Relief passed across Rebecca's face, as though she hoped the diversion might ease her sister's pain, might slow the momentum of their conversation. "Remember my telltale twitch?"

Rachelle recalled her sister's cheek muscle and its predictable spasm. It was true. Rebecca couldn't lie, at least not lie and get away with it, not with those who knew her. "So you think I'm proud?" She returned to the thrust of her sister's accusations. She would ferret out this dangerous tumor and remove it.

"I do. Only God is perfect. And he can help you through this, if you let him."

"I should have guessed you'd bring God into this." Becca was still a child, living in a fantasy world. "God can't help me—he can't bring the man back. And God doesn't exist anyway."

"You still don't believe? After all your healing, all the suffering you've seen? You clearly believe in the moral law, or you wouldn't be in such anguish now—where do you think that law came from? Who gave it to us?"

"You just never grew up." Rachelle stood, turned, and headed for the chateau.

How could Becca presume to preach? She was no more than a simple homemaker who never finished college. What did she know about

80

hard work, realizing your dreams, accomplishing miracles in peoples' lives? And what did she know about failure? Knowing despair...feeling helpless...accepting the ordinary. Rachelle was astounded, outraged. Her blood raced, and she fell into a heavy jog down the mountain path as the sun slipped behind a cloud.

Her run slowed to a walk as she climbed the lane to Crillon-le-Brave, her anger smoldering. She crossed the square and paused before the stone church, not ready to return to the chateau. Pulling on the heavy wooden door, she read the scripted sign, *Saint-Romain*, listing this week's calendar. She slipped into the musty dark and sat in a back pew, her heart pounding, glad for the shadows. In the dim light, a red candle wavered on a stone altar, and Rachelle recalled its significance—the Sacrament was reserved in the tabernacle, that miniature house with the bronze door. Was God really there, in that communion wafer they called the host? Unlikely. But Rebecca believed he was, and Father Benedict too for that matter, as well as his nephew, Anthony.

Why had she fought with her sister? As children, Rachelle achingly recalled, they had been inseparable. They dressed each other and combed each other's hair, tenderly working through each snarl. They read to each other and finished one another's sentences. Rachelle dictated the activity, chose the song. Rebecca followed happily, immersed in her sister's game, singing her chorus. When they attended different colleges, they phoned daily. But when Rachelle was accepted by Harvard Medical and Rebecca settled in Crillon-le-Brave, they drifted apart, removed by choices as well as distance.

The heavy air smelled of damp and dust. Why had she been so nasty to her sister? Could Becca be right? It probably *was* the first time for her, and the fall was long and hard.

A muscular arm wrapped about her shoulders. *Pierre*. How long had she been sitting here? A half hour? An hour? Silently, her nephew guided her outside, into the harsh sunlight, across the square to his home.

"*Merci, mon Pierre, merci.*"

He led her to their vegetable garden, a small plot behind the kitchen, then excused himself. Rebecca stood near the chateau wall, leaning down and filling a pail with water from a low spigot. The cat, curled in a spot of sun on the kitchen stoop, was washing her face with her paw.

"Becca, I'm sorry. I didn't mean it. I realize you work hard, probably harder than I shall ever know."

"It's okay, Shelley," she said. "How about helping me? Here—trim these while I talk." She handed Rachelle a bucket of string beans, a paring knife, and a clay bowl. "I'm peeling potatoes. It helps me think, and Alphonse hates the job."

Rachelle stared at the green beans and waited.

"Somehow, my dear sister," Rebecca said, "I knew this moment would come, and I knew you would find me. This home can be yours, too. You will always have a place at our table. It's a good life, as I've said, full of sun and growing things, making babies, oil, and wine. And there is love, don't forget love. Love of family. Love of the land. Love of country."

Rachelle began to work slowly, cutting off the tips and dropping the beans one at a time into the bowl. "I know," she said softly, "but medicine has been my life, my soul. I think I'm dying." As the words slipped out, she was certain they were true. She was gray inside, ashen, grizzled.

"Dying? Maybe part of you is dying." Rebecca frowned and rose to add more water to cover the peeled potatoes.

"Who *am* I, Becca? Who are *we*? You know, don't you? I haven't a clue. I thought I was a doctor, a good one. But now? What's left?"

"I can't tell you, Rachelle, but I *can* tell you about our family. Do you remember our imaginary games, trying to figure out who we were and who we would become?"

"When we found out we were adopted." How old were they then? Rachelle couldn't recall. Young, though.

"Right. When we understood why we were named DuPres and our adoptive parents named Kennedy. And how we were smuggled out of Nazi France."

"So where are you going with this?"

"When Daddy died, and Mom was diagnosed with Alzheimer's, I researched the DuPres history further. I didn't want to hurt Mom and Dad Kennedy; they loved us, raised us. They were our real parents, Shelley."

Rachelle concentrated on her beans, listening to each word.

"Philippe learned we have four uncles on our father's side, the Catholic side. Three fought and died in the war, two in Vence, near Nice, and one in Reims, up north."

Rachelle glanced up. "The Catholic side? What other side was there?"

"Shelley," Rebecca said, pausing as she turned, her eyes bright.

82

"Our mother Leah was Jewish."

"Jewish?" Rachelle stared at her sister and set down her knife.

"She was Jewish. She married a Catholic boy in the village, Alain DuPres—what a scandal that must have been. Philippe found out from local talk. It took awhile to confirm the rumors, but they appear to be true." She carried her bucket to the kitchen stoop and set it beside the cat.

"So the Underground, the French Resistance. They felt more than sympathy or love of justice."

Rebecca sat by Rachelle on the stone bench. "Right. Probably other family members were hidden and smuggled to freedom, just like us, through Lourdes into Spain, through the western ports, by Catholic families. And I'm sure many died in the camps." She reached for a handful of Rachelle's beans, deftly nipping the ends and dropping them into the bowl.

Rachelle considered her sister's words. Her Jewish colleagues were often the brightest and most driven. She had felt a kinship with them in so many ways.

"Why didn't you tell me?"

"I wrote you about it, but you didn't reply. It was only last year that Philippe was able to confirm some of the facts."

"You said you were finding your roots...what else did you learn? What about the fourth uncle you mentioned?"

Rebecca smiled. "He's Alain's twin, fraternal, like us."

"His twin? Our father had a twin? That's amazing."

"But that's really all we've learned. He seems to have disappeared without a trace. I've been intending to ask Clarice about him—Aunt Clarice."

"Clarice?" Rachelle struggled to absorb the new names, her new family.

"We have an elderly aunt who survived the war, our mother's sister. Her name is Clarice Laurent. She lives in a chateau-hotel, a larger version of our little place. It's in Vence, in one of the hilltop villages of the Côte d'Azur above Cannes. I haven't met her—I only located her last year—but I've spoken to her on the phone. She sounds frail. I wanted to visit and ask about Leah and Alain. See where our uncles died. I haven't found the time so far." She gazed at the kitchen, then the vineyards below, and a weary resignation swept over her features.

Rachelle breathed deeply. "Thank you, Becca. Perhaps this is why I came here, came home, in a way." She wrapped her arms around the bowl and stood. "I'd like to see where our parents lived."

"Their homes were destroyed in the war."

"Then can I see their graves?"

"There are only memorials—in the square and Saint-Romain, the village church. We'll show you in the morning."

"Thanks, I'd like that. And I'd also like to visit this Aunt Clarice."

"I'll call her tonight. Come, we'd better help Pierre set the table." Rebecca looked up at the gathering clouds, dark and threatening. "I don't like that sky."

The Alpine hail hit hard that night, as gale winds slammed the chateau. Staggering out of bed, Rachelle reached to close the heavy wooden shutters and stared at the drama before her. Lightning lit the vineyards and small farmhouses. A quarter moon emerged, then slipped away. The flashes in the dark sky marched down the mountain and descended upon Crillon as heavy clouds rumbled through the heavens, booming and clashing, finally deluging the earth. Against the force of the wind, Rachelle jerked the shutters closed and fastened them with iron hooks.

Leah and Alain had lived in this village of Crillon-le-Brave. She wanted to know them. Did she, Rachelle, think like Leah? Did she look like Alain? Who were these people who conceived her and then saved her life by giving her up?

She crawled back into the narrow bed and pulled up the quilt. Wondering if the workers had brought in the grapes, she drifted into a dreamless sleep.

Chapter Eleven
Saint-Romain

Who shall separate us from
the love of Christ...
Romans 8: 35

The storm left a saturated and sparkling earth and an urgency to finish the picking. The men began at dawn, filling the white vans and driving their purple loads to the barns. Rachelle followed Pierre and Rebecca to the village square where a weathered bronze sculpture of a grieving woman, bent low in sorrow, cried over the valley of grapes. Behind her, the *Mairie*—the town hall—flew the red-blue-and-white flag of France. Only a distant motor scooter broke the silence.

"She grieves," Rebecca said, "for all the village boys killed in the wars, both the first and the second World Wars, and for the victims of the Holocaust." She pointed to a list on the cement slab under the figure, moving her finger down to *Les Morts de la Résistance*.

Rachelle read the names engraved on the plaque: Leah Laurent DuPres, 1918-1943; Alain DuPres, 1914-1943.

What would Alain and Leah have thought of her today—fleeing the hospital, fleeing her job, fleeing herself? She studied the monument in silence. "And the church? You said the church..."

"*Oui*," Pierre said, "*allons-y*, we go there now."

They crossed the square and entered the dim sanctuary. The red candle still flamed, and through a high window, light streamed onto the tabernacle. Rachelle followed Pierre to a side bay where he flipped a switch, illuminating a wall plaque. Saint Francis stood in a niche, his open palms raised to a seraph in the heavens, his features open and unguarded in adoration.

"Francis," Rebecca whispered, "asks to suffer the wounds of Christ, and Christ appears to him and gives him his wish. You see the crucifix in the heart of the angel? That's Christ. He comes as an Angel of the Lord."

Rachelle felt Pierre's eyes on her, as though he waited for her reaction. "Really?" she said.

Rebecca continued to gaze at the figure, as though meditating. "Francis is an appropriate saint for this memorial. We believe Christ redeems our suffering, turns it into good. Leah and Alain also suffered the wounds of Christ."

"How so?" She couldn't understand how one could glorify suffering. This beggar in rags asked to be wounded. Wasn't that masochistic?

"By acting out Christ's love to others and suffering for it. The same happened in other holocausts: the early martyrs of the Church, the religious wars of Europe, the martyrs of Asia and Africa, the Communist purges of our century."

Hoping to sidestep her sister's piety, Rachelle turned to the marble plaque. Here, again, were the names of the dead, the children of the parish: *Les Enfants de Paroissiens à la Mort*. She found Leah and Alain.

"Here are more DuPres." Pierre traced the names with his finger.

"François, Antoine, and Robert," Rachelle read.

Rebecca also touched the letters and inhaled deeply, as though the touching pulled her into their lives. "Our other uncles. And these Laurents are Leah's family, unaccounted for and presumed lost in the camps."

"So much death." Rachelle looked away, toward the red glow on the altar and the dim musty nave. Death. Darkness and death.

"Come, let's rest a bit." Rebecca touched her sister's elbow and motioned to a pew.

Pierre raised his brows. "I wait in the back." He strode down the aisle with the air of a practical man.

The women sat near the altar. Rebecca pulled down a wooden slat from the pew in front of them and knelt. She made the Sign of the Cross and bowed her head, her lips moving silently. Rachelle waited with unease, as the altar and the candle and the tabernacle, all objects from her past, intruded powerfully into her present. The bell tolled and Rebecca rose. The sisters stepped outside into the bright, windswept square.

"The light and the dark," Pierre said as they walked back to the chateau. "We remember them outside and inside. We never forget."

Rachelle pulled her jacket tight against the cold breeze. "You could be a poet, Pierre, or a very creative doctor."

Pierre grinned.

"Becca, thanks for contacting Clarice," Rachelle said. "And I'd better gather my things—it's late."

"She sounded happy you were coming. I wish I could join you, but I'm needed here. Do you still want to catch the early train to Nice? I think you can make it."

"I'd like to try. Thank you. Thank you both for everything."

Rachelle was zipping her bag when Pierre appeared in the doorway, a cordless phone in his hand. "It is for you. You know a Dr. Lau?"

"Yes, I work with him." She took the phone. "Connie? Is that you?"

Pierre paused, then turned to go.

Rachelle covered the mouthpiece. "It's okay, Pierre. Stay. It's only a colleague from work."

Pierre flopped in the easy chair, fingering its green slipcover and watching her closely as though she held the key to his life.

Conrad briefed her on Jack Seymour's case. "Rachelle, he and his wife have left for France. I'm sorry. *I* didn't tell them where you were going."

"How did they find out?"

"I don't know. Your nurse said they were asking questions. Did you leave anything in the office they might have seen?"

"The Lourdes book might have been out. You don't think they put it together from that?"

"Possibly. He's a man who enjoys a challenge and is used to winning. Rachelle, he's very sick. Could you at least consider his request? I urged him to take Goldberg or Sanders but he wouldn't. Too young, he said."

"They *are* under thirty." Pretty wet behind the ears, too, she thought.

"But they know their stuff. They're good. They're talented, scored highly in school."

"So where are these Seymours now?"

"I believe they're heading for your village. I traced them to Benedict O'Reilley, who said they were following you to Rocamadour. Father O'Reilley gave me your sister's number. It won't be long before Jack Seymour hears about Crillon as well. By the way, Father O'Reilley thinks you should return to surgery, 'get back in the ring' were the words he used."

"You talked to Father Benedict? How did you locate him?"

"I used the amazing Knights of Malta network."

She laughed. "Of course."

"Just looking out for you, my dear."

Rachelle could see him saying that, eyes twinkling, finger wagging. She missed him. Conrad Lau had worked hard to reach department head. She admired his drive and envied his good humor through it all.

"Thanks for warning me," she said.

"Will you think about it?"

"Not if I can help it."

"And will you have Jack Seymour call me? I didn't expect them to leave the country like that. I need to talk to him."

"I'll tell him, if I see him."

"Rachelle, he doesn't know how serious his condition is."

"What?"

"Just have him call me."

She could hear the panic in his voice. "I will. But why didn't you tell—"

"Take care of yourself, Rachelle. Where can I reach you?"

"I'll be in touch, Connie. You take care too."

With some confusion as to the judgment of her old friend, she handed the phone to Pierre. "A patient—a Jack Seymour—is following me. He requires surgery and wants me to operate. What do you think, Pierre?"

"I think you need more time for your vacation, *ma tante*. I will help you. I will keep this Jack Seymour away. I will tell them you go to Paris. Ha!"

"Thanks, but you mustn't worry about me."

"I want to come with you."

"I've got to go alone, Pierre, deal with my own problems my own way. And your mother needs you here. I've intruded too much already. I'd better catch that train."

He frowned and helped her with her bags.

Rebecca was waiting in the front hall, wiping her hands on her apron. "Thanks for coming, Shelley. I can't tell you how much it meant to me. You *will* return to Crillon before you go home to the States?"

"I promise."

"And you'll call and keep in touch on this journey of yours?"

"I will."

"And Shelley...keep your heart open." She fingered the cross about her neck.

"I'll try."

They kissed cheeks and hugged. Rebecca handed her a woven bag. "For your journey. You can't visit our aunt empty handed."

Rachelle peeked inside. "Wine. And cheese. And a sandwich."

"Our red wine. Our neighbor's cheese. Give Aunt Clarice my best wishes and tell her I'll visit soon with the children. The sandwich is for you. You still like tuna salad?"

Rachelle smiled. They had split many tuna sandwiches over the years. "I do."

The aroma of the cheese was pungent, and Rachelle pulled out the wine. *La Domaine du Crillon* was scripted above a drawing of a chateau. Mount Ventoux rose behind.

"Thank you, Becca, thank you."

Pierre held the car door open for her, and she lowered herself onto the torn seat. She strapped on her seatbelt and looked out the open window, back to her sister. The car sputtered forward. Rebecca waved with one hand as she held the other over her heart. The radio blared, and Rachelle waved back, knowing part of her had been restored already.

Chapter Twelve
La Sainte-Baume

That ye, being rooted and grounded in love,
may be able to comprehend with all the saints what is the breadth,
and length, and depth, and height...
Ephesians 3:17

Madeleine counted the wasted days as Elena maneuvered the sedan up the hill to Crillon-le-Brave. It was already Wednesday evening, September 22, a week since their flight and two weeks since Doctor Lau's visit. Still, she told herself, they were close to finding this elusive Rachelle DuPres, closer each minute. Here, surely, in the village of her sister, their search would end. She squinted through the gathering dusk, trying to read the French signs as the quarter moon rose over Mount Ventoux. They made two wrong turns, then she read the words *Crillon-le-Brave*, wondering, from force of habit, how the town was named.

"Whew!" said Elena, as she pulled the car to a stop. "Here we are. We arrived."

Jack looked about and rubbed his eyes. "I must have dropped off a bit."

"I'm glad you slept." Madeleine looked at the neat stone houses emerging from the shadows.

Jack got out and opened the back door for Madeleine. His smile was forced, but he held her shoulders tenderly and kissed her forehead. "You've been patience personified, darling. Thank you. And I'm sorry; I'm not very good company these days."

Madeleine searched his eyes. "It's okay, Jack, I understand."

"The important thing is that we're here." Elena led them up the street, reading the house numbers, and pointed to a green door with *16* painted neatly in black.

They climbed the stairs. Jack pulled the bell rope, glancing at the knotted end buried in a pot of geraniums. The bell jangled, the door opened, and a young man looked at them with a worried expression.

Madeleine smiled nervously. "Pierre Morin?"

"*Oui.*"

In the dim light, Madeleine squinted at the note Brother Anthony had given her and looked up at the dark-haired boy. "Is this the home of Rebecca Morin?"

Pierre frowned. His denim shirt was rolled to his elbows, and he planted his hands on his hips.

"*Morin? Oui.*"

Jack leaned forward. "We're searching for Doctor Rachelle DuPres."

"Elena," Madeleine said, "could you help us with the French?"

Elena looked up at Pierre. "*Nous cherchons pour Rachelle DuPres.*"

"*Entrez, s'il vous plaît.*" He led them into the small foyer. "Please wait here."

Madeleine watched Pierre enter an adjoining room where a fire burned in a stone hearth. The young man spoke rapidly to two men and a woman holding steaming mugs. A tortoise shell cat slept on a rug in front of the fire.

The woman stood and approached Madeleine. "I'm Rebecca Morin," she said, smiling, "Rachelle DuPres's sister. How do you do?"

Seeing the silver cross in the vee of her blouse, Madeleine was encouraged. "I'm Madeleine Seymour, and this is my husband, Jack, and our friend, Elena Coronati. Please forgive us for intruding. We tried calling but the line was busy." They shook hands.

Madame Morin's grip was firm and her face thoughtful. "Pierre said you were looking for my sister. Please, join us by the fire. We've just finished dinner." She led them into the parlor. "Philippe and Alphonse, could you begin the dishes? I must speak with our guests. Pierre, stay for a minute, please." The two men sauntered into a back room. "The harvest is a busy time for us. Won't you sit down? Would you care for some tea?"

They sat in overstuffed, mismatched chairs slipcovered in worn damask and chintz. Pierre stood beside his mother and regarded Elena with undisguised interest.

Jack leaned back in the chair. "Thanks, tea would be great. We appreciate your time, Mrs. Morin." He slipped two tablets into his mouth, chewing slowly.

"I'd love some tea if it's not too much trouble. You are kind,"

Madeleine said.

"*Mais oui. Merci,*" Elena said.

Pierre disappeared through a door.

"You've missed my sister," Rebecca said, her eyes wide, her tone tense. "I'm afraid she left this morning—for Paris." Her cheek muscle twitched and she raised her hand to cover the side of her face as she turned toward the fire. The cat jumped onto her lap and pawed her stained apron, purring loudly.

"We've missed her again?" Madeleine said. *More days disappearing.*

Jack laid his hand on Madeleine's. "Could you tell us how we might reach her? Or could you call her for us? I'll give you our number in Paris." His words faded into husky syllables.

Flames crackled in the grate, sending sparks up the blackened chimney. Madeleine walked to the fireplace where an icon of the Virgin and Child rested on the mantel. The image was familiar and comforting, the face tender, and she thought it might be Our Lady of Vladimir, a popular Russian icon. Madeleine felt for her gold cross under her sweater. Rebecca Morin sounded American and appeared to be a Christian, if her silver cross and this icon meant anything. One could never tell these days. But she seemed to be hedging for some reason, possibly protecting her sister.

"I'm not sure where she is exactly," Rebecca was saying, massaging her cheek, "but forgive me, you must be tired. Do you have a place to stay tonight?" She looked toward the kitchen. "And here is Pierre with the tea."

"Thank you, Madame." Elena pulled a paper from her bag. "We have reserved with the Hostellerie de Crillon-le-Brave. Could I use your phone to tell them we are here? We have come from Rocamadour."

"Rocamadour? All that way? Pierre will call for you." Rebecca appeared to be in some distress.

"We met with a Brother Anthony."

Rebecca smiled, her face relaxing. "Brother Anthony—a fine boy. He visited us with his uncle, Father Benedict." Stopping abruptly, she looked away, as though she had revealed too much.

"And we saw Father Benedict in Lourdes." Madeleine reached for her steaming tea, fragrant with rose hips and orange, and returned to her chair. "It smells wonderful," she said to Pierre as she inhaled the vapor.

Jack sipped his tea and turned toward Rebecca. "Your sister is a difficult person to find."

Pierre tapped a number on his cell phone and spoke in rapid

French.

"Is this your home village?" Elena asked Rebecca. "Did you and your sister grow up here?"

"No, but our parents did, and Philippe and I settled here."

Madeleine searched for a route through the words of delay. She gazed at Pierre, who remained on the phone, whispering and nodding.

Elena sipped her tea. "We couldn't see much of the village. It was getting dark."

"Crillon-le-Brave is very small, only one main street, but people live down the hill in the valley too."

"Where did the name come from?" Elena glanced at Madeleine. "Who was Crillon-le-Brave?"

"It's an intriguing name," Madeleine said. How could she resist such a story?

Rebecca looked relieved with the change of subject. "General Crillon, Duke of Crillon, sixteenth century, fought for King Henry IV. His family name was Louis de Berton Balbe. They named the town after him at the end of the nineteenth century for he was brave in battle. The village name Crillon actually goes back to Roman times when it was called Cillonium."

Pierre clapped his phone shut and frowned, but shades of relief flickered over his face. "They do not have your reservation, *Messieurs*."

"Wouldn't you know it," Jack said to Madeleine.

Madeleine reached for his hand. "Oh dear."

"But you can stay here," Rebecca said.

"We couldn't intrude." Yet Madeleine wasn't sure what else they could do.

"But I insist. We have extra rooms we let out in the summer. It would please us if you would stay. You've come so far."

"It's most gracious of you," Jack said.

"It's the least we can do."

Madeleine glanced at Jack. "We should tell you our story."

Pierre shifted his gaze to Madeleine and sat beside his mother.

"You want her to do your surgery," Rebecca said, stroking the cat. "Doctor Lau called her this morning."

"Did he really?" Madeleine said, grateful. "Doctor Lau called?"

Jack stood and walked toward the fireplace. "Good! She's been briefed then. That helps. You see, I have an illness—Barrett's esophagus— and I need this procedure done relatively soon."

"Why must Rachelle be the one to do it?"

He turned to face Madame Morin. "She's experienced. I don't like these young fellows. I know about experience. I managed a chain of stores in my working days."

"Stores?" Pierre leaned forward, brows raised.

Jack approached Pierre, taking a seat opposite. "Wine stores. We imported from this region, as I recall, through a local broker. What was his name, Maddie?"

"Douliers, I think. He drove down from Beaune—in Burgundy—to meet you, remember?"

Pierre rubbed his hands together. "Douliers! He is a successful man. I have heard his name. You must be a great American businessman." He glanced at Elena.

Jack smiled with pride. "Not that great, really. But we did grow from nothing, and I must say, we did pretty well in making a profit, not a huge profit, but a satisfying one nevertheless."

As Jack and Pierre chatted, Elena turned to Rebecca. "We visited Lourdes and met Father Benedict. Lourdes was wonderful."

"Father Benedict was your parish priest?" Madeleine glanced at Jack and Pierre. Her husband's face was alight with the challenge of those productive years, as he basked in this sudden and unexpected admiration. Pierre looked at him with obvious envy.

Rebecca smiled with the memory. "In Massachusetts. Father Benedict taught in our parochial school. Everyone loved him." She turned to Elena. "Lourdes is remarkable, isn't it? The cures are real, you know."

A shadow crossed Elena's face. "I've never understood suffering, why it has to happen. But I'm glad for places like Lourdes that give people hope."

Rebecca studied Elena. "But there *are* reasons for suffering. Just not easy ones. For one, suffering is the price of freedom."

"And your sister, Madame," Madeleine said, trying to stay on track, "your sister—would it be possible to call her? You said she was in Paris?"

"I'm sorry, you can't call her. I don't know where she's staying." She raised her hand to her cheek, massaging it.

But Elena continued to follow her own line of thought. "The price of freedom—did you mean free will, Madame?"

"*Oui.*"

"Sister Agnes said much the same thing," Elena said, half to herself.

"Sister Agnes?"

"A dear mother to me. I was raised by nuns in a convent in Rome."

Pierre looked up from his conversation with Jack.

"You were an orphan?" Rebecca asked. "Forgive me, that's a personal question. We were orphans, too, of sorts, but adopted. Even so, that doesn't excuse my rudeness."

Elena looked wistfully into the fire. "That's okay, I was...never wanted by anyone but the nuns, you see." She glanced at Madeleine. "I was crippled from birth, but with surgery two years ago—and God's grace—I'm fine."

Madeleine put her arm around Elena. "May, 1997. A time to remember! And you could say the convent has been your family. Not to mention Michelangelo, your beautiful golden retriever."

Elena grinned. "They are my family and the Seymours and many others have been like family too. I have been blessed."

Rebecca lifted the cat off her lap and onto the rug. She stood, smiling. "Family can be found in surprising places. But please, will you excuse me? I must say good night. I need to prepare lunch for tomorrow's workers."

"Of course," Madeleine said as Jack reached to pet the cat.

"Pierre will show you your rooms. I wish you *une bonne nuit*." Rebecca disappeared into the kitchen.

"*Bonne nuit*, and thank you," Madeleine and Elena echoed.

Madeleine snuggled close to Jack in the narrow, soft bed. "It was nice of the Morins to let us stay. Now we'll head for Paris and find this doctor." She pulled up the comforter.

"That Pierre is a bright young man," Jack said.

She snuggled closer. "He was interested in Elena."

"I noticed. She's a beautiful girl, so that's no surprise. He was also interested in my career. He appreciates hard work and success." He coughed in sporadic jagged gasps, and his chest convulsed.

"It's worse, isn't it?"

"I'll manage. Let's get some sleep...." His words trailed, drugged with exhaustion.

Dear God, Madeleine prayed into the dark, *help us find this doctor soon, for my heart is in knots. Our Father, who art in heaven....* Her prayers tumbled, one after another, ritual phrases holding her love, giving form to her feelings, carrying her to God. But what did God want of her? Simply trust? Simply obedience? Was there more?

Unable to sleep, she rose and tiptoed to the bath. There, in the half-light, she turned on her laptop and worked on her manuscript, searching for words to express the inexpressible. Provence was Mary Magdalene country; she would focus on that chapter. She loved the story of Mary Magdalene finding the empty tomb on Easter Day: how she spoke to the gardener, who, she soon discovered, was Jesus himself. Madeleine thought of Mary Magdalene as a sister, a spiritual sister from another time.

Holy Manifestations: Mary Magdalene
There is much we do not know about Mary Magdalene, in spite of continued research and speculation on the part of New Testament scholars. She is considered to be the woman from Magdala, possessed by demons, whom Christ healed. She is thought to be the Mary Magdalene present at Christ's crucifixion and resurrection. Until 1969, she was identified with other women in the Gospels as well—the woman who washed Christ's feet, the woman nearly stoned for adultery, and Mary of Bethany (the sister of Martha and Lazarus). But today the Church claims there is no direct evidence to support these latter identities. It is presumed she became a disciple and was among the women who followed Jesus through Galilee and Judea.

Madeleine hoped Mary Magdalene *was* the one who washed Christ's feet and the woman nearly stoned. That woman had nothing and gave all. Like the widow who gave her last "mite" in the temple offering.

While she may not have been the fallen woman of the Bible, she was, like each of us, a fallen human being. She stands in contrast to the Virgin Mary, who, according to the doctrine of the Immaculate Conception and numerous Marian visions of the nineteenth century, was conceived without sin. It is no wonder "the Magdalene" is the endeared patron saint of Provence. She is one of us; she was close to Christ, and we can be too.

Legend claims that around 44 A.D. Mary Magdalene arrived on the shores of Les Saintes-Maries-de-la-Mer, the Roman fort, the

Oppidium Ra, west of Marseilles. Fleeing persecution by Herod Agrippa, she traveled with Martha, Lazarus, Maximinus, Mary Jacobé (mother of James the less), Mary Salomé (mother of James and John), Sedonius (the man born blind), Sarah (Mary Salomé's servant), Joseph of Arimathea, Zaccheus, and Veronica.[11] Over the next thirty years, Mary Magdalene preached in Provence, finally retiring to a cave in the Sainte-Baume Massif, east of Marseilles.

Maximinus built a sanctuary in the valley near Sainte-Baume,[12] gave Mary last rites, and buried her. He was buried some years later, and the shrine over their tombs survived until threats of Saracen invasions forced the relics to be hidden by the monks. Some bones were taken north to Vézeley. Some were buried deeper under the church, to be discovered by Charles of Anjou in 1279. Today the head of Mary Magdalene is venerated in the crypt of the Basilica of Saint-Maximin.

Twenty minutes south of Saint-Maximin, a wide path climbs through a protected forest to Mary Magdalene's cave and farther up to Mount Pilon, where legend says angels carried her to hear them sing. Dominicans look after the shrine from their monastery in the valley. Set in a cliff face above the broad massif, the grotto-chapel reserves the Blessed Sacrament on a humble altar in the dark, lit by vigilant flames. Dripping walls hold thanksgiving plaques. Behind the altar is the massive rock where Mary slept and prayed. Against the back wall of the cave, votives flicker at the foot of her marble image.

Madeleine sensed she was in a cave too, longing for the light, for the fluttering of angel wings, the sound of their song. How could she be like this Mary, how could she draw closer to Christ, to know his demands? The Virgin Mary obeyed. Bernadette trusted. Mary Magdalene gave herself.

Madeleine thought she was close, so very close to understanding what she was called to give. How could she be obedient when she didn't know what the demand was?

She closed her screen and turned to her prayer book to read the evening Psalms, always a soothing ritual. At this point she would settle for Bernadette's trust and belief. When the time was right she would know how she must obey.

She slipped into bed and fell into a deep sleep. As she slept, she dreamt of a damp cave and whirling, fluttering lights that pulled her out of the dark—high, high, higher, to the mountaintop, where music filled her, music like she had never known, a sweet, yearning joy, full of longing. If she could only hold on to that moment, that song, that fluttering light....

The morning was chilly, the air moist from earlier rains. Madeleine gazed up to the blue sky, then down to the geraniums spilling over the Morins' stoop. Jack was loading the car trunk with the luggage, carefully laying the garment bags flat. She handed him a bottle of water from her canvas tote and a tiny pink pill.

Elena took her seat behind the wheel.

Pierre, in khakis and a white shirt, descended the stairs two by two and approached Jack. "Perhaps, Monsieur Seymour, you like to see our local abbey, the Abbey of Mary Magdalene in Barroux, before you leave for Paris? My mother says to ask. They sing the ten o'clock mass in one hour." His eyes shifted to Elena.

Jack gazed fondly at the boy. "We might as well. I'm sure Madeleine would like that."

"Mary Magdalene? An abbey mass?" Madeleine tried to summon the images of the night from her memory. "I dreamt about Mary Magdalene." It would be good to go, and she sensed she was returning to a beloved place. "How about you, Elena?"

"*Mais oui.*" Elena inserted the key in the ignition.

Jack opened the car door for Madeleine, then took the front passenger seat. "We'll follow you, Pierre?"

"*D'accord.*" Pierre jumped into a small Renault parked up the street and led them down the hill.

As they followed Pierre's car, regret stabbed Madeleine. "We should go directly to Paris."

Jack cleared his throat. "It will only take another hour to go to the abbey. We have to stop near Lyons tonight, anyway. I don't want to drive to Paris from here in one day."

"Did you make a reservation," Madeleine asked, "for Chateau Bagnols?"

"Pierre made it."

"Bagnols?" asked Elena.

"Bagnols is a castle near Lyons in Beaujolais country," Madeleine said. "We stayed there once on a wine buying trip. But I thought we would have found the doctor by now. I'd rather go straight to Paris— that's where she went."

"I always wanted to see Lyons," Elena said, her eyes on the Renault as they maneuvered the narrow country road. "Sister Agnes often spoke of the martyrs of Lyons."

"We may not have time to go into town," Madeleine said.

Elena glanced back at Madeleine. "Maybe you're right. Let's go straight to Paris, Mr. Seymour."

Jack coughed again, this time a thick and congested cough. "Madeleine," he said hoarsely, "there's no reason we can't take a day or two off and see Lyons, enjoy Bagnols. It's a great place."

Madeleine's chest tightened and she breathed deeply, hoping to ease it. "Sure, why not?" The hours weighed heavily, yet were teasingly, flippantly light, like feathers blowing away. She wanted to grab the days and hold them tightly, stop them from passing, control her world. She wanted to crawl from beneath the huge boulder pinning her to earth, inhale fresh air, once again see light. The two opposites—the weight and the weightlessness—collided, numbing her, paralyzing her. *Six months. Only six months. And it was soon to be five.*

Chapter Thirteen
Abbaye Sainte-Madeleine, Barroux

*We cannot help conforming ourselves
to what we love.*
Francois de Sales

They drove through tiny Modene, past Caromb's imposing basilica, then up through foothills, vineyards, and stands of pine and alder. They passed a large sign with the letters *BARROUX*, standing at the foot of a towering fortress. Continuing for several miles, they followed signs to the monastery. Finally, Pierre led them up a newly paved lane bordered with thyme and rosemary.

Pierre jumped out of his car, and they walked down a path lined with cypresses, through beds of browning lavender. At the end of the path stood a Romanesque abbey, its ocher stone supporting a graceful dome. In the abbey's porch, a wooden plaque announced *Le Monastère de Sainte-Madeleine*, listing the hours of the sung offices and masses. A sculpture of Mary Magdalene, her face thoughtful, her robes colorful, occupied a corner of the portico.

They paused in the portico and Pierre pulled out a paper. "My mother gave me this news article. It tells about the abbey. But it is *en Français*. Perhaps Mademoiselle Coronati will translate." He handed it to her.

"*Bien sûr.*" Elena blushed as she studied the newssheet:

In 1970 on the slopes of Mount Ventoux, a few monks gathered in the Chapel of Mary Magdalene in the village of Bedoin. Following the rule of Saint Benedict, they prayed the daily offices and worked the land. Soon others joined them. They built a new monastery with their own hands in neighboring Le Barroux. By June 1989 fifty monks and fifteen novices offered their ora and labora to God.

"Their *ora* and *labora*?" Jack asked.

"Latin for prayer and work," Madeleine said, "the rule of Saint Benedict. Go on, Elena." She was fascinated that the community was doing so well in a time when religious orders were declining.

Elena continued:

> They celebrate daily mass and sing the prayer offices of Matins, Lauds, Prime, Terce, Sext, None, Vespers, and Compline, beginning their day in the dark of the night. They grow lavender, harvest honey, and press olives for their aromatic oil. They teach, toil, and pray beneath the windy mountain. Nearby a group of nuns does the same, in the Convent of Notre-Dame de L'Annonciation.

Jack rubbed his chest and looked over the grounds. "Maybe we can visit the gift shop later and sample their olive oil or lavender honey."

Madeleine checked her watch and moved toward the open doors. "Maybe so."

They entered the north aisle and blinked in the abbey's dim light. A short nave led to a long wooden choir. Columns of cream and brown stone under vaulted arches lined the side aisles, and a high ceiling ran from the western loft to the eastern apse. A Madonna stood on a pedestal to the left of the altar, holding the Christ Child on her hip in the country manner, a figure of greens and golds. The sculpted image reminded Madeleine of the Madonna in Saint Thomas' back home, but the lofty symmetry of the sanctuary echoed Saint Antimo's in Tuscany. All was balance and harmony, calling the soul to peace.

They squeezed into the second pew. Jack knelt, mumbled a few words, then sat back. Madeleine knelt and prayed her thanksgivings for the clergy, the people, and the freedom to worship, an opening prayer she learned in her Confirmation class many years ago. Elena knelt next to her, and Pierre sat next to Elena.

As her eyes adjusted to the low light, Madeleine focused on a lone monk, hooded and robed in black, kneeling in the dark choir. He rose, switched on the lights, and joined another monk. They took positions at each end of the altar, reached for thick ropes hanging from the bell tower above, and pulled. At first there was no sound, and Madeleine watched the black figures pulling down and letting go, pulling down and letting go, pulling God through the heavens down to the earth in a tranquil arc, a dance of silent preparation.

On the third pull the bell rang, releasing its mellow tones through the countryside. *Come to mass....* The monks pulled and let go, pulled and let go, calling God down and sending their prayers up.

A wooden crucifix hung suspended over the altar. The figure of Christ the King was draped in blue-and-red robes and wore a golden crown. Here, the humble carpenter became a royal and omnipotent sacrifice. In the dim light, the swinging ropes threw shadows on the crucifix, at once scourging and celebrating, and Madeleine knew that soon the eternal would sanctify the bread and the wine, the real Christ appearing under the carved one. The red sanctuary lamp hung to the side and six thick candles flamed upon the altar. In the apse, stained glass windows glimmered with ruby and sapphire.

The apsidal vault was frescoed in pastel images, nearly translucent in the shimmering light: the twelve apostles formed a half circle under Andre Rublev's *Trinity*. The beloved and profound Russian icon, here frescoed in pastels, depicted three angels gazing upon a tiny lamb in a chalice, the cup of sacrifice, of offering. Madeleine recalled the icon's significance. The Old Testament angels were the three persons of the Trinity: the Father, the Son, and the Holy Spirit. They were the Angels of the Lord who visited Abraham, foretelling the birth of Isaac and promising the numerous descendants that would become the People of Israel. The three angels, the three persons of God, gazed upon the lamb in the chalice on Abraham's table. Who would be the sacrificial offering, the Lamb of God, slain for the People of Israel and for all mankind, the price of man's eternal life? The middle angel, God the Son, points to the lamb.

Madeleine smiled as she watched the dance of the bells beneath the shimmering vault. She knew the price had been paid for her too, that God would accept the pulling-call, that once again the Lamb would be offered in this liturgy of sacrifice. She knew he would transform them all, and that they, as new creatures, would fly like those notes released in the tower, like doves let loose from a cage of self and winging for heaven. Yes, the monks let loose the ropes just so, just like that.

Madeleine nudged Elena and pointed to a door opening off the south aisle.

Silently, fifty-four brothers processed into the long wooden choir, their black robes dusting the stone floor. Their hoods were raised, signaling prayer, and their hands were hidden, clasped in their wide sleeves. A few were observers or novitiates, for their street clothes could be seen under simple capes.

The brothers sang *a cappella*, and the Psalms soared through the

102

vaults, a tenor journey into prayer, into the soul, and into God. The Latin chants framed a French gospel and sermon preached enthusiastically from the chancel steps.

Madeleine studied the faces of the young men. They led a stern life, rising at 3:15 a.m. for the night office. In the hours between services, they tended lavender beds and olive orchards, carved crosses and painted pots, baked bread and harvested honey. Their gaunt, strong faces were chiseled with work and discipline, yet softened with an amused and serious serenity. They had found something they had searched for. They had been fulfilled.

As always, Madeleine traveled into the mass like a northerner visiting the tropics. Here, Christ filled her; here, the Creator gave himself to his creation, and his creatures offered themselves to him. In these mysterious moments, Christ the groom united with his bride the Church in an earthly feast, a foreshadowing of the banquet in heaven. Madeleine prayed her thanksgivings and again asked that she might ease Jack's pain, that he might experience that banquet on earth. She had glimpsed heaven through windows opening slowly in her soul; she had dined with the saints through the mass.

As the last prayer songs soared through the abbey, Madeleine reached for Jack's hand. She had learned, through the years of their marriage, that somehow their union involved one another's salvation. They were mystically entwined by love, the love of God weaving through his people. Prayer, sacrifice, and not least, suffering, forged these links stronger than steel. Like the warm pulse of Jack's fingers, God's love beat within them, uniting husband and wife in joy and suffering, in spirit and flesh. Christ was indeed a third person in every sacramental marriage, a divine strength, a holy bonding.

Lord, receive my offering for Jack. Penetrate his soul with mine, that he may know my joy, your joy, that he may offer his pain back to you.

They walked to the cars, following the gravel path through the brown lavender.

Elena glanced at Madeleine. "It was beautiful."

"It was." Madeleine's words, silenced by the holy, felt their way to the surface.

"Our church in Rome is so different—mostly baroque, with paintings and statues and layers of history, probably an artist's nightmare. But it is loved."

"And colored by centuries of sacrifice. I envied you today, Elena."

"Why is that?"

"You received the Eucharist. Sometimes I wish I was Roman Catholic, just so that I might receive in all these churches."

Elena grew thoughtful. "The Eucharist...makes me happy."

Madeleine smiled. "Me too."

"Being present is good as well." Elena's eyes were large with sympathy.

"It is. Somehow I know I'm part of the Eucharistic sacrifice."

"Sister Agnes said we are members of the communion of saints."

"One body, the Body of Christ." As they approached the cars, Madeleine put her arm around Elena. "You understand, little one." With a twinge, she thought of Mollie, and as often happened with these surging reminders, the drowning of so long ago swept through her with incredible force. But now she gazed at Elena thankfully. Indeed, God took our crooked lines and straightened them. He redeemed yesterday's sorrows with today's grace.

Jack opened Madeleine's door. "Pierre invited us to lunch in Modene—a good truffle place, he said. You remember truffles—those black mushrooms? They're very rare. Shall we go?"

"What do you say, Elena?" Madeleine glanced at Pierre, waiting by his car.

"I don't know," Elena said, following her gaze. "Perhaps we had better move on to Bagnols."

Jack frowned. "We have time for lunch. Let's enjoy the day a bit. After all, we went to church, and now we can go to lunch."

But Madeleine heard Elena's hesitancy. "We do need lunch, Elena, and we might learn more about the doctor's whereabouts. Pierre may have a secret treasure of a restaurant too, which would make Jack especially happy."

Elena smiled. "*D'accord.* I *am* hungry."

Jack insisted on driving the short distance. "Don't treat me like a child, Madeleine. It's okay. I'm giving up *some* control, like Conrad said. I let

Pierre choose the place, right?"

Madeleine looked at his flushed face and noticed the bottle of antacids protruding from under the passenger seat. They pulled up to a small café where a red sign over the door announced *La Maison de la Truffe*. Pierre led them to one of six tables in the front room.

"I know the chef." Pierre headed to the kitchen and soon returned, announcing with a grin, his eye on Elena, *"Mes amis, un festin, simple mais grande!"*

Madeleine noticed the color rising in Elena's cheeks. Was she embarrassed by the young man's attention? She couldn't have had many boyfriends, Madeleine thought, being crippled most of her life, and living in a convent. She seemed nervous.

Pierre took a seat. "The chef is owner too. He is waiter too. He is clean-up too. This happens often here, *en Provence*."

"Like Italy," added Elena.

Pierre opened his napkin. "We were in school together. He liked cooking even then."

"Cooking is honored in France," Madeleine said. "I like that."

"What do you mean, *honored*?"

"Respected, looked up to," said Jack.

"Oui. Cooking is honored. Chefs, they are like movie stars."

An apple walnut salad was followed by *les omelettes*, fluffy eggs laced with truffles. The sweetly rich aroma of the mushrooms filled their senses, and Madeleine thought of moist forest beds gently touched by the sun. They sipped a house wine, a fruity red, poured from a carafe into balloon glasses.

The chef paused at their table as he stacked the dishes. "Good, no?" he asked. He wiped thick fingers happily on his smudged apron, then smoothed his black mustache. He poured Jack more wine.

"Jack...," Madeleine protested, as a dull ache formed behind her eyes.

"Just a taste, Maddie. This is special—special place, special people." He raised his glass to the chef. "You, Monsieur Chef, are an angel of the kitchen."

"Un ange de la cuisine," Pierre translated.

Jack twirled the goblet, inhaled the bouquet, and sipped slowly. The chef nodded, satisfied.

"Monsieur Seymour," Pierre said, "how do you learn about wine? In school?"

Jack smiled and leaned back in his chair. "Not at all, my son, not at all. I worked my way through school and learned about wine on the side. Why I remember packing fruit in Colfax—that's a small factory town in California."

"Packing fruit?" Pierre's face held amazement tinged with satisfaction.

"Indeed...bought my first car at seventeen. And what a car." Jack examined the rosy depths of his glass, then eyed Pierre meaningfully. "Dark blue '39 Chevy!"

Pierre nodded, and Madeleine wondered if the young man knew the model—he was far too young and Chevrolets were rare in Europe even today.

"And," Jack continued, "I bought my family—my sister and mother—our first TV."

Madeleine's gaze returned to Jack. Her own dull ache had moved deeper, the familiar pressure pushing against her forehead. She rubbed her right temple with her index finger.

Jack closed his eyes, smiling with delight. He raised his glass to Pierre. "Thank you, Pierre, for your interest in the life of this old man. And for the abbey. It was wonderful. I feel renewed."

"*Je vous en prie,* Monsieur." Pierre glanced at Elena, as the chef arrived with steaming platters. "You are welcome."

The linguini was dressed with butter and truffle shavings, and as Madeleine twisted three strands with her fork, she observed Jack. As his pain receded, hers seemed to increase. Maybe it was the wine.

"Not to worry, *ma chèrie.*" Jack sipped a bit more, then a bit more.

There were no truffles in the next course. A tangy *chèvre,* the local goat cheese, was arranged on a cutting board, alongside thinly sliced nut bread and bunches of red grapes.

They spoke slowly so that Pierre could follow the conversation. Jack smiled as he sipped, reassuring them with his good humor and insisting he was much better. He branched often into stories of his threadbare days, war rations and blackouts. Madeleine's throbbing head swirled around Jack's happiness and she was strangely at peace.

Pastries filled with lemon puree arrived with a large pitcher of vanilla sauce.

"Bagnols," Jack said to Elena, "is close to Lyons. You mentioned you were interested in the Lyons martyrs?"

"They were terribly persecuted, weren't they? I believe Lyons was part of the Roman Empire then."

Jack looked at Madeleine. "Ask our historian."

Madeleine recalled the tragedy; the martyrs stood before her like a Greek chorus, demanding witness. "Forty-eight Christians were tortured, burned at the stake, and fed to the beasts under Marcus Aurelius. Twenty years later, eighteen thousand were massacred."

"Eighteen thousand—why so many?" Pierre asked.

"Envy, really. The Christians in Lyons were prosperous merchants from Asia Minor, and the locals were jealous. Christianity had been illegal since Nero in the first century, but the edict was not usually enforced unless pressured by the community. It was the classic scapegoat scenario. Every culture finds one." She had not touched her dessert, lost as she was in the scene.

Jack mopped a bite of pastry in the sauce pooling on his plate. "So the law was a political tool—a tool of jealousy, greed, racial hatred."

"Exactly," Madeleine said, grateful to be pulled into the present. She tasted the lemon tart. Light and fresh. The flaky pastry floated on her tongue.

"I want to pray over their graves," Elena said, "for Sister Agnes. She wanted to make a pilgrimage to Lyons, but never did. I'll make it for her."

Jack turned to Pierre. "Son, let's keep in touch. Maybe I could help you with your career choices. There are many opportunities in business, with room to advance. It's important to realize your full potential, to get the most out of life. I didn't have two pennies to rub together when I started out, believe you me."

"Do you have e-mail," Madeleine said, "or a phone number?" As she rummaged in her bag for a pen and paper, she found some aspirin. She needed to calm this surge before it became a full-blown migraine.

They exchanged addresses and numbers.

Madeleine washed the aspirin down with her water. "Let us know when you hear from your aunt. We'll be at Chateau Bagnols near Lyons tonight, and the Paris Ritz in a few days. Could you ask her to call us?"

"The Ritz?" Pierre asked, his eyes large. "You stay at the Ritz? It is very grand!"

Jack smiled with pride. "A friend from home is putting us up. A special treat."

"You will call, Pierre?" Madeleine hoped her tone wasn't too demanding. It sounded like someone else speaking, far away, beyond the throbbing.

Pierre paused. "*Oui, Madame, avèc plaisir.*"

Madeleine reached for her bag. "We'd better go—it's nearly two.

Elena, could you drive, please?" Perhaps she could close her eyes, lean against her sweater bunched in the window corner, rest a bit before the nausea hit.

The chef set the check on the table, and Jack picked it up. "Please, Pierre, let me get this. It would make me happy."

"Merci, Monsieur." He turned to Elena, taking her hand and brushing it lightly with his lips. "It was a pleasure to meet you, Mademoiselle Coronati. I wish you a safe journey to Lyons."

Elena blushed and withdrew her hand. "Merci, Monsieur, *et au revoir.*"

Would they ever find their way to Paris and the elusive doctor? Madeleine asked herself. How many other diversions would there be, both sacred and profane, not the least of them being Lyons, a site of suffering and sacrifice? Was God truly directing her path? Was she listening to him? How could she know? From far away, a little voice sang, *Trust and obey, for there's no other way...* Then she saw in her mind the Rublev *Trinity*, the great sacrifice, the *Agneus Dei*. Was her headache something she could give to God, a kind of suffering sacrifice?

"Are you okay, Maddie?" Jack said, as he opened her car door. "You look pale."

"Just a little headache, honey."

Madeleine navigated from the front passenger seat while Jack napped in the back. Elena drove north on the A7, exited at Villefranche-sur-Saone, and wound through vineyards to the farming village of Bagnols about thirty minutes west of Lyons. They passed houses of golden stone, *pierres dorées,* built to reflect the harsh sun and blunt the icy mistrals from the Alps. Soon, climbing a gentle hillside striped with vines, they came to a medieval castle, complete with a deep grassed-in moat and four crenellated towers. They drove through iron gates and parked in a gravel yard.

Madeleine recalled that a Lyons merchant restored the castle in the sixteenth century, adding formal Renaissance gardens and decorating the grand salons to receive silk dealers and royal guests. But it still looked like a medieval castle to her, something from the fairy tales of her childhood, maybe Perrault's *Sleeping Beauty.*

108

Two porters opened the car doors and unloaded their luggage from the trunk. Madeleine followed Elena and Jack across a drawbridge, through heavy iron-studded portals, and into a cobbled courtyard. Jack left for *Réception* and the ladies waited in the court, looking up at the massive walls anchored by the four towers.

"This reminds me a bit of Quattro Coronati," Elena said.

"Your convent in Rome? How so?" Madeleine recalled the medieval church, rather odd shaped, sitting on the bluff looking over Rome, and the convent-turned-clinic and orphanage attached.

"Remember the courtyard as you walk in?"

Madeleine smiled. "Of course—it too was a fortress at one point, with the outer court built for defense."

"I wonder if we ever had a moat and drawbridge—I don't think so."

A pretty brunette returned with Jack, her heels clicking on the stones. "We have nice rooms, Messieurs," she purred. Jangling two giant keys from red fingernails, she led them up steep uneven stairs, worn smooth, to the top floor. "You visit the chateau before?"

Jack rubbed his chest. "Once on business."

The clerk worked the key into the huge lock and pushed a thick wooden door. They entered Elena's room, a long, narrow space, the walls frescoed with crosses and lilies. The bed lay in a vaulted alcove.

Madeleine recalled the room. "I believe this was the chapel. This rounded end was the apse and chancel."

Elena walked to the bed and stared at the alcove. "Really? A chapel on the roof?"

"My theory is that the Catholic Lyonnaise worshiped here secretly."

"Why secretly?" Elena asked.

Madeleine glanced at Jack chatting with the clerk. "This was Protestant territory."

"So Lyons was Protestant?"

"It was, being so close to Geneva." Madeleine looked about the former chapel. "Plus the trade guilds were strong here, and Protestantism was favored by the emerging middle class. Catholics were drowned in the freezing Rhone. Of course, other French towns saw the reverse, Catholics drowning Protestants. The Reformation and the Religious Wars were an ugly time in France."

Elena pointed to the long vertical windows. "These must have been for crossbows and this roof the parapet."

Jack was moving toward the door. "Let's check out the other room."

They entered a similarly shaped room in the corner of the castle, once an extension of Elena's former chapel. Elena ran her hands over the carved angel bedposts and examined an old sarcophagus-chest. She spoke quickly to the clerk in French and Madeleine caught a few words—Lyons, church, martyrs—but could not understand the rest.

Jack gazed through a window slit to the surrounding countryside and cleared his throat. He rubbed his forehead and pulled out his wrist monitor. The sound of Velcro scraped the air and Madeleine moved to his side, watching him. The quiet whir of the tiny machine came to a stop and numbers appeared on its face. Jack nodded his approval.

Jack slipped his arm around Madeleine's waist. She breathed deeply as she recalled other trips, happier trips. Their worries had revolved around finding a reasonably priced Beaujolais or appropriate souvenirs for the grandchildren. How the passage of time could change one's life.

She gazed at the mist hovering over the rolling vineyards, refracting the sunlight, a halo crowning the valley. A walled village of amber houses clustered around a steeple. Beneath their window, in the pear garden, a fountain bubbled, and church bells chimed six from the valley below.

"How soothing beauty can be," Madeleine said.

"That's so true." Jack pointed to the village in the distance. "Isn't that the town of Bois d'Oingt?"

"I believe so. Remember the mass there?"

"You never forget a mass. But the village was nice, too. Quaint."

"The priest was short; his sermon was short. He spoke like a grandfather to his children—tired, but wise and revered. And the congregation was a real farming parish, with heavyset men, and women with babies on their laps. After the service, they poured through the doors four-abreast to the market square for their coffee hour. The *boulangerie* across the street did a booming business."

"I remember the bakery."

"Jack, let's have an early dinner."

"Sure."

"We need to head for Paris tomorrow."

"I promised Elena we'd go into Lyons, Maddie."

Elena joined them at the window, looking at Madeleine with hopeful eyes. "It's up to you."

Madeleine was torn. "We can decide in the morning when we see what the weather's like."

110

Chapter Fourteen
Chateau Saint-Martin, Vence

And his love is perfected in us...
1 John 4:12

It was nearly noon when Rachelle's taxi ascended the road from the sea into the Alpine foothills, the driver chatting in stilted English about the Knights Templar and the castle that would become the hotel-chateau. "Very old," he said as though he possessed great knowledge worthy of a great tip, "and very famous." He paused, tapping the steering wheel and glancing sideways. "You maybe need a guide? Saint-Paul de Vence very nice art village. Grasse is village with perfume factory. Very nice."

They wound past walled villages perched on hilltops and through more modern communities of white stucco and red tiles, French vacation rentals, Rachelle thought. So this was the Riviera, the Cote d'Azur, the sunny escape from the cold north to the warm south, the azure coast. The pace was faster than the agricultural basin surrounding Ventoux, the cars speeding and honking, rushing somewhere, everywhere.

The taxi maneuvered through a narrow gateway, passed crumbling ruins, and parked in a garden of overgrown lavender in front of a three-story manor house. Jasmine covered a stone wall on one side of the garden, and silver-tipped olive trees circled a spouting fountain.

The taxi sped away. All was quiet now, here in the front garden, as though the white stucco mansion built on the medieval ruins rose over the fray of the coastal towns, choosing to face heavenward. Rachelle carried her backpack, her duffel, and Rebecca's woven tote through the canopied entrance and set them before a deserted reception counter. Beyond the counter, in an adjoining salon, a sculpted soldier on his mount stood on a fireplace mantel, unsheathing his sword, ready to carve his cloak in two. Rachelle guessed he must be Saint Martin.

Through a distant archway, she glimpsed tables covered in coral linens, laid with silver and crystal. Beyond, a panoramic window beckoned. With her backpack over her shoulder, she walked through the elegant salon to the archway and passed through a paneled bar with giant tapestries set into the walls. Entering the empty dining room, she crossed over to the window.

Rachelle caught her breath. The sea spread far below, hugging the coast under a swirling mist. Up the canyon to her right loomed the Alpine foothills, rocky gorges tamed by cypresses, umbrella pines, olive trees, and terra cotta villas. Between the mountains and the sea, the hilltop villages commanded the valleys descending to the Côte d'Azur. Immediately below the chateau, the red roofs of the village of Vence surrounded a church steeple.

"Bonjour, Madame," a deep voice purred behind her. *"Comment desirez-vous?* We do not open for ten minutes more. Perhaps an aperitif in the bar?"

Startled, Rachelle looked up.

A tall man of significant presence, with rimless glasses increasing his stature, inclined his silver head toward her. He smoothed his neat mustache and touched his yellow tie. He waited with an air of authority softened by courtesy.

"Monsieur, I'm so sorry. I just wanted to...could you direct me to Madame Laurent? My sister phoned earlier, I believe?"

He grinned, his teeth white against his tan, and bowed gallantly from the waist. *"Vous êtes Madame DuPres. Mais oui.* She expects you. Allow me to introduce myself. I am the manager, Bertrand Olivier." He extended his hand. "Please, follow me."

Monsieur Olivier led Rachelle to the front salon. "I shall advise her at once. She will be here shortly. Please be comfortable." He bowed again and stepped away.

Rachelle retrieved the woven bag with the wine and cheese and waited in the salon with Saint Martin. She recalled the story Benedict had related once, about a Roman soldier who gave half his cloak to a naked beggar. At the time—she must have been a precocious ten-year-old—she had asked why Martin didn't give his entire cloak to the beggar. Benedict had laughed, his deep lovely laugh, and said something about God having more work for Martin, so Martin needed to care for himself as well.

Rachelle smiled with the memory, but the present moment with all of its strangeness commanded her attention, and she looked about the room nervously. She had entered a rich refined world of silk and antiques, unlike her simple condo at home, unlike the tract house in which she grew up. She picked at her hands, wondering why she had come. Rebecca. Rebecca had sent her here. She could say she had come because of Rebecca. She would give her aunt the woven bag.

Soon an old woman, leaning on a cane, emerged from a door in the wall. A few strands of white hair, thick and frizzy, had escaped her French braid, and a gray fringed shawl draped her gauzy black dress. The folds at the neck lay softly open to reveal a delicate crucifix on parchment skin. Clarice Laurent's eyes were full of longing as she smiled timidly and proffered a cool limp hand. She kissed her niece on the forehead, a light feathering touch, barely felt, and Rachelle caught a brief scent of rosewater mingled with cedar.

"*Bonjour,* my little one. You have come."

"*Bonjour,* Madame...or rather, Aunt?"

"I am pleased to be called Aunt. You are one of Leah's babies. Let me look at you. Come, we will sit. I have lived eighty-five years, and I cannot stand for long."

They sat on a delicate love seat, its legs curving into an Oriental rug. Rachelle stared at the fine-lined face turning toward her own, the brown eyes under folded lids, the pursed lips.

"You have come from America?" Aunt Clarice asked.

"Yes."

"For a holiday?"

"Sort of."

"You visit your sister, no?"

"Yes—Rebecca sends her regards. She wishes to come someday too...with the children."

"When she called...I was so happy. And here you are!"

Rachelle was unsure what to say. She reached for the woven sack. It reminded her of macramé from the sixties. "This is for you. From Rebecca...and me."

Clarice set the bag on her lap and looked inside. "Ah, wine...and cheese...thank you. Do they make the wine and the cheese? Your sister, my niece and her family?" Her eyes were wistful, as though she could bring back the lost years.

"The wine is theirs. Not the cheese."

"The wine?" She pulled out the bottle and held the label toward the light. "Crillon...it is the chateau!"

Rachelle watched her aunt's delicate skin flush deeply. Was she all right? Seeing a picture of her village must have startled her. Rachelle had not foreseen the perfectly natural reaction. She was definitely losing her doctor's touch.

Gently, Clarice set the bottle down, her eyes fixed on the etching. She raised a hand to her heart. "I am sorry, *ma chèrie*, but it is a good likeness. It has been many years since I have been back...and the mountain too..."

Rachelle repacked the bottle in the sack with the cheese. "Perhaps I should keep this? Do they bring bad memories?"

"No, it is good and I thank you. We shall share some tonight." She took Rachelle's hand. "My dear, it is very fine to see you. You look like your father, Alain."

"I supposed so, somehow." Rachelle was grateful for the insight. "I would like to know about them. What was...my mother...Leah...like?"

"Leah was dark," she said softly, as she slipped into the memory, "with thick curly hair we pulled up high on her head. Ah, we had such a time. I was four when she was born, and born with that head of hair. I was sent from the room, but I watched through a crack in the door. *Je pense*...seeing her come into the world...such a wonder. We loved our little Leah, but we spoiled her."

Clarice's eyes rested on the yellow roses on the low table before her, as though her thoughts tumbled through the petals, and she would follow soon to retrieve them.

"There was Samuel, the oldest. Then came Francine and Jean, then me, then your mother. I think she was, how do you say, not expected? We had a good family, a devout family with synagogue, Sabbath, prayers. But Leah fell in love with a Catholic boy—Alain." Clarice shook her head. "Papa did not understand and refused his blessing. It was a terrible thing, to refuse the blessing." She tapped one long finger on her knee. "They ran away to Paris, but returned to Crillon when Hitler invaded."

She sat back, relaxed her shoulders, and closed her eyes. Rachelle waited. A grandfather clock ticked, its pendulum swinging, its face showing the wrong time.

Monsieur Olivier appeared at the old woman's side. "Madame," he whispered, "perhaps I show Madame DuPres to her room?"

"Do not whisper, Monsieur," she said, squinting at him. "I am not sleeping. The wine and cheese, they are for dinner. My niece must be tired. And I will rest, too." She turned to Rachelle. "Please to dine at six? I eat light and early, at my age. *Á bientôt, ma chèrie. Merci* for coming...to see this old lady. *J'espère que je peut t'aider.* I hope I can help you." Her words crackled, and she coughed lightly as she shuffled through the low doorway.

Monsieur Olivier carried her bag, and Rachelle followed him up a winding staircase. They entered a spacious corner room with *Sans Souci* lettered on the door. She walked out to a small roof terrace. Leaning against the low stucco wall, she drank in the startling vista of land, sea, and sky. She inhaled deeply. "I feel like a bird in a tree."

"*Oui, Madame, un oiseau.* It is an aerie, or maybe a nest?" He smiled, and they returned to the room. "Do you require anything, Madame?"

"No, thank you, I'm fine. What does *Sans Souci* mean?"

"Without care, Madame. Please, call for anything. I wish you a most pleasant stay." He bowed and closed the door behind him.

Rachelle opened a leaflet on the desk describing the pool and gardens. Changing into her swimsuit, she slipped into a thick terry robe hanging from a hook in the bathroom and headed downstairs. She followed a gravel path through a garden of hibiscus, jasmine, and pines to an olive orchard where tables under white umbrellas tilted in the grass and jacketed waiters served lunch. Beyond the garden, she found the pool, a pane of water pouring over an infinity edge, seeming to disappear into the meadow beyond. How did they do that? A few guests sunbathed on striped lounge chairs.

Rachelle set her bag, robe, and slippers on a chair and crossed the warm flagstone. The sun beat hard, warming her skin, turning the meadow greener and the pool bluer. She dove in, slicing the glassy surface, and swam to the rim where the water poured into a long basin, the cascading torrent tumbling into the silence. At the far side of the meadow a row of cypresses intersected the sky. Who was she? She had no faith and no profession; she belonged to no one, to nothing. She was like those clouds over the mountain, cut off from the earth, wispy and vague, rootless. She had come here to find herself, but what—or where—was she? She floated, free from meaning or identity. Perhaps her soul would tumble out of control, like this water falling, with nothing to impede her descent, no hands to hold her, no one to rescue her. Would Alain and Leah watch, or help, or were they truly gone?

She pushed off from the wall of falling water and began a rhythmic crawl, her muscle memory taming her thoughts, the familiar movement massaging her body. *Exercise will cure you*, said a remote voice from a distant depth, as she exhaled into the water and lifted her face to inhale the sunlight.

They dined outside on the terrace as the sun dropped toward the western range and a smoky haze drifted through the air. Other guests sipped champagne, murmuring as though in church. A rooster crowed, and a scooter buzzed up the hill. Rachelle wore her black sheath and was grateful for the shawl her aunt loaned her, for the evening air was chilling.

A young man in a red jacket and bow tie appeared with the bottle of Chateau Crillon and poured two glasses.

"They burn the leaves from the garden," Clarice said. "What day is it? September is so hazy."

Rachelle tried to remember. "It's the twenty-second, I believe. September 22." *1999,* she added to herself. So close to the Millennium. Would the world end as some said? She thought not. Still, it was both an end and a beginning, of something, she supposed.

"A burn day." Clarice turned to her glass and sipped the wine. "A good wine. Fruity. Light. I enjoy country wines such as these. And made by one of my Leah-babies."

Rachelle held the glass to her nose: flower petals drenched with rain. She sipped and let the wine linger in her mouth. It tasted of cherries and oak and a hint of some spice she couldn't name. Conrad would know—he had tried to educate her. What were the words he had used time and again? Promise? Full bodied? Something about legs. Rather sexist language, she thought. This one wasn't full bodied—there was an ethereal thinness to it, a trace of strawberries. Nutmeg? She stared into the rosy liquid glimmering in the round glass, then turned to her aunt. "Aunt Clarice..."

"*Je pense.* You want to know about your mother."

Their plates were placed before them—lamb loins bathed in blackberry puree. Fennel stalks and baby potatoes clustered to the side.

"Aunt Clarice..."

"Perhaps there are some things you do not want to know."

"I *do* want to know, if you don't mind speaking of them. I want to know everything about them, please—my father too, and my uncles. They fought near here?"

Clarice's eyes darted about the terrace. "The hotel is full, I believe. Many tables are taken, and it is so early..."

"We should speak of something else. I'm sorry."

Clarice settled her gaze on Rachelle. "No, you are right. I should tell you. It is time."

Was she pushing too hard? Rachelle asked herself. Her aunt was old and frail, and these were not pleasant things for her. "Please, only when you're ready."

Clarice pulled herself up, straightening her spine. She studied her niece. "We are the last, and you must tell the story, you must carry us forward so no one forgets." She paused. "I was in Switzerland—Basel—it was a great center for my studies, psychiatry, when they came, those barbarians. They even took Crillon-le-Brave. Our little village. It was 1942."

She gripped her glass and stared into its rosy depths. Rachelle, poised on the edge of her seat, waited for each word.

"Leah and Alain had joined the Resistance. They sent you and your sister away. They sheltered many others. Then they were shot in the winter of 1943."

Rachelle waited, her throat tight.

"Why wasn't I with them?" Madame Laurent wailed. Other diners turned to stare as her high whine pierced the tranquil air. She leaned forward and grabbed Rachelle's shoulder with bony fingers, her voice rising. "To this day I do not understand. How could they disappear so suddenly? Papa wrote to me, telling me to stay in Basel. He asked me to send money. Why did I listen to Papa? I left school. I worked in a clinic. I sent home what I could—but the letters stopped. In 1944 the Allies freed our villages. They came up from the coast in August. But they were too late."

"Too late?"

"I returned to Crillon. My family was gone. The village looked the same. It wasn't the same. Many were missing. Those who remained were full of shame. They told terrible stories, the same story—the fear, the hiding, the grief. The Nazis shot Monsieur Pinot, the old blacksmith. They shot his grandson too. A little boy. In the village square. For no reason but to show their power."

Clarice's eyes brimmed. She shook her head, and two trickles found a path along her wrinkled skin, moving slowly, unhurried. She seemed unaware and sipped her wine, leaving her food untouched. Rachelle waited, suddenly shivering.

"I searched for my family, not believing they were gone, sure I would find someone. Mama, Papa, my brothers, my sisters, and Jacob, the boy I thought I would marry. How I loved *ma petite* Leah, my dear baby sister. She wanted the life of the home, she cooked, she sewed. She wanted Alain and she wanted children. But I never saw her babies, until now."

Clarice covered the back of Rachelle's hand with her own, so cool and frail. Rachelle turned her own hand over and tenderly held her aunt's in her rough palm.

Rebecca was like Leah. Home and family. Children. Rachelle swallowed hard. She was glad she had come, if only to give her aunt, and herself, this moment.

"I learned later of Alain's brothers. They died here, fighting up the canyon, just before the Allies arrived. Their names are listed on a plaque up the road." Clarice pulled her hand away and pointed toward the mountains.

"I'll look for it. Aunt Clarice, what of Alain's twin?"

"His twin?" She shook her head and stared out to the foggy valley. "His twin died too, in a way."

"How?"

"I cannot say." She coughed, shaking her head. Her face grew red and puffy.

Rachelle feared she was choking. "Are you all right?"

"A bit of bread caught in my throat. I must take care to eat slowly. The doctor says to chew each bite twenty times. I don't always do that."

"Aunt, how did you find out about us? About Rebecca and me?"

Clarice sipped her water, then her wine. "I tried to find you many times, but the records were sealed or...destroyed. Sometimes this was done for safety. The day I left Crillon-le-Brave, our town of death, I received a letter. I do not know who wrote it. But it told of you and your sister and your escape."

The old lady reached for a paper in her pocket and unfolded it. "Do you read French?" At the shake of Rachelle's head, Clarice said, "No? I translate." She recited the words, etched in her mind, as she gazed out to the darkening sky.

Madame,

I am too ashamed to tell you who I am for I did nothing to stop it.

But you should know of Leah's babies. They were sent through Lourdes. Probably America.

I am old and it does not matter now—pray for me, Madame, for I have much to repent of.

A friend.

Carefully, she folded the yellowed paper and handed it to her niece. "You keep this and you do not forget."

Chapter Fifteen
Le Col de Vence

Many want me to tell them
of secret ways of becoming perfect...
the secret is a hearty love of God,
and the only way of attaining that love is by loving.
Francois de Sales

The following morning, Rachelle walked through the front garden, around the gate, and turned left on the road that wound under the Col de Vence, the mountain rising above the chateau. Stepping slowly, she searched along a dry-stone wall that bordered the property. Soon she found it—a plaque embedded in the stones, listing the names of the fifteen boys who died *Pour La France* in 1944. Here were the brothers, François and Antoine. She calculated they were twenty-three and twenty-two when they were shot.

Rachelle stood with her hands on her hips and leaned toward the stone memorial. She stared at the names, absorbing their lives and deaths like bitter medicine, penicillin that would heal her soul, destroy the bacteria attacking her. These were her uncles, Catholics fighting for their country, for their freedom, and for their Jewish brothers and sisters. Shaking her head in puzzled sorrow, she shifted her pack and continued uphill, her stride determined.

Rachelle didn't know how long or how far she walked. The brisk mountain air slapped her cheeks and the deserted road wound higher and higher above the tree line. The wind surged and she welcomed it, the colder the better. She broke a sweat, and finally, reaching a plateau where the road branched, she stopped, wiped her brow, and turned toward the valley.

It wasn't your fault, Connie had said. Then Mrs. Steinhoff, her eyes red and steely, appeared in her mind. The stricken woman refused any apology and walked silently away.

Suddenly, there was Father Benedict, the bushy-haired, ruddy-faced priest fondly shaking his head. *To love is to suffer*, he said. More of his Catholic mumbo-jumbo. Love should redeem suffering, not cause it. Why do people want to fall in love, to be loved, if it means suffering? Rachelle recalled her disappointment when Benedict had only given her sympathy and sayings. How embarrassed she was that she sought him out at all—so different from the teacher she remembered from her childhood, much shorter and much less impressive. *To love is to suffer—* whatever had he meant by *that*?

And there was that other platitude he repeated: *God writes straight with crooked lines*. Why couldn't God write straight with straight lines? It looked to Rachelle as if God mostly wrote crooked with crooked lines.

She sat on a rock and drank deeply from her water bottle. Then she opened the bag lunch Monsieur Olivier had prepared. She unwrapped the goat cheese and pulled out a slice of bread and a bunch of purple grapes. She ate quickly, slipped on the pack, and headed down the hill.

As the bells in the village rang four, Rachelle recalled she would dine again with her aunt at six. But she would go for a swim first. She would face one day at a time. At least that advice made sense, advice she regularly prescribed in her other life as a doctor. Perhaps time would heal her, time and, of course, exercise.

That evening they dined inside, for the air had grown too chilly for Rachelle's elderly aunt. The wind had cleared the smoky haze, and again Rachelle could see through the window, down to the village and beyond to the pale blue Mediterranean. The evening light had lessened, muting the landscape's colors, and the rolling hills darkened before her, falling into shadow now, but the coast was still bathed in the last of the sun dropping in the western sky. Was that Antibes, the old Roman port, far to the right? She could see high-rises along the waterfront.

Rachelle's muscles felt looser with the hike and the swim; some tension had been released. The Alpine breezes had been a healing tonic, swirling with the salty air from the sea. But her mind was not soothed, holding fast to the burden of memory; her exercise prescription was not as simple as it promised to be.

She looked about the nearly empty dining room as her aunt spoke in French to Monsieur Olivier, her frail hands flying through the air like sparrows, her voice husky. Peach damask panels, tied back with braided tassels of green and blue, draped the windows. A coat of arms hung over a fireplace between heavy wall sconces. Other tables—around twenty she thought—would soon be occupied.

She tried her white burgundy, tasting the cold crisp fruit, and waited for her aunt to begin. She didn't want to miss a single, raspy syllable.

"You will like the sea bass, my dear. Our local style." Clarice sipped her wine and smiled, her thin lips purposeful.

"I love fish." Rachelle returned her gaze to the view. "This is so beautiful, Aunt Clarice."

"They are good to let me stay here."

"They—you mean the owners?"

"I gave them many years of my life. I brought in good customers. They are grateful."

The sea bass arrived, swimming in olives and capers and chopped tomatoes. Rachelle breathed in the pungent aroma of lemon and, perhaps, the bittersweet of fennel.

With her knife, Clarice moved a miniscule bite onto her fork. "I will tell you of the other one now, *ma chèrie*."

"The other one?"

"He is at the abbey."

"The abbey? Who is at the abbey?"

"Gilbert, Alain's twin."

"But...you said he died."

"He died to me, and, as they say, he died to the world. He became a monk. He survived the war and joined the Cistercians. Now he is Abbot of Lèrins. He took a new name, as they sometimes do—Augustin. I have not seen him in many years. He lives another life on that island of prayer. He would not want to see *me*."

"A monk—and with another name? That's why Rebecca couldn't trace him."

"That is why." Clarice looked out the window. "The good people who raised you—they were Catholic, were they not?"

"Yes, the Kennedys were Catholic. But I stopped believing when I grew up. Rebecca believes. I don't know why, but she does."

Clarice turned to her with a piercing gaze. "And these Kennedys? Do you not love them? They are your family, my dear, are they not?"

122

"I'm sorry, I don't mean to sound ungrateful. They shall always be my parents and I shall always love them—although we didn't take their name—they wanted us to keep DuPres."

"Why did they wish such a thing?"

"They said we had so little of our past that we should keep what we had."

"I see. They are truly selfless people. And are they still living, your mother and your father?"

"Dad died two years ago and Mom doesn't know me. She has Alzheimer's. But I had a loving family, a good upbringing." Riding the yellow school bus, assembling class projects on the lace-covered dining table, practicing Mozart on the warped piano in the den. A simple childhood, but a good one.

"But you are looking for something else?"

"Yes." Rachelle paused, suddenly tense. Her cheeks grew warm.

"What are you looking for, Rachelle? Why did you come? You are searching, *ma chèrie*, you are sad."

Rachelle looked at her hands with resignation, her surgeon's hands. "It's a long story, but you were in medicine, perhaps you will understand." Could she trust this woman with such a story?

She told her aunt about her career, her love of healing, of putting things right that had gone wrong. She told her how, when she practiced surgery, she moved in a mysterious world of miracles, in a partnership with an unseen power, how she knew the force of resurrection, of new cells coming to life. She explained how she journeyed into the sources of creation as she stitched together lives shattered by disease.

She had improved upon a useful procedure—the Cobel wrap—and had received recognition for her technical success. There had never been a problem; she had a 100 percent record of happy patients. Until last month.

"Samuel Steinhoff was thirty-three with a wife and children. It was his third surgery in a delicate area, the esophageal lining and opening to the stomach. We scrape off the dead cells, sometimes precancerous, that have been formed by the rising acid, the reflux." Rachelle breathed deeply as she recalled the routines and methods of her past that had formed her very being.

"Go on, my dear." Clarice touched her chest, as though experiencing the rising heat herself. "It is a wonderful thing that you do. I see that."

Rachelle shook her head ruefully, but continued. "We tighten the sphincter muscle, which has become loose, or 'lazy,' with lining material from the stomach, and the reflux is largely controlled, at least for a time. In Mr. Steinhoff's case, I knew the scar tissue, so close to the opening, could be a problem. Still, I refused to admit it. Other doctors warned me. I thought myself invincible. I even operated in front of students...and I couldn't stop the bleeding. We never even started the wrap."

"Were you responsible?"

"I was."

"Did he know the risks?"

"He did."

"Then *he* was responsible."

Rachelle glanced at her aunt. "Maybe."

"And you have come here because of this failure?"

"When he died, part of me died too. I'm searching for *me*. Is that crazy?"

"It is not crazy. Your identity was your work. I have seen this before."

"Who *are* we, then, if not what we do, what we make of our lives?"

"I once believed, like you, that what we do is who we are. But today I believe our identity is based on what we choose, and that choice governs what we do." Clarice's eyes held a careful reserve, as though she feared to trespass.

"What is the difference between choosing and doing?"

"What we choose to believe. Who or what we choose to worship. For that choice orders our doing." Clarice tapped the table with her long index finger as though the linen could testify to her thesis.

A familiar disquiet filled Rachelle. Was her aunt religious?

"Do you believe in God, Rachelle?"

"Do I believe in God?" she repeated, tossing it back. How should she handle such a question? Her aunt was old and frail and *needed* to believe.

"God will heal you, if you choose him. He will show you who you are. You will be reflected in his love."

"Is it that simple?"

"I think it is that simple. If I had known his love earlier, I would have known myself earlier. You cannot know yourself without knowing God. You knew him when you healed others. You must find him again. Do not let your heart empty into nothing. The Evil One will fill it up. Choose God instead. There is no middle way. No being lukewarm."

"Have you always believed?" Did her aunt really say "the evil one"?

A phrase from the middle ages. Sorcery. Witchcraft. Crones with black cats.

"No, not at all. It was fashionable to believe in nothing when I was in school. We studied Freud. We read Camus and Sartre. We learned that faith was a fairy tale, a problem of transference."

"I studied the same thing. We formulate our idea of God from wishful thinking, from images of our fathers, images we don't want to lose in adulthood."

"*Exactement.* And our Jewish home had many laws to keep, laws I did not choose to keep. I wanted to escape that world, and I did escape. I trained with the Freudian institute."

"You never married?"

Clarice opened the dessert menu. "Would you like some coffee, my dear?"

Rachelle ordered mint tea and her aunt asked for her usual.

"Jacob was my first love, and he was gone," Clarice said, shaking her head, "but there was one other, much later." She stared at the single peach rose in the vase as she rubbed the age spots on the back of her hands. "After the war, I came to Vence to put flowers on your uncles' graves—Jewish flowers for my Christian brothers. And I stayed, changing sheets and serving guests, trying to forget, to start over. I could not afford to finish school. I worked hard, and one day they made me manager."

"And Gilbert...Augustin?"

The old woman's face reddened. "Have you guessed? He was the other one, my dear, but he believed in God. He said the war proved man's need for God, his need to be told right from wrong, his need to feel shame. I said the war proved that right and wrong were relative. That we must make our own meaning. That guilt and shame were sense-less and...harmful. The gap was too great. I wanted to be free—to dance and go to parties and have many lovers. I wanted to go to Paris, forget those hard, terrible years. He wanted to marry, have a family. Later, he joined the Cistercians. But I never went to Paris."

"Did you love him, Aunt?" Rachelle wondered at her own boldness.

Clarice's speech was high and skeletal, her words escaping in a kind of wheeze. "I loved him more than my life." She looked around, frowning, and gripped the table. "Where is Bertrand with my coffee?"

"He's coming. I see him now."

Her aunt's eyes begged Rachelle to make sense of it all. "But you see, love was not enough. Today, I understand Augustin's choice, for I now believe as he does. Finally, at eighty-five years of age, I begin to believe, to understand. A slow study, some would say." Her closed smile held both irony and sadness.

"To understand what exactly, Aunt?"

"To understand why we suffer. We suffer because we are fallen. But we still have the choice to hurt others, to fall farther. Even so, I have seen man's courage in the face of suffering, his sense of right and wrong, of injustice. Where did this knowledge come from? The Ten Commandments are written on our hearts, and we do not doubt them."

"You mean the moral law?" Rachelle recalled Rebecca's words, *You clearly believe in the moral law.*

"*Oui, exactement.* The Jews have always had the Commandments. The question for me is this: Has the Chosen One come? I believe he has. Augustin tried to convince me and I wish I had listened. Because, my little Rachelle, I believe his Christ is indeed our Messiah."

"I'm sorry, Aunt, I'm not a believer." Rachelle would not argue, not now, not here, not with *her.*

"Do not be sorry. You are honest and you use the free will that God gave you." She pointed her finger at Rachelle's heart. "I cannot make you believe, my dear. I can only tell you what I have seen, what I have learned, and what I think is true. That is all."

"I understand. Thank you."

"You are a doctor. I will give you a medical analogy, one I heard in a sermon. It is a vision I have carried a long time since. A good sermon, it is like that, no? Like Jesus' parables. This one goes like this. God is the doctor of our souls, just as you and others are doctors of our bodies. Our souls were born with a fatal illness, just like our bodies, which were born to die, no? Just so, our souls are born to die. This Soul-Doctor has given us medications and prescribed exercises and appointments to keep. Should we choose to ignore his regimen, our souls will die with our bodies. Should we choose to follow it, our souls will be raised to heaven. And our bodies as well."

Rachelle smiled. "That is very neat, Aunt, but I like it. I don't know if I believe it, but I like it. I wish it was true, that it *was* that simple."

The old woman rubbed her bony fingers together. "It *is* that simple."

As they spooned their last bit of *crème brulée,* Rachelle turned to her aunt. "I don't know how to thank you, Aunt Clarice." She paused, and added, "But I think I should leave tomorrow."

"Where do you go? Back to Crillon-le-Brave? Back to America?

First, please, see your Uncle Augustin. He and I, we talked far into the night," she whispered to herself as she stared into her empty dish. Then she looked into Rachelle's eyes, challenging her. "It would be only fair to let him see you, Alain's baby. He loved his brother very much."

Rachelle considered her words as she walked Clarice to her door. The elderly woman turned and unclasped a silver necklace.

"Here, *ma chèrie*, I want you to have this. I have few years left on this earth. It may do you more good than me. And keep your heart open, *ma chèrie*."

Rachelle looked at the finely wrought crucifix laying in her palm. "Thank you," she said, unable to refuse. "It's beautiful."

"I shall inquire about Augustin." Clarice kissed Rachelle on each cheek. "Go in peace, *ma chèrie, ma petite* Leah-baby. And go with God."

Chapter Sixteen
Lyons

Love, after all, makes the whole difference
between an execution and a martyrdom.
Evelyn Underhill

Madeleine woke early as light streamed through uncovered windows. Where was she? She turned to Jack, who slept fitfully. *Bagnols. Lyons.*

Judging from the partially clear skies, it looked as if they would be going into Lyons. She reached for her robe and moved to an antique table at the far end of the room. Opening her file on the French martyrs, she prayed to be led along the right path. *Lord, teach me thy will.* Soon she knew she would be taught—taught by the martyrs themselves.

She would accept the moment granted her. She would trust and obey.

Holy Manifestations: The Martyrs of Lyons
Cicero writes that Roman Lyons was founded at the convergence of the Rhone and the Saone Rivers, where Celtic tribes had settled. In 44 BC Roman veterans from Vienna were given land overlooking the western banks of the Saone, and streets were laid out. This area came to be known as Fourvière, *forum vetus*, the ancient Roman forum. Stones from the forum would later be used in the apse of the twelfth-century cathedral.

The Romans called it Lugdunum, or "the hill of the Celtic god Lug." In 27 BC Caesar Augustus decreed that the Emperor be worshiped instead of Lug and he made Lugdunum the capital of the "three Gauls"—today France—ruled by his son-in-law Agrippa. Lugdunum became a compulsory site of imperial worship.

Madeleine was thankful for the freedom to worship. What was it like when Christianity was illegal? She often took such freedom for granted, and knew she shouldn't.

Agrippa built four highways, a crossroads that would link Lyons with the Empire, spokes that promised a flourishing hub of trade. He then built the Amphitheater of the Three Gauls for gladiator competitions, oratory, and the annual meeting of the sixty Gallic tribes. The area came to be known as La Croix Rousse, "the russet cross," named after an ocher stone cross that stood at one of the intersections, since destroyed by the 1789 Revolution.

In the middle of the second century, Christian merchants from Asia Minor settled in Lugdunum. They refused to worship the emperor and were branded atheists and subversives. Thought to have angered the Roman gods, they were made scapegoats for natural disasters. On Good Friday, 177, the townspeople rounded up the Christians and "tried" them, accusing them of cannibalism and incest. The venerable bishop Saint Pothinus was beaten to death. Twenty-four others were beheaded. The rest were tortured and fed to the beasts in the arena.

The bodies were thrown into the Rhone so that relics could not be honored, a cult not created.

Twenty years later, the new ruler Septimus Severus set the town on fire and massacred the remaining eighteen thousand Christians, including Saint Irenaeus, one of the great Fathers of the Church.

These were France's first known Christian martyrs.[13]

Madeleine shivered. Such sacrifice. Such suffering. She felt small and insignificant, her worries and fears petty. How could she complain to God when she enjoyed such religious freedom? Elena was right. Madeleine would lay flowers of thanks over the graves of these holy men and women. Perhaps some of their courage and sanctity would rub off.

Jack stirred in bed and looked up. Madeleine moved to his side. "How are you feeling, honey?"

He rubbed his face with both hands and sat up. "Lousy."

"Bad night?"

"I can't seem to get comfortable." He ran his hand down her arm and she touched his cheek.

"We'll find the doctor," she said. "I know we will."

"Maddie, I keep thinking of my father."

"You were so young when he died."

Jack pulled himself out of bed, slipped on his robe, and stepped slowly to the window. "Maddie, I'm scared."

Madeleine put her arm around him and gazed at the lime trees below without seeing them. "Of dying?"

"Not so much dying, but suffering. My father suffered a long time. At least it seemed an eternity to Meg and me. It wasn't fair. He was a good man. He was a believer too—God didn't help him at all."

Jack hadn't spoken much about his father's last days. Would he share this now? This was a piece of Jack's story she longed be a part of.

"It was cancer, wasn't it? They couldn't medicate him?" She hoped she wasn't pushing into a tender area.

"Not enough. He groaned a lot. Meg and I tried to get as far away as possible."

Madeleine felt his tears were near. "And Meg was only...seven?" Her sister-in-law lived in Florida, divorced. She drank too much and was far too gaunt, moving in and out of rehab as though it were a second home. Perhaps she too raced against the clock. Terrified of a slow death. She must be fifty-nine now.

"She was seven."

"That explains a lot."

"She was thin even then and bulimic all through high school. It was as though she needed complete control over her body."

"We should see more of her, Jack."

"She says I remind her of Papa."

"Oh dear. So it's her choice to avoid you?"

"Pretty much. When Nathan died, that gave her a cause she couldn't give up. That's when she really started drinking. And she was jealous of my boys, too. She called us the 'perfect little family.' My first wife hated her."

Madeleine ached with Meg's suffering. Nathan was her only child, and a reckless, headstrong boy, left alone most afternoons after school. One day he rode his bike in front of a car and was killed instantly. After that came the divorce. She remarried twice, but didn't want to deal with children "cluttering her life."

"Let's try inviting her for Christmas, Jack. Let's fly her out to San Francisco."

"It would be good to see her, if she would agree to come—with me the way I am, somewhat like Papa. I tried to protect her." His speech grew hoarse. "Papa told me to, and I tried, but she backed away." He shook his head and wiped his eyes with the back of his fist. "I'm hitting the shower. Why don't you order room service and call Elena."

Elena joined them in their room for a breakfast of croissants, fruit, yogurt, lavender honey, bowls of rich café-au-lait, and pulpy orange juice. Madeleine had laid the table, moving each item from the huge trays carried upstairs by the waiter, setting Jack's place just right.

Jack looked out from behind the *Tribune*. "Our Neotex dropped again—another point and I call our broker."

"Did we decide about Lyons?" Elena's timid tone was edged with hope as she passed Madeleine the bread.

Madeleine smiled. "We need to move on to Paris, but another day can't make a great difference."

Elena reached for a tiny raisin swirl bursting with butter. "You could ring Madame Morin and see if she has reached her sister."

Jack set down the paper. "Pierre thought the doctor would be in Paris for some time, probably visiting relatives. Maybe Pierre could join us, Elena? He seems like a fine young man."

"I don't know—if you wish."

"You don't like Pierre?" Jack asked.

Elena was silent as though searching for an appropriate response. Her dark eyes were troubled, and she glanced at Madeleine.

"We'll decide about Pierre later," Madeleine said. "Providing Rebecca has no news, we'll visit Lyons. We have time."

We have time? The lie ate at her.

While Jack was faxing his broker from the hotel office, Elena read Madeleine's Lyons chapter, and Madeleine dialed Rebecca Morin.

"I'm sorry, Mrs. Seymour," Rebecca said, sounding far away, "I left a message for my sister. There's been no reply."

Madeleine watched the door for Jack. "We're at Chateau Bagnols near Lyons. Could you call as soon as you hear? It's very important."

"I must go, Madame."

"My husband is very ill, dangerously so."

Silence.

"Madame Morin?"

"I understand. I'm sorry."

The phone went dead.

Jack appeared in the doorway. "Ready? Any news?"

"No news." Madeleine looked out the window. "It might rain, but let's go."

They walked to the car, umbrellas in hand, and Madeleine sat in the front passenger seat. Jack drove, his face determined. Elena took the seat in back.

As they wound east through the hills, Madeleine wondered what this ancient city would tell her, for she was beginning to see God's hand in many things, common things, sudden appearances of the divine in ordinary life. She paid increasing attention to the world about her, opening her heart and stamping down self-centered thoughts, leaving room for fresh breezes and new lights revealing the dark, neglected corners of her soul.

Jack maneuvered through Villefranche and followed the A7 south to Lyons. Exiting the freeway, he drove along the river to Fourvière, the historic center, and parked behind the medieval Cathedral of Saint John.

Entering the cathedral's cold, colossal space, Madeleine stared at the dirty stained glass and dark side chapels. A freestanding altar stood barren of cross or crucifix. She recalled the Protestant influence so near Geneva. It seemed iconoclasts had purged image and beauty here too.

In a side chapel, a crowd gathered around a tall fourteenth-century pendulum clock, as they waited for the noon performance of the Annunciation, enacted by tiny wooden figures hidden above the face. Suddenly a miniature cock crowed twelve and the Archangel Michael darted through a tiny door to greet the Virgin Mary. Madeleine turned away, uncomfortable with the frivolous treatment of the holy, with this mighty act in history turned into a mechanical toy.

Jack chuckled. "It's a religious cuckoo clock, like the Swiss ones, with the little figures running out and hitting a bell. And made in the fourteenth century!"

Madeleine frowned. "Before clocks, church bells kept the village time."

Elena looked from Jack to Madeleine. "Bells sound better."

Madeleine felt a twinge of desire to have lived in that simpler, more melodious time. "They rang at dawn for morning prayers, for the start of the workday, and for noon break. They rang at the end of the workday and for evening prayers."

"Sweeter than alarm clocks," Jack said, scratching his chin.

"We measure our day by the minutes, sometimes seconds, always in a hurry." And she was no exception, Madeleine thought.

"Like rats on a wheel," Jack added.

Elena gazed at the empty altar. "We don't always pause to reflect."

Madeleine wondered if many people ever considered the larger questions of life—why we are here, why we suffer, what happens when we die. She recalled her own busy days as a young single mother with an eight-to-five clerical job. She had no time for such reflections. She could barely keep up with work and Justin: Saturdays she cleaned their apartment and did the laundry, shopped for groceries and thrift-store clothing; Sundays, after church, they visited her father, slowly dying, and her grieving mother.

And now, *Jack* was slowly dying.

Elena turned toward the chancel. "Do you think there's a connection between the Protestant work ethic and clocks and plain altars?"

Jack pulled out his monitor and strapped it on.

Madeleine watched him, waiting for the results. "Let me think about that one." She paused, listening to the predictable hum. "You mean the work ethic's desire for efficiency?"

Elena looked thoughtful. "When you make things simple, more can be done."

"And clocks organize our day efficiently, as well as our work," Madeleine added.

"Italy is Catholic and not very efficient." Elena grinned.

Jack was satisfied with the monitor's numbers. Madeleine was relieved. "And America is a Protestant nation. We're the world's manufacturers, organizers, defenders."

Elena opened her palms as though the proof lay there. "But Italy has art, and music, and *la dolce vita*. Catholics drink and dance, and many Protestants don't. Catholics enjoy life."

Jack steered them to the doors.

"But I do like my laptop and e-mail and electric appliances," Madeleine admitted.

Elena's raised her finger. "An Italian invented the volt for the battery, and don't forget Leonardo da Vinci and Galileo."

"Where are you two going with this?" Jack ushered them outside. "It's time for lunch. You can discuss the pros and cons then." He shook his head as though traveling with such women had become a challenge indeed.

Madeleine and Elena exchanged understanding glances. Elena had indeed become like a daughter, Madeleine thought. Did mothers and daughters talk like this?

They rode a funicular up the cliff face to the towering nineteenth-century basilica, Notre-Dame de Fourvière, built in 1870 in thanksgiving for the end of the Franco-Prussian War.

Pausing in the narthex, they gazed at the immaculate sanctuary. Covering the side walls, Byzantine mosaics depicted heroic faith-stories, from the second-century martyrdom of Bishop Pothinus to the nineteenth-century doctrine of the Immaculate Conception. Stars speckled the vaulted domes.

Elena scanned the nave and side aisles. "It's too perfect. Like it's never used, a museum perfectly kept."

"But it's incredibly beautiful," Madeleine said, "and beauty can be inspiring, too."

They wandered through a side door and into a small chapel. Seeing the red candle burning on the altar, Madeleine genuflected. Others knelt before the tabernacle.

Madeleine could feel the prayers of the penitents through the years. She turned toward the south wall, where a garden of white tapers surrounded a sculpture of the Virgin Mary, her arms outstretched, beckoning. A woman in a patterned headscarf and baggy sweater lit a candle, bowed her head, and turned to kneel before the Blessed Sacrament.

Elena smiled, her face full of confidence. "I think this Madonna is one of the miraculous ones."

"Miraculous, and somehow more real," Madeleine said. She looked about. "Elena, where's Jack? I thought he was with us."

They walked outside and scanned the terrace. Madeleine rubbed her hands nervously. Why did he disappear like that? Without a word? "I don't see him, but let's hope he'll find us here. It's such a wonderful view."

Elena focused her camera on the old town below her, the pitched roofs, the meandering lanes packed tightly with medieval houses. "He'll find us," she said and repacked the camera carefully in the canvas case on the strap around her neck.

The wind had died down, and the noon sun burned their cheeks as they gazed over Lyons. The Saone and Rhone streamed between leafy banks; church spires rose modestly amid steeply pitched red roofs. In the distance, conical buildings witnessed to modern Lyons, and farther out, high-rises covered distant hills. The two women gazed at the panorama in the comfortable silence of their deepening friendship.

Madeleine adjusted her glasses. "Elena, what do you think of Pierre?"

Elena paused. "I'm not sure. He's attractive, isn't he? And ambitious."

"He was sitting at Jack's knee, waiting on every word."

"I don't understand him. He has a wonderful family. Why would anyone want to leave Crillon-le-Brave?" Elena looked puzzled as she glanced at Madeleine, then turned again to the view.

Madeleine's heart ached as she observed Elena's pretty profile. Her thick hair was pulled back in her red scarf and her white sweater set off her olive skin. "Sometimes we don't appreciate things until we leave them...or lose them."

"Or never had them."

"I know. You never had family in a traditional sense. I do know what it's like not to have the family one had envisioned or planned. My life didn't turn out the way I thought it would."

"What do you mean?" Elena sounded careful, as though she didn't want to intrude.

"I always wanted a house full of children." Madeleine ran her finger over the surface of the cool stone wall, feeling its rough spots.

Elena turned, her eyes searching. "You have Justin—and he'll have children one day."

"I know. And I love Jack's grandchildren—they've been such a joy; they've saved me from myself. How easily I slip into my old sadness. I suppose Mollie is never far from my thoughts."

"Have the nightmares returned?"

"No, thank God," Madeleine said, suddenly shaky. "I'm sorry—I was trying to say that I understand a little of what you're feeling. Family is important."

"Thank you." As Elena moved a strand of hair behind her ear, her scarf slipped off and she reached for it. "I'm envious when I see a home like Pierre's—the fireplace, the dining table in the next room, the gathering of generations. I want that someday. I really do." She studied the square of cotton as though it held her future. Her hair blew freely in the breeze.

"And you'll have it one day. You're no longer thinking about becoming a nun?"

"I guess not." She smiled thinly. "Sister Agnes gave me this scarf on my twelfth birthday. She said it was in the basket when they found me."

Madeleine touched the faded burgundy pattern, a paisley with flowers and vines.

Elena looked up, returning to the present. "And did you notice Pierre at the abbey? I don't think he's a believer."

"I wondered about that too. Would you mind, though, if I asked him to join us on our trip to Paris? He's going that way, and he could help us with his aunt. Jack is keen on the idea and I'm so worried about him."

Elena looked resigned but wanting to help. "Invite Pierre if you think he might lead us to his aunt."

"Thanks."

"How *is* Jack? He coughs a lot. Should he be drinking wine?"

"It's a familiar pattern. He goes on his regimen—no wine and a restricted diet—feels better, thinks he can drink and ignore his diet, and slides into trouble."

"He's taking antacids. That should help."

"Actually, he's not supposed to take them." She hated to nag, but she would have to say something soon.

"How can we help?"

"We can't tell him what to do. No one can, it seems. We let him have his fling and be there when he crashes. And here he is now."

Jack approached, waving his hat. "Come along—I've found the perfect spot for our noon feast, but not until you see what you came for."

They followed the road along the spine of the silent hill. The wind picked up and sudden sun beamed through the fast-moving clouds. Soon the ruins of a Roman amphitheater appeared; two semicircles of stone and grass descended to a stage.

"The great dramas were held here." Jack scanned his guidebook. "Aristotle, Virgil, Aristophanes."

Madeleine studied the arena as Elena took a picture. "Is this where the Christians died?" She pulled out a small folded map.

Jack kept reading. "They don't really say."

Madeleine grappled with the irony, the opposites merging in this dry grass. "How could such art coexist with such blood? Doesn't art civilize man, control his animal passions, his blood-thirst? The action of catharsis was to purge suffering."

Jack raised his brows. "Oh boy, here we go."

Elena looked doubtful. "But is this the Amphitheater of the Three Gauls? The map shows it's on the other side of the river."

Jack scowled. "Wrong arena? You're kidding. How many Roman arenas could there be in one town?"

"How far is it?" Madeleine asked.

"Not far." Elena traced the route with her finger.

"Could I see?" Jack coughed as he studied the map.

Madeleine searched her pocket for a tissue. Her fingers touched a folded sheet of paper. The biopsy report. Should she destroy it? She shoved it deeper into the pocket and found a tissue for Jack in her handbag.

Jack led them back up the hill, hailed a taxi in front of the basilica, and helped Madeleine and Elena inside.

"*Amphithéatre des Trois Gaules, s'il vous plaît,*" Elena said to the driver.

They drove down the hill, crossed the Saone and wound through medieval streets scrawled with graffiti. Finally, they arrived at another arena, this one nearly surrounded by chicken-wire fencing. A sign announced that this was the site of the Christian martyrdoms of 177 AD.

They stood in front of the bleak field and stared at the gates that had released the beasts. Madeleine walked the silent paths between the stone seats, Elena at her side, Jack following. They descended stairs to the stage. From there, Madeleine looked up to the terraces as she imagined the times. She could hear the crowds roar, as bravery and blood and Christ mingled in that sacrificial altar. The blood of the martyrs, Tertullian said, became the seed of the Church, feeding the growing new faith, and encouraging other Christians. Many witnesses of these terrible ordeals became converts: jailers, executioners, those watching from the terraced arena.

Madeleine shivered. She fingered her cross, its cool gold warmed by her heart. *Show me thy will, Lord, show me how I can help Jack.* The sun disappeared behind a cloud and a dark shadow moved over the stadium. There was no answer, only silence, but Madeleine knew those men and women were strengthening her. They had remained steadfast. They had sung hymns glorifying God as they died. They had not demanded release from their ordeal, but had borne the full weight of the Cross. She too would glorify God. She too would live in the moment, enshrined by his light, a shimmering golden pool.

As the prophet Jeremiah said, "The Lord's mercies...are new every morning." Each day would grant her greater light as she lived as the saints had lived, lived each minute in the heart of God.

Elena looked lost in her own thoughts, perhaps her prayers. She touched her rosary, her camera lying still against her chest, forgotten.

"The taxi's waiting," Jack shouted from the street.

They lunched at a restaurant overlooking the old city and shared salads of potatoes and marinated herring, fish with mashed leeks and cream, and veal medallions with mushrooms. Jack poured a white burgundy, and Madeleine listened to the whispering graves of Lyons.

Chapter Seventeen
Lèrins

Prayer is...
a simple look turned toward heaven,
it is a cry of recognition and of love, embracing both trial and joy.
Thérèse of Lisieux

Friday morning Rachelle boarded the eleven o'clock ferry in the Cannes harbor. White yachts floated between wooden piers, their red-blue-and-white flags rippling in the breeze.

She stood in the bow, her windbreaker zipped tight, her backpack at her feet. Her aunt had learned that Father DuPres still resided at the abbey, although he was no longer abbot. At eighty-four, age had granted him rest as well as honor, Clarice explained, and Monsieur Olivier had whistled through his teeth. "A holy man," he said, "known to be wise."

Rachelle leaned over the front rail and watched the froth foam where the ferry cut through the saltwater. Farther out to sea a mist blanketed the horizon, hiding the Isle de Saint-Honorat, the home of her uncle. She could not refuse Clarice, and seeing Augustin might give her one more piece of herself.

Rachelle balanced herself against the roll of the ferry and maneuvered to the square stern in back. Beyond the wake, the bay of Cannes receded beneath the lower Alpine hills. Except for the faraway haze out to sea, the day was clear and cold, and she welcomed the drum of the motor in her ears. Other passengers had retreated to the warm cabin, and she found herself alone on the deck, enjoying her isolation. She sat on a plastic chair bolted to the deck and wrapped her jacket tighter. As she pulled her guidebook from her bag, something fell out.

The silver crucifix and chain caught the sun as she picked it up and slipped it into her pocket. She should have left such a precious thing at the chateau.

She opened the guide and skimmed the entry for Lèrins Islands. There appeared to be two, Sainte-Marguerite and Saint-Honorat, the latter the home of the Cistercians. Saint Honorat had arrived on the island by the end of the fourth century. He lived as a hermit and soon attracted others to his life of prayer and penitence. No longer a solitary, he established a monastery that became famous in the medieval world for its learning and influence. Pilgrims, including a pope, walked barefoot along its shoreline path. Over the years the island was raided by Saracens, sacked by pirates, and finally closed by the Revolution in 1788. Cistercians restored the monastery in 1869.

Rachelle returned the book to her bag and felt for the chained crucifix in her pocket. She slipped it around her neck, letting it fall under her shirt, safe. She would try to keep her heart and mind open, for, after all, she was a modern woman, receptive to all points of view.

As the ferry approached the small harbor, Rachelle could see that Saint-Honorat was forested, with a white shoreline that met the blue sea; a stone steeple rose above the trees in the distance. She disembarked onto a concrete dock and, following signs, walked up a dirt road to a stone archway on her right. She passed through the carved portal and continued up a long straight drive bordered by tall cypresses and surrounded by lush vineyards. The abbey with its bell tower stood amidst the vines with their rich green foliage and dark dusty grapes not yet picked. Rachelle walked faster, striding with purpose along the uneven path as the bells clanged in the crisp autumn air, a sound both sweet and shrill.

She entered the dim abbey, and could make out only a few people in the shallow nave. A service was beginning. A dozen white-robed monks filed in from a side door into a long choir. Rachelle sat in an empty pew toward the back and studied the men. None could be old enough to be her uncle.

Her aunt said the community was Cistercian. The sanctuary was certainly plain with white walls ascending to stone vaults. High opaque windows filtered a pale light. She recalled her childhood church of Saint Mary's, with its statues and stained glass. Here only one statue, a sculpted Virgin holding the boy Jesus on her hip, hung from a column in the left aisle. An unadorned tabernacle rested on a plain altar, and above the tabernacle hung a simple wooden crucifix. Rachelle pulled her eyes away from the suffering figure nailed to the cross, his head angled, his body collapsing, his arms outstretched.

A man and a boy, possibly father and son, knelt in the front pew.

An elderly woman in a flowered dress, her shoulders hunched from bone loss, sat in front of Rachelle. She had braided her hennaed hair and arranged it on top of her head, exposing silver roots that fanned her neck. Rachelle copied her movements, standing and sitting when she did. She could not remember the last time she had gone to mass, but she recognized enough of the liturgy to know it *was* a mass, even if it was in French and in a monastery.

The monks chanted the opening prayers, branching into pleasing harmonies. One monk stood and read from a large missal. Another monk moved about the altar as he intoned the consecration—at least Rachelle thought it was the consecration, her memories stirring—then raised a large chalice. Outside, bells clamored in a kind of delirium. A third monk walked through the choir, entered the nave, and shook the hand of the man in the first row, who in turn shook hands with the boy. The boy walked to the woman and pumped her hand vigorously. Rachelle recognized that moment in the liturgy when the "Peace" was passed among the people in the form of a ritual greeting and handshake.

The woman turned to Rachelle. Her eyes beamed as she laughed the words "*La paix du Christ!*" and gently squeezed Rachelle's hand. Rachelle forced a half smile and quickly withdrew her hand. She shook herself and stared at the monks. What was happening to her? A sweet warmth lingered, washing through her mind, smoothing the sharp edges. She turned her eyes to the crucifix.

Here, in this plain church, the body on the wooden cross commanded her attention. He was the focus, and no matter how Rachelle tried to avert her gaze, she continually returned to his agony. She sensed that the others in the abbey shared his suffering, or he shared theirs. She shook her head again, and, as they lined up to receive the Eucharist, she wrenched her gaze from the image. Silently, she slid from the pew and stole through a side door, her heart pounding.

She found a bench in a quiet garden and caught her breath. Beds of rockrose and red geraniums circled a spluttering fountain, and she decided she must be in the cloister. She breathed deeply and her heartbeat slowed. As she saw in her mind the wooden corpus on the wooden cross, she assured herself that these were material things, not living, with no power over her. Without thinking, she pulled out the crucifix from under her shirt, touching it lightly.

The moment of weakness, the moment of almost-belief, unsettled her. Perhaps she would walk around the island, then return. She would gather herself together, collect her thoughts, and ask about her uncle.

She followed the path through pines, eucalyptus, and cypress, past bays of deep blue, maneuvering around trees uprooted by the storm and pruned branches piled like funeral pyres. The air smelled of sea salt and damp earth, and a cold gust blew over the surface of the sea from the mountains. Coming upon a stone hut in the shape of a chapel, she found the door locked and tried to see inside through a small window. The interior was bare but clean. Was this one of the hermit houses? She returned to her clipped stride, her useless hands tightening in fists as they swung at her side.

A fallen tree blocked the path. Grasping a branch for support, she climbed over the trunk, scraping her palm. The cut was shallow but dirty, so she sat on the log, opened her bottle, and poured water over the wound, cleaning it with her cotton neck-scarf. As her blood washed away she saw the other blood, the blood of Sam Steinhoff, the blood that wouldn't stop flowing.

The students had formed a ring around the operating theater, taking notes, watching the procedure from the balcony. Well-placed monitors zoomed in. The anesthesiologist stood by, administering measured doses. The surgical nurse waited, handing instruments automatically. They had done this procedure so many times—it was routine. She cut into the carefully marked area and removed the damaged tissue. It was time to begin the wrap.

When did she know the bleeding was out of control? She issued orders and demanded clamps, but the line flattened across the screen, that monitor of life and death. Alarms sounded, their beating beeps shooting through the air like bullets. Other medics arrived, and they worked as a team. They staunched the blood. The nurses' eyes held raw fear and the anesthesiologist stared helplessly. They were all eyes behind their masks, eyes that told everything. She looked at her people, her team, their scrubs bloody, and they shook their heads, each one confronting the terrible truth. Her forceps fell to the floor with a loud clang, and she turned from the body as her own life drained away.

How could she have taken this patient on, made him insane promises? Conrad had advised her against it. Even Jorgenson, who took chances on a child, told her to forget Sam Steinhoff. But did she listen?

The wound on her hand looked clean. She recapped her bottle and continued along the dusty path strewn with branches. The wintry air bit into her cheeks. She pulled her memory away from that arena of blood, and she thought of Father Benedict.

The old priest had shaken his head in dismay, steepling his thick fingers. She had pulled away then too, had adeptly shifted the conversation and asked why he never went home to Saint Mary's. He said he simply couldn't leave Lourdes once he arrived. He had come with his flock to the shrine of Bernadette and had seen the healings, had believed they were real. Then he spoke of the changes of heart, as if those were more important than changes of body—*her* surgeries had removed cancers, had given people *real* changes of heart *and* lives, *real* hope. Until now.

Rachelle sat on a stretch of pebbled beach, digging her heels into the smooth shingle as the two-o'clock bells rang. Father Benedict was her real father. Dad was never there but to scold and set limits and frown. Rarely did her father find her praiseworthy, and rarely did Benedict find fault. How she looked forward to her history class when the energetic priest sat on the edge of his desk in his blue jeans and polo shirt, his legs swinging, the white collar cinching his thick neck. And how she loved his laugh that included the world, embraced every sorrow, reached for every hurt. He healed her often of the many wounds of childhood; he gave her the confidence to become a doctor, to heal with her hands just as this miraculous priest healed with his words.

A sailboat skimmed toward her. It winged across the whitecaps, catching the breeze neatly. She had sailed like that, through school, through twenty-five years of caring and curing and making a difference. But suddenly, she had grounded.

Benedict had held her shoulders in his coarse hands as she sobbed. He had looked into her eyes, trying to fill her with something he possessed and she desperately needed. Was it love? Maybe, but she sensed something else, something more, something she couldn't grasp on her own.

"Come to mass, my little Rachelle," Father Benedict had said. "Come and meet him. We celebrate tomorrow in the grotto. He will take your burden, Rachelle."

"Yes, Father," she had replied, as she had replied as a child, enthralled by his voice, his eyes, his strength, his *knowing*.

Then she was on the train first thing in the morning, without so much as a thank-you or a good-bye. Again she had fled, run away from the silliness of belief, from the intangibility of faith. How much better it was to embrace the known reality of atoms and molecules. But he meant well. How could she be so rude to him? And here she was, on a monastery island of silence, fleeing again.

Rachelle watched the sailboat motor into the harbor up the coast, the sails taken in. Weary, she pulled herself up, reshouldered her pack, and walked slowly back to the abbey. This time she would speak to someone. This time she would find her uncle.

The 2:30 office was short, according to the sign outside, fifteen minutes of sung prayers called *None*. This time she sat in the front to better study the monks' faces. They filed in, knelt in the choir, and began to chant. At the end of each Psalm, they bowed their heads and sang a *Gloria Be, Gloire au Père, et au Fils, et au Saint-Esprit*, a neat punctuation. Rachelle liked that. The order and the timing was pleasing, a kind of perfection.

She studied each face. Then, late, a young monk entered, pushing a wheelchair that cradled a fine-boned, aged man with wisps of silver hair. The elderly monk's legs were tangled in the footrest and his long fingers touched one another in prayer. His face was creased like dry leather but his eyes did not belong to his aging body. Even from her pew, Rachelle could see the soft amber pools, the eyes of a boy, the eyes of a dreamer, the eyes of a young lover seeing his beloved.

The young monk knelt beside him and joined in the chants. The old monk bowed his head as the Gloria was sung, his fingertips suspended in the space above his lap, his eyes far away. Rachelle stared at him, up to the crucified Christ, and down to him again.

Uncle Augustin.

Rachelle stood in the doorway of the Chapel of the Holy Sacrament, where, they said, Father Augustin received visitors. Sunlight fell through a window onto the tabernacle, a filmy ray catching the dancing dust. A sanctuary lamp hung from the ceiling, and its red candle burned with a soft glow. There were no pews and no altar rail, only benches against the walls. Augustin sat in his wheelchair before the altar, moving his lips silently.

"Father Augustin?" Her words sounded frail, hesitant, far away. They echoed lightly over the stone floor. "Is that you?"

He wheeled his chair around to face her. "Speak, my child. What do you desire? Do you need counsel? Would you like to make your confession?"

Did no one tell him of her visit?

She breathed deeply and tried to summon her normal voice. "Nothing really, Father. Didn't anyone call you? Or tell you I was coming? You see I am...I came...this is difficult for me to say. I don't want to upset you."

"Nothing surprises. Nothing changes. God is always love."

Rachelle wrung her hands and paced. "Yes, Father, but...oh, what can I say?"

"Please, *ma chèrie*, what troubles you?"

"Father, you are my uncle."

"What do you say?" The old man stared at her.

The words tumbled out. "I'm Rachelle DuPres, one of Leah and Alain's twins sent to America. I've come from Aunt Clarice, Clarice Laurent."

The monk blinked several times and turned his head toward the tabernacle. He closed his eyes, and one hand clenched the back of the other. *Would he be all right?* Rachelle stepped closer and watched him carefully. He was sweating, or was the moisture tears? Tears streamed from his closed lids, and his face perspired in the cool chapel.

He opened his eyes and gazed at her through those deep amber pools. "Rachelle, Rachelle, welcome home." He opened his arms.

Rachelle bent over the wizened, crippled old man and carefully wrapped her arms around him, feeling his bones. She kissed each wet cheek and smiled a crooked awkward smile, like a girl at her first confession.

"Alain would be so glad," he said, his voice choking. "He never knew what happened to you...but then perhaps he has known all along."

The old man wept with sobs that rose and racked his frail shoulders. Rachelle held him, gently, firmly, as best she could. Finally, she wept too, as she knelt on the cold stone floor and rested her head in his lap.

He gave her a room in the retreat house, clean and sparse. She called her aunt to let her know she was staying over, and Clarice sighed with relief.

"That is good," she said, and agreed to send Rachelle's bag to the abbey.

In the morning Rachelle met her uncle for brown bread and black coffee in a small conference room. She told him of Rebecca and her family in Crillon-le-Brave, of their childhood with the Kennedys in America. He listened carefully as though to memorize each word.

Rachelle explained that she wanted to see Robert's grave in Reims. She had paid her respects to Antoine and François; she would say good-bye to Robert as well.

"Robert was the wild one," Augustin said. "He had no faith. Mama said he would come to no good, and sometimes, *je pense,* her saying this changed him and his life. We cringed when she said those words, as if she could tell the future. Ah, the power of motherhood. It is so...forming. Alain and I, and in their own ways, Antoine and François, were *good* boys. That is, we went to mass and did not argue." He shook his head sadly as he stared into the past. "But Robert, he questioned, always. Mama did not appreciate his questions, said he would go to hell, so he ran away. He was eleven the first time, but the third time, he was sixteen. He never came home."

Rachelle pictured these boys growing up in Crillon-le-Brave, her birthplace, Leah and Alain's home, now Rebecca's. Why did they choose to fight? Some French had chosen not to fight; some had chosen to accept the occupation.

Augustin handed her a slip of paper. "Visit Anne-Marie. She is Robert's daughter, your cousin. She may still be in Reims. She will know, if anyone does, where his grave is. I help Anne-Marie from time to time as I have the others. Visit the Saint-Remi Basilica and light a candle for your father."

"I will. You said you help the *others?*"

"Pierre, and some of the cousins. School is costly, and I have saved a little money, for I have few needs, with no wife, no children. The family trust came to me, and the Cistercians allowed me to keep the trusteeship, as long as I help discreetly. We take vows of poverty. Otherwise our property is communal."

"You know Pierre? And Rebecca?"

Augustin smiled. "I have held them in my prayers, and helped them from time to time. But they do not know *me.*"

"Of course." Her new family was still so foreign.

"I trust you too will be discreet?"

"I will."

He gestured toward the delicate chain about her neck. "What is that you wear, my dear? My eyes are not good."

Rachelle fingered the crucifix. "Aunt Clarice gave this to me." She moved closer so that he could examine the finely hammered silver.

The Christ was an intricate one for its size, fused to a cross of gold. "It is unusual, the silver on the gold." He studied the crucifix as though held captive, then his face went deathly white.

"Father...Uncle...are you all right?"

"Child," he whispered, "did your aunt say anything about me?"

Rachelle spoke slowly, measuring her words as she watched him carefully, "She said that she...loved you once. I think she still does."

He looked into her eyes. "Did she say that, after all the years? She never told me. We parted, for I could not marry an unbeliever. Christ was too real to deny him, the betrayal too great. And during the war, betrayal was a familiar demon."

"I think I understand."

With great tenderness, he touched the crucifix. "I gave this to her the last time we met." He buried his face in his long fingers.

She stood and wrapped her arms about him. "Why is life so hard?" Her words trembled in the air, as though his loss—and Clarice's—had been piled on her own. The weight was nearly unbearable.

He shook his head. "We are fallen creatures, and we make our choices; God's love allows us to choose. It could be no other way. And in the end he redeems us and gives us joy." He looked up at her, his eyes brightening. "But I loved your aunt. I will always love her, Rachelle."

Rachelle swallowed hard, imagining her aunt and uncle when they were young, when they chose their separate paths. "Augustin, she told me something else you should know." She returned to her chair and leaned forward, her hands clasped, her eyes on his.

"Yes?"

"She believes what you believe...now."

"What do you say, my dear?" He inclined his head as though he had not heard the words correctly.

"She believes that...*your Christ is the true Messiah*. I think that is how she put it."

Augustin smiled, closing his eyes. "Thank you, Lord," he whispered, folding his hands. He opened his eyes and turned to Rachelle. "And you, my little one? Do you believe that Jesus is God's son?"

"No, Father," she said, surprised at her sudden sadness.

"Keep your heart and mind open, my child."

"Will you see her again?"

"I shall try. It is time. Our days are numbered, and it must be over ten years since she visited."

They sat in close silence. The fountain outside dripped slowly, tapping through the open window.

"Dear Augustin, what was he like—Alain, my father?"

"He was my fraternal twin. We were different from one another. How I admired him—he was so driven. He wanted to do big things, be successful, but he never had the chance. Perhaps his work in the Resistance, organizing the villages and the escape routes, was his great success."

"Aunt Clarice says they were shot. Do you know any more than that?" Rachelle could ask this of her old uncle, so full of life but so close to death.

"You ask difficult questions, but you have the right." He turned and looked into her eyes, his love singeing her heart. "Leah and Alain were machine-gunned in the barn, with Leah's family, but they were together, they were never sent to the camps, and their babies were safe. And," he added, as he fingered a small wooden cross on a leather thong, "I will see them soon. I will ask forgiveness. For you see, I heard the soldiers banging on the doors, and I was afraid. I did nothing."

Rachelle caught her breath. "There was a note—was it *you* who sent Clarice the note?"

"A note?"

She pulled the paper from her bag and showed him, and as he whispered the French words, she recalled some of the English.

I am too ashamed...I did not stop it...Leah's babies were sent through Lourdes...to America...Pray for me....

"This is my father's writing," he said. "I wish I could burn it, but it would make no difference now. We were cowards." His face held anguish and bitter remorse.

Her grandfather. Rachelle reached for matches on the table. She lit the note, dropped it into a tarnished brass bowl, and watched it flame and burn to ash.

"Thank you." He looked up as the last spark died. "But, perhaps, you too are dying, *ma chèrie.*"

Rachelle was startled by his directness. Yet Father Benedict had said nearly the same thing. She stood and walked to the window, her turn to clutch the peaceful cloister and the dripping fountain.

"But it is not my business," he said. "Although, sometimes I think, death is more my business than life."

She felt his eyes on her back, pleading not to push him away, no matter the pain. She turned, then slowly began to say the words that needed saying. She relived the operating room, the anguish, the fear, the panic, the realization that her life was gone, that *she* was gone.

"You feel guilty, *non?*"

"He was young, with a family." She rung her hands and paced.

"So this is why you come so far? To lose? Or to find?"

"Both, I suppose. I don't know. Something pulled me here, perhaps Becca, perhaps I'm searching for a shred of myself, hoping there might be something left when my doctoring is taken away, to begin again."

"Is doctoring impossible?"

She felt his gaze as she circled the room. "Of course it's impossible. How could I face another patient, having let one die?"

"Perhaps you are too perfect."

Rachelle paused and turned to him. "That's what Rebecca said."

"Maybe she is right."

Augustin's careful words continued to lead her down a safe path, his shepherd's instinct protecting her thoughts from straying. For the first time she saw herself as human, as full of error—some said sin—and accepting the condition, albeit briefly. A tiny flame lit her soul, and as Rachelle peered within, she saw a cluttered room, a dusty space.

Augustin said good-bye at the door, where a young monk waited to wheel him into the abbey. "Go in peace, my Leah baby." He extended his bony hands, then pulled her down to him, kissing her on each cheek. He touched her crucifix tenderly.

"Please, Uncle Augustin, I want you to have it." She unclasped the chain and pressed it into his withered palm.

"Thank you, Alain's daughter." He smiled and traced the Sign of the Cross on her forehead. "Thank you for coming to see me. I shall hold you in the heart of my prayers. You are a gift from God to an old man; you are the New Israel, my Rachelle DuPres, and God will use you. *Á Dieu*, and may Our Lord be always with you." He clasped the crucifix against his chest.

Rachelle remained rooted on the spot with a silly grin she could not control. She waved as the young man wheeled her uncle toward the chapel.

Dear Augustin. Whatever did he mean by the *New Israel*?

Chapter Eighteen
Nevers

I shall not live one day without loving.
Bernadette of Lourdes

The chateau dining room, once the massive *Salle des Gardes*, the medieval guardroom, was awash in soft candlelight. Madeleine, followed by Elena and Jack, sat at a table before the huge stone fireplace and unfolded a damask napkin. Crooked candelabra wobbled on bleached linen and flames flickered over lilies bunched in small white vases. Giant logs burned on a grate where game once turned on a spit. Above the mantel, a carved coat of arms bore a crown that marked the 1490 visit of King Charles VIII. Tall windows opened onto the courtyard on one side and gardens on the other.

Madeleine opened her menu. "Elena, we reached Pierre."

"Oh?"

"He's agreed to come to Paris with us."

Jack smiled with pride. "I talked him into it."

"He'll be a great help," Madeleine said. She watched Elena, who appeared pleased in spite of herself.

"And he speaks my language," added Jack, as he slipped on his reading glasses.

"Your language?" Elena tossed a thick strand of hair over her shoulder. She wore it loose, and it streamed over her brown arms. She looked at Jack with undisguised curiosity.

"He appreciates success."

"Maybe he wants to be like his aunt," Madeleine said.

Elena opened her menu. "That's good, I suppose." But her tone was shadowed with doubt.

"I think Pierre likes you, Elena." Jack motioned to the waiter. "We'll have the local Beaujolais, your house vintage."

"And two large bottles of water, *s'il vous plaît*," Madeleine added. "Don't tease her, Jack."

Her concern for Jack's choices collided with her pleasure in seeing him enjoy himself. He presided over their table like a country squire. For the moment, this castle was his, and all the manors 'round about. It was a working class dream, she thought, to be an aristocrat. The fact that Americans harbored such desires in secret made them no less powerful. Indeed, the secrecy intensified the power, the mystique of wealth.

They dined on fresh *foie gras* pan-fried with truffles, venison in wine, and river perch in tarragon vinaigrette.

Jack ordered more wine to go with dessert. "So, my ladies, what shall we do tomorrow? I rather fancy a drive in the country, then another nice dinner like this one."

"I thought we were going to Paris," Madeleine said, eyeing her husband.

"Pierre can't join us until Sunday," Jack explained, "so that gives us time to see the countryside."

"But Jack—"

"Is Nevers near here?" Elena asked. "That's where Bernadette died."

Madeleine gave in. "It's about a two-hour drive, I believe."

"Well then, Nevers it is," said Jack.

The rain hit that night, hard and straight with no wind, a sudden deluge from the heavens. Madeleine lay in bed and listened to the torrent striking the roof. She was looking forward to seeing Nevers, the place of Bernadette's death, and it was said her body remained incorrupt.

She slept fitfully and woke in the dark, early hours of the day. Pigeons cooed. It was a comforting sound, as though angels cradled her. She adjusted the bedcovers over Jack's sleeping form, tiptoed to the table, and opened her laptop. Bernadette's suffering had touched her deeply.

Holy Manifestations: Bernadette's Death
The Virgin Mary told Bernadette that she could not promise her happiness. Still, Bernadette could retreat from the world with no

151

regrets, for she had met the Mother of God.

In May of 1866, eight years after her visions, Bernadette attended a Solemn Mass with forty thousand pilgrims in the new chapel crypt. In July she took the train north to Nevers and joined the Sisters of Charity in the Convent of Saint-Gildard.

She worked in the kitchen and nursed the sick in the infirmary. She suffered from asthma and tuberculosis; a tumor grew on her knee, and finally bone disease confined her to her bed. On April 16, 1879, at the age of thirty-five, she died in great pain.

The Church considered canonization. They examined her body three times in the following years and found it incorrupt. The first "Identification of the Body" occurred on September 22, 1909. The Bishop of Nevers and a church tribunal presided; three witnesses from the convent, doctors Jourdan and David, stonemasons Gavillon and Boué, and carpenters Cognet and Mary, swore to tell the truth. When the stonemasons opened the coffin, Bernadette appeared in amazing condition with no odor.

The second "Identification of the Body" occurred on April 3, 1919. The body was covered with a light mildew and there was some loss of skin.

The third "Identification of the Body" was held on April 18, 1925, forty-six years after Bernadette's death. The organs were intact, some skin remained, the muscles and bones were whole.

In 1933, Pius XI proclaimed Bernadette a saint.

Madeleine's spine tingled as she read the words. Here was a holy, tangible intervention in the world. What was required for such intervention? Bernadette had indeed been trusting, obedient, accepting.

Madeleine gazed at Jack's sleeping figure. He breathed in jagged gasps. How could she help him? *Bernadette, teach me your patience. Your simplicity. Your acceptance.*

Saturday morning Madame Morin did not answer the phone, and Madeleine pushed the urgency to head for Paris—and to tell Jack—to the back of her mind. As she followed Elena and Jack to the car in the gravel lot, she breathed in the clear air and gazed up to the few clouds scuttling across the sky. Sunlight sparkled on the lemon trees in the front garden, their lemons long ago picked and stored. Madeleine took the front passenger seat, and Elena, the back.

"I found a place for lunch." Jack coughed, reaching for his handkerchief with one hand and turning the ignition with the other.

Madeleine studied the hollows under his eyes. "Good."

They drove through rolling farmland, finally arriving at medieval Nevers. Parking near the cathedral in the town center, they wandered about, unable to find the Convent of Saint-Gildard.

Madeleine frowned. "It's not clear in the guidebook where it is, but I had thought there would be signs. It should be famous."

"Not to everyone, my love." Jack scanned the entry on Nevers.

"But this is where Bernadette Soubirous spent her last years, *where she died.*" Madeleine could see her, in a chair by the fire, her feet propped on a stool. She recalled the description vividly: *Bernadette Soubirous died in the cold spring of 1879, in gasping pain, tuberculosis tumors racking her body.*

They paused at the entrance to a park, and Elena asked an elderly man for directions. "It's on the opposite side of the square," she reported.

They walked along a straight gravel path between wide lawns and leafy sycamores, passing suited ladies leading dogs and pushing prams. On the far side of the park, across the street, stood the Saint-Gildard Convent, a simple two-story building. A small sign announced that Bernadette's shrine was in the chapel in the back.

They found her body in a side bay off the southern transept. It was, indeed, unspoiled by time. Her face and hands were glazed with wax to prevent darkening by the air.

Madeleine and Elena moved closer to the figure behind the glass. Jack stood back, rubbing his chest. Bernadette looked like a child, Madeleine thought, so small, and so at peace, her hands folded, her head turned a bit toward the living who gazed at her, pilgrims seeking her secret, her joy.

Outside, they paused before a replica of the Lourdes grotto. Ivy climbed the sides of the cave and flowers in pots rested beneath the sculpture of Mary. A scrawny tabby slept at the Virgin's feet in the weak sunlight.

Jack squatted, beckoning with his finger. "Here, kitty, kitty." The cat stood, stretched, and allowed him to pet her. "You're so skinny. I wish I could take you home and fatten you up."

Madeleine watched, absorbing her husband's pleasure.

He stood and studied the grotto. "This Mary is smaller than the Lourdes Mary."

Madeleine gazed at the peaceful, hopeful image of the Mother of God. "It's a reminder, a revisiting."

Jack glanced back at the chapel. "Was that body for real?"

"It really *is* Bernadette's body, if that's what you mean." Madeleine shook her head as they headed for the gift shop, amazed once again at the power of miracles. "She died in 1879, and they exhumed it three times. The body's preservation led to her beatification."

Jack rubbed his chin. "And that's why she's a saint? It seems to me it should be her life, not her death, that makes her a saint."

Madeleine recognized the Calvinist tenet. A person is known to be a member of the elect, the saved, by one's works. "The Catholic view is that a saint is one who loves God totally, gives himself or herself to God completely. Of course this would mean he or she would obey God's commands. And the incorruption of the flesh is simply another reflection of this love. As are miracles performed by the saint, before or after death."

"I think it's a sign from God," Elena said.

Jack turned toward her. "How so?"

"It's a reminder that God exists, and that he loves us. It's truly a public miracle that we all can witness."

Madeleine looked back at the chapel. "He's loving us through matter."

"It reminds me of the dark time before my surgery."

Jack looked thoughtful. "We were in Rome, finishing up Madeleine's pilgrimage."

Elena turned to Madeleine. "You let me borrow your altar cloth."

It was two years ago last spring, Madeleine thought, but it seemed much longer. "The cloth with the spilled consecrated wine, the Blood of Christ." Had she really carried that linen cloth through Italy, the cloth of Father Rinaldi's last mass at Saint Thomas'? She had prayed before so many ancient shrines, asking to be healed of those terrible nightmares. The demon dreams had been so real, so powerful: her drowned baby girl took phantom shapes and disappeared. She shivered. But the pilgrimage *had* healed her. No—if she was honest—it was Christ who healed her, once she asked. The pilgrimage encouraged the asking.

Elena's eyes were large, as though seeing beyond, to a far country. "The linen helped me, Madeleine. Christ was there in a mysterious way."

Jack looked back toward the chapel. "Perhaps," he whispered, "God *does* work through the body, through material things. I only wish I could believe that. Another tall order."

He opened the gift shop door. "Let's see if the nuns have a book in English on Bernadette. Would you like some postcards, Elena, for your friends in Rome?"

They lunched near the park at a small café. They lathered croutons with garlic mayonnaise and dunked them in bouillabaisse; they savored warm goat cheese on greens and spread chunky pâté on baguette slices. Pleasurably weary, they drove home through the Bourbonnais countryside and through medieval Moulins. The N7 led to the Roman textile town of Roanne, crossed the Loire, and wound through rolling hills toward Tarrare. As they rounded a bend, a rainbow appeared. The pastel streaks of promise curved from the heavens into the earth.

Tomorrow, Madeleine thought, they would be in Paris. But first they would meet Pierre's train in Lyon. Surely he would lead them to the doctor.

Chapter Nineteen
Les Crayères, Reims

If we love one another, God dwelleth in us.
1 John 4:12

Rachelle rubbed her hands as she looked through the wide window of the train. Heading north to Reims, they sped past villages and vineyards: they must be in Burgundy. The grapes would be in by now, so what was next for these vintners? She had heard of the *Nouveau Beaujolais*, the popular festival of the first pressings. The image of celebrating the harvest, the work of one's hands, attracted her in its simplicity. If only she could embrace that simplicity, abandon the complications of her own world. But not yet. First she must face her ghosts. She picked at a finger where the rash had scaled the skin and looked at her palms as though she were a psychic. The scales were turning into angry eczema patches. She found her cortisone cream and massaged it in.

Her ghosts had led her to Augustin, and she was grateful. It was Saturday, September 25, and she had been traveling nearly two weeks. Was that why a gray fatigue seemed to wrap about her? She had dozed on the train, and had awakened with a start again and again. The strange dull distance from things, the separation, had lessened, and she was beginning to feel again. It was tears, she thought, that had melted the ice about her center: her own tears, her aunt's tears, her uncle's tears.

As the train rolled into Dijon, Rachelle reread Augustin's slip of paper: *Anne-Marie DuPres, Les Crayères, Reims.* Before visiting, she would check the names on the memorial plaque in the basilica. Perhaps Robert's name was written on a dark chapel wall. Would that give her what she wanted? What *did* she want?

Now, as the train neared Reims, Rachelle gazed upon fields open to the broad sky. Forests of pine and alder grew so innocently in this northern landscape, this land of war. Here, boys had shivered in muddy trenches as they waited for hissing mortars to find their targets, smelling the inevitable stench of the living and the dead. Machine guns fired staccato bullets, as the wounded screamed and friends panicked. Did Robert lie in this mud, like so many others?

The train came to a slow halt. Rachelle reached for her bags, stepped off the train, and found her way through the station to the taxi queue.

"Saint-Remi, s'il vous plaît, le basilique," she said to the driver.

The radio blared an American tune as the taxi accelerated through a green park and passed a graceful town square. They continued up a broad boulevard, the driver whistling and tapping his palms on the wheel, and Rachelle's heart lightened.

She entered the ancient Basilica of Saint-Remi as bells rang five and set her bags in a shadowy corner by the side door. An immense brass chandelier—a giant wheel with candles in holders—hung in the center of a vast nave. A few tourists stepped beneath the soaring arches, as the sun chose privileged spots to enshrine: a folding chair and half its neighbor, a sculpted angel's face on a stone column, a pane of jewel-toned glass.

Rachelle walked slowly up a side aisle and paused to read a history panel. Saint Remi, a fifth-century bishop, baptized Clovis, a young Frankish warrior-king, and his army of three thousand men. One of those early church-state liaisons, she supposed, the beginning of centuries of mutual power-building. The basilica was built over the bishop's relics, bodily fragments—surely no more than dry bones—that, they claimed, healed the living.

She sat in a caned chair, one of hundreds filling the nearly empty nave, and focused on the giant wheel of candles above. In the silence she could feel her heart beat; she waited, waited for something, something she couldn't identify, as though there were answers here she could not access. Other seekers, like her, rested in their flight through life, some kneeling, some sitting, some gliding through the vast space. How quickly we move through time, she thought, scarcely touching one another in passing, strangers in a common country. She breathed deeply, inhaling the cool musty air. It was good to pause for a moment in this peaceful place with no demands to choose. Demands to choose what?

She *did* promise to light a candle, she recalled.

She found the Holy Sacrament Chapel, dropped a coin in an iron box, and lit a small blue votive. Now what? She sat in the back and stared at the red flame on the altar. *If you are there, God, help me. Help me find you. And take care of Alain and Leah, and Robert, Antoine, and François, and comfort Clarice and Augustin. And I pray for Dad Kennedy's soul and Mom in the rest home, those who loved me all those years, those who raised me.*

Rachelle returned to the side aisles, to search for war memorials. Bells clanged their discordant tones in the distance, and a few deep notes sounded from an organ, grunting fits and starts from an upper gallery. She found Saint Remi's tomb behind the high altar. As she glanced down the nave, she saw people streaming through the entrance doors. A service was beginning! The organ thundered an introit and she stepped quickly into the side aisle. She retrieved her bags and slipped outside. She paused in the fading light to collect herself.

Her slip of paper said *Les Crayères*. Asking directions in a *charcuterie* up the street, she learned that *Les Crayères* was a restaurant, a restaurant in a chateau, and not far away.

A young porter showed Rachelle to a room that overlooked the back garden. He wished her a pleasant stay, excused himself, and closed the door quietly. She crossed the room to French doors and pulled down hard on a thick cord. Heavy red-and-cream floral draperies, swooping from the ceiling to the floor, parted slowly. She opened the doors and peered over a balcony. Formal beds of yellow and purple pansies bordered an expansive lawn and gravel paths disappeared under lofty shade trees. In the gathering dusk, a three-quarter moon climbed above the basilica spires in the distance.

Antiques had not been a passion of hers—they seemed a frivolous waste of time and money—but here, in this old chateau, she ran her rough palms over the smooth chair legs with their carved lion-feet and admired a gilt-framed mirror. Ornate candlesticks perched on the mantel of a closed-in fireplace. Oil paintings hung on the silk-covered walls. She thought one must be Venice. Another seemed to be the Riviera, another an Alpine lake.

She picked up the phone on the desk and dialed. "Becca?"

"Shelley, it's so good to hear from you. Where are you?"

"Reims. You can't guess where I'm staying. I'm a guest in a chateau, Les Crayères. It's a long story."

"You're in Reims in a chateau? Did you see Aunt Clarice?"

"I did and learned a great deal about our family...she loved the wine." How could she describe their aunt? *Frail. Clever. Religious.* "You would like her. And Becca, I found our Alain's twin."

"Gilbert? Really?"

"He's a monk on Saint Honorat, one of the Lèrins Islands."

"That's amazing. Did you visit?"

"I spent last night in their retreat house. He was so happy to see me." Rachelle recalled his tears, his love. "You should visit them, Becca. It would mean so much to them both. They are very dear. But they may not have much more time."

"I'll try to go soon, when things settle down here. Rachelle, Pierre wants to talk to you. But he's gone out. So tell me about this chateau."

"This place is from another world. I wish you could see it. It has a gourmet restaurant downstairs, and I have a reservation."

"That's nice."

Rachelle could hear her sister's disapproval.

"Do you realize," Rebecca said, "what those restaurants cost? You could feed a family for a week. And the food is terribly high fat." There was a pause, then, "I'm sorry. You *are* a guest, enjoy the experience. Why are you there? Whose guest are you, anyway?"

"We have a cousin here—she manages the chateau. Her name is Anne-Marie DuPres, the daughter of Robert, Alain's brother."

"Robert, the one in Reims. Of course. He had a daughter?"

"I'm hoping she knows where her father is buried and his story. What does Pierre want? Is he worried about those Americans again?"

"They showed up here. I told them you went to Paris. It was difficult. You know I hate to lie. But now Pierre is joining them tomorrow in Lyons. He thinks he'll keep them off your trail, that somehow it's his job to protect you. And he likes the young lady in the party, though he won't admit it. In fact, that could be the real reason for all of this."

"Tell him I appreciate his efforts. I can't deal with these people now, maybe never. Let them find another doctor."

"Pierre says not to go to Paris since they're heading that way."

"I don't know why I would, except to see his school."

"I need to go. Keep in touch, okay? Call. I love you."

"I love you, too."

Rachelle pulled her rumpled black dress from her bag. She called housekeeping. What was French for *iron?*

"Come this way," Anne-Marie DuPres beckoned Rachelle.

Her cousin was close to Rachelle's five-feet-four. Her straight, strawberry blonde hair fell neatly over a tailored black suit that clung to her curvaceous body. She was both friendly and businesslike, and seemed curious about her new cousin.

Anne-Marie had to be close to Rachelle's age, but she looked no older than forty-something. Her lids may have been lifted and her laugh lines filled, Rachelle thought. And then there was makeup.

They sat at a table in the corner of the formal dining room. Soft light fell from gold-fringed lamps and green satin draped from oak-paneled walls. A bay window, framed by ivory Roman shades cascading in frilly tiers, looked out to the garden, now cast in early evening shadow. Guests spoke in subdued tones as they waited reverently for the next course to be placed soundlessly before them.

Her cousin whispered to a waiter; another young man unfolded linen napkins and spread them carefully on their laps. A third poured champagne, his white-gloved thumb placed deftly in the hollow of the bottle's base.

Her hostess sipped, her long pink-polished nails wrapped about the flute's stem. She held her glass up to the soft light to watch the bubbles ascend, then turned toward Rachelle.

"So, you are one of the Leah-babies. Augustin spoke of you."

"Yes—Rebecca and I. Do you know Augustin well?" Rachelle took a bite of smoked salmon pooled in cream and caviar. It melted on her tongue.

"No, but he has been my guardian angel. My father did not get along with his family, and they cut my mother out of the will. But Augustin has made up for it over the years. He thinks I do not know this, but I do. I would not be here if it wasn't for him."

"This is a beautiful restaurant...chateau...dining..."

Anne-Marie laughed, showing perfect teeth. "It is all of those, and I do enjoy working here. Now, tell me, you search for my father's grave? Your uncle's grave? Why, may I ask?"

Rachelle looked into Anne-Marie's dark eyes, the lids shadowed in a smoky gray, the thick lashes long and curled. She was suddenly aware of her own wayward hair, her own scrubbed face. "I don't know, exactly. I

160

experienced a great failure in my work at the hospital."

"You are a nurse?"

"A doctor, a surgeon."

"A doctor, yes, of course. You said you knew a great failure?"

"I came to Reims to find my uncle, your father. Do you remember him?"

Anne-Marie shook her head sadly. "I was born after his death. I know only stories of him. But I know where he died. I visit often."

Early Sunday morning the two women walked through amber leaves to a Tudor-style castle with crenellated towers and faux half-timber siding. *Pommery–Greno* was forged in script over imposing iron gates. Anne-Marie opened a side door with a large steel key and led Rachelle down a long hall to an arched entry. A wide staircase descended to the caves.

"One hundred and sixteen steps and eleven miles of caves dating to the Romans." Anne-Marie's words echoed in the tunnel of stairs. "One hundred and twenty chalk pits—*les crayères*—were joined. The chalk came from calcified shellfish left behind when the seas receded thousands of years ago."

Rachelle slipped her jacket over her shoulders, impressed with her cousin's knowledge. "Is the temperature natural?"

"Yes, around ten degrees Celsius, fifty degrees Fahrenheit, perfect for champagne."

They descended, stepping slowly past wall lanterns casting pools of light in the dark.

"These caves have seen so much," Anne-Marie said as they reached the bottom and turned down a corridor. Small bays opened on either side, stacked with black bottles caked with dust. "The early Gallo-Romans excavated the chalk to build their houses, and later, third-century Christians hid here with their bishop, worshiping in secret when their faith was illegal."

"I had no idea."

Their speech echoed in the damp halls, as their shoes tapped the cavern floor.

"Local history is an interest of mine. I give private tours occasionally to special guests at the chateau. Augustin paid for schooling in Paris where I learned English."

"I suppose Christians were persecuted, much as the Jews were persecuted."

Anne-Marie paused and turned. "They were, and Christians, as well as Jews, continue to be persecuted in many parts of the world. Stalin's purges sent twenty million, many of them Christians, to the gulag camps in Siberia."

"How awful." Rachelle was suddenly aware of major gaps in her education. Had she ever taken a history course? She must have had Western Civ in college. Could she recall any of it?

Anne-Marie stared up the dark corridor. "In 1662 twenty thousand Christians were massacred in Japan, many crucified. In 1900 in China, the Boxer Rebellion killed over thirty thousand Chinese Christians. All such massacres are true crimes against freedom, freedom of belief. You are half-Jewish, are you not? So you understand."

"My mother was Jewish." How strange the words sounded.

"It was terrible during the war. The Jews were loaded on trains and fear was everywhere. My mother hid many in her family's cellar and many in these caves. Which brings me to my father, your uncle."

They turned a corner. In a side cavern lit by a single lamp, Rachelle read the words carved into the chalk wall: *Les Morts de la Guerre de la Résistance.* Anne-Marie shined her flashlight onto the name *Robert DuPres, 1923-1942.* He was only nineteen, Rachelle thought sadly.

Anne-Marie touched Rachelle's shoulder. "They fought bravely, these boys. Thank God, there were few here at the time. But their hiding place was discovered, and my father shot. I was born six months later, in late 1942."

"The same year we were born." Rachelle traced the name slowly with her finger. Here was the last of her uncles, and just as brave as her father, Alain. She swallowed hard, as she struggled to control her tears—such loss, such grief, such a place to hide and to die, lying in the dark in the cold and the damp, so young. The cumulated loss pounded her. She sat on a stone bench, covered her face in her hands, and sobbed.

Anne-Marie joined Rachelle on the bench and wrapped her arm about her shoulders. "He was a good man. Brave. We should be proud."

Rachelle's trembling eased, and she wiped her cheek with a tissue from her pocket.

"He worked in the cellars," Anne-Marie explained, "and my mother gave tours. They were married as the first Nazis swept into Reims."

Rachelle stared at her cousin, unable to comprehend the times, the terror.

Anne-Marie stood and gazed into the damp dark. "A Jewish family cooked in my grandmother's kitchen in our house in town. My mother was friends with her girls, slightly younger. The Gestapo came. She followed secretly and watched the soldiers shoot the entire family in the cathedral square. An example, the commandant said. My mother—she was only eighteen."

A loud clattering echoed through the cold air.

"The carts," Anne-Marie said, "for transporting bottles and equipment."

"They sound like rattling bones." Rachelle stood and dusted herself off, the sadness still clutching her.

"I am glad I have this place...to visit...and to share, although I do not know where his body is." She turned to Rachelle. "We must remember, cousin, that they are the dead, but we are the living. We go forward with our lives, and then, we meet them in heaven. We must not forget this." The whites of her eyes were luminous in the shadows. "I know I will see my father one day."

"Maybe I will too." Did she believe that? She wanted to.

They returned through the cavernous halls, following the lantern light, and Anne-Marie maneuvered the conversation toward less painful territory. She spoke of grapes, skins, and twice-over fermentation—a process discovered by the monk Dom Perignon in the neighboring village of Épernay. She explained that, today, workers called "riddlers" turned the larger bottles to settle the sediment, but machines turned the rest. Soon the two women arrived at the foot of the stone stairway.

As Rachelle climbed, she wondered if she could be transformed like those grapes, if she could be changed into another creature. She felt her heart pump harder as she pulled herself up. Resting a moment to catch her breath, she turned and gazed back down into the caverns. The lanterns burned bright against the thick, nearly tangible, darkness.

Could lives be transformed like grapes? Did she have enough sugar in her soul to ferment something new? *God only knows,* she thought, *if he even exists.*

Anne-Marie checked her watch. "It is 10:45. I go to Sunday mass at Saint-Remi. Would you like to come?"

"Yes, I'd like that."

They emerged into the light, stepping onto the amber carpet of leaves.

Chapter Twenty
Vézeley

The reason for loving God is God himself
and how he should be loved is to love him without limit.
Bernard of Clairvaux

On Sunday morning, Madeleine, Jack, and Elena met Pierre's train in Lyons.

"It is a pleasure to see you," Pierre said. "Thank you for inviting me. I hope I can help. I have business in Paris with my school."

"It is good to have you with us," Madeleine replied, grateful for this solid link with the elusive Doctor DuPres.

Elena grinned. "You are welcome."

Pierre blushed. "Have you visited Paris before, Mademoiselle Coronati?"

"I have not."

Pierre bowed his head slightly. "It would be my honor to show you this most beautiful city."

Jack reached for Pierre's backpack. "Welcome, son. Is this all you have?" His face was alight with satisfaction.

"Allow me to carry it. I travel with little."

Madeleine and Elena followed the two men to the car. Jack opened the front passenger door for Madeleine, and Pierre opened a back door for Elena.

"Merci." Elena slipped into the seat behind Madeleine.

"Je vous en prie, you are welcome." Pierre walked to the opposite side and took the seat behind Jack. He touched the leather and looked around. "This is a beautiful car."

"Have you heard from your aunt, Pierre?" Madeleine buckled her seatbelt.

Jack maneuvered toward the A6, following the signs to Paris.

"We have not, Madame." He glanced out the window.

Madeleine pursued her questioning. "Do you know where she might be staying in Paris? With family or friends?"

"I have ideas, Madame. I will make calls." He turned toward Madeleine. "But *je pense, peut-être*, you like to see another Madeleine church, very famous, the Basilica of Vézeley?"

"Perhaps," Madeleine said, suddenly aware of the increasing speed of the car. She glanced at the speedometer. The arrow pointed to 130 kilometers—80 miles per hour—the legal limit, and they were in the slow lane.

Madeleine heard Elena speaking quietly behind her. "Bernard of Clairvaux preached there, didn't he?"

Jack shifted into fifth and pulled into the left lane, the sedan purring smoothly. "Great car," he said. The arrow pointed to 140 kilometers.

"Jack," Madeleine protested. Turning toward Elena, she said, "He did, calling for the Second Crusade." Another Mary Magdalene church? Would this saint of Provence speak to her, guide her?

Jack's eyes darted from the rearview mirror to the sideview mirrors. "I'm just having a bit of fun, Maddie. Pierre, Vézeley sounds good— there's a three-star restaurant nearby—L'Esperance. Maybe we can lunch there."

"D'accord. Parfait." Pierre was quick to agree.

Madeleine pulled out the guidebook and they drove in silence as she scanned the entry on Vézeley, looking for something that might shed light on her life.

Vézeley, named after the fourth-century landowner Vercellus, sits on a hill overlooking the rich farmlands of the River Cure. In 858 Girart de Roussilon and his wife Berthe founded a convent of nuns in the valley where the town of Saint-Père lies today. After Normans destroyed the convent, Benedictine monks established a monastery on the more defensible hilltop.

For many years, Vézeley remained a quiet community. In the tenth century, when Saracens invaded the south, one of the monks traveled to Saint-Maximin to rescue the relics of Mary Magdalene. In 1037, Vézeley's abbot displayed the relics, and many sick were healed. Word spread, the abbey was re-dedicated to Mary Magdalene, and pilgrims crowded the village.

Vézeley became an important stop on the Via Lemovicensis,

one of the pilgrim routes to the shrine of Saint James in Santiago de Compostela, Spain. When the basilica was rebuilt in the twelfth century, a large narthex was added to shelter travelers.

Others had sought shelter in Vézeley. Others had been healed by the bones of Mary Magdalene. Madeleine recalled the story of Mary in the cave at Sainte-Baume and the mountaintop where she heard the angels sing. It would be good to pray before her relics, to ask for her intercession.

On March 31, 1146, the town of about six thousand, including eight hundred monks, witnessed the preaching of the legendary Bernard of Clairvaux. Bernard stood on the northern slope and called for the Second Crusade, addressing a crowd of one hundred thousand, including King Louis VII and Queen Eleanor of Aquitaine, later Queen of England. He called them to save Jerusalem from the Turks, for the Turks were on the march to conquer the West.

The Crusades have been overly maligned, thought Madeleine. Europe had been preserved by the Crusaders marching to Jerusalem, in spite of the bloodshed. Today, who would protect the continent from invasion? Who would stand and fight for the freedom to believe? The birthrate wasn't even replacing Europe's population, let alone increasing it.

And the same could be said for America's "great experiment" in democracy and freedom. The birthrate was below replacement levels there as well. And with America's kind desire for inclusiveness, rightly defining the nation's identity, there was a frightening indifference to terrorists who would deny religious freedom. One way or another, it seemed Western Civilization was imploding, self-destructing. Could freedom ever prevail for long against the force of tyranny? Freedom by definition contained the seeds of its own demise. It seemed a miracle to Madeleine that freedom had prevailed for over two centuries. Freedom had sometimes burned dimly, but it had always been fanned back to life. A true miracle.

Madeleine smiled with the comforting sense of God's presence in history and returned to her text.

During the religious wars of the sixteenth century, Vézeley sided with the Protestants; the town's ramparts with its seven gates and fortified towers were often under siege by Catholic armies. In 1790, the Revolution struck the final blow by closing the basilica, mutilating statues, and selling the furnishings. In 1840 restoration began.

What would historic, holy Vézeley reveal? As Madeleine closed the book, she heard Elena's uncertain speech, breaking the long silence.

"You go to Paris for your school?"

"Oui," Pierre replied. "I hope to start medical school in the spring."

"Like your aunt?" Elena said.

Madeleine turned, interested.

"Oui, I need three more years."

"What kind of medicine do you want to practice?" Madeleine asked.

"For the heart? How do you say?"

"Cardiology."

"Oui."

"Why cardiology?"

"It is the big field, no? It is very important. There is great demand."

Jack nodded. "You could do well, Pierre. I've heard transplants are the future."

"Oui, transplants—a good field."

"You don't want to practice in Crillon-le-Brave?" Elena asked.

"Crillon is too small. And you, Mademoiselle Coronati, do you work? Maybe you are too young...and too beautiful..." He laughed nervously.

Madeleine searched his face for disrespect. He simply looked uncertain, as though speaking to Elena was like speaking to a goddess.

Elena blushed. "I'm an accountant." She seemed unaware of her power.

Madeleine could hear the tension in Elena's speech and remembered how awkward she herself had been as a teen, not knowing what to say, fearing too much or too little, but most of all fearing silence. Small talk had not been part of her growing up; her pastor father and teacher mother debated politics and religion, history and theology, over the dinner table, passing ideas back and forth like tennis balls—or boiled potatoes—and she and her younger brother had listened silently. It wasn't until she left home that she realized her great social handicap; she copied others' lighthearted comments and learned to enter a conversation slowly, talking about weather and sports, books and movies. As a teen, she practiced lines from advice columns, but when actually on a date, found herself tongue-tied. She sensed that, although Elena was nineteen, her social skills were closer to fourteen, or even younger, by today's standards.

Pierre's words could be heard over the hum of the car. "You work for a big accounting company?"

"I work for Coronati House, an orphanage in Rome. It is a long story. Would you like to hear it, Monsieur Morin?" Her tone was fragile as though she were testing herself as well as him.

"I would very much like to hear your story, Mademoiselle."

The speedometer read 145. Madeleine listened to the murmur of their speech in the back seat, but kept her eye on the road.

A horn blared from behind. Headlights flashed, and Jack moved into the right lane. He took his foot off the accelerator. "This guy thinks he's some kind of race driver."

Madeleine groaned and eased her grip on the dashboard. The road signs flashed past and she watched for Beaune: Bourg-en-Bresse, Tournus, Chalon-sur-Saône. "Here, Jack, the turnoff is coming up, where the A6 branches northwest toward Paris."

Pierre leaned forward. "This is correct. A few kilometers on the A6, then turn off at Avallon."

They exited and wound through the Cure Valley. The road followed the river and through the old town of Asquins.

Jack pointed to a giant basilica crowning the hill before them, the medieval village surrounding the church. "There's Vézeley, just like in the postcards."

"You come the best way," Pierre said, "for the view."

The narrow Rue Saint-Etienne climbed through town to the great stone abbey at the summit and Jack parked in the broad square facing the church. Emerging from the car, they paused as Jack coughed a heavy, loose cough. He pulled out his hanky.

"Are you okay, honey?" Madeleine slipped the guidebook into her bag.

"Sure, no problem."

She squinted in the bright noonday light and looked up to the basilica's façade, as she watched Jack from the corner of her eye. "Where's your hat?"

"Don't need it."

Elena focused her camera on the abbey. "I'm too close, but I'll try anyway. Maybe get a picture of the doors."

Pierre pointed to the shortened left steeple. "The Huguenots—the

French Protestants—destroyed the second bell tower."

Madeleine rummaged through her memory. "Didn't they use the apse as a riding school?"

"*Oui.*"

"How horrible." Elena repacked the camera. "They must have hated the Church."

Jack rubbed his chin. "It's a good thing to remember. You can't force people to believe, or in this case, how to believe."

They walked up the basilica steps and into a massive narthex, partially separated from the nave by a wall. In this space, Madeleine recalled, pilgrims once found lodging on their way to Spain. Here Crusaders gathered, heading for Jerusalem. A huge tympanum arched over the nave's entry, its frieze telling the story of Pentecost. Christ descended upon the disciples, his outstretched arms sending spirit-flames upon them.

They followed Pierre into the long nave and found seats toward the front. Noon prayers would soon begin.

Twelve young men and twelve young women, robed in white, entered the chancel and took their places in the choir. Then, into the waiting silence, an ethereally high note soared. They chanted in Latin, singing Psalms of thanksgiving, complaint, and praise, composed long ago by the shepherd boy David. They sang antiphonally, a spiritual dialogue made corporal.

Sun streamed through the chancel's clerestory windows and bathed the choir in a pale light. Pillars supporting limestone arches led solemnly toward the altar. Did the early pilgrims sing the songs of David? Did the Crusaders pray in this dusty space? The chants moved through time, linking her with those earlier travelers, and for that moment, she shared their pilgrim path, transfixed and suspended in the chancel light.

Jack reclined in the pew, holding his restaurant guide in a shaft of sun, studying it with particular interest. He touched Madeleine's shoulder, pointed to a side door, and slipped out quietly. Bells rang one.

"Madame Seymour," Pierre whispered, as the young people processed out, "would you like to see the relics?"

"Mary Magdalene's?" Madeleine whispered.

Elena's eyes grew large. "Are they in the crypt?"

"*Oui, allons-y.*"

They followed him up the south transept to a life-size sculpture of Mary Magdalene.

Pierre pointed to the statue's base, where candles burned. "Some of her relics are here, but come this way."

They descended stairs into the crypt, once the ninth-century church. Directly beneath the high altar, a glass sarcophagus held Mary Magdalene's bones. At the opposite end of the crypt, in the ancient apse, a tabernacle rested on an altar. The red candle burned steadily.

Madeleine knelt before the tabernacle with Elena. A young nun, robed in pale blue, entered and carefully opened the tabernacle door. She removed a glowing monstrance in the shape of a golden cross, the white host in its center, and placed it before the tabernacle.

"Thank you, Lord," Madeleine said, then prayed an *Our Father*, lifting her eyes to the host. *Do not speak*, he said. *Be silent and adore.* Madeleine obeyed, her eyes drawn into Christ, her self pulled into love. Outside, bells clanged, vibrating through the buried stone, a sound of earth tempered with heaven. At moments such as this, Madeleine felt so sure, so suffused, so complete. She had been touched by the holy. All would be well.

Madeleine turned to Elena, kneeling beside her. "Where's Pierre?" she whispered.

"He went to find Jack."

They made their way up the stone stairs, into the great abbey, and down the long aisle. They passed under the soaring vaults and into the huge narthex that opened onto the square. Jack was deep in conversation with Pierre, the elder leaning toward the younger, the younger listening with rapt atention.

Jack smiled when he saw them. "I have great news! L'Espérance can take us at 2:30 for lunch. We're in for a treat."

"It sounds wonderful," Madeleine said. "And that gives us time for one more stop." She led them down a narrow gravel path. "La Cordelle," she said as Elena caught up with her, "is this way, I believe."

"La Cordelle?" Elena was close behind.

Madeleine led them through the Porte Croix in the medieval wall and continued down the hill to a rustic chapel. Beyond the chapel, on the edge of a promontory, a rough-hewn wooden cross, anchored by a large boulder, towered over the countryside.

"Saint Bernard preached the Second Crusade here." Madeleine walked to the edge, and, standing under the arm of the cross, gazed at the valley below. "The crowds were too large for the basilica, so he preached from this mountainside, much as Christ did, I suppose."

Jack joined her near the foot of the cross. "As I recall, the Crusades were bloody rampages."

170

"They were and they weren't." Madeleine imagined the times as she raised her hand against the bright sun. "Many Crusaders sought commercial gain, some sought expiation, some sought adventure and honor. But many, if not all, wanted to save Jerusalem, their Christian Mecca, from the infidels. And the Church in Italy feared the Muslims marching west. Even peaceful Saint Francis crusaded to Egypt and tried to convert Saladin. It's a miracle Francis came home alive."

"Sister Agnes," Elena said, "claimed that more Christians were slaughtered than Muslims. And those who survived returned defeated."

"An army crossing land hurts it," Pierre added quickly, as though eager to be included in Elena's circle. "They stole and killed. They were not ready to travel so far."

Jack ran his hands over the rough wood of the cross. "I like this cross. It's simple and direct, better than that huge basilica." He glanced at his watch. "We need to move along."

Inside the small chapel, a jug of dried poppies sat on a dusty floor before a slab altar. Light filtered through a dirty window.

Madeleine handed Elena a leaflet she found on a table at the entrance. "Could you translate?"

Elena studied the text. "This chapel was built to remember Saint Bernard. Then, in 1217, two Franciscans, Brother Pacifique and Brother Louis, settled here. They were allowed to use the chapel and a hermitage next door. They built a monastery in 1232. Saint Louis came here four times."

Pierre stood behind Elena's shoulder. "King Louis IX. A holy king. He built Sainte-Chapelle in Paris, *vous savez.*"

"The stained glass chapel," Madeleine said, "to enshrine the crown of thorns. The one near Notre-Dame on the Île de la Cité?"

"Oui." Pierre stared at the leaflet, his head close to Elena's.

"Oh, my," Elena said, skimming the rest of the text, "this little chapel survived the Hundred Years War, the Reformation wars, and the Revolution of 1789."

"So what about the name?" Jack asked, moving toward the door.

Madeleine followed. "It was called Sainte-Croix after Bernard's cross, but has become popularly known as La Cordelle, for the corded belt the Franciscans wear."

Elena ran her finger down the page. "The Franciscans returned in 1949. But I guess they're not here now."

"What order *is* here?" Madeleine would not forget the singing in the great abbey, the crypt with Mary Magdalene's relics, and the host in the monstrance.

"The Brothers and Sisters of Jerusalem," Elena said.

"I've heard of them." Madeleine searched her memory. "They're new—a young Benedictine group."

Jack paused at the door and turned. "We must continue this exciting discussion over lunch. It's two o'clock, and I'm not giving up this chance with L'Espérance." He ushered them into the bright light.

They sat on a broad wooden veranda, shaded by leafy sycamores, that wrapped around the farmhouse-restaurant. As they sipped champagne, a jacketed waiter brought them menus.

"They were so young," Madeleine said.

"Who were young?" Jack's eyes roamed the tables, studying the guests.

"The Brothers and Sisters of Jerusalem, the monks and nuns singing today."

"You're still on the Brothers and Sisters."

Elena leaned forward. "Madeleine, according to their pamphlet, they're in Paris too, at the church of Saint-Gervais."

"Saint-Gervais? Maybe we can visit. Their singing is wonderful. And Jack, the monstrance in the crypt glowed like liquid gold. It filled my heart." *God gave me patience, a patient certainty. If I could only hold on to it.*

Jack tapped her unopened menu. "You had better fill your head with lunch choices, my dear."

"What do you suggest, Monsieur Seymour?" Pierre asked.

"Every dish should be excellent. It's a miracle we got in."

Pierre consulted with Elena, and she pointed to several possibilities.

"Please—call me Pierre," Madeleine heard him say quietly, and glanced up.

"*Bien sûr,* Pierre," Elena said, her eyes unguarded, "and call me Elena."

Madeleine returned to the menu, trying to concentrate. "I'll have what you have, Jack," she finally announced, as the abbey, the menu, and now Elena, competed for her attention.

The young people ordered the lamb; Madeleine and Jack tried the turbot in bone marrow sauce. "A specialty," Jack said. He turned to the sommelier and pointed to a bottle of red burgundy on the wine list.

Pierre smiled, raising his dark brows. "My brother Alphonse speaks of this way of cooking. He *marries* fish and meat juice. It is strange, no?"

Jack raised his glass. "Your brother sounds like a very bright young man, Pierre. Once we find the doctor, we must find Alphonse."

"*D'accord*, but allow me to repay you for this wonderful hospitality. I will take you to a nearby chateau tonight. It is a hotel, run by a girl I know. It is my thanks to you."

Madeleine shook her head. "We have reservations in Paris." How she hated to push, wheedle, whine. She was swimming against a swift current, lost in eddies, pulled back to her starting point. But progress, after all, *was* being made, she told herself. *Patience.*

"One more night won't hurt," Jack said, raising his glass. "I'll call the hotel. They'll understand. We might like Pierre's chateau, after all."

Pierre's face lit up with satisfaction. "Felice Dubois runs *Le Château de Cure*. Ten minutes from here. She buys our Crillon wine. She has—how you say—*peacocks*, and chickens, and horses."

"Felice—" Elena said nervously.

"She was once engaged to Alphonse, but no more. She was too wild for him."

"Too wild?" Elena blushed.

Madeleine scrutinized Pierre. Who was this young man, after all?

He turned to Elena. "She has family, a little girl. You will like Felice."

Their courses arrived silently, sliding onto the floral linens, as the light chatter of other diners mingled with the clink of silver and porcelain. The sun had burned through the haze, warming the air.

Madeleine savored the delicate sauces laced with butter, inhaled rosemary and thyme, and tasted hints of lavender and lemon. The oxtail *au jus* swirled around opaque filets of turbot. Such flavors and textures astonished her, as though they fused the material with the spiritual. Man had recreated creation with foods that nourished not only the body, but the heart and soul as well.

As she sipped the red burgundy, she accepted the chatter of Elena and Pierre as a good thing. She would trust God and allow their growing friendship to water her parched heart. She saw how the young man worried over her, searching, in conversation, for secure roads to travel. She watched as he then found common experience to share with Jack, and she smiled as Jack laughed heartily at something Pierre said. She could see how Jack missed his sons, grown now and nearing middle age, with families of their own. With that thought, she wondered how Justin was doing with his Lisa Jane; it had been only six days since his e-mail, but it seemed much longer.

How good God was to grant such grace that he gave each of them what they needed. Jack, though, was drinking and it was only lunchtime, but she was grateful he would not be driving the four hours to Paris that night. She said a double prayer of thanksgiving and intercession, and in her mind returned to the soaring songs in the marble vaults, the bright host in the dark crypt, the hefty wooden cross in the blue sky, and the dusty chapel of the first Franciscans.

For the moment, God held her in his palm.

Felice's sixteenth-century chateau occupied a large parcel of land, at least several acres, Madeleine guessed. The young woman lived with her aging parents and her little girl, and kept the family home intact by letting out rooms to tourists. After mingling with other guests in the Great Hall before dinner, they sat at a common table before the former kitchen hearth. Thick logs blazed, shooting flames up a blackened chimney.

Madeleine could see that Elena had taken extra time with her appearance. She had plaited her hair into a French braid and applied a little lipstick; her green silk blouse set off her smooth olive skin. But Madeleine winced at Elena's expression as she observed Felice. Elena's eyes held envy, distrust, and a hesitant fear that she could not be nearly as attractive as her hostess.

There were ten diners that evening: an American couple, loud and brash, at the far end; a German family of four in the middle, who, by speaking in their native tongue, created their own world. Felice presided from Madeleine's end of the table, keeping an eye on her guests. In her husky English, she spoke with animation to Pierre and the rest of the Seymour party. Her brows rose and fell and she angled her face to create different effects.

Felice's yellow tee fell low, revealing full breasts and freckled skin. Her orange highlighted hair was cut short, tapered in layers toward her face, giving her the look of a cat peeking out through dry grass. As she leaned forward, Pierre's eyes roved to her cleavage, then escaped upwards. Felice smiled as though she had won a small victory.

"Little Charlotte's father is in Brussels," Felice explained. "He works in the diamond business. We are no longer...together."

Madeleine wanted to change the subject, move away from Felice, put Elena at ease. "Are the gardens here extensive, Madame?"

Felice turned to Madeleine. *"Oui.* There are walking trails and horses and peacocks and a stocked river for fishing. One hundred acres!" She raised her brows for emphasis. "It used to be much larger. But we manage." Her eyes roved to the back room where pots and pans rattled. "Mama cooks. Bernice who serves us is Mama's sister. Papa cares for the garden and the animals. You like the *lapin?"*

"It's very good," Madeleine said. "I haven't had rabbit stew in ages. I'd forgotten how sweet it can be, especially with the carrots."

Jack raised his glass. "And you have a nice fruity house Burgundy. Ready to drink."

"Merci. I do the wine buying." She grinned at Jack.

Elena's face relaxed and she spoke quietly to Pierre. He laughed in apparent agreement. A slow flush rose in her cheeks.

"I am glad everything is good," said Felice, raising her glass to the assembled guests. "A toast, Mesdames and Messieurs, to old friends and new." She winked at Pierre, then at Jack.

Chapter Twenty-one
Saint-Remi, Reims

God is love.
1 John 4:16

From the narthex, Rachelle could see the mass had not yet begun. A large crowd settled restlessly in their woven seats, rustling papers and whispering prayers as they knelt on wooden slats hanging from the chair backs in front of them. Babies whined, mothers shushed, and fathers lifted toddlers over their shoulders, rocking them gently. Rachelle smelled incense and jasmine and damp stone.

She followed her cousin to the second pew. Anne-Marie handed her a missal, turned to the correct page, then pointed to a bulletin that listed the lessons and responses for that Sunday. Rachelle studied the French, and, admitting defeat, decided to imitate her cousin's movements.

The crowd quieted as the organ opened with a lilting prelude. Rachelle watched, waiting. The altar, covered in white linen, held six thick flaming candles on either side of the tabernacle and, behind the altar, Rachelle recalled, Saint Remi's relics lay in their jeweled tomb. Light streamed through high clerestory windows into the chancel.

The mass began. A priest chanted the opening prayers and a choir sang from a gallery. The congregation responded, their chorus weaving through the vaults. Rachelle listened to the French phrases and watched the people sing, as the language took on a life of its own. *The Word was made flesh*...maybe in some way these words were paths linking man to God.

A young woman approached the lectern on the right and began the first *lecture*, the Scripture reading. Other *lectures* followed, each read by a member of the congregation, each person adding words to this communal celebration. Four women, their eyes shining, passed the collection baskets, smiling cautiously as though they carried secret joys.

They walked up the aisle and handed the gifts to the priest who turned and raised them up to God.

The celebrant began the *Canon of the Mass*, a phrase Rachelle recalled from long ago, the most sacred part of the service. Vested in a green cape embroidered with gold, the priest raised the host and the chalice, as bells jangled wildly in the tower.

She tried to open her heart and mind, and to her surprise, found herself singing the *Our Father*, her heavy English weighing down the lilting French, her red palms open and outstretched, like the others. Could some form of the Eternal be present here? Falling into childhood habits, she made the Sign of the Cross and found comfort in the familiar motion, thinking fondly of Father Benedict.

As Anne-Marie joined the line to receive the host, Rachelle gazed upon the altar, its surface flat like an operating table. *Dear God, help me.* She thought of Augustin and his calling her the New Israel. She looked up at the golden crucifix, the son of God sacrificed, another death, and for those who believed, one that paid the price for their sins, their many mistakes.

Anne-Marie returned, her face alight with some interior happiness, her golden hair swinging.

The communicants bowed their heads solemnly, their hands folded as they stepped forward. The priest, standing near Rachelle, held the cup of hosts with his left hand and pulled individual ones out with his right, placing each holy wafer on one person's palm and into another's mouth, saying *Le Corps du Christ, Le Corps du Christ, Le Corps du Christ.* One after another reached the head of the line, and the priest repeated the words, again and again. Rachelle looked behind her and saw another priest distributing hosts halfway down the center aisle.

The line moved on, young people in jeans and tee shirts, middle-aged women in shawls and scarves, old men in tight vests and scuffed leather shoes. A woman pushed a stroller, opening her mouth to receive the host on her tongue. A bearded man with a worn baseball cap and red nylon trousers, his too-big army jacket soiled, took his place too, received his God, and shuffled out the side door. A boy with Down syndrome returned to his seat, his head tilted to the side, his arms swinging, his large eyes peaceful. It was a melting pot of humanity, different outsides next to similar insides, humanity traveling...home, it would seem.

The organ trilled and the choir sang.

Rachelle looked beyond the celebrant to Saint Remi's tomb lit by the streaming light, then back to the tabernacle on the altar as the priest returned, his job done. He turned the fringed key that opened the small door and placed the remainder of the hosts inside, closed the door, and turned the key. *Open your heart*, her sister had said.

Suddenly Rachelle sensed a rushing love, a love emanating from...was it the altar tabernacle? A man had died on her hospital altar, but she was *lost* in that death, not saved. A man had died on this altar too, but out of love, not negligence. This was an offered sacrifice, a willing sacrifice, a loving sacrifice in its truest sense. Love settled upon her like a cloud of roses, sweet smelling, caressing, desiring, holding. If only she could keep it, stay here under its protection. It was the first peace she had known since Sam Steinhoff's death.

Rachelle chanted with the others, following the French on her yellow sheet. *"Tu nous donne ton pain, tu nous donne ta vie, Seigneur tout vient de ta main, et nous chantons: merci..."*

The crowd poured through the basilica doors and onto the courtyard. Rachelle followed Anne-Marie to a café on the Place Drouet d'Erlon in the center of town and found an outside table. A rotund waiter, looking too busy to take their order, agreed to note two *chèvre chaude* salads and a large bottle of sparkling water. *"Pas de vin?"* he asked. "No wine?" He frowned in disapproval and moved to the next table, flipping his pad to a new sheet and mumbling under his breath.

"It's crowded out here, but I like to watch the people," Anne-Marie said.

"It's like a movie set. The square is so perfect." Neat townhouses lined the plaza. Cafes and shops occupied the ground floors; bistros with bright awnings opened onto broad sidewalks. A fountain played and a carousel circled. Students ambled toward the park at the far end, and tourists sat at tables, watching with slant-eyed sophistication, their cigarettes dangling, Sunday Reims stroll past. It was a scene from fifties' Paris.

Their salads arrived: toasts layered with baked goat cheese nestling in beds of rocket, radicchio, and endive.

Rachelle inhaled the pungent aroma. She had never tasted warm *chèvre* before. "It was an amazing service, a beautiful church."

Anne-Marie considered Rachelle curiously. "It *is* amazing, and

178

beautiful."

"May I ask you a personal question?" Rachelle's own boldness astonished her, but she wanted to know. She would be direct.

"Of course, cousin." Anne-Marie smiled, and Rachelle sensed an openness.

"Do you believe God is really there?"

"Really where?"

"In the host?"

"Do you?" Anne-Marie tossed the question back, but Rachelle knew she wasn't teasing, wasn't treating it lightly; her expression was thoughtful, serious.

Rachelle tried to be honest. "I don't know."

"Do you want to believe?"

Rachelle winced. Did she? She paused before answering, spearing a bit of lettuce. "I guess I don't know the answer to that either."

"Something is troubling you, my cousin. Do you want to tell me? Sometimes it helps to share."

Rachelle gazed into her kind eyes. "I told you I'm a surgeon?"

"Oui."

"I...had a tragic accident...during a surgery. As a matter of fact, it was exactly two months ago, July twenty-sixth." She stared at her salad, then her empty fork. "It's difficult to talk about..."

"You don't have to."

"No, I want to. I trust you. You see...my patient bled to death. He was a husband and a father. It's been difficult to deal with." Rachelle studied her cousin's face.

Anne-Marie blinked hard, as though absorbing Rachelle's pain, then looked away. "That is terrible. I am so sorry for him...for his family...and for you." She looked back at Rachelle with a calm intensity. "You must feel guilty, no?"

"I do feel guilty. I should not have let it happen. I thought that here, in France, I might...I might find..." Rachelle began to cut her lettuce into long strips.

"You are looking for forgiveness for your deed? If you do not believe in God, you do not need forgiveness." She dabbed the corners of her mouth with her napkin.

"But there are still standards of right and wrong, and this was terribly wrong."

"Accidents are not right and wrong, and you say this was an accident. Did you intend to kill this man?"

"No, but—"

"Then you have false guilt." She sipped her water and refilled their glasses. "Only God can cleanse you, Rachelle, really cleanse you, even of your *false* guilt."

"So you *do* believe God is there? Is that why you go to mass?"

"I do believe God is there. He is in the host as God the Son, and he weaves through his people as God the Spirit. He is in his Church; his Church is his body in our world today. Would you like to know how I learned these things? How I found him?"

"Please. I would."

"I was raised to fear the Church, for my mother married my father in secret, and with my birth, the town gossip was unkind. She considered the Church and the town one and the same. She hated them both."

"Being judged like that must have been awful."

"It was. So I knew little about Christianity. When I was in school in Paris, I walked by a small chapel and saw a crowd going through an open gate. I was curious, so I followed them. The drive led to the Chapel of the Miraculous Medal. A statue of the Blessed Virgin stood against the back wall. The Virgin was so lovely and the chapel so filled with light, that I sat in the back and stared at her, watching the crowd sing the mass. Later I inquired and took a class from the nuns. I learned about forgiveness and found a God of love. I only wished my mother had found him too. She had many to forgive. She grew hard in her hate."

"Forgiveness?"

"Do you see? That is the whole secret to happiness! Forgiveness. We must first see we are sinners and need help. That is hard for many. We must be sorry and ask forgiveness. When God forgives us, we forgive ourselves, and we forgive others."

"But you just said my guilt was a false guilt."

"You may have other guilts that are real, other sins, to use an unpopular word."

"Oh? Like what?" Rachelle shifted in her chair. Who was this woman to accuse her of other sins?

"Pride—belief that every surgery you do will be perfect."

"That's what my sister said, or words to that effect." And so did Augustin. Rachelle breathed deeply, trying to calm her racing heart.

"We need to sort out what is truly wrong and truly right. It is not always clear. The Church helps with that. God helps with that."

"But we must believe in God first," Rachelle said.

"And that first step can be a great leap for many."

"Was it a leap for you?"

Anne-Marie smiled, seeming reassured by the memory of such a happy time; she appeared eager to share her story. "It might have been a leap, but I was so lonely then, and the nuns so loving. I wanted what they had, their community and their hard work, their sacrifices full of meaning, their answers, their joy. Those things I could see, they were real, and they took no leap to understand."

"Then why didn't you join them?"

"Because I soon saw that those things were not the source. I could have all of that and live anywhere, or do any work." She tore a bit of bread off her roll and mopped the last bit of dressing at the bottom of the bowl.

Rachelle leaned forward. "And the source?"

She looked up. "God was the source, *is* the source, *bien sûr*. He was the only reason for their lives, and they would be the first to tell you that. He gave them the answers, the love, the joy." Anne-Marie unclasped a chain around her neck and handed it to Rachelle. "Take this. It is their medallion, Our Lady's medallion. She will help you if you pray to her for faith. Once you make that step, Rachelle, everything else falls into place, and there is no longer any confusion about all of these things."

Rachelle examined the silver oval. A capital M wrapped about a cross. She turned it over. The Virgin Mary stood with her arms spread out, palms open.

"Thank you," Rachelle said. A medallion—wasn't that superstitious? She recalled Clarice's crucifix and supposed such things could be comforting, metaphors for something else, holding joy or pain, containers for one's experience.

"Perhaps you will come to Paris with me?" Anne-Marie asked. "I go Tuesday to order new fabric for the rooms. I will introduce you to the nuns, especially Sister Marguerite, my dear Mother-in-God." Anne-Marie beamed.

Rachelle considered her cousin's words and saw the fire in her eyes when she spoke of her faith. She saw her intense desire to help. She didn't want to leave her newly found cousin, not yet. Anne-Marie was one who had been there, who had experienced God.

"Yes, thank you. It's been many years since I've been to Paris." Pierre and the Seymours wouldn't find her. Paris was big enough. "This morning I sensed something wonderful on the altar."

"*Oui*, that was the love of God," Anne-Marie said. "Yes, the burning love of God."

Chapter Twenty-two
Paris

For I am persuaded,
that neither death, nor life...
nor things present, nor things to come...
shall be able to separate us from the love of God,
which is in Christ Jesus our Lord.
Romans 8: 37

Felice gave Madeleine and Jack the Kings Room, the room kept ready for royal visits. They slept in a deep feather bed with a carved canopy, ensconced behind heavy brocade curtains; when they awoke, chickens squawked and a rooster crowed in the yard outside. A cat scratched at their door and joined them for a breakfast of homemade breads and jams, tea and coffee.

Through their window, Madeleine glimpsed Pierre and Elena walking a path into the parkland. She turned to Jack and studied him. "Honey..."

Jack looked up from his toast. Monday's *Herald Tribune* lay open to the stock page.

"Shouldn't you go lighter on the wine?" she asked, approaching her subject with caution.

His eyes were red, his face puffy. He rubbed his chest. "I suppose. I'll try and be good in Paris. My chest *is* burning up—but being here and enjoying a nice country meal...it's hard, Maddie. Part of me wants to enjoy the last years I have and part of me wants to live longer."

"I know." She reached for his hand. "Jack..."

It was time. Time to tell him about the biopsy. The moment opened before her and she simply needed to seize it. But she hesitated once again, torn between magnifying her husband's despair and the terrible passage of time. Would his despondency grow like cancer itself?

Uncontrollable? Would she blame herself forever?

"Have you looked up your Paris notes yet?" he asked in those brief seconds.

His eyes held hers and she smiled with a twinge of relief, the confrontation postponed, the window closed. "I'll do that. With my last cup of coffee."

She would think more about it. They were *so close* to finding the doctor; it could wait a few more days. Maybe Jack would *never* have to find out.

Madeleine removed *The School of Charity* paperback and her prayer book from the nightstand to make room for her coffee cup. She settled herself on the bed and opened her document on Paris. As it loaded, she gazed at the Underhill book, now occupying the pillow, and considered the words she had read the previous evening: "Human beings are saved by a Love which enters and shares their actual struggle, darkness and bewilderment, their subjection to earthly conditions." She must not, would not, forget this—that God loved her and shared every problem, every suffering. With that thought, her Paris document flashed on the screen. She adjusted her glasses and leaned forward, her finger on the down arrow.

She had visited Paris only once before, on one of Jack's buying trips, but she would never forget it. The historic and romantic city sang a sweet, tender song, calling her. When she thought of Paris, and time with its choices changed her own rhythms over the years, the city's tune had become her own, a melody of memory that clung to her soul as eau de cologne lingered on the fingertip. Paris was a lacy, feminine city with curving wrought iron, leafy sycamores dappling old stone, and poetic monuments at the end of open vistas. Yet under the surface lay centuries of struggle, centuries of searching, centuries of passion for the right way. Today, these ancient rivers still flowed under a sophisticated surface of nihilistic style, and the Church still spoke to her people.

But would Paris speak to *her*? Would her saints guide her through these difficult hours and minutes? Would God open doors that seemed so tightly closed? If Christ lived in the heart of her pain, would, could, he lead her out of it?

Madeleine studied her words with a new ferocity. On this trip, she had become the reader, not the writer, and she waited for the Holy Spirit to move through her words and into her heart and mind, informing her soul...and her conscience.

Holy Manifestations: Saint Denis, Saint Genevieve

The history of Christianity in Paris is interwoven with the history of the French monarchy. With the baptism of Clovis, the first Christian king, on a Christmas Day at the end of the fifth century, Christianity spread through the countryside, uniting tribes devastated by war. From that time, the Church would share the fate of the State.

Indeed, political man could not embrace belief without using it to his advantage. As the State and the Church united, the Church became a tool of the powerful, at times forgetting it was the Body of Christ. Soon, the people of France looked for a kinder route to God, and they welcomed Mary into their hearts.

But long before Clovis and long before Mary, Paris, the City of Light, was born the village of water. Called Lutetia, Celtic for "habitation surrounded by water," its earliest citizens were from the Parisii (boat people) tribe, one of many Celtic tribes in Gaul that followed druidic practice. The Druids—the Celtic priests—decreed religious and civil law. They worshiped nature spirits and practiced human sacrifice to appease the gods and to read omens in victims' entrails.

Madeleine shivered. There had been a renewed interest in the Druids today, as though human sacrifice had never been a part of their rites. Animism. Omens. Witchcraft. If one's power didn't come from God, where did it come from? If the tenets of a faith weren't scriptural, what was their source of authority? What made them true?

In 53 AD, Roman legions settled on the Ile de la Cité and created a Gallo-Roman city, eventually suppressing the Druids and any Celtic resistance. They built a temple to Jupiter and the Emperor on the site of Notre-Dame. They martyred Christians on Mons Lutetius (today Montagne Sainte-Geneviève) in a ten-thousand-seat amphitheater, which remains today.

In the third century AD, the Lyonnais Christians sent Bishop Denis to Paris (renamed after the first tribes). The old bishop and his companions were martyred shortly after, but the episcopal see remained. The young church, at first an illegal gathering of men and women converted by Roman merchants and soldiers, survived persecutions until legalization in 313. The Church grew.

Fifth-century Bishop Germaine of Auxerre, stopping in

Nanterre on his way to preach in Britain, met a young girl who, he foretold, would do great things for God. At age fourteen, Genevieve traveled to Paris where she lived a life of prayer and sacrifice, helping the poor of the city. One day she had a vision of Attila and his Huns heading their way.

Attila marched from the east, crossed the Rhine, burned Metz, continued through Verdun, Laon, Saint-Quentin, Reims, and bridged the Marne. The governors of Paris fled to Bordeaux to ally with the Visigoths. The townspeople fled as well, crowding the streets leading out of the city. But Genevieve told those remaining to trust God, hold their ground, and do works of penance. Attila turned southwest and Paris was spared.

Jack coughed, a deep thick cough. Did Genevieve, Madeleine wondered, have this sense of time caving in? Belief. Trust. Obedience. Adoration. All aspects of a holy life. All aspects of joy.

Next came the conquering Franks, called the Merovingians after their leader, Merowig. Genevieve converted Merowig's descendent, Clovis,[14] who moved the capital from Reims to Paris. Clovis established a rule of law and soon Christianity spread throughout his kingdom, south to Toulouse, east into Germanic lands, and southeast into Italy.

Genevieve died in the early sixth century and was buried alongside Clovis in his church of Saints Peter and Paul. The Parisians renamed the church Sainte-Geneviève-du-Mont and named their beloved Genevieve their patron saint.

Madeleine was amazed at the power of another young girl. It was as though Genevieve could see beyond her own life to a greater life, a greater purpose. Or perhaps because she focused on God, God was able to use her in her unknowing state, in his great plan of redemption. For she converted Clovis, and Clovis converted France. Could—or even should—Madeleine see beyond her own narrow landscape, to God's greater purpose for her as well? Should she simply focus on the moment? At the moment, all she could see was time spinning. Perhaps she didn't need to see, but simply trust. And obey.

"Better get packing," Jack said, stacking the dishes on the tray. "We're meeting Elena in an hour."

There was more on Paris, but Madeleine closed her document.

Tomorrow would be Monday, September 27. Surely, they would end their search in Paris.

The rain poured as they drove through the city's slick streets. Pierre insisted that he be dropped off at his room on the Left Bank. He promised to keep in touch, shouldered his bag, and stepped onto the wet pavement. Madeleine and Elena waved to his retreating figure and their car headed for the Seine, the Right Bank, and the Ritz Hotel.

They turned onto the Place Vendôme, and Madeleine recalled that the Ritz had been founded by the thirteenth child of mountain shepherds. She smiled. *Catherine of Siena, twenty-fifth. Beethoven, ninth.* How many others of large and humble families had done great things?

A gray-green column, forged from Napoleon's melted canon, rose in the middle of the neoclassic square. Chopin lived in this square; Hemingway, Coco Chanel, the Duke and Duchess of Windsor, had all stayed in the Ritz. Princess Diana dined here the evening of her fatal accident.

Elena peered through the foggy window as she retied her red scarf.

Jack pulled up to the entrance, turned off the motor, and waved to several porters. Madeleine reached for her bag as a gloved hand opened the car door.

Sheltered from the rain by a porter's giant umbrella, the women moved toward the portico, leaving Jack with the bellman. They passed plainclothes guards, handguns bulging from their pockets. A liveried attendant spun a revolving door, greeting them with *"Bonsoir Mesdames."* They entered a world of gold, velvet, and silk, and walked past the concierges' gleaming counter and on to *Réception.*

They sat on a satin settee as Jack negotiated with the clerk for the most reasonable rooms. Could there even *be* reasonable rooms, Madeleine wondered. A harpist played in the distance.

"Wow." Elena eyed the dark blue carpet, the gilt moldings, the antiques.

"Beautiful, isn't it? We once stayed here as guests of our Paris broker, and now Joe McGinty, the Board Chairman of Coronati Foundation, insisted on it. Awfully nice of him."

"He's thankful for the fundraising you do for our Coronati House."

Madeleine was appreciative of the elderly millionaire who had taken such an interest in their Rome project. "Jack said staying here would be our special treat. He thinks this will be our last trip." It was bittersweet, she thought, the beauty and the worry at odds with one another. But more bitter than sweet.

"I wonder if Pierre has ever been here."

"He seemed happy to be dropped off at his room. I can hear the harpist. I think I know where she's playing."

They stepped past a sweeping staircase to the shadowy Bar Vendôme. Velvet banquettes lined an oak-paneled wall, and bowls of white roses sat on tables covered with linens striped in red and green. A mahogany bar glimmered before a wall of jewel-toned bottles. Waiters moved briskly from table to table as men in tailored suits, women in black silk and pearls, and girls in skintight jeans and jerseys, sipped afternoon tea and nibbled delicate sandwiches arranged on three-tiered silver trays.

The harpist, a brunette in flowing green taffeta, sat on a stool in the center of the room. She embraced her harp, her head tilted toward the sheet music on a stand to her side; her fingers plucked the strings in rhythmic arcs, releasing the sweet tones into the room. Light chatter wove between the notes, and through the far windows Madeleine glimpsed the garden, where wet leaves brushed against the French doors, inviting one outside, had the day been fair. Instead, the rain fell steadily. Elena breathed deeply, and Madeleine put her arm around her.

Paris–home of saints and sinners, light and darkness, historic hope and modern despair. City of light and surprising–exquisite–beauty.

That afternoon, as Jack studied the stock page, Madeleine reopened her Paris chapter. She had hung her dresses in the antique armoire and stuffed a Louis XV chest with tee shirts. The rain still poured but one could sense the dimming of the light as the afternoon faded to evening. The traffic in the square had receded. Soon she would run a bath, but not yet.

The mystery of Paris was her mystery too. She would learn all she could about where she was, where she and Jack were, at this moment in their lives.

In the later fourth century, Ambrose of Milan claimed that Mary was a type of Church, for when she gave birth to Christ she also gave birth to Christians who became his body. In 431, the Council of Ephesus pronounced Mary the *Theotokos*, the "God-bearer." When Charlemagne, in the late eighth century, built the stunning basilica Aix-la-Chapelle in Aachen, he dedicated the church to the Holy Mother of God. His example inspired others, and "sermons in stone" dedicated to Our Lady rose throughout Europe: Notre-Dame of Amiens, Notre-Dame of Reims, Notre-Dame of Laon, Notre-Dame of Chartres, and Notre-Dame of Paris. The sacred feminine had found glorious expression.

The great Gothic cathedrals of Europe soared through Madeleine's mind like giant sculptures with wings. She longed for that solidity paired with that lightness, surely a fitting reflection of her own body and soul, the earth and heaven that made up her being. And she loved that these churches were dedicated to Mary, a human being touched by the holy, indeed, bearing the holy within her body.

Madeleine was filled with something she couldn't describe—something promising, pulling her.

In 1163, Bishop Sully began Paris's Notre-Dame on the Isle de la Cité, near the royal castle. Stonemasons, carpenters, ironsmiths, sculptors, and glaziers worked on the massive church. They also built the neighboring Hotel-Dieu, a hospital for the poor. Louis IX brought back Christ's crown of thorns from Jerusalem and enshrined it in his palace chapel, the exquisite stained glass Sainte-Chapelle. The king founded more churches, hospitals, and a home for prostitutes, the Filles-Dieu. He established a house for poor students, which evolved into the Sorbonne.

Yes, Madeleine thought. Soaring cathedrals weren't enough. Hospitals and schools must be built alongside, for love was active, not merely artistic and grand.

Late medieval Paris crossed the Seine to the right bank, filling the marshland—the Marais—with luxury townhouses, fashionable squares, and, farther upriver, monasteries. The kings lived in the damp Louvre Palace and governed their Île de France with the aid of the Church. It was an age of faith, a faith taught to an illiterate people through stained glass story and wondrous ritual by a Church at once glorious and corrupt, reformed and power-hungry.

"Down again!" Jack's words exploded into the quiet. He ran his finger along the newspaper's lists of microscopic numbers and symbols.

Madeleine looked up from her screen, a sadness washing over her. She bit her lip and returned to her text.

To be sure, all Europe saw the Church rise and fall, then with more reform, rise again, only to find her on the street once again selling her wares. Ninth-century Cluniacs cleansed the abbeys of superstition and greed. Eleventh-century Cistercians followed ascetic rules; they reclaimed agricultural lands, draining the swamps and clearing the forests. They cultivated the soil and fed starving villages decimated by plague and famine. They invented new technology and developed the scientific method, observing the heavens through telescopes in cathedral towers.

Here again, the action of love—clearing, farming, feeding—breathed life into the Church. Without such life, there could be no love. And the life of giving and sacrifice opened new doors of discovery probably not directly sought. Such discoveries would have come suddenly upon the lone monk who simply looked for a better way to plant and harvest, a means to gage seasons as he studied the night skies with his telescope.

They trusted, thought Madeleine. They obeyed the call of love and God did the rest.

Thirteenth-century Francis and Dominic fought pride and heresy with their new orders. But by the fifteenth-century, a few popes lusted after gold and territory, glory and power, causing an Augustinian monk, Martin Luther, to nail his objections to the chapel door of Wittenberg castle.

Luther's followers denied the power of relics, saints, and sacraments. They claimed man could meet God through faith; works were no longer necessary. They rejected clerical authority and church tradition, ignoring fifteen hundred years of labored thought. The individual could decide matters of truth on his own.

Madeleine sympathized with Luther. It was easy to find fault, major fault, with the Church. But was he too extreme? Or his followers? He set the pendulum swinging, and it would be centuries before things would calm down, before the streets of blood would be washed clean.

The ensuing Religious Wars bloodied the streets of Paris. In the end, the Catholic crown subdued the protesting Huguenots and created an absolute theocracy that invited revolution two hundred years later. By the end of the eighteenth century, the Church hid in fear, as abbesses and nuns, bishops and priests, were guillotined on the Place de la Revolution, today's Place de la Concorde.

On Paris's Right Bank, Napoleon Bonaparte moved into the Tuileries Palace. He sold Church property, but eventually struck a useful peace with the bishops and brought them under state influence. He crowned himself not merely king, but emperor, and returned France to a divine monarchy. Again, revolution pitched France between empire and commune for another sixty years.

In this troubled nineteenth century, the French sought manifestations of the holy to give them hope. The saints became paths to God as they channeled prayers through their common humanity. God worked through the French Church, through the muddled motives of rulers and people. He cleansed and he cured. He was a beacon in the dark, in the City of Light.

Madeleine closed her laptop. The suffering of France moved her: the many wars fought on French soil, the fervent belief, and finally the curious appearances of Mary, a mother who cared for her children. She prayed that Mary would speak to her too, that Christ would use France's holy men and women to turn her own suffering—and Jack's—into good.

Jack was dialing the old-fashioned black phone. He spoke quickly, then hung up. "We have a reservation at Le Grand Vefour tonight. Remember, Maddie? The little jewel box restaurant in the Palais Royale. They had a cancellation."

The exquisite café was a place of past suffering, yet today a place of great beauty and nourishment. Another transformation.

The rain had stopped as Madeleine stepped from the taxi, and she sensed she was in one of those pivotal places of history. She glanced at Elena as they waited for Jack to pay the fare. Elena looked curious as she peered through the iron gate to the formal gardens enclosed by arcades and shops on four sides, once the grounds of an elegant estate.

Madeleine recalled the story of the old palace. Built by Cardinal Richelieu in 1624 and given to Louis XIII, the Palais Royale was home to the queen, Anne of Austria, and her young son, Louis XIV. The English Queen Henrietta Maria lived there as well, having fled to France when Charles I was beheaded. Today shops and cafes occupied the rooms that lined this square of trees and fountains.

Jack held the door open for the women and they entered a small foyer where a young lady took their coats and the maitre d' smiled, his eyes twinkling. *"Bienvenue—*welcome. This way, please."

They followed him into a small ornate room. Burgundy velvet curtains draped the windows. Porcelain wall panels portrayed neoclassic ladies in flowery togas and towering hats with bowls of fruit. Other frivolous fancies of a decadent age looked down from the ceiling. Such erotic flippancy, Madeleine thought, gave patrons escape from the times, from the threat of political intrigue and revolution. Not unlike today.

Madeleine slid into a banquette with Elena; Jack took the chair opposite. The dapper maitre d' presented menus and explained in quiet tones the imaginative cuisine. He folded his fine-boned hands. "I return," he said and pivoted to another table. The expert sommelier hovered close to Jack's elbow, and the two men conferred over the wine list.

Others entered the foyer, kissing cheeks, chatting excitedly, sliding into their banquettes. Gilded mirrors reflected the guests who watched one another, assigning a ranking. The volume increased.

"This is so civilized," Jack said as he looked about the room.

"It certainly is." Madeleine sipped her champagne and turned to Elena. "But it's such a contrast to the café's past; this little restaurant saw the beginnings of the French Revolution."

"This restaurant?" Elena's eyes widened in disbelief.

"Right here, in this square, the Duc d'Orléans, the envious brother of the king, printed pamphlets that enraged the people, encouraging them to revolt. He got more than he asked for."

"And now," Jack said, "the chef is up for another star, they say. It *is* a jewel box with all these reds and greens and mirrors. So, ladies, what do you fancy?"

Madeleine considered the choices. She admired a great chef, just as she admired a Renoir or a Monet. She would appreciate the moment.

They began with an *amuse-bouche*, an appetizer of cod with leeks on a tiny bed of greens, then ravioli pockets of *foie gras* bathed in a creamy truffle sauce. Jack beamed as his *parmentier* arrived: layers of beef, mashed potatoes, and truffles in a rich red wine reduction, a gourmet hash. Madeleine and Elena chose lamb loins infused with chocolate.

Jack ordered more wine. "Just a half bottle to go with dessert."

Madeleine shook her head, and Elena eyed Madeleine.

"Not to worry," Jack said hoarsely, "I'm feeling just fine." He tasted the wine and nodded his approval. "But I *am* worried about my tech stocks. They're dropping fast." He tipped his glass, swirled the ruby liquid, and watched it slide down the sides in perfect streams. "Good legs."

Madeleine turned to Elena. "Pierre is contacting his aunt tomorrow?"

"He has an idea where she might be, but wouldn't explain."

"I'll call him in the morning," Jack said, "but Maddie, we must show Elena Paris."

Elena blushed. "Pierre wants to take me around the Left Bank on Wednesday."

"Just the two of you?" Madeleine asked.

"Let her go, Maddie," Jack said. "After all, she's a grown woman, and we can tour the Right Bank tomorrow."

"It *is* my first time in Paris," Elena said, "and Pierre knows the city."

"Should we come with you?" Madeleine asked. "Would you like that?"

Jack raised his brows in protest. "Maddie, it's a date, that's all, and it's Paris! But Elena, if the weather's good, go to Notre-Dame and climb the bell tower. We climbed one in Florence once, in my younger days. It's a wonderful feeling up there, and you can see for miles."

Elena grinned. "Maybe we will."

"I trust your judgment, Elena. You'll be careful?" Madeleine looked at her husband who sat back with a contented smile. He would forever be a romantic, enjoying life to its fullest, waltzing through his days. How could she not let him have the moment?

But suddenly, pain flashed across his face. Wiping his mouth with his napkin, he coughed a rough, loose cough, and excused himself. "Get the check, please, Maddie," he gasped, "and have them call a taxi."

"It's the wine, Elena," Madeleine said as she watched him head for the restroom.

192

She signaled for the waiter.

She was sure there was blood on the napkin.

They said good night to Elena at the door to her room and entered their own suite. The coverlets had been neatly turned down, and a chocolate wrapped in gold foil lay on each pillow. Madeleine hung their coats, then faced her husband, who was undoing his tie in front of the dresser mirror.

"Jack, why are you doing this?"

"Doing what?"

"Drinking, eating the wrong foods."

"Oh, Madeleine, who are we kidding?" He looked at her, his eyes red and puffy.

"Kidding?"

"I've been thinking about the operation...and..." He slipped the tie over the metal bar on the back of the closet door.

"And?"

"...what life will be like on the other side of it."

"And what will it be like, Jack?" A steady throb pulsed in the upper right corner of her forehead. Soon, she knew, it would spread through her skull to the back.

"I'll never be the same man."

"I don't expect you will."

"So what's the point?" Jack sat in an armchair. He rubbed his face with his hands as though he could erase her questions.

"The point is that you will be living, and we'll still have a life together. *That's* the point, Jack."

"You won't want the debilitated, crippled Jack." He turned away, as though lost in the past. "My father—"

"I'll have you any way you are. *Please* don't do this." She fought a rising panic.

"They'll scrape my dead cells off, along with the dangerous living ones, then do the wrap to tighten the hole. I'll really be handicapped; the gas won't know which way to go. I've watched Bruce—on the Scout board—go through it, Maddie. He's bloated and full of gas and choking more than ever." He gripped the sides of the chair, darting his gaze back and forth between Madeleine and the walls.

Madeleine sought his eyes. "Let's take it one day at a time, okay? Let's not borrow trouble." She massaged her scalp, pushing her index finger into the tender spot.

He turned and looked out the window into the dark square. "If I ever got the big *C*...I don't want to stick around. I'm not that brave, and you'd be better off without me."

"Don't say that. I didn't hear you say that." Madeleine tried to move toward him, but helplessness paralyzed her.

Chapter Twenty-three
Chapelle de la Medaille Miraculouse

It is only by feeling your love
that the poor will forgive you for the gifts of bread.
Vincent de Paul

Tuesday morning Rachelle and Anne-Marie drove out through the iron gates of Les Crayères and headed west for Paris on the A4. Anne-Marie gunned the motor, moved the Citroen into the opposite lane, overtook a big rig, and slipped back into the right lane, narrowly missing an oncoming car.

Rachelle breathed deeply, grasped the edge of her seat, and watched the Épernay exit speed past. She had enjoyed her Monday in Reims visiting the famous cathedral and walking through the Eisenhower Museum where the peace treaty had been signed. She had studied maps covering the walls, markers showing past and future battles, numbers tracking the dead and the missing.

"Épernay is where champagne was discovered," said Anne-Marie, "by the monk Dom Perignon."

"A monk invented champagne?" Rachelle shook her head in disbelief, then recalled the vineyards on her uncle's monastery island. Alcohol taboos must have been more Protestant than Catholic. "How far is Paris?"

"About an hour—not far—the traffic is not bad on Tuesdays."

"Thank you for taking me." Rachelle looked out to the gray-green hills and wondered what Anne-Marie's chapel would look like.

"It is my pleasure. But I must return to Reims tonight. Where would you like to stay? The nuns may have a room, but be warned, their rooms are not like my chateau's!"

"That would be perfect."

"Their convent is part of the Daughters of Charity, founded by

Vincent de Paul. They run a hostel and clinic for the homeless and the poor. And for pilgrims. Today the chapel is a shrine."

"A shrine?"

"Millions come each year to pray before Catherine's body and the relics of Vincent de Paul."

"Catherine?"

"Saint Catherine Labouré. Our Lady appeared to her when she was a novice. Her body is incorrupt—not decayed. You can read about it there. They have materials in English." She glanced at Rachelle. "Remember the medallion I gave you?"

"Yes," Rachelle said as she felt for it beneath her shirt.

"Our Lady told Catherine to make them."

They drove up Boulevard Saint-Germaine and turned right on Rue du Bac as a light rain misted the windshield. Anne-Marie edged the car into a tiny space, close to the curb. The street was lined with small shops: *Meubles, Boulangerie, Charcuterie.*

Anne-Marie pointed toward a busy intersection. "On the corner is the Bon Marché, a large department store, if you need anything."

Rachelle recalled she'd promised souvenirs for Conrad's children. Later, she thought.

They walked up the sidewalk to *140* and entered a gated drive. A number of visitors moved along the drive toward a portico in the back. Others stopped to view a row of white sculpted figures. A short, graying nun in a dark habit and white headscarf hurried toward them.

"Sister Marguerite, how good to see you," Anne-Marie said as she bent down to kiss the nun on each cheek.

"And you, my daughter. *Comment ça va?*" Marguerite's eyes shone from beneath her banded headscarf and she clapped her hands together with a child's delight.

"I am well, thank you. Please allow me to present my cousin, Rachelle DuPres."

Rachelle shook the tiny hand, its birdlike bones fragile in her own. "Sister, I am pleased to meet you."

"And I am pleased to meet *you*, Madame."

Anne-Marie spoke quickly in French to Marguerite, and they led

Rachelle into the chapel.

"This is where Catherine had her visions," Anne-Marie said. "Marguerite will show you around, and yes, she does have a room for you, the last one—you are in luck. I am sorry, but I must go. I have much to do before I return."

"Of course," Rachelle said, somewhat absently. Visitors—pilgrims, she guessed—knelt in the large nave. Blue mosaics covered white walls and statues stood in alcoves. Above her, along each side, wide balconies with wrought iron railings overlooked the sanctuary. All was pale blue and creamy white. The light lifted her.

"It was so very good," Anne-Marie was saying, "to meet you, cousin. Please, you will keep in touch?"

Rachelle pulled her eyes away from the luminous space. "I will. And thank you for everything. You've helped me more than you know."

Anne-Marie embraced Rachelle, kissed Marguerite, and turned toward the door. Feeling both regret and gratitude, Rachelle watched her cousin leave.

"You must be tired, Madame DuPres," Sister Marguerite said. "Would you like to see your room?"

Rachelle followed the elderly woman upstairs. A wooden crucifix hung over the bed; a pitcher and washbowl rested on a chest. Linens lay folded at the foot of a lumpy mattress. Through a foggy pane of glass, she glimpsed an alley. Turning to the little nun, she smiled. "Thank you, Sister."

Marguerite stood in the doorway and pointed down the hall. *"La salle de bain."* She checked her watch. "It is eleven. Mass is at noon. May God bless you, my child." She closed the door behind her.

Rachelle unpacked. She hung her dress on a rusty hanger in a dark closet and placed her folded clothes in the warped chest. She made up the bed, splashed water on her face, and descended to the chapel.

She picked up a leaflet by the door and sat in the back. The sanctuary was awash with light, a clear, breathable air. A vault of blue mosaic rose over a white marble altar and tabernacle. A life-size Saint Joseph, holding the boy Jesus on his hip, stood in a tall niche to the left, and on the right, Mary, draped in white, held a golden sphere in her hands. A glass sarcophagus rested at her feet.

Rachelle opened her leaflet.

On July 19, 1830, the feast day of Saint Vincent de Paul and six days before the streets of Paris were barricaded by the July

Revolution, the Virgin Mary appeared to twenty-four-year-old Catherine Labouré.

Catherine, one of ten children born to a poor farming family in Burgundy, had joined Vincent de Paul's Daughters of Charity. One night, three months after she arrived at the motherhouse on the Rue du Bac, an angel-child led her to the chapel. There, Mary appeared to her and predicted terrible times for France. She wore a white robe and held a globe representing the world.

She instructed Catherine to have medals made of a certain design with the words *O Mary, conceived without sin, pray for us who have recourse to you.* The Blessed Virgin promised graces to those who wore her medals and to those who prayed before her image in the chapel.

Catherine told her confessor and urged him to have the medals cast. The archbishop agreed, seeing no harm. She told no one else about the visions until her deathbed confession in 1876, forty years later. Decades after her death, the body of this "Saint of Silence" was found to be incorrupt, untouched by time.

Rachelle walked to the glass coffin. Through the side panel, she could see Catherine's body, clothed in black with a white headdress. Her face was coated in a wax-like substance, but the body certainly appeared whole, Rachelle thought. How could this be? By now, over a century after her death, it should be nothing but dust and bones.

Rachelle returned to her pew. The chapel was nearly full, and the standing crowd thickened behind her. All these people were here for a weekday mass.

An elderly nun stepped to the microphone and led a pre-mass rehearsal. She chanted a tune that floated over the people, and wove her hands through the air as though inviting them to join a great work, to give themselves to God. Rachelle looked up to the wide galleries above, now packed as well, where screens broadcast the service to those who could not see into the chancel. What brought all of these pilgrims here? There must be hundreds. Was this another Lourdes? Would the sick be healed?

The crowd was mixed, every race and class, gender and generation; the crippled leaned on canes and slumped in wheelchairs; faces reflected worry, exhaustion, devotion, adoration. A priest began the liturgy and the sisters sang from the front pews. Rachelle followed the songs on the yellow sheets and joined in the *Glorias.* Another priest preached from the center aisle, bellowing and waving his arms. She wondered what he said and regretted her poor French, but sensed he called his people to action.

Rachelle turned to Mary who gazed over her children. She was a loving mother, a powerful, caring mother. She was a mother who understood all: the beginnings, the middles, the ends; where Rachelle had been, where she was now, and where she was going. *Hail Mary, full of grace...guide me, help me.* Rachelle studied the faces in the crowd as they listened to the preacher. These were ordinary people seeking the extra-ordinary, searching for miracles of body and soul, wanting more than the everyday reality of their lives, wanting to be filled with something beyond themselves. Could she be filled too? How empty she was of late, except for that moment in Saint-Remi.

As the French prayers danced through the vaults, Rachelle's eyes were drawn to the crucifix above the altar, then to the white tabernacle, and finally, to the bread and wine of the mass. The celebrant raised the chalice, offering the *Agneus Dei*, the Lamb of God, and the crowd surged forward, receiving the host on their palms and placing it carefully in their mouths.

Rachelle pulled Anne-Marie's medal from her pocket. Catherine's vision of Mary was engraved on one side—it was the Madonna in the chapel with the outstretched hands. Rachelle examined the other side. The *M* wrapped around the cross, as though enclosing it in mother love, tangible love. Two hearts rested at the base of the *M*. A sword pierced one heart and thorns pierced the other, uniting love and suffering, love and sacrifice. What did it all mean?

Rachelle found the little nun waiting in the courtyard.

"We welcome you, Madame," Sister Marguerite said, "and we hear you are a doctor." She bowed her head as though studying her sandals, her hands folded.

"I am."

"Should you wish to see our clinic, we would be most happy, *vraiment heureuse.*"

"Certainly, Sister. You have been kind to let me stay."

"It is a good work, a great work, and we feed the hungry too. We feed and we heal, *nourrissons et guerissons.*"

Marguerite led her through a courtyard, into another building and a long dormitory. "You see that we are full."

A few patients glanced up from their cots. Silently, nurses checked charts and dispensed medications.

Rachelle wanted to escape the familiar scene. "And the kitchens? You feed the hungry, you said?"

The little nun shrugged and shook her head, mumbling. She led Rachelle out to a street entrance. "Our soup kitchen."

The line of the hungry straggled down the block. Rachelle followed Marguerite inside where attendants ladled thick stew from steaming tureens. This was better, she thought, a safe distance from the nurses who healed.

"Do you need help?" she said without thinking.

"Oui." The little nun led her into the kitchen and handed her an apron. *"Merci, Madame, Merci."* She disappeared through a side door.

Rachelle tied the stained sacking around her waist as a girl with orange hair and a nose-ring motioned to Rachelle to take her place in front of an iron pot. *"Merci, Madame."*

Rachelle reached for an empty bowl, filled it, and handed it to the next person in line, a weathered woman with trembling hands. She wondered if Mary was present, if she was with them, there, in that kitchen, and, as she repeated the motion again, she thought, Yes, *mais oui*...and if Mary, perhaps, too, her son. Maybe Anne-Marie was right.

Rachelle spent the afternoon in the kitchen, preparing supper and sharing a meal with the nuns and volunteers. Her legs ached and her muscles throbbed. That evening, as she soaked in the bath at the end of the hall, a light tap on the door woke her from a warm reverie. The bath was not hers alone.

She dressed and found a wall phone downstairs. Pulling out a slip of paper, she dialed the scuffed black face with her index finger, feeling the disc roll back into place with each number, whirring and clicking.

"Becca?"

"Rachelle, I'm so glad you called. Where are you now? Another fabulous chateau? Hold on a minute..."

Voices and footsteps came and went. The line clicked.

"Sorry, Shelley, I changed phones. This is quieter. We finished the picking today, and they're celebrating downstairs."

"That's good to hear."

"So where are you?"

"Paris."

"Paris? But Pierre said—"

"I know what Pierre said, but Paris is a big city, Becca. I'm at the Chapel of the Miraculous Medal with the Daughters of Charity. Have you heard of them?"

"I have. I've visited a number of times. Philippe knows one of their priests from the men's order around the corner, on the Rue de Sèvres, I believe. Vincent de Paul's body is in the chapel there, you know."

"The thrift store saint?"

Rebecca laughed. "The very same. The location is remarkable. They have the sarcophagus resting *above* the altar, quite high up as I recall."

"How did they do that?"

"Go and see for yourself. Pierre, by the way, has a room down the street, number 73. It's not much but serves him for school. Did you read about Catherine Labouré?"

"It's quite a story. And they have a soup kitchen here. I helped out a bit this afternoon."

"What are you doing there, Shelley?" Rebecca's tone was at once skeptical and full of hope.

"Anne-Marie brought me. She came here years ago and liked it. I wanted to see it for myself, and the nuns gave me a room. It's remarkable, really remarkable." Rachelle searched for words to describe the chapel but found none, lost in unfamiliar territory. She must learn a new vocabulary. "The chapel is so light."

"I remember. Philippe took me there the summer we met."

"On a date?"

"Well, not exactly."

"That's amazing."

"He wanted to be a priest then, you know."

"I'd forgotten. I guess you changed all that." Rachelle noticed a nun waiting for the phone. "I've got to go, Becca, I wanted to let you know where I was."

"Keep in touch, Shelley. I love you."

"I love you too."

Rachelle set the mouthpiece on its cradle and walked slowly up the stairs, achingly tired, but oddly content with her day.

Wednesday morning Rachelle looked at the peeling paint on the door of *73 Rue du Bac*. She pushed a button next to *P. Morin* on a side panel, heard a distant buzz, and waited to speak into the intercom.

"Oui?"

"It's your Aunt Rachelle, Pierre."

"Oui, un moment."

Soon the door flew open, and Pierre stood tall and serious, his hands on his hips. *"Ma tante*, what are you doing here?"

"I decided to come to Paris, after all, and wanted to see where you lived."

"But you should not have come. Did not my mother tell you this?"

"She did. But it's okay, Pierre. Paris is big."

Pierre shook his head. "Very well, come in. I must go soon, but I show you my room."

They climbed and climbed.

"Small, *mais pas trop chère*, cheap." Pierre lowered his head as he stepped through the door. *"Voila*, my home in Paris."

It *was* cramped. Clothing, books, and papers were strewn on a narrow cot. A miniature fridge was wedged between the wall and a hotplate. It reminded Rachelle of her summer at the Sorbonne with Becca.

"The bath is down the hall."

Rachelle looked through the cracked window as she rested her hands on the sill, its paint flaking. "You've a great view of your neighbors."

She dropped onto the low bed, her legs angled onto a ragged throw rug. "I'm staying up the street." She watched his reaction.

"Up the street?" He scooped instant coffee from a jar into two mugs, poured hot water from a kettle, and stirred in milk and sugar.

"At the hospice."

He handed her a mug. "You stay with the nuns? *Pourquoi?"*

"It's a long story, Pierre, and you said you have an engagement?"

"I am showing Elena the sights."

"Elena?"

"She is with the Seymours. She is...nice."

"Your mother said something about a young lady. How nice *is* she, Pierre?"

"You should not have come to Paris, but I have done all I can. They will not find you because of me."

"And this Elena?"

He blushed and turned away, then stared at the floor.

"Sorry," Rachelle said. "Sensitive subject? We'll talk about it another time." She sipped her coffee, strong and sweet.

"No, it is okay." He turned toward her. *"Ma tante*, she is wonderful, she is beautiful, she is smart. *Je pense...*"

"I see," Rachelle said, smiling.

Pierre's eyes lit up the room, and as she watched him speak of Elena, a twinge of loss pinched her heart. Had she missed the greatest event of all? Had she bargained and lost when she chose career over marriage? Was she a fool to assume she could have both, have it all, that time would wait? Forgotten faces passed before her as she listened to Pierre: faces from school, from her internship at Harvard Medical, faces she had rejected.

"Pierre, if you care about her, don't lose her. I still regret...but there's no point in going there, as they say. You need to be honest with her. Tell her everything in your heart."

"Oui, ma tante." Pierre looked vacantly out the window. His coffee remained untouched.

"I must get back. I promised the nuns I'd help today, and I don't want to be late. Would you like to have dinner with me tonight?"

"Thank you. I call later."

"Good," she said as she rinsed her mug out. "Have fun and don't forget what I said."

Rachelle kissed Pierre on the cheek and let herself out. She trundled down the stairs and walked into the bright sunlight, back to the soup kitchen, and perhaps, the noon mass.

Chapter Twenty-four
Sacré-Coeur

My God, behold me, wholly thine; Lord,
make me according to thy heart.
Brother Lawrence

Wednesday evening, the Café Saint-Honoré bustled with activity. Madeleine, holding Elena's hand, followed Jack through the crowded bar to a table in the back. The waiter handed them large menus with an insert that listed the specials of the day.

Confronted with the French phrases, Madeleine said, "Jack, I'll have the special."

Elena raised her dark brows in doubt. "You're having pig's feet?"

"I guess not. No pig's feet. Or snails. Or frog's legs."

Elena scanned the menu, twirling a thick strand of hair around a finger. "Let me find something. How about the vichyssoise and the grilled sole? That's what I'm having."

With her hair waving over her shoulders, Madeleine thought once again how she looked like a country Madonna, but this evening a deep sadness lingered over her features.

"Perfect." Madeleine waited. Elena would explain when she was ready.

Jack tapped the menu. "And I'll have the veal medallions and fish soup. Where's the fish soup, Elena? They always have a fish soup. And a bottle of the house red."

Elena ordered for them.

Jack slipped his reading glasses into their case and turned to their young friend. "Okay, Elena, how was your day with Pierre?"

Elena looked from Jack to Madeleine. "Not good. He's not what he appears, not at all. I don't know where to start."

"Did he find his aunt?" Madeleine asked.

"No."

"I was afraid of that."

"He's been lying to us, Madeleine."

"Lying to us?"

"I don't believe it," Jack said. "Pierre is an outstanding young man. He must have a very good reason if he's hedging a bit."

"Start from the beginning," Madeleine said, her chest tight.

A server poured the wine and Elena waited until he left. "I agreed to meet Pierre halfway, on the Pont Neuf. I followed the concierge's map: crossed the Place Vendôme, headed for the Rue de Rivoli, and walked up through the Tuileries."

"A nice day for the park since the rain finally cleared," Jack said. "Maddie and I walked up the Champs-Elysee. We didn't see much yesterday."

Madeleine frowned, anxious. "Shush, let her tell."

"It *was* a lovely walk. A brisk breeze blew falling leaves. It was magical. I passed a large pool and fountain where people lounged in the sun; then I reached the Louvre—wow—and turned toward the Seine. It was so romantic. Couples strolled along the river. I saw him on the Pont Neuf. He lifted his head and waved."

Their first courses arrived, and Elena paused. "He took me to Saint Genevieve's church. I thought I was in heaven."

Madeleine reached for her spoon to taste the vichyssoise. "Saint-Etienne-du-Mont, next door to the Pantheon? It's beautiful—Gothic, I believe—with exquisite stained glass and curving staircases to the galleries and lots of white stone. I'll never forget that one." The soup was creamy and cool, the flavors delicate.

Elena tasted hers, working her spoon through the potato cream with determination. "That is the one, but Genevieve's relics aren't actually there. The Revolution burned them, threw them into the Seine. All we could see was the stone on which she lay in her tomb. But I was touched by her life, the way she came from the countryside and did so much for the people of Paris."

"God uses the innocent and the weak, those with uncluttered hearts." Madeleine glanced at Jack, who was listening intently, having finished his *soup de poissons,* Parisian bouillabaisse.

"I like that," Elena said. "It's encouraging, isn't it? So we talked about the Revolution and Genevieve and the saints. I asked him if he believed in God. His answer should have warned me."

"Warned you?" Jack sipped his wine and watched her intently.

"He wasn't sure. His parents believe, and he went to Catholic school, and France is full of saints' stories, he said. But his aunt doesn't believe, so he thinks he shouldn't believe either."

"He wants to be like Doctor DuPres?" Madeleine asked. The pieces of Pierre's character were beginning to form a pattern.

"That's not a bad thing," Jack said. "More power to him."

Elena set down her spoon and dabbed her mouth with the napkin. "He wants her to take him to America, to oversee his schooling. He worships his aunt and he worships America. And another thing. I wish he was a believer. Belief in Christ is so important to me. How could I be close to someone who didn't believe?"

Madeleine rested her hand on Elena's shoulder. "It does create challenges." How grateful she was that Jack was a believer, even if they disagreed on some of the implications of that belief. Still, he believed that Christ was the Son of God. He believed that Christ would save them from sin and death, was his "personal savior" as the evangelicals would say. She and Jack shared a strong foundation.

What was that Scripture reference about being unequally yoked? Saint Paul, she thought.

"Then he gave me the second clue."

"The second clue?" Madeleine asked.

"He said we must find another doctor for Mr. Seymour." Elena looked at Jack with some nervousness. "I asked him where his aunt could be reached, but he changed the subject. I should have left right then."

"You wanted to trust him, Elena, that's all." Madeleine finished her burgundy and studied the empty glass.

Jack leaned forward as though he could soothe her with his words. "And leaving him wouldn't have helped the doctor search." He refilled their glasses and ordered a second bottle.

Elena breathed deeply. "I didn't want to believe what I was hearing. So he took me to a little fish restaurant near the Luxembourg Gardens, and I told him more about my upbringing, the convent and the orphanage and the clinic in Rome, even about my paralysis and my operation. He told me about his family, how they were persecuted, and how so many were lost in the camps."

"Is he Jewish?" Madeleine asked, feeling sympathetic toward the boy.

"A quarter Jewish from his grandmother Leah. Evidently his mother is Doctor DuPres's fraternal twin. The twins were smuggled out as babies during the Second World War and adopted by an American family."

Madeleine recalled Rebecca's warm hospitality. "That's quite a story. I've heard of the children sent to the U.S. but never knew any personally."

Jack turned to Madeleine. "Remember Joe Riesen who worked with me on our stock portfolio? He was a child survivor."

The story had touched Madeleine with the reality of history. "He survived Auschwitz and was adopted by an American GI in northern Italy. He was around fourteen, I think. But go on, Elena."

The veal and sole arrived, and the waiter poured the second bottle as Elena continued.

"We walked all over the Left Bank and saw where the famous artists gathered, and toured an old abbey, Saint-Germaine-des-Prés, and I forgot my misgivings, the way we chatted back and forth. It was so easy." She paused. "It was like we were in our own personal world."

Madeleine saw the depths of her fall. "Oh, Elena."

"We took a cruise boat—a *vedette*—and sailed up the Seine. He wiped down a chair for me. I was Cinderella with her prince. It was on the way back, as we approached the dock, that it all came to an end." Elena paused, hesitant to continue.

Jack's face was flushed. "What happened, Elena?" He pulled out his wrist monitor and strapped it on firmly.

Madeleine watched him with concern.

"Mr. Seymour, don't worry, he was the perfect gentleman. He said he liked me very much, so he had to be honest. Then he said he had been keeping us away from his aunt on purpose."

"On purpose? What do you mean? Why would he do that?" Madeleine asked.

"Ever since Lyons, he has been diverting us. She isn't in Paris at all. Who knows where she is, probably China."

Madeleine groaned. "There must be a reason, Elena." She looked at Jack, who was frowning at his blood pressure numbers.

Elena looked into Madeleine's eyes, as though searching for refuge. "He said she is on vacation and shouldn't be bothered, or words to that effect."

"Jack, we should settle for one of the other doctors...please..."

"We've got time, Maddie, we'll find her. Maybe she needs more space. We only want to talk to her, buy her dinner. Surely Pierre can be reasoned with—he must have his reasons as you say...and we've come all this way."

"I don't think she's in Paris," Elena said, "and I don't want to see that man again. He lied to me."

"I understand, Elena," Madeleine said. "You feel betrayed."

"I do. He was so caring, and it turns out for a reason I didn't guess. I was such a fool. He only cares about himself and his aunt, his *wonderful* aunt." Elena paused and moved her plate away; she had eaten little. "I stopped by Notre-Dame on the way home. It was comforting to sit before the Blessed Sacrament in one of Our Lady's churches. Mary had a trying time with Joseph at first—she would understand."

Madeleine put her hand over Elena's and looked into her dark eyes. "That's good. God will help you through this, Elena. And you're no fool. It's just as well you found out now, right? There are many devious people in the world, but we don't stop trusting, we don't stop loving." With a start Madeleine realized she was one of those devious people, lying to Jack, or at least hiding the truth. Her head began a slow throb.

Elena tried to smile; her lower lip quivered. "Thank you, Madeleine. I left him on the dock. When I crossed the bridge, I looked back. He was walking along the river, his hands in his pockets, his head bent in that thoughtful way he has."

They finished their dinners in silence. As Jack paid the bill and they slipped into their coats, Elena added, "And I lost my scarf."

"Not the red one?" Madeleine asked. "The one from Sister Agnes?"

"I'm afraid so. It's somewhere in the Seine or maybe the park. I don't know."

Jack opened the door for the ladies. "We'll look for it in the morning."

As they stepped into the cool evening, Madeleine pointed up. "Look!"

A full moon lit the night sky, casting the street in a pale glow.

Elena flashed a wide smile. "And you know what today is?"

Madeleine paused. "September 29?" She was sure it was a feast day, but which one? Saint Francis' was coming up next week, she thought.

Elena grinned. "It's the Feast of Saint Michael and All Angels, and a full moon!"

Madeleine watched a cloud move toward the moon's rim. "The great defender of those who believe. He kicked Lucifer out of heaven."

She turned to Jack, who stared at the sky, mesmerized.

Jack had stacked the breakfast dishes neatly on the tray, and now he clutched Thursday's *Tribune* between tight thumbs and forefingers, holding it at an angle to catch the light. Madeleine could see he was concentrating, probably calculating sums in his head. His eyes ran down the stock lists. His face was flushed.

Elena's story had added another layer of worry to her own assorted troubles, and Madeleine had prayed for the young girl as she read her morning Psalms, "praying the Psalms" as they said, simultaneously interceding and listening and absorbing the ancient laments and praises. Now, filled with the rhythm of those phrases as though the song continued to weave a new cloth, a fine one of silk, many-colored, in her own soul, Madeleine turned to her Paris notes. Could God speak to her through these words? *Trust and obey, for there's no other way.* But one must surely listen, too, and surround oneself with the material things of God— his Word, his saints, his sacraments.

Madeleine poured the last of the coffee, finished off the milk, and settled cross-legged on the bed. They were meeting Elena at eleven to taxi to Sacré-Coeur, the church of perpetual prayer at the top of Montmartre.

Holy Manifestations: The Sacred Heart of Jesus
The Basilique du Sacré-Coeur rose from Montmartre, the Roman Mound of Mercury, the medieval Mount of Martyrs. Legend says third-century Saint Denis was martyred here. The feeble bishop, over one hundred years old, was beaten, grilled on an iron grate, hung on a cross, and decapitated. He was buried in the village of Catalliacus where, two centuries later, Genevieve built his basilica. In the years following, wave upon wave of persecution spilled more martyrs' blood on the slopes of Montmartre.

Madeleine tried to see through the thick mists of eighteen hundred years. She saw rivers of blood and tears, and she thought of the many martyrs of the early Church she had encountered in Italy and more recently in Lyons. She considered Christ's blood, poured out for her, for Jack, for Elena, *his* life given for *their* lives, his death suffered so that they would not die. And the martyrs, those witnessing to the first blood—

Christ's—continued the rivers of healing waters.

Would she have such courage? Such trust and obedience? To give her life for Jack? So that he might live?

> The Rue des Abbesses winds up Montmartre, named after forty-three Benedictine abbesses of a twelfth-century convent destroyed by the Revolution. The convent chapel, Saint-Pierre-de-Montmartre, survived and today stands behind iron gates on the Place du Tertre, home of silver-draped mimes and art fairs.
>
> The Franco-Prussian War and the Commune Rising of 1871 devastated Paris, especially Montmartre. When peace was restored, Catholic Parisians, in an offering of grief and thanksgiving, built a church dedicated to the Sacred Heart of Jesus, that icon of love, life, and blood. A white Romanesque basilica emerged from the martyrs' mound. Its Byzantine domes fused East and West, a home to perpetual prayer. Through the last century—through two world wars—the vigil continues, as the faithful pray before Christ present in the golden monstrance. They pray for peace, and they pray for those who suffer, as they meditate on the love of God in the sacred, suffering heart of Jesus.

The sacred, suffering heart, the cleansing blood of the cross, the gift of life. Was she called to carry the cross too? Could one even contemplate loving without carrying it? For that matter, could one truly *live* without carrying it? *If any man will come after me let him take up his cross and follow me...for my yoke is easy and my burden is light.*

Their taxi wound up the hill, along shady streets lined with apartments and shops, to the top of Montmartre and the white basilica.

The church was a place of healing, and in Madeleine's admitted helplessness, she reached for what she knew. Jack had withdrawn, had exiled her to a distant country, a place of detachment. Her loneliness grew, for without Jack, close and real, she was alone, alone except for God, and, as she was sensing more and more, Mary, the God-bearer.

But she was thankful for Elena, her new daughter, who suffered in her own way. Together she and Elena would offer their wounds to

210

Christ.

Joining a thick throng, she led Jack and Elena through a narrow scaffolded entrance. They emerged into a brightly lit nave. The noon office had begun and song flooded the air: *Dieu, viens à mon aide! Seigneur, à notre secours!* God, come to my aid! Lord, help us! The Christ Pantocrator—Christ, creator of all—spread his arms across a blue mosaic apse, welcoming and embracing, his sacred heart bleeding love. They maneuvered through the crowd, found seats at the end of a packed pew, and knelt on wooden slats.

Madeleine gazed at the domed chancel. Some fifty nuns led the chants. She glanced at Elena, who leaned forward to capture every word, every motion, every sound of the scene before her. Madeleine then looked at Jack, who, slumped and staring at his leaflet, was far away. He scratched his chest and shifted to find a comfortable position. He tapped his foot.

Dear God, teach me what to do. I am so helpless in helping him. Should I tell him the truth or not? She stared at the giant monstrance hanging from the startling mosaic in the apse. The monstrance held the host in its center, surrounded by golden rays, not reserved in an ornate tabernacle but visible for adoration. She recalled the humbler Vézeley crypt where the host was exposed, then gazed at Christ's bleeding heart in the mosaic above. She considered his suffering, his love. What was expected of her?

Must I suffer with you, Lord? Was she connected to all who suffered? *I am the Way, the Truth, and the Life,* Christ said. *No man cometh to the Father but by me.* Must she follow Christ's sacrificial way? Perhaps that was the only way to redemption, to joy.

In her mind Madeleine saw Christians climbing a steep hill to heaven. Each one carried a load of souls upon their backs. *Perhaps, through love, we help save others and continue doing so after we die, until all have been offered or re-offered salvation.* Somehow, as she saw those hikers with their people-loads, she knew the load was light and the load was necessary.

The crowd was mixed, every color and class, with faces of penitence and hope. A nun, her arms outstretched, led the chant as she gathered the voices together. She then turned to Christ and offered the song-prayers as one might release doves into the heavens.

Suddenly Jack stood, frowned, shook his head, and left through a side door. She and Elena would pray for him. They could carry him a ways, but in the end, she knew, he must choose, he must choose on his own to trust God.

Five minutes passed, and Elena touched Madeleine's arm. "I'll check on him," she whispered, "and meet you outside." Madeleine nodded.

The service was ending, and Madeleine recognized the words of Thomas Aquinas in the last hymn, the otherworldly tune soaring into a mystical union of earth and heaven, body and soul: *Therefore, we before him bending, this great Sacrament revere; types and shadows have their ending, for the newer rite is here; faith our outward sense befriending, makes our inward vision clear....* She left quietly, ahead of the departing crowd, and, as she neared the exit, she turned and gazed at the white-robed Christ. *Make my inward vision clear...and give Elena hope.*

She found Jack and Elena in the taxi as the meter ran. "Sorry to keep you waiting." She clambered in and closed the door.

"It took you long enough." Jack turned to the driver. "The Hotel Ritz, the short route, please."

Trembling at his tone, Madeleine stared through the smudged window. Yet in the soaring basilica she had grasped a ray of light in her fog of near-despair. Christ touched her, and she knew he would not let her go. She rocked in his arms, cradled.

They followed the Rue des Abbesses down the hill, past graffiti, souvenir shops, neighborhood parks, and corner groceries. Soon they came to the Galleries Lafayette and the Opera House, and finally pulled up in front of their hotel with the familiar red carpet and spinning doors, the gloved hands and friendly guards.

The digital clock read 3:35 a.m. Madeleine reached for Jack in the bed, but the space was cold, empty. She slipped on her robe and found him by the window, looking into the square. Under the full moon, Napoleon's column rose, an eerie gray pillar of pride. The Victorian lampposts remained lit and the jewelry shops shined security beams above their barred windows. A siren howled in the distance and a scooter droned; car doors slammed against raucous laughter. Night sounds in the city.

"I'm afraid, Maddie."

She wrapped her arm around him and drew close. "I know. I am too." She had to tell him about the biopsy. *Now.*

"Jack, I need to tell you something—"

"I don't want to live like this, with all this pain, but I don't want to die either."

"There's something you should know—"

"Can't it wait? I'm going back to bed."

"But Jack—"

"In the morning, Maddie, we'll talk in the morning."

Chapter Twenty-five
Le Mémorial de la Deportation

Love worketh no ill to his neighbour:
therefore love is the fulfilling of the law.
Romans 13:10

Rachelle met Pierre at the convent gates on Thursday morning. "I got your message canceling dinner and ate with the nuns. What's up? How was your date?" The sun slanted between billowing clouds, warming the breeze.

His face reflected both hope and despair. "I will tell you, Aunt Rachelle, but can we walk? Mama says we walk together when we have troubles."

They headed toward the Seine, striding silently, as though each step required their full attention. When they reached the river, Rachelle drank in the moist air, thinking of her remarkable days, serving soup, going to mass, serving soup, going to mass, eating in silence with the sisters as a nun read aloud in French.

How good it was to be doing something again, something useful. A new spirit coursed through her, and now her body responded to the vigorous walk. The men and women in the food line were grateful, and helping them fed her hungry heart. Perhaps she would stay awhile.

The rhythm of the hours, punctuated by bells and chants, soothed her, but the services perplexed her: the great devotion of the hundreds who worshiped, the intact corpse of the peasant saint, the altar with its tabernacle and divine hosts. She could not yet make sense of it all, but the music lingered in her head, and she found herself singing French Psalms in her sleep, waking to an odd delight.

When they reached the Seine, they turned right. Notre-Dame loomed before them, the towers bridging earth and sky.

"I like to walk when I think," Pierre said seriously, "especially along the river. It is so open here, so free. The skies, they are *plein d'espérance,* full of hope."

"And you, Pierre, you are not full of hope?" Should she ask again about Elena?

He shook his head. *"Non, pas d'espérance."* They turned left onto the Pont Saint-Martin and he motioned upriver to the Pont Neuf. "That is where I saw her last."

"Oh, Pierre. What happened?"

"I was honest, like you say. She was angry, but she does not understand my heart. If only I may see her, show her my heart."

"What did you say?"

"Why I come with them to Paris. You know why."

"I think I see."

"Elena believes that is all the reason."

"Then find her and explain. Don't give up. I don't know this young woman, but I'm getting to know you, Pierre. You have my drive. You could be a great doctor or lawyer or anything you choose. And you can have love too. Don't let one eclipse the other."

"Eclipse?"

"Take over by replacing. Push you away from. Don't give up, Pierre."

"I *not* give up? *Ma tante,* it hurt me to see her angry. I wanted only to run away."

"Never give up on someone you love, Pierre. I did many times. Only recently have I truly learned about love." Rachelle hardly knew what she was saying to this boy, except that it was true. Her mind raced to catch up with her experience, one she could not analyze and classify. And what, exactly, had happened to her? The altar of Saint-Remi filled her mind, merging now with the sisters' chapel, both places of love and suffering, life and death.

A minute passed, then two.

"You are far away, Aunt Rachelle. Come back, I need you."

"I'm sorry, Pierre. Someday I'll explain. It's a confusing time for me."

Rachelle turned toward the cathedral and, to divert Pierre's thoughts, said quietly, "I heard there was a Jewish memorial behind Notre-Dame. Did you know some of our cousins came from Paris? Have you ever visited to see if our family is listed?"

"I have not. Let us go."

They crossed the bridge and headed to the cathedral, both glad to have a purpose outside themselves.

Pierre paused by a wall plaque commemorating the death of a fighter in the French Resistance. "Look—many died here." He read the tiny etched letters. "Machine-gunned."

"We shall never forget, Pierre."

They circled the cathedral, and beyond a small park, a severe cement structure protruded into the Seine like a ship's prow. Descending steps into an underground cavern bordered with barbed wire, Rachelle read the names of the concentration camps carved on the walls. They peered through glass into a tunnel of more names.

"They list only the camps," Pierre said, sadly. "There are no names of people."

"There would have been too many and too many unknown. I should have thought of that. But there must be over forty camps listed here."

They climbed the stairs into the light, having added their grief to the grim memorial, and walked silently back to Notre-Dame.

As they entered the cathedral, bells rang eleven. Pierre walked the side aisles, but Rachelle paused to light a candle in the Holy Sacrament Chapel. The stained glass panels glimmered ruby and sapphire, and sent splashes of color upon the altar. She knelt and prayed for the Laurents, and for all those who died in these terrible wars.

She thought suddenly of the Kennedys and their love. When had she last visited Mom in Florida? Since Dad's death, she must be lonely. Rachelle sat back in the pew.

She recalled Sam Steinhoff. But she remembered, too, the many she had helped, a procession of grateful patients who now led better lives. She saw the Paris soup kitchen, all those thankful souls.

Rachelle considered her Catholic uncles and why they had died. Really, they died so she could be free, free to help people, so that she could, she supposed, practice love. All these years she had never understood. She was practicing love, even a suffering love. Perhaps this was the only kind of real love, after all. Sacrifice and suffering and love intertwined like muscles and tendons around a bone, like the M around the cross on the medal. A weight lifted from her heart as though chains had been cut.

Pierre slipped into the pew, a red scarf entwined in his fingers. "This is Elena's. I found it in the aisle."

"She was here."

"*Oui*, she was here."

Rachelle looked at the burning candle on the altar. Pierre knelt beside her and crossed his head and heart. He whispered, *Notre Père*.... She bowed her head and murmured, *Our Father*....

That evening Rachelle sat with Sister Marguerite in the nun's sparsely furnished room. The elderly woman, slumped in a rocking chair, pulled her tattered shawl about her shoulders. She arranged her hands carefully in her lap and gazed at the embers glowing in the fireplace. Rachelle put another log on the fire, poking the charred bits to life. It was good they gave her a warm room, she thought.

"Thank you, my dear," the nun whispered.

Rachelle returned to her footstool, clasped her hands around her knees, and looked into the fire as though it held answers to her questions. "So what should I do, Sister? I trust your decision."

"Your cousin Anne-Marie was like that, in the end. Once she let God into her heart, she made him master of the house. No halfway for her. You too, I think?"

"We shall see. He's definitely in the guest room."

"That may not be good enough, *ma chèrie*."

"For the time, it has to be. Now, what should I do?"

"*You* must decide that, but to not give all is to give nothing. You can help Monsieur Seymour. Why don't you?"

"I'm afraid, I suppose."

"Afraid, my child?"

"I'm afraid...I will fail again."

"And what if you fail, trying?"

"I would blame myself."

"You do not blame yourself. You give it to God, and he takes care of it. False guilt is a sin, so you must learn to live without it."

"Ah."

"Rachelle, I cannot make you believe, but I must testify to that which is true."

"But what is true? How do I know?"

"Keep your heart open, and use your mind to sort true from false."

"I have a lot to learn about this God."

"But you know much already. For you are the New Israel."

Rachelle studied Marguerite as the words echoed in her ears. "That's what my uncle Augustin said. What do you mean?"

"The New Israel is the converted Israel, the fulfillment of ancient prophecy. You are half-Jewish and half-Christian. So you embody the *entire* Chosen People: the Old Covenant People and the New Covenant People. You see, you are the New Israel."

"But I know nothing about being Jewish." And even less about being Christian, she thought.

"This may be true, but you will learn. The Chosen People were headstrong, but God chose well in the end. Abraham changed the world, *ma chèrie.*"

"How did he change the world, Marguerite?" What did Abraham have to do with all this?

"Abraham was the first, in the Sumerian world of many gods, to believe in one God. And Jehovah sent him out of the great city of Ur into the desert. He was a wealthy man. His caravan of family and servants numbered over three hundred. His descendents, as you know, are the Jews. They are also the Arabs, but that is another story."

"What does all this have to do with me?"

"Through Moses, God gave Abraham's descendents the Law and expected them to keep it. And with law, time is important. Man becomes responsible, he must *choose*, for what he does today will be judged tomorrow. Never before had man worried about judgment. His world was circular, not linear. And his gods demanded innocent sacrifice, often virgins and children."

"Those ancient civilizations sacrificed children?"

"History is not always good, not always pleasant. Man in Ur, in Sumer, was bound by the wheel of fate, his life fixed. But Abraham left Ur and traveled into the desert. His people sacrificed animals instead of humans, and with the new law, time became linear, progressing to a destination."

"And Israel?"

"Israel was Jacob, Abraham's grandson. Oh, the stories I shall tell you! God changed Jacob's name to Israel. Israel's descendents were the twelve tribes of Israel, the People of Israel, the Hebrews, the Jews. But enough." She patted her rosary, content for the moment.

"But, Sister, you called me the *New Israel.*"

Marguerite grinned, showing her yellow teeth, "The New Israel. You see, my dear, the Church did not begin with Christ. The Church was already there. It has been the People of God since the earliest days."

"What?" Rachelle concentrated on the wizened face. Marguerite's words were so full of meaning and so unfamiliar, that she feared she would never understand.

"It is not difficult, my Rachelle, *pas dificile*. Do not worry yourself. You see, it is this way. Christ redeemed the Church. With his death and his resurrection, he filled the Church with his own life, so that the Church today continues his life. He worked through the People of Israel, and now he works through the Church which came out of that People."

"Like an extension?"

"Like an extension, an extension of Israel and of Christ's own Body. Your ancestors' faith was Abraham's faith, and yours will be Christ's faith, the continuation, the extension, of that." Marguerite barely mouthed the words, her breathing growing difficult.

"I think I see. I'll let you rest. Thank you, Sister."

Rachelle stood, laid another log on the fire, and gently wrapped a blanket about Marguerite's knees. She kissed the old woman tenderly on the forehead and let herself out.

"Sleep well, my New Israel," Marguerite wheezed.

"And you, my new Mother-in-God." Rachelle heard the squeak of the rocker and the rattle of beads as she carefully shut the door behind her.

In the cold hall, Rachelle inspected her hands. One of the cracks was bleeding, and she pressed a tissue against it. She sighed as she walked to the chapel, her step light, her heart thankful.

Chapter Twenty-six
La Madeleine

Our only business is to love
and delight ourselves in God.
Brother Lawrence

Friday morning they met Elena for breakfast in the hotel restaurant.

"The doctor's trail is cold, I'm afraid," Jack said.

With a tight heart, Madeleine studied her husband's deeply lined face. His eyes were pinched and red with dark circles.

"I'll call Madame Morin," Elena said.

Madeleine spooned yogurt on her fruit salad. "She may have news."

"She knows where we're staying," Jack said. "Let's enjoy the week and go home. I need to make reservations with the airline. I'm not made of money, you know. We can't live like this forever, even with Joe McGinty's help."

"Are you settling for another doctor?" Madeleine asked.

"We'll see."

"You still want to have the surgery, Jack, don't you?"

"We'll see." He sipped his coffee and reached for a chocolate croissant. "Now, where do you want to go today? It's overcast, but dry."

Madeleine dropped two brown sugars into her cup and followed his gaze to the high molded ceilings, the gilt and mirrors, the swooping draperies, the soft luxury that cushioned life's rough edges. A waiter refilled Jack's glass with orange juice and poured him more coffee.

"I don't know," Madeleine said. *I'll tell him today.*

"How about visiting La Madeleine, the church up the street?" Jack asked. "We saw the other Mary Magdalene churches at Barroux and Vézeley."

"Pierre mentioned La Madeleine," Elena said wistfully.

"Then let's go," Madeleine said.

The neoclassic church looked down the broad Rue Royale to the Place de la Concorde. A wide flight of steps led to a pillared porch with massive bronze doors.

Jack paused at the foot of the stairs. "I'm going to Fauchon across the street to see if they have some canned truffles to take home, and maybe some of those brandied raspberries I've heard about. I'll meet you ladies there in an hour."

"Fauchon?" Elena asked as she watched Jack's retreating figure.

"A gourmet market. Elena, I'm worried. Jack's worse. He didn't sleep at all last night, and you see the wine he's drinking, not to mention juice and coffee."

"And I couldn't reach Madame Morin. I agree, he looks exhausted."

They climbed the wide stairs and entered the narthex where a booth sold icons, crucifixes, and rosaries. At the foot of the nave they contemplated the vast interior as they waited for their eyes to adjust to the dim light.

"Louis XV," Madeleine whispered, "modeled this church on Saint Peter's in Rome, but the Revolution halted the construction. Then Napoleon turned it into a temple to his army. He never finished it."

"But *now* it's a church."

"Yes," Madeleine said, comforted. "When Louis XVIII came to the throne after the war, he wanted the church to honor his slain family. Even so, it wasn't completed until 1842, years after his death."

"It's as large as many basilicas back home."

"The people love it. The size could make it cold and overwhelming, but I think that red candle on the high altar makes all the difference. Having the Sacrament available and central makes the space personal, warm. At the same time, it allows us to experience the glory of the holy here on earth, the vision of God."

"And look at the gleaming tabernacle. With a spotlight on the doors. And look at Mary Magdalene above the altar."

The towering Magdalene raised her arms in joy. Three angels circled her, dancing, holding her up with powerful wings.

Madeleine smiled. "It's the story of her time in the Saint-Baume mountains in Provence. Do you know it?"

"Just that she spent her last days in a cave."

"Farther up the mountain, above the cave, is Mount Pilon. Tradition says angels carried her there to hear them sing. Later, when she was near death, the angels brought her to Saint Maximin in the valley for last rites."

"What a lovely story. She's beautiful, here, over the altar."

"Today the Saint Baume cave is a shrine, dripping and dark, with the Sacrament reserved in a niche. You can see the stone where she slept and prayed."

"I'd like to visit someday."

"You should. You can hike to the top of Mount Pilon."

They walked down the central aisle and knelt in the front row of caned chairs. *Accept my offering, O Lord,* Madeleine prayed. *Use my love to heal Jack, or at least to give him faith, acceptance, and peace. Heal Elena's broken heart, and if it be thy will, grant her a husband, someone to love her and someone she can love back, someone to banish her loneliness.*

The organ boomed, signaling the noon mass. A priest entered from a side door and began the liturgy. As he consecrated the bread and wine, bringing Christ into their midst, the holy into the ordinary, Madeleine was again surprised by her delight in the amazing action of God.

As they left, she lit a votive to Our Lady of Lourdes in the north aisle. Mary stood in a grotto, where banks of candles flamed at her feet. "*Hail Mary...*" Madeleine placed a coin in a metal box and lit a tall tapered candle. As she prayed she sensed a motherly love, a feminine understanding of heartbreak, for indeed, a sword had pierced Mary's heart. Then Madeleine saw in her mind that torch-lit night in Lourdes and Jack's tears before the giant crucifix, as his heart opened. She gazed at the Blessed Virgin, fearing the bars of steel jailing her husband's soul, keeping God out, were nearly impossible to penetrate. A helpless panic rushed through her, and she sobbed, her head in her hands, her shoulders shaking.

Elena wrapped her arm about her. "What is it?" she whispered. "Come now, Jack will be okay, I'm certain everything will be fine."

"I'm sorry, Elena, you don't understand."

Elena led Madeleine outside and they sat on the porch steps. Madeleine wept as Elena held her, rocking gently.

Madeleine breathed deeply and wiped her cheeks. "Jack will never trust God. He'll never find peace. He's like Sisyphus, rolling that stone up the mountain and never making it to the top. He has to do everything himself."

"Some of us have a more difficult time." Elena handed her a tissue.

"Jack's a believer, but it's as if his faith is only for Sundays."

"You're saying he doesn't walk with Jesus?" Elena looked thoughtful.

Such a touching phrase, Madeleine thought. And an accurate one. "Exactly. For Jack, trusting God is a monumental leap like jumping from a plane with no parachute. He'll never let God into his real life."

"Never is a big word."

"Maybe so..."

"And it's a despairing word, not a godly word." Elena's eyes pooled with tears. She looked out to the obelisk but seemed to see another time.

"I'm sorry. *You* don't despair, do you?"

"Sister Agnes said it was a tool of the devil."

"When you were paralyzed?" Madeleine asked, ashamed of her cowardice.

"There were some dark times. Something would overpower me." Elena regarded her legs as though they belonged to another person.

"What did you do?"

Elena turned, her eyes thoughtful. "We prayed and we waited. Agnes said that, after all, we had all eternity."

"And that was when you decided to risk the operation?"

"Agnes would not let me despair. She said God didn't allow it."

"So we don't give up on Jack," Madeleine said, "no matter how we feel. I knew that, but sometimes it's difficult to feel what you know to be true."

"We pray and wait and trust God."

They paused in silence as they watched clouds scuttle across the sky.

"But Madeleine," Elena asked, "how serious *is* Jack's condition?"

Madeleine's heart beat hard. "Doctor Lau said to keep it from him, but I should tell you. It's time. He has esophageal cancer. And I haven't told him."

"No! You can't keep that from him, can you?"

"The doctor made me promise. I believe that in some cultures it's routine procedure. But I'm having serious regrets. I don't know much longer I can do this."

Elena's face held mixed feelings. "That's a terrible choice for you. I don't know what I would do in your place."

Madeleine folded her hands. "I've been praying about it, but I can't seem to find my way. I feel so lost and alone."

"I'll pray too, so you won't be alone, will you? We'll be lost together."

Madeleine smiled and squeezed Elena's hand. "Thanks. I'm sorry to burden you with this—but it was time." She stood, shouldered her bag, and looked down the Rue Royale. "This is a wonderful place, here at the top of the steps."

"A great view." Elena followed Madeleine's gaze.

Madeleine waved her hand toward the panorama before them. "We look straight down the stairs of a beloved church. Then we look down the Rue Royale to the Place de la Concorde, once the Place de la Revolution. So the church points to death, then to life. Robespierre guillotined Marie Antoinette on that square. Later, he suffered the same fate. The renaming of the square is a hopeful statement of peace. Beyond the Place de la Concorde is the National Assembly, France's democratic government. And beyond *that* is Napoleon's golden dome church where he's buried. In many ways Napoleon Bonaparte represented it all: the Republic, the Empire, the Revolution itself, man's greed and ambition."

"He didn't represent the Church, though."

Madeleine looked at Elena thoughtfully. The young woman's education had been better than most. "No, his peace with the Church was political. But at each end of this vista, what is it that presides? Two churches—ha! How about a picture?"

Elena focused and carefully squeezed the tiny button, as though sealing their troubles in the camera.

Madeleine stood slowly, feeling a little off balance. "Let's go find Jack and pick up some lunch."

They dined that evening at the Café de la Paix near the Opera. Small tables lined the windows fronting the sidewalk. Jack downed the better portion of the bottle of wine as he watched Madeleine thoughtfully. She wanted to object, but what could she say that hadn't been said so many times? Should she give him his freedom to do as he pleased? Should she keep the peace or constantly nag? Hard choices. But she was so tired of nagging. She hated herself, for it went against the image she had of herself, the self she wanted to be.

Several times that afternoon, when she and Jack were alone, she had begun the sentence that would explain everything, make it all clear. Each time she allowed a diversion to stem her words. Now Elena's presence became her excuse.

Sole, mashed potatoes, and steamed vegetables were followed by profiteroles and coffee. Madeleine and Elena chatted about the basilica, and Jack responded quietly, seeming to be glad they had enjoyed themselves. He had, indeed, found his canned truffles, but the brandied raspberries were glass-bottled, not something he wanted to pack.

Their conversation skated the thin, icy surface of the moment.

Chapter Twenty-seven
Saint-Gervais

There is no fear in love;
but perfect love casteth out fear.
1 John 4:18

S aturday morning they met Elena in the lobby to plan the day.

"I booked our return flight for Monday," Jack announced, returning from the concierge's counter.

"Good." Madeleine was relieved. Surely this meant he would take another doctor. But her husband's face looked twisted, preoccupied.

Jack turned to Elena. "You're going on to Rome, right? And making the arrangements yourself?"

"Cristoforo is working on it," Elena confirmed, her tone carrying a touch of regret.

Jack buttoned his coat. "So we have two days left. I'd like to browse wine stores this morning. You two can visit a church, or whatever, this morning. I'll meet you in the bar for lunch at 1:00."

"Okay," Madeleine said, disappointed. "Have fun." She watched him nod to the gloved doorman and enter the revolving glass panels.

She knew he enjoyed browsing wine—it was the merchant in him, the buyer Jack of the old days. It would give him pleasure, and knowing that would give her pleasure.

"How about visiting Saint-Gervais?" Elena asked. "The Brothers and Sisters of Jerusalem are there, according to the brochure from Vézeley. It's walking distance."

"Good idea. Maybe they'll sing an office." But should she be finding the doctor? Wasn't this still a priority? Madame Morin had not answered her phone; nor had Pierre answered his.

The two women made their way down the Rue de Rivoli, past the Louvre and the Hotel de Ville—the old town hall—following the map.

Pausing in front of the church, Elena skimmed a page in her guidebook, running her finger down the entry. "This square was used for executions—for hangings."

"It's near the courts of justice. What a place for a church. God's justice on one side and man's on the other. One would hope they were the same."

They stepped inside the soaring Gothic basilica. Massive columns rose to fan vaulting. Far beyond the high altar, in the apse above the ambulatory, stained glass glimmered. Low wooden stools filled the long narrow nave. Unusual, thought Madeleine, no pews or chairs, but stools. Madeleine and Elena joined the congregation of forty or fifty faithful that waited for the next office to begin. Madeleine focused her eyes on the golden icon of Christ on the altar.

Elena shared with Madeleine an English brochure she had found by the door.

The six-century church on this site was dedicated to the Roman martyrs Gervais and Protais, whose relics were brought to Paris by Saint Germaine. Today's building is seventeenth century. In the Middle Ages, public trials were held in the square in front of the church.

Today the church is home to the Brothers and Sisters of Jerusalem, a monastic order serving the community, founded in 1975 by Fr. Pierre-Marie Delfieux and Cardinal Francois Marty. Their mission is to bring the contemplative spirituality of the desert into the heart of the city.

The brothers and sisters hold part-time jobs and rent housing. They offer daily mass and sing the morning, noon, and evening offices. They follow rules of love, prayer, work, hospitality, and silence as well as chastity, obedience, and poverty. Lay orders, defined by interest, age, and profession, form the Family of Jerusalem. The order has communities at Vézeley, Blois, Strasbourg, and Magdala.

Services are open to the public daily except Mondays. A shop sells books, crafts, icons, honey, and jams.

Madeleine looked up from the glossy leaflet as young monks and nuns processed silently in, their white robes dusting the stone floor. Their hoods were raised, framing expectant faces. They took their places in the choir and began to sing. The notes soared in four-part harmony through the vaulted stone. They sang with purpose and joy, bowing from the waist and touching the ground during the *Gloria Patri*, as if dancing. Lessons were read and more prayers sung.

As the young people filed out, Madeleine was thankful, for she had been pulled into their worship; she had soared on the wings of their melodies like a bird riding the wind. For the time she had escaped her prison of worry.

So this was their desert in the city; this was their peace in God. She would cultivate her own desert garden with her own flowers of prayer. She would learn to fly too.

The women returned to the hotel, and Madeleine paused at the entrance to the Bar Vendome. "It's 1:05, and Jack's not here yet. Ask for a table, and I'll look for him. He should be back by now. He's probably in the room."

She took the elevator up, walked down the narrow hall, and turned the key in the lock. The maid had not yet cleaned the room; the bed was rumpled, the towels still heaped in the bath hamper, the air stale. Her tan slacks lay in a heap on the floor. Jack stood by an open window, his back to her. He turned. The look on his face made Madeleine gasp. She had never seen such fury in her husband.

His red face was twisted with hurt and betrayal as he clutched the biopsy report, waving it in the air. "Can you explain this?" he choked.

Madeleine reached for the bedpost. "I can, Jack. I've been trying to tell you—"

"You've been lying to me." His speech was thick, his throat tight.

"I wanted to tell you but—"

"Then why didn't you?" he shouted. "I've got cancer and you haven't the kindness—or the Christian obligation, if that's what you need—to tell me?"

"Doctor Lau—"

"Conrad? You've been in on this lie together? Tell me, does Elena know as well?"

"It's not the way it looks, Jack...he was worried...and Elena—"

"Right." Jack threw the paper on the floor and reached for his jacket. "I don't believe what I'm hearing. This time you've gone too far,

228

Madeleine." He slammed the door behind him.

Madeleine stood still, wanting to follow, wanting to move, caught in the moment like a deer in the headlights.

The room shimmered. The *School of Charity* rested where she had left it the night before, open at the spine. "Suffering," Evelyn Underhill had written, "has its place within the Divine purpose, and is transfigured by the touch of God."

She wasn't sure how long she leaned against the bedpost, staring at the book on the desk. *Lord Jesus, have mercy* were the only words that came to her, and she repeated them again and again, as though weaving a protective shawl around her. Slowly, she focused on the biopsy report, a white crumpled wad on the rug, picked it up, and moved toward the door. Slowly, she made her way to the elevator, rode down to the lobby, and found Elena in the bar.

"I ordered salads and tea," Elena said. "Hope that's all right. I didn't order for Jack. I guess he's running a little late?"

Madeleine sat next to her, shaking her head, stifling her tears. "I just saw him. He's furious. He stormed out and I don't know where he's gone. He found the biopsy report."

"Oh no."

"I wish I could explain things to him. He said something the other night."

"What was that?"

"He wouldn't want to live if he was diagnosed with cancer."

"You don't think...he would take his own life?"

Elena put her hand over Madeleine's. Their salads came, and they picked at the food in silence. Madeleine turned over the events of the week again and again in her mind, praying for an answer, watching the door, hoping Jack would return.

Finally, as she signed the check, she said, "Let's go to Notre-Dame. You said you might have left your scarf there, and we can pray before the Sacrament in a grand, holy, and historic place. I don't know what else to do, Elena."

With a dull migraine forming at the base of her skull, Madeleine stepped outside through the twirling doors, Elena close behind.

"Look, there's Pierre," Madeleine said under her breath, "leaning against a lamppost. He seems lost. I don't want to see him."

"Let's keep walking. We can find a taxi up the street."

"Too late. Here he comes."

"Elena, wait!" Pierre bounded up to them, waving the red scarf.

"Pierre, this is not a good time," Elena started to say—then, startled, exclaimed, "You have my scarf!"

"I found it in Notre-Dame." He handed it to her, his face full of anguish.

"Thank you." Elena looked at Madeleine, her hurt clearly at war with her hope, and the women turned away, heading for the taxi stand.

Pierre blocked their path. "I must talk to you."

"Please," Madeleine said, "we need to find Jack."

"Monsieur Seymour? What is wrong?"

"He's been gone too long. He's been tense and in a good deal of pain." *And he found out I lied to him. That he has cancer.*

"*Alors*, I see. Let me help."

"You can't help, Pierre; it's too late." Madeleine tried to control her anger and rising panic. Why hadn't she told Jack when she had the chance? And why hadn't this boy helped them instead of lying to them? Things would have been so different now.

Pierre touched Elena's shoulder. "Let me take you to my aunt. Will that make up for all the wrong I have done? I am sorry."

"So she *is* in Paris," Elena said, her eyes narrowing. "How do we know you're telling the truth now, Pierre?"

Madeleine saw his misery was genuine. "What harm can it do, Elena, to find out?"

Elena frowned. "Where *is* she, Pierre?"

"She stays with the Daughters of Charity on the Left Bank. The Chapel of the Miraculous Medal. They have rooms for pilgrims."

Madeleine searched her memory. "Didn't the Virgin Mary appear to Catherine Labouré? Is that where it happened?"

"*Oui*, Madame."

They met Sister Marguerite in the chapel's driveway. Pierre spoke rapidly in French, then introduced Madeleine and Elena. The little nun looked up at Madeleine. "You wish to see Doctor DuPres?"

"Please, Sister, if it is possible."

"Your husband is ill? He is Monsieur Seymour?"

"Is my husband here?"

"No, he is not here. But Doctor DuPres has spoken of him. We have talked of these matters." She studied her sandals seriously.

"You have talked?"

"We have talked. Come. She expects you."

"She expects us?" Madeleine's questions were multiplying.

Elena was talking animatedly to Pierre, her hands on her hips.

They followed the shuffling Marguerite to the soup kitchen.

"This reminds me of home," Elena said. "We had a soup kitchen once in Rome. Brother Cristoforo wants to reopen it."

Madeleine recognized Rachelle DuPres from her photo. The doctor was ladling stew into a plastic bowl. When she saw Sister Marguerite, she set the ladle aside, pulled off rubber gloves, and followed them into a large kitchen. They found a quiet corner where a few stools lined a long cutting table.

Marguerite introduced them, bowed, and left silently, a quiet satisfaction settling over her features.

Pierre kissed his aunt on each cheek. "Is it okay, *ma tante*? You said to bring them?"

"It's okay," Rachelle DuPres replied and shook their hands. "I'm pleased to meet you." Her eyes rested first on Madeleine, then lingered on Elena. "How can I help you?"

Madeleine searched the doctor's face. "My husband, as you may have heard, wants you to do his surgery."

"Doctor Lau briefed me." She rubbed her hands and adjusted a bandage that wrapped her palms.

"Will you speak to him?" Madeleine asked.

"Certainly. Where is he?"

Madeleine glanced at Elena as her confusion and concern collided. "He would be here if he knew we'd found you. We don't know where he is actually—at this moment—but I'm sure he'll return soon. He's been extremely upset this last week, and not following his diet, and he just found out..." The words tumbled out, unstoppable. Madeleine swayed and settled on a stool. Elena laid a steadying hand on her shoulder.

Doctor DuPres leaned forward, her gaze close and penetrating. "He just found out?"

Madeleine groaned as she set down her handbag. "He found the biopsy report," she said, looking at the green linoleum. "I kept it from him. It was Doctor Lau's idea."

"I can see this has been hard on you," the doctor said. "Mrs. Seymour, do you know why I came to France, why I left my practice?"

"You aren't on vacation? You left your practice?" Madeleine touched her chained cross with her index finger. She noticed a small silver medallion hanging over the doctor's apron.

"Mrs. Seymour..."

"Please call me Madeleine."

"Madeleine, several months ago I lost a patient in surgery."

"Oh dear." *Another piece of the puzzle. And not a welcome one.*

"I should have stopped the bleeding." The doctor picked at her palm.

"But you're so experienced..."

"There were risks and he knew them, but, even so, it was my responsibility."

Madeleine saw the doctor's anguish, but how could this woman operate on Jack? She paused. "Will you tell this to my husband?" Then, once Jack understood, he would choose another doctor.

Doctor DuPres felt for her medallion. "I will speak to him, and I will pray about the surgery."

Madeleine smiled and breathed deeply. "Thank you. That will be enough. So will I."

The doctor turned to Pierre. "Why don't you show the ladies the chapel? It's lovely." She turned to Madeleine. "It's full of light."

Pierre pulled his eyes away from Elena. *"Bien sûr."*

"I'd like that," Elena said, blushing slightly.

"I would too," Madeleine said, suddenly full of hope. "Doctor, perhaps you could join us for Sunday brunch tomorrow? Or come to mass with us?"

"I would be happy to join you for mass. Where?"

"Saint-Germain l'Auxerrois, behind the Louvre, eleven o'clock. The monks sing in Latin."

"In Latin? Really? I'll be there, and maybe Pierre will come too."

"Bien sûr, ma tante, bien sûr." Pierre smiled sheepishly.

"Good," Madeleine said, a huge weight lifted. "And you can speak with my husband then."

Doubt flickered across Elena's face. "Maybe we should go back and check the hotel."

"Yes," Madeleine agreed, "we need to get back."

Chapter Twenty-eight
Notre-Dame

He that loveth his life
shall lose it.
John 12:25

Jack walked briskly, heading for the river.
Cancer!
Why had Madeleine kept this from him? They were close, he thought, not always seeing eye-to-eye, but even so, close. She had never lied before, at least not to his knowledge. In fact, her honesty had at times been unintentionally brutal. She wore her feelings on her sleeve, as his mother would have said.

She sure loved churches. For that matter, they had met at a church, so he was forewarned. But how cute she was that day at Saint Thomas' with her swinging short skirt and auburn hair, her pert face and teasing eyes. Clean cut. He liked that. And he liked her determination, always wanting to do the right thing. He wined and dined her at the best places in San Francisco, but she never really appreciated how fashionable they were, how upscale. Then one evening, early on, as he recalled, she proposed—wanted to know his long-range intentions, since she had a young son and a job and didn't want to date just to date. She didn't have time to fool around, she said.

Jack breathed deeply with the memory. He was crossing the Tuileries now, almost to the river. The afternoon sun shot through broad plane trees lining the wide gravel walkway, then disappeared behind a cloud. He reached the river and descended steep stairs to the cement quay along the embankment. The water rushed by, rolling to the sea, under bridges that crisscrossed for miles.

Madeleine was like that tide—quiet, steady, strong. How he loved her earnestness, even in religious matters. For, after all, he had been raised a Methodist by a devout mother. What would his mother have thought of all these Catholic shrines they had been visiting? At Lourdes, the bright steeples, the darkness and light, the chant and song, had unnerved him, as though an interior wall had been breached. He felt exposed, just like this open river, and vulnerable. He had been near tears. But the crowd of believers lifted him up and he rode the crest, pushed by a powerful wave. His mother would have frowned, distrustful of crowds, distrustful of tears, and most of all, distrustful of Mary.

Did she watch him now, from the heavens? Did the dead visit the living? She had been his model with her constant whirl of activity, forever on the phone organizing this and pushing that, spreading her do-gooder creed throughout the community, politicking for school lunches and collecting shoes for poor children. How proud he was when Oakland elected her Mother of the Year, and they engraved her name on a plaque in the City Rose Garden.

Would she have understood his experience at Lourdes, then at the abbey in Barroux? This sudden welling up of love, inside and outside, that overcame him? Such a foreign experience, and yet now he mourned the moment. He wanted to pull it back from the past and relive it.

And little Bernadette. Did he believe her? Her visions of Mary? The intact corpse? The evidence was there, and he was one to look at evidence, trained to do so. Like the martyrs in Lyons. Why didn't they recant and escape those tortures? Such powerful belief, that it could control one's life completely. He had always kept his distance, saw religion as a civilizing duty, a pleasant ritual perhaps, something added on to one's life, not something consuming it.

Jack passed couples sunning themselves on benches, tourists taking pictures. He continued along the river, his long legs determined as though he could work out his grief with each stride.

Cancer!

Jack returned to his past, summoning images that might hold answers, hidden, waiting for him. Like Madeleine and her martyred saints, he had been determined. His Uncle Harry, when he heard that Jack at twenty-five had plans to better his life, had sneered, "So you want to be a lawyer, do you? Just who do you think you are?" Jack had shown him, all right. Even with Pamela and the boys to take care of, he'd worked his way through Hastings Law lifting boxes in an Oakland warehouse. Was it all worth it? So hungry and so driven—so many sacrifices. He passed the California Bar on the first try and landed a job in Gilpin's contract department. He worked long hours, rose quickly, and ventured out on his own as a wine importer. In the process, he lost Pamela. Well, she found a guy who would stay home with her.

And Jack found Madeleine. Were the seventeen years of their marriage a lie? Madeleine had often said that marriage went beyond two people. It meant children possibly and even went further to include greater circles of society. It was an institution in the truest sense—a social group formed to strengthen and inform the culture. It was in the family, she said, that children learned how to behave with others, a true "school of civilization," where all were forced to live under one roof with those they might not like or agree with. Ideally, the family taught us duty, charity, giving, self-sacrifice.

Would his death affect others besides Madeleine? There would be his sons, including Justin, and their families, and Meg. There was innocent Elena. And Pierre who seemed like a fine young man in spite of everything. Elena should give him another chance.

But Jack wasn't brave enough to be the long-suffering example of how to die a good death. He wasn't brave enough to hold on to a few more years for such a meager, painful, and embarrassing existence. They could manage without him. Self-sacrifice, indeed.

Cancer! He was only sixty-four. Would he leave Madeleine a widow at fifty-two? It wasn't fair.

Jack thought back over the last week, her concern over his drinking, the worry lines pulling together over her eyes. It all made sense.

And Doctor Lau. Trying to get Jack to take one of the younger fellows instead of Doctor DuPres, as though time was of the essence. Why didn't Conrad simply tell him? Jack recalled one of Conrad's cases, a terminal illness, and the doctor's self-blame when the patient overdosed. Jack had taken Conrad golfing to take his mind off it. *Too precious a conscience,* Jack had thought at the time. *Overactive guilt. Way overactive.*

So where did he go from here? Jack wondered. What were his choices? He rubbed his chest as though he could erase the burning. Maybe Conrad's fears were justified. He'd sure like to escape all of this.

The towers of Notre-Dame rose in the distance. The view from the top must be tremendous, he thought.

Jack coughed as he leaned against the cathedral's rampart railing. He gazed over the City of Light.

He had thrown his heart monitor into the Seine. He wouldn't need that anymore. Why bother checking numbers when the game was over? His fury had abated, his roaming thoughts had settled down, but his chest churned. He could taste the sour reflux as it rose and filled his mouth, then spilled into his lungs, choking him. How long had he been standing there, gazing over Paris? His legs throbbed from walking all afternoon, but here he was, on top of the world. Notre-Dame's bell towers were wonderful, so high. He'd made it to the top, with a few rests along the way—had to let those kids pass him—but hey, here he was. What a view.

Notre-Dame meant "Our Lady." Would Mary be his mother too, as Madeleine said? It would be comforting to have a mother again, even at his age—especially at his age. He'd felt such peace at Lourdes that night.

That was the river down there, snaking past the Eiffel Tower. And there, to the right on Montmartre, was Sacré-Coeur that Madeleine loved so much. Below to the left was the tourist trap restaurant Maddie had wanted to go to, but he'd refused since their wine list was lousy. Ah, Paris! Such a city! Could he love it without the fine wines? Did he want to try? To be sure, he'd had his share. Importing the best. Drinking the best. He had worked hard and played hard. Now it was time to go. Curtains, as they say.

Maddie had lied to him. Lau had lied to him. They pushed, controlled, and lied. That wasn't love.

How many other secrets do you have, Maddie?

He'd sit here in this corner for a bit. Watch the clouds drift by. Maddie said suicide was the great sin against the Holy Ghost, the breath of life. She would say, her face so earnest and supplicating, that because God gave him life, he had no right to take it. But did he believe in God? He did believe, sort of, but God would understand, wouldn't he? He was supposed to be a God of love and mercy, after all.

What would happen when he died? Would Saint Peter meet him at the pearly gates? Would Our Lady greet him? Or help him travel between worlds? Would he have to account for his life? Would he go to hell? Or purgatory to be purged, cleaned up a bit? Or simply go unconscious and become part of the universe like the Buddhists said? At least he thought that's what they said.

The surgery wouldn't solve anything. It would just give him a slow death. A living death. He'd be so handicapped with gas and a restricted life that he wouldn't be able to enjoy himself or do what he wanted to do. After all, it was the quality of life that counted, not the quantity. He had the right to determine his own way of dying, to die in dignity, after all.

"Papa, Papa!" he whispered. "Are you there?"

His father had suffered so. Jack didn't want to suffer like that.

But a sin against the Holy Ghost. He wondered if Maddie was right. She might be right. "Papa, is she right?"

She'd be much better off without him, even if the insurance was cancelled. She'd be better off. He'd been pretty grumpy, with his chest churning and his lack of sleep. Everyone would be better off.

Oh, Maddie! They'd been so happy. Until this last lying bit. Why did she lie? He had a right to know, to deal with his own suffering in his own way. It was his life.

Maddie said they were linked in their suffering. Maybe. Linked through Christ, she often said. But just who was Christ, anyway? A charismatic preacher from long ago. A wandering carpenter. Who knew what, or who, he was?

Maddie said you have three choices. Call him a madman. Call him a deceiver. Call him the Son of God. Jack supposed Jesus couldn't really be crazy and still be admired, even by atheists. And he supposed Jesus wasn't intentionally deceiving anyone. Was Jesus then the Son of God, the Christ?

"Maddie, oh Maddie," Jack gasped, "get out of my mind, and let me do what needs doing." He rubbed his chest and stared to the cityscape that intersected the horizon.

Two doves landed on a gargoyle. How easy it would be easy to climb out there and—whoosh—fly, soar into the air, freefall into peace.

But would he find peace?

Maddie said that if Jesus is God's son, you'd better listen to what he says. You'd better do what he says, too. Jack could see her—so sweetly straightforward, shaking her head, adjusting her glasses.

"Dear God, help me," he prayed.

The sun was setting. He'd been there awhile. Napoleon's golden dome was reflecting the last light. A cold place, kind of creepy, with the tomb in the pit, surrounded by all that marble. Maddie's churches were better.

"Dear God, help me."

Jack rubbed his hands, then steepled his fingers. "Jesus, Jesus, Jesus, you died for others, why can't I die for others too?"

He knew the answer as soon as he asked the question: his life was not his own. Yet he wanted it to be his own. But it wasn't. That was just the fact of the matter. He must face the facts; yes, he must face the facts.

"So I go when you choose, is that it, Lord?"

He wasn't brave enough, not nearly brave enough.

"Dear God, help me."

Maddie said give up control. Was that the secret? Give up his life? Trust God?

"Dear God, help me."

Maddie said face the truth. Face his sins. Face the fact he's not perfect. That took courage. That took bravery.

"Dear God, have mercy."

He wanted the truth, though. He'd always faced facts squarely. So he'd better step up to the plate here, too.

"I've been selfish and proud, Lord. I've been greedy and arrogant."

When did ambition slide into greed? When did self-esteem balloon into arrogance?

"I've pushed and I've shoved, and I haven't loved nearly enough, Lord. Show me how to love. Dear God, have mercy."

Maddie said he should open his heart. She sounded like his Sunday school teacher at Melrose Methodist. She'd have said to ask Jesus in, too.

"Should I ask you into my heart, Lord? Would you want to live there? In my dark heart? It's not very pretty in there, Lord. But you know that, don't you?"

Jack watched the birds soaring and diving about the gargoyles—there must be at least seven or eight, now. His fingers interlocked tightly, his knuckles white.

"Come in, Lord, come in—and live in my heart. There, I said it."

The doves flew off, gliding into the twilight. Pretty things.

"Lord, I do feel better. I feel a peace I haven't known in a long time. Is that peace coming from you?"

Maybe the peace was from something else. His consciousness working out his problems. Freudian self-therapy.

"I believe this peace is you, Lord. Is your mother here, too? High up here on top of her church? *Hail, Mary...*" He wished he knew the rest. He would learn it.

He'd better face it. He was going home. Home to Maddie.

Jack Seymour wiped his eyes on his sleeve, and as he stumbled to the door, he glanced over Paris once more.

The full moon rose over Montmartre, its pale translucence shimmering against the early evening sky, a moon full of promise.

Chapter Twenty-nine
Saint-Germain l'Auxerrois

And walk in love, as Christ also hath loved us,
and hath given himself for us
an offering and a sacrifice to God.
Ephesians 5:2

Madeleine returned to their room and sat at the antique desk overlooking the square. Surely, Jack would calm down, be home for dinner, and allow her to explain. She fought her rising panic, the sense that something was terribly wrong, and this time could not be righted. *Despair is the tool of the devil,* Elena said. *Bless Elena. She has been such an angel of mercy.*

She opened her laptop and tried to work, tried to occupy her mind or at least its surfaces. She would pretend, for a time, that everything would work out, at least until she had proof it wouldn't. *Trust and obey.* What was the next piece of her manuscript? *Speak, Lord, speak!*

Holy Manifestations: the Fire of God
The appearances of Mary throughout the last two thousand years, the working of God through saints' bones to heal man—these visits since Adam's fall—have all been manifestations of the holy on earth. They have continued to express God's love for us, ever since he came to us in Bethlehem. While the greatest manifestation was his Incarnation, his Holy Spirit working through his Church has sustained man ever since.

But perhaps the most frequent manifestation of God's presence has been in the Eucharist, which has truly become man's daily bread. For here Christ himself enters the molecules of matter, again and again. Here the Creator unites with his creation. Because of the Eucharist's repeated celebration, it has often been taken for granted, but the power of this manifestation is not lessened by man's lack of awe.

Madeleine was filled with a rush of heat as though wings fluttered through her flesh. To her, the body and blood of the Eucharist fed her, and it had been too long, thirteen days, since she was fed like that, in Lourdes. She was weak, she thought, simply weak, her soul becoming a listless, filmy creature. But even now, her own words reminded her of the sacrament's joy, its fulsomeness, its peace. There would be other times, other celebrations, hopefully not too far off, where she would once again be made whole.

Come home, Jack.

God created man and continues to recreate him. He breathed his life into Adam, and he breathes into each of us that choose him. And once we choose, we follow.

We experience nothing less than the breath, the fire of God, a fire that does not consume but revives. The alternative to God's fire is the consuming fire of our own selves, our own passions. God's fire perfects us and draws us closer to him. His is the fire of the burning bush, the fire that led the Israelites out of Egypt, the fire that came upon the disciples at Pentecost. Just so, he comes upon each of us. It is this breath of God that prompts us to pray, urges us to love, and beckons us to sacrifice. He breathes life into our minutes, hours, and days.

In the end, manifestations of the holy need not be sought in the past, however comforting and instructive. They need not be found in distant countries or miraculous shrines, although these give tangible hope. Manifestations of the holy are found in the simple stuff of our daily lives, through matter and spirit. Christ enters the bread and wine and we receive him. The Holy Spirit enters our thoughts and prompts our prayers. On a grand altar and beside a lowly bed, this God enters our world and sets it on fire, on fire with himself.

But there is a catch. We must give all, we must offer all. Only then, will God offer himself back to us. And we learn a surprising secret. All that we gave up is returned a thousand fold. When we seek God first and happiness second, we receive both, and the pleasures of this world increase, a truly holy manifestation.

Madeleine had written those words in a happier time, but this moment would prove them true or false. She realized now the piece of her life that was missing, what God demanded, the answer to the nagging question. She knelt by the bed and prayed.

She said a last *Glory be...*and offered her entire self to God as a *living sacrifice*, the only way of love. The sufferings of this world, both little and great, would be offered to him. She would not seek suffering, but the everyday variety that came her way she would accept. Soon she was overwhelmed by love, as though a white cloud had settled over her, a warm glow had filled her. How long she knelt there, she did not know. Time disappeared.

She heard a key in the lock. "Jack?"

He stood in the doorway.

She rose from the desk and moved slowly toward him, her heart pounding. He opened his arms wide and she slipped into them. "I was so worried." She rested her cheek on his chest, feeling the wool of his jacket, cool from the evening air.

He rubbed her back and stroked her hair. "I'm sorry, Maddie. I'm sorry."

She stood back and studied his face. There was no anger, only relief. "I'm sorry too. I didn't know what to do. Doctor Lau believed we shouldn't tell you, and I went along with it, and then I regretted it, and then I was stuck..."

He shook his head with regret. "I was so angry at first, darn angry, but I've cooled down. I'm just glad to be here, back with you. How I love you, Maddie."

Madeleine breathed deeply and reached for his freckled face with her palms. "And I love you." She paused, then asked, searching his eyes, "Where have you been?"

Jack moved to the window and gazed at the dark square. "Walking. I don't know, down by the river. Just walking."

"You forgive me?"

He turned and smiled, his features oddly peaceful. "I forgive you. Do *you* forgive *me?*"

"There is nothing to forgive. Just your anger, and I understand that."

"Let's get some dinner. It's nearly eight." He found her coat and wrapped it around her shoulders.

"Elena and Pierre have gone out on their own. She's giving him another chance."

He opened the door. "A wise choice."

"Jack, I've some good news—we found Doctor DuPres." Madeleine searched her mind for any other information that might lie hidden away.

"Really? After all this time?"

"We're meeting her tomorrow after mass."

"Excellent. After mass."

They headed down the hall for the elevator.

"She had a failed surgery, Jack. A patient died on her operating table."

"That explains a good deal."

"It does. Does this mean you'll choose another surgeon?"

They headed through the revolving doors out into the night.

"We'll see. I'll do what needs doing. How did you find her? Where is she?"

"We waited for you at lunch and when you didn't show up, we decided to go to Notre Dame, and there was Pierre in front of the hotel and he had Elena's scarf and..."

They dined in a restaurant near the Champs Elysee and strolled home in the moonlight through the Place de la Concorde, past the Hotel Crillon. They paused at the Rue Royale to gaze at the floodlit Madeleine church, then continued down the Rue Saint Honoré.

When they entered their room, Jack turned and kissed Madeleine on the forehead, then traced his finger down her cheek, as though memorizing her bones. "How could I have been so blind?"

"How could I have been so secretive?"

"You acted out of love. I understand that now. It was misguided, I think, but well intended. And I know how stubborn Conrad can be. It must have been so hard for you."

"And for you. Even with your surgery, it will be difficult. I know that. Our lives have taken a new turn, but we'll face each turn together."

Madeleine hung her nightgown on the bathroom door as the moonlight filtered between the drapery panels onto the sheets, marking a golden path. She slipped into bed and snuggled her back into her husband. He wrapped his arms about her. She turned and pulled him close, her face buried in the hollow of his neck, Armani spice mingling with his own sweet aroma. He led her up the path of wanting and of filling, slowly, carefully, with attention to moment and measure, place and part, touching her smooths and her roughs. Finally, flesh joined flesh and spirit joined spirit and they were one, no longer two.

Sunday morning, hand-in-hand, they walked down the Rue de Rivoli toward Saint-Germain l'Auxerrois behind the Louvre Palace. They passed souvenir booths selling tees and tiny Eiffel towers, colorful scarves and lacy lingerie, as they stepped through the shadowy colonnade.

Madeleine recalled the previous evening, wanting to hold the time forever. In her memory she would, knowing her present was formed by her past, indeed *contained* her past, owned it. She slipped her arm about her husband's waist and leaned her head against his shoulder.

"So Doctor DuPres is meeting us at the church?" Jack sounded cheerful. "That's great. And Elena too?"

"We're meeting both of them at the church. And Pierre, I think. I've been so worried about Elena and worried about you. I pray things will come together soon."

"Maybe you should learn to trust a bit more, my Madeleine."

"Trust? Did I hear that coming from you? I rather like it." What had come over him?

"And I have some news I can't hold back any longer. I was going to surprise you. But you should know right away."

"Yes?" Madeleine gazed into his blue, blue eyes. What now?

"I spoke with Justin earlier this morning—you were sleeping. He wanted to talk to *you,* but couldn't wait."

Madeleine's pulse quickened. "Has something happened? Is everything all right?"

"Whoa, my dear...it's okay. It's *good* news. At least I'm beginning to think so. I don't think I would have said that last week." He coughed and pulled out his hanky.

"Jack, would you please *tell* me?"

"Maddie, they're expecting a baby."

"But that's wonderful. You're not upset? It's not too soon? Are they happy? I must call them..." Madeleine was suddenly giddy. *A baby.*

"It's the middle of the night there. Justin said it was a bit of a surprise. But they are, my dear, ecstatic, and, after all, a child is a child! A great cause for celebration, one among many."

"One among many." Madeleine's heart was full as they walked in contented silence. "You're different, Jack," she finally said, looking up at him.

"Am I? I feel different, my love. I think the bell tower did it. Did I mention I climbed Notre-Dame yesterday?"

"Did you really? And did it clear your mind? That's what you said when we went up the one in Florence."

"It cleared my mind, and...maybe my soul."

"Oh?"

"I'm going to try prayer, Maddie. In fact, I've already begun. And I think there may be something to it after all. I feel stronger already, more at peace."

"Especially in the mass."

"Now why is that?"

Madeleine chose her words carefully. "They say that the faithful are connected through Christ in time and space, so when we pray together in the mass, we offer and we receive. We offer ourselves as the Body of Christ, and when we receive the host we receive ourselves back, a thousandfold. Does that make sense?" Madeleine glanced up at him, nervous at his sudden interest, expecting a teasing twist that would diminish her words.

"No, but then prayer doesn't really make sense either, does it?"

"You understand better with practice."

"Now *that* I can relate to."

"Me too."

"So why was I so slow to try? Why are so many so slow?"

"Sometimes fear. Mostly pride. Will."

"Free will? I've heard you mention that many times, but how does it fit in here? I suppose we have the choice to pray or not."

"And the choice to open our hearts, to unfasten the bolts and locks, to tear down the scaffolding we erect about ourselves. God has a hard time reaching us, buried, self-imprisoned as we are."

"We erect defenses, I suppose."

"And the irony is that our defenses destroy us. Our own chains of worry and pride restrict us, strangle us. The saints are those who tear down the walls, opening themselves wide to God."

"My sweet Maddie, how patient you've been with me. Did you know

I owe God a church? I may not be *physically* healed, but something happened in Notre-Dame yesterday. I think I'd better pay up, whether or not Doctor DuPres does my surgery."

"You owe God a church?"

"I made a vow in Lourdes, when I saw the crutches. I'd better come through, I guess."

"You made a vow to God? I should say so. And where will this church be?"

"I'm not sure. I trust we'll find out when the time comes."

"Another fundraising challenge?"

"Another challenge, but one that I know will be different, more of an adventure, an exciting adventure. One never knows where God may lead us."

They approached the church steps, and Jack pointed to a woman in a tweed jacket, waiting. "Is this our elusive doctor?"

Madeleine introduced them.

"Mr. Seymour, it's good to meet you," Rachelle said.

"Doctor DuPres, it's indeed a pleasure. But I must apologize. I'm terribly sorry. I should have left you alone."

"It's all right, Mr. Seymour. *I'm* sorry for my cowardice."

"We'll talk after church?"

"After the mass."

They entered the Gothic nave, took their seats on caned chairs next to Pierre and Elena, and knelt on wooden slats. The stone floor, smoothly polished by penitence, patience, and time, dipped unevenly. Four parishioners stood at a lectern, on the Epistle side, and sang Gregorian chant as a choir echoed antiphonally from the loft. Slowly, the sun lit the jeweled windows above the altar. Madeleine looked up at the lofty columns bordering the aisles and craned to see the organ in back. She then focused on the tabernacle.

Exhausted, she prayed her thanksgivings. Jack had been walking about town—but he should have left a note—and Pierre and Elena were getting along. They had found Doctor DuPres. A baby, a new life, had been created. And Jack was changed. He welcomed his grandbaby. And he seemed to be saying his prayers.

The clergy and acolytes processed up the center aisle to the altar. The shortest acolyte carried the crucifix high and a priest elevated the Bible as though waving a lantern in the dark. The lessons and prayers sculpted the hour into a sacred offering as the celebrant solemnly wove the people with their God, the bride with her groom. The chants echoed as they prayed *Lord have mercy...*

Madeleine was grateful for this moment of oneness with her husband, with Elena, and now with Pierre and his aunt. Her heart opened, and she confessed her fear, her lack of trust, and offered herself to join Christ on his cross. His wounds absorbed the remnants of her pain, and once again she was reborn and made whole as love filled her.

They sang the Latin creed, following phrases in their leaflet, and attempted some of the French responses, *et avèc votre esprit*. They shared the Peace, turning to a young couple behind them, shaking their hands and saying *la paix du Christ*. In this mass, in their offering to their creator and his offering to them, they caught and shared past and future offerings, other offerings of sacrifice and celebration. They were one with the Church, Christ's Body, throughout time and space.

Pierre, Elena, and Doctor DuPres joined the line of communicants. Madeleine watched, her heart full, as the doctor opened her palms to receive Christ.

The mass ended and the congregation processed to the Lady Chapel, the home of the *Saint-Sacrament*, singing *Je vous salute, Marie*. Incense billowed about the altar as the faithful sang the lilting hymn, and Madeleine thought tenderly of the many comforting Madonnas she had encountered on their journey. Here, appropriately, Mary presided over the altar home of her son.

She would not forget Mary, the mother of God, nor that other Mary, the Magdalene. The one offered her body to bear God's son and the other offered her tears and her hair to wash his feet. Together they wove a healing presence in her soul. She would continually give thanks.

They left the church, and Rachelle walked with Jack through the Tuileries gardens, the others following. Squinting in the bright Parisian light, the sun warming her skin, she listened to the crunch of the gravel. At the far end of the wide path an obelisk marked the Place de la

Concorde.

Rachelle spoke first, her words carefully parting the crisp silence. "Again, let me say, I'm truly sorry, Mr. Seymour, to be so evasive. I needed time."

"Please call me Jack." He moved cautiously toward a gray cat creeping from behind a bush.

"Did you know—Jack—that I lost a patient recently?"

"I learned only last night. But you're still the best. I want you to do the surgery, if you'll consent, but...I'm willing to take someone else." His big hand smoothed the thin coat as the cat nuzzled his fingers.

"Thank you. Your words are kind, if not true."

"I'll live with whatever you decide."

They walked on and Rachelle studied him. "Have you had a change of heart? You don't sound like the Jack Seymour that Pierre described."

"I'm not the same man I was two days ago, doctor." He regarded her with startling blue eyes. "I think I found God, or he found me. He...changed my heart, as you say. It's a long story. But tell me, are you saying you'll do my surgery, after all?"

Rachelle paused. "I'll make you an offer. If you'll tell me your story, I'll consider doing the procedure. I would like to hear about your finding this God." She gazed at her red palms. The host had laid there, right there, the flesh of the Son of God. Could it be true? Her bleeding hands had become a crèche.

They passed an ice cream stand and pony rides, then a carousel, the tall graying man waving his arms and pointing to the skies, the short graying woman folding her hands peacefully, much like Marguerite, as she contemplated the ground and listened.

Jack shook his head with obvious regret. "My story is a common one. I wanted it all."

"You wanted it all?" That part was familiar.

"I wanted to run my life and those lives around me in my own fashion, have my own way. But my old methods don't work anymore."

"I know what you mean."

"I wanted to control every outcome and trust no one else."

"Control and trust. There's such power in those words, Jack."

"It's difficult to let go, isn't it?"

"We can't do it by ourselves. I'm only beginning to understand. But God will help us."

Jack Seymour grinned. "I believe you're right, Doctor DuPres. And I accept your offer. I will tell you how I found God, or he found me."

Chapter Thirty
Saint Thomas'

But God...
for his great love wherewith he loved us...
hath quickened us together with Christ.
Ephesians 2:4-5

On the second Sunday in October, Madeleine and Jack knelt in the third pew, Gospel side, in their little church of Saint Thomas'. Light fell through skylights upon oak pews and green floor tiles. White roses, celebrating the Feast of Saint Francis, were bunched in terra cotta vases on classical pedestals. Candles flamed on the altar beneath the wooden crucifix.

Soon Father Michaels would process up the aisle, following the crucifer and torchbearers in their white cottas. Soon the organ would play the opening hymn. Soon the great liturgy would begin.

In the pile of mail that greeted them when they arrived home, Madeleine had found an envelope of pictures. Justin and Lisa Jane on the beach (who took that one?). Justin raising a glass of beer. Lisa waving prettily at her new husband. A number of sunsets, crimson stripes against cerulean skies. Close-ups of flowers—coral bougainvillea, white jasmine, an orchid on white linen. And to think, a *baby!* Maybe, just maybe, there would be another family celebration, here at Saint Thomas', next summer. *This* sacrament would welcome their grandchild into Christ's Body. Through water and the Holy Spirit, Christ would enter this child and fill him with grace so that he would never be ashamed to confess Christ crucified. Another holy manifestation, another offering. *Baptism.*

Elena had remained a few more days in Paris, staying with Sister Marguerite. Madeleine prayed she and Pierre would find the right way, the right path to their futures. But did their paths involve one another's?

How would they know? She glanced at the stone altar and the marble tabernacle, the red candle aflame alongside. Of course they would know. At least she was confident that Elena would listen to God, as the young woman prayed her way through the hours and days.

Jack's surgery was scheduled for the following week, and even with the experienced Doctor DuPres, Madeleine worried.

The organ pounded the opening notes of the hymn and the congregation rose. Jack pointed to the number and she found it in her book. She looked up at her husband. His eyes were tearing.

He winked and put his arm around her. "Good to be home," he said, his voice husky.

He was changed. Was she?

She turned her eye upon the Madonna and Child in the Gospel corner. The green-robed Mary gazed upon her, confident all would be well. The blue votives flickered hopefully, as though reflecting the certainty of the Madonna's gaze. Madeleine said a silent *Hail Mary....*

She gazed at the tabernacle, embedded with amber and aquamarine, holding the Presence of Christ. *Thank you, Lord,* she prayed. *I offer you my worries. I offer you myself. Transform my heart, again.*

Madeleine knew that today she would indeed be transformed. For when the priest turned to the altar and offered his people to God, Christ would offer himself to them. As they received his Body and Blood, they would be made whole. All of the troubles, all of the worries of life, all would be absorbed by him and redeemed into something new, something holy, something that would change even the world outside and set all creation afire.

With that thought, a fiery peace filled Madeleine's heart, like embers glowing, and she turned toward the narthex. The procession was beginning, moving steadily, joyfully. The organ thundered its rich tones, spreading an amber carpet beneath their feet.

Madeleine breathed deeply and handed Jack a tissue. With the others, she rose and began to sing. *Crown him with many crowns, the Lamb upon his throne....*

Chapter Notes

Chapter Two: San Francisco Medical

Epigraph: Underhill, Evelyn, *The School of Charity* (Longman Group UK Ltd., Morehouse Publishing, 1991), by kind permission of Pearson Education Ltd., Harlow, Essex, U.K. Evelyn Underhill (1875-1941), English mystic, became known for her writings on the spiritual life, arguing that one sought God and sanctification in one's daily experience.

Chapter Four: Alameda

Epigraph: Underhill, Evelyn, *The School of Charity,* ibid.

Chapter Five: Lourdes

Epigraph: Bernadette Soubirous, as quoted by Melanie MacMitchell in *Sacred Footsteps* (Encinitas, CA : Opal Star Press, 1991).

Chapter Six: The Esplanade

Epigraph: F. Fenelon, as quoted in *The New Encyclopedia of Christian Quotations,* compiled by Mark Water (Grand Rapids, MI : Baker Books, 2000), used by kind permission of John Hunt Publishing, Hampshire, U.K. Francois de Salignac de la Mothe Fenelon (1651-1715), Archbishop of Cambrai, promoted the idea of selfless love and contemplative prayer. His writings strongly influenced John Wesley as well as the Quaker movement.

Chapter Seven: The Grotto of Massabielle

Epigraph: Charles de Foucauld, as quoted in Evelyn Underhill's *Mystics of the Church* (Harrisburg, PA : Morehouse Publishing, James Clarke & Co. Ltd. 1925) used by kind permission of James Clarke & Co., Cambridge, England.

Saint Charles de Foucauld (1858-1916), "Hermit of the Sahara" lived a solitary life of prayer, serving the desert tribes of Algeria, and was martyred there. He was greatly influenced by Abbe Huvelin of Saint-Augustin's, Paris, and a shrine, with a display of his life, can be found today in this church near La Madeleine. After his death, many orders formed that followed his rule: the Little Brothers of Jesus, the Little Sisters of the Sacred Heart, the Little Sisters of Jesus, among others. He was beatified in 2005.

Chapter Eight: Crillon-le-Brave

Sigmund Freud (1856-1939), founder of psychoanalysis, systematically attacked Christianity; *Bertrand Russell*, the third Earl Russell (1872-1970), believed in the power of the human mind to solve mankind's problems, articulating the popular modern belief in the natural progress of man; *Paul Tillich* (1886-1965), Protestant theologian, believed that God was merely the life force running though man, having no authority. He believed that man could be taught to be good.

Others countered these opinions, saying the wars of the twentieth century proved man cannot better himself, that traditional belief creates order out of chaos, gives man hope in his despair, and transforms selfishness into love. Belief that God is only a force within man removes moral imperatives and creates a vacuum of meaning, forcing man to create his own values.

Existentialism arose in the wake of Freud, Russell, and Tillich, as man sought to create his own meaning, to find answers apart from an outside authority, answers invented to suit one's own needs. Nihilism followed, for eventually one must despair and believe in nothing, since to face that meaning is invented, created for our use, is to face that meaning doesn't exist. Many have followed this thought process and committed suicide.

Christians thankfully believe that history proves these theories fraudulent.

Chapter Nine: Rocamadour

Epigraph: Jane de Chantal, as quoted by Melanie MacMitchell in *Sacred Footsteps.* Jane Frances de Chantal, Saint (1572-1651), with Francis de Sales, founded the Order of the Visitation, which allowed religious women to visit the sick and poor. At the time of her death, eighty-six houses had been founded.

"Be it unto me according to thy word." Luke 1:38

Chapter Thirteen: Abbaye Sainte-Madeleine

Epigraph: Francois de Sales, as quoted in *The New Encyclopedia of Christian Quotations,* ibid. Francois de Sales (1567-1622), Bishop of Geneva, spiritual director to Jane de Chantal, encouraged in his writings the sanctification of everyday life.

Chapter Fifteen: Le Col de Vence

Epigraph: Francois de Sales, as quoted in *The New Encyclopedia of Christian Quotations*, ibid.

Chapter Sixteen: Lyons

Epigraph: Underhill, Evelyn, *The School of Charity*, ibid.

"The blood of the martyrs..." Attributed to Quintus Septimius Florens Tertullian (c.160-c.225), a Church Father, brought up in Carthage as a pagan, but converted to Christianity before 197.

"The Lord's mercies...are new every morning." Lamentations 3:22-23. Pope John XXIII said this prayer each day.

Chapter Seventeen: Lèrins

Epigraph: Therese of Liseux, as quoted in *The New Encyclopedia of Christian Quotations*, ibid.

Lèrins: In the 5th and 6th centuries learned brethren from Lèrins guided the Christian world. These men would form and reform European civilization, as it struggled through the dark ages of war and famine. Here on Saint-Honorat, one of Lèrins islands, the British-born Patrick trained before returning to Ireland, the scene of his boyhood slavery. Here, Augustine of Canterbury stopped on his way from Rome to Britain where he re-established episcopal ties with a church weakened by Saxon conquest.

Others sowed seeds of orthodoxy that would feed the Church over the next fifteen hundred years. Saint Vincent of Lèrins, fifth century, wrote the *Commonitorium,* which provided standards for interpreting Catholicity, called the Vincentian Canon: "what has been believed everywhere, always, and by all." Lèrins produced other writers and great bishops who shepherded the early church: Saint Hilaire of Arles, Saint Eucherius of Lyons, Saint Maximus, Saint Faust of Riez, Saint Veranus of Vence, and Saint Benedict Biscop of England who founded the Jarrow monastery, home to the Venerable Bede. Lèrins was truly a "school of bishops."

Fifteen centuries after Saint Benedict, the monks have reinstituted the rule of *ora* and *labora*—prayer and work. They sing the *ora*—the hours, the prayer Office—to the glory of God and invite visitors to join them, asking only that they observe "the silence" by speaking quietly or not at all, as they walk the island.

Chapter Twenty: Vézeley

Epigraph: Bernard of Clairvaux, as quoted in *The New Encyclopedia of Christian Quotations*, ibid.

Chapter Twenty-one: Saint-Remi, Reims

"*Tu nous donne ton pain, tu nous donne ta vie, Seigneur tout vient de ta main, et nous chantons: merci.*" Translation: *You give us your bread, you give us your life, Lord all comes from your hand, and we sing: thank you.*

Chapter Twenty-three: Chapelle de la Medaille Miraculouse

Epigraph: Vincent de Paul, as quoted in *The New Encyclopedia of Christian Quotations*, ibid.

Chapter Twenty-four: Sacré-Coeur

Epigraph: Brother Lawrence of the Resurrection as quoted in Evelyn Underhill's *Mystics of the Church*, ibid. Brother Lawrence (1614-1691) was a lay brother in a French Carmelite monastery. He is known today for his *The Practice of the Presence of God,* saying everyday actions can bring us to the heart of God.

"Be ye not unequally yoked together with unbelievers: for what fellowship hath righteousness with unrighteousness? and what communion hath light with darkness?" 2 Corinthians 6:14.

"If any man will come after me let him take up is cross and follow me...for my yoke is easy and my burden is light." Matthew 16:24; 11:30.

"I am the Way, the Truth and the Life. No man cometh to the Father but by me." John 14:16.

"A sword shall pierce through thy own soul also..." Simeon prophesying to Mary, Luke 2:35.

Chapter Twenty-four: Sacré-Coeur

Epigraph: Brother Lawrence, as quoted in *The New Encyclopedia of Christian Quotations*, ibid.

Selected Bibliography

Abbaye Sainte-Madeleine du Barroux (Moisenay: Editions Gaud, 2000).

Butler's Lives of the Saints, Eds. Herbert J. Thurston, S.J. and Donald Attwater (Allen, TX: Thomas More Publishing, 1996).

Caujolle, Marie, tr. Alison Hebborn, *Lourdes* (Vic-en-Bigorre Cedex, France, 1998).

Cole, Robert, *A Traveller's History of Paris* (Gloucestershire: The Windrush Press, 1994).

Cole, Robert, *A Traveller's History of France* (London: The Windrush Press, 1988).

Coloni, Marie Estelle, *Notre-Dame in Paris* (Strasbourg: Editions du Signe, 1996).

Johnson, Paul, *Intellectuals* (New York: HarperCollins, 1988).

Jones, Colin, *The Cambridge Illustrated History of France* (Cambridge, UK: 1999).

Knight, Jeremy, *Roman France* (Charleston, SC: Arcadia Publishing Inc., 2001).

MacMitchell, Melanie, *Sacred Footsteps, a Traveler's Guide to Spiritual Places of Italy and France* (Encinitas, CA: Opal Star Press, 1991).

Martin, John, *Roses, Fountains, and Gold* (San Francisco: Ignatius Press, 1998).

Moreaux, Roselyne, tr. R. Field, *Les Saintes Maries de la Mer* (Septèmes les Vallons: Editions PEC, 2000).

The New Encyclopedia of Christian Quotations, compiled by Mark Water (Grand Rapids, MI: Baker Books, 2000).

Nicholi, Jr., Armand M., *The Question of God* (New York: Simon & Schuster, Inc., 2002).

Oxford Dictionary of the Christian Church, Eds. F.L. Cross and E.A. Livingstone (New York: Oxford University Press, 1997).

Russell, Paul S., *Looking Through the World to See What's Really There* (Bloomington, IN: Authorhouse, 2004).

Underhill, Evelyn, *Mystics of the Church* (Harrisburg, PA: Morehouse Publishing, James Clarke and Co. Ltd. 1925). *The School of Charity, Meditations on the Christian Creed* (New York: Longmans, Green and Co., 1954).

Werfel, Franz, tr. Ludwig Lewisohn, *The Song of Bernadette* (San Francisco: Ignatius Press, 2006).

Endnotes

Holy Manifestations: God's Presence in Our World

[1] www.lourdes-france.com.

[2] On November 27, 1830 the Virgin Mary appeared to Catherine Labouré and asked that a medal be struck bearing the words *O Mary, conceived without sin, pray for us who turn to you*; on December 8, 1854 Pope Pius IX announced the doctrine of the Immaculate Conception; on March 15, 1858 the Virgin appeared to Bernadette and named herself the Immaculate Conception.

[3] Caujolle, Marie, tr. Alison Hebborn, *Lourdes* (Vic-en-Bigorre Cedex, France, 1998) 24.

[4] It is interesting to note that genetic research has found that character traits are passed on physically in the gene, and Adam's fall could very well have been passed on physically, so that mankind is born with the sin gene, the gene for pride, selfishness, greed, etc. Who would have guessed modern Science would validate the Fall of Man?

[5] www.lourdes-france.com.

[6] The Druids were the priestly class of the Celts. In France, these tribal Celts entered Gaul from the east beginning in the eighth century—the Scythians of the Steppes and other groups from the Near and Middle East—and swept south and west, so that by 400 BC, they had left their iron traces north of Carcassonne and Geneva. The Arverni tribe settled and dominated the Massif Central, where Rocamadour was carved from the limestone cliffs. It is possible that a shrine to a mother-goddess once occupied the site of the Black Madonna. Christianity often took over existing shrines, "baptizing" them with the new faith.

[7] Many rescues at sea have been recorded, amazing for this mountaintop, inland shrine; sailors returned with thanksgivings, having prayed to the Virgin Mary for safety.

[8] The veneration of the relics of the saints has been practiced since the first martyrs were buried outside the walls of Rome and Christians prayed over their graves. When Christianity became legal under Constantine, the faithful built their churches over these graves, and soon it became customary and highly desirable to have relics under every altar in Christendom. The Second Council of Nicaea (787) said relics must be present for a church to be consecrated. This led to the relic trade of the Middle Ages, which encouraged the body's dismemberment. Since then Roman Catholic canon law forbids the cutting up of the body and the sale of relics.

As in all of man's enterprises, corruption took hold in the relic trade, and many fakes found their way to Europe's altars. It was a time of little science, and the lure of fame and income to the abbey or monastery proved a great temptation. Unfortunately, the real and the fakes have merged, and it is through a foggy glass that we must assess each one. Legend along with contemporary accounts of healings (which do exist in historical documents) must provide the historian with his only lens.

[9] Miraculous Madonnas appear throughout Europe, particularly in Spain, France, and Italy. They are pronounced miraculous by the parish faithful who have received answers to their prayers and are surrounded by hundreds of *remerci* plaques, or in some cases, paintings and gifts.

[10] Other destinations bestowed other emblems—Saint James Compostela in Spain sold scallop shells, which became the pilgrim's talisman (shells were carried as drinking vessels about the neck and are associated with Saint James' legend).

[11] Legends concerning these figures of Christ's life flourish throughout France, but most can only be traced to the Middle Ages. Lazarus is said to have preached in Marseilles, and was possibly buried in Autun, Burgundy (he is venerated in the cathedral). Mary Salomé and Mary Jacobé with the servant Sarah settled in Les-Saintes-Maries-de-la-Mer. Martha traveled north to Tarascon where legend says she subdued a water dragon with the sign of the cross. Joseph of Arimathea continued up to Cornwall, Britain where he planted his flowering staff on the top of the ancient Tor and settled in Glastonbury. There he built the first Christian church. He brought from Jerusalem the Holy Grail, the cup (or cups) of Christ's last supper, cups that also caught Christ's blood at the foot of the cross. Circumstance and oral tradition from varying parts of the Mediterranean basin reinforce these tales, but it is also true that the Greek Orthodox claim this group settled in the East.

Tradition says that Sarah, an Egyptian servant, begged to accompany them. Upon reaching the shores of France, Mary Salomé threw her cloak over the water so that she could reach the boat. Sarah remained in Les-Saintes-de-la-Mer with the elderly Mary Salomé and Mary Jacobé. They preached and performed miracles, and a freshwater spring still flows. They were given the last sacrament by Saint Trophime from Arles and buried close to a small oratory they built. In 1448 King René, Count of Provence, excavated the area and found several human heads arranged in the form of a cross, the bodies of two women, and an earthen altar, all under the main altar of the first church built in the Middle Ages. Since it was the custom to celebrate mass over the relics of saints, these remains were probably the two Marys. Miracles have been documented over the years.

Today, one can visit the basilica honoring Mary Jacobé and Mary Salomé in this quaint beach town on the sea, at the edge of the vast Camargue region. Their relics reside in two reliquaries in an upper chapel behind the main altar. Sarah's relics are in the crypt, the ancient church. Every May the townspeople join many other pilgrims and people from nearby Arles to process to the sea with the saints' relics housed in life-like models. The Arlesians wear period costumes and the saints are accompanied by a guard of Camargue horses and riders.

[12] The massive Basilica of Saint Maximus can be seen from the A8, rising from the valley floor, and is worth a visit. One can also climb to the cave where Mary spent her last years (about a 30-minute walk up a wide path to the ledge) and can hike farther up to Mount Pilon.

[13] Major state persecutions of Christians in the Roman Empire prior to Constantine's conversion occurred from 54-68 AD (Nero), 81-96 AD (Domitian), 161-180 AD (Marcus Arelius), 180-193 AD (Commodus), 235-238 AD (Maximinus), and 284-305 AD (Diocletian).

[14] Clovis was also influenced by his Christian queen, Clothilde, a Burgundian princess. He agreed to baptize his children Christians, but still wavered. During a battle, however, he invoked "Clothilde's God" and won the day. He was converted.

Don't Miss

PILGRIMAGE

Christine Sunderland

It was a day
when nothing should have gone wrong...
but everything did.

Madeleine Seymour will never forget what happened twenty-two years
ago in her own backyard. She's still riddled with guilt. Hoping to banish
the nightmares that haunt her and steal her peace, she travels to Italy
with her husband, Jack, on a pilgrimage. As a history professor,
Madeleine is fascinated by the churches they visit...and what they live
about the lives of the martyrs. But can anything bring her the peace that
her soul longs for?

For more information:
www.ChristineSunderland.com
www.MyTravels.ChristineSunderland.com
www.oaktara.com

Coming Soon...

INHERITANCE

Christine Sunderland

She risked everything to save a life...
But who would save hers?

Vietnamese-American Victoria Nguyen, seventeen, flees to England with a powerful secret.

Madeleine Seymour, a history professor, and her husband Jack, a retired wine broker, travel from San Francisco to London to found a children's home.

Brother Cristoforo, a black Franciscan from the Seymours' Quattro Coronati orphanage in Rome, disobeys his superior, and must face his penance.

Woven through the mists of Lent to new life on Easter Day, *Inheritance* draws the lives of these four characters together to a stunning, unforgettable conclusion.

For more information:
www.ChristineSunderland.com
www.MyTravels.ChristineSunderland.com
www.oaktara.com

About the Author

CHRISTINE SUNDERLAND, also the author of *Pilgrimage* (the first book of the trilogy and the story of Madeleine's journey through the grief of losing her young daughter, Mollie), has been interested in matters of belief since she was sixteen and her father, a Protestant minister, lost his faith.

Today she is Church Schools Director for the Anglican Province of Christ the King and Vice-President of the American Church Union (*Anglicanpck.org*). She has edited *The American Church Union Church School Series, The Anglican Confirmation Manual,* and *Summer Lessons.* She has authored *Teaching the Church's Children* and seven children's novellas, the Jeanette series, published by the American Church Union.

"In order to write *Offerings,*" Christine says, "I traveled extensively in France to Christian historical sites. It was a fascinating quest."

Christine holds a B.A. in English Literature and is an alumnus of the Squaw Valley Writers Workshop and the Maui Writers Retreat.

Inheritance, the third book of the trilogy, will be set in England.

For more information:
www.ChristineSunderland.com
www.MyTravels.ChristineSunderland.com
www.oaktara.com

Printed in the United States
147432LV00002B/6/P

3 1901 04859 2184